The Perfect Find

Tia Williams

BROWN GIRLS BOOKS

Houston, Texas * Washington, D.C. * Raleigh/Durham, NC

WHAT OTHERS ARE SAYING...

The Perfect Find

"This juicy page-turner is the ultimate beach read ...with characters you'll think about long after the last page. The chemistry is so steamy." – *InStyle*

"You're always clear that it'll end up happily, and sometimes, especially with characters of color (who often seem disproportionately predisposed to suffering) – an unyielding lightheartedness is the best gift a romance novel can give you." – *Washington Post*

"Adorable heroine. Great plot. A delightful book." – *Essence*

"Tops our collection of can't-put-down page-turners. Our new favorite beach read!" -*People StyleWatch*

"Tia Williams has revived the black chick lit genre. The summer read." - *Ebony*

"Sexy, fashionable, quirky." – *Madame Noire*

"*The Perfect Find* is a deliciously good time!" – *Nicola Kraus, National Bestselling co-author of The Nanny Diaries*

"Epically witty, juicy and irresistible. What a perfect, fresh take on the high stakes that come when we fall, pick ourselves back up, and step unsurely into the future."— *Denene Millner, New York Times Bestselling co-author of Act Like a Lady, Think Like a Man, and The Vow*

"A saucy, cutting-edge love story amidst the backdrop of the New York City fashion world, with delicious dialogue. Refreshing and engaging with a cast of characters that stayed with me long after the last page had been turned." — *Sadeqa Johnson, author of Second House From the Corner*

"A fun romp through the world of new media fashion reporting. Tia Williams writes with juicy, behind-the-scenes details that let us know she's been there and survived." — *Virginia DeBerry and Donna Grant, authors of Tryin' to Sleep in the Bed You Made*

"The story of 40-year-old former It girl Jenna Jones stumbling upon that giddy kind of passion will have you longing for someone to sext — even if you haven't sexted since 2008. Equal parts heartwarming and electrifying, when you really get into *The Perfect Find*, make sure you have a fan ready." — *Helena Andrews-Dyer, columnist and author of Bitch is the New Black*

"A funny, fashion-filled, fiercely provocative read perfect for the grown and sexy woman."— *Niobia Bryant, National Bestselling author of The Pleasure Trap*

The Accidental Diva

"A randy new read." — *Cosmopolitan*

"Could not be more perfect for the beach." — *Lucky*

"Former Elle beauty editor Tia Williams scores big with this debut novel." — *Marie Claire*

"Williams [has a] gift for sexy prose and an insider ear. A sharp new talent." — *Publishers Weekly*

It Chicks and It Chicks: Sixteen Candles

"Williams, who has an ear for the way teens speak, has created a hip series filled with heart and sass." – *Essence*

"Over-the-top, fun, lively!" – *Children's Book Reviews*

"Revolutionizing literature for young girls." – *Uptown*

Tia Williams

"Known for her smart, funny, tell-it-like-it-is writing." – *The Huffington Post*

"Part of an elite group of beauty mavens." – *Allure*

"Tia really knows her glitz and gloss." – *Refinery 29*

Acknowledgements

I couldn't have written word the first without the love and support of the Williamses, Gantts, and Shareefs. Endless thanks to Tricia, Renae, Abby, and Lori for refusing to let me give up when the road got rocky—and to Charlotte, for the web series brainstorm. To my agent, Brettne Bloom, I bow down to your dedication and uncanny literary instincts. You helped me breathe such big, juicy life into Jenna's story! And to my editor/homegirl Cherise Fisher—there'd be zero book if it weren't for your passion, patience, and therapy sessions (#allhats). I'm here because of you. Period. Nerissa and Chris, this cover is truly one of the prettiest I've ever seen. ReShonda, Victoria and the Brown Girls team, bless you for making my dream a reality. Dawn, you're a P.R. goddess. And Lina Lina Bobina, my darling little girl, you are my greatest inspiration. You're not allowed to read this until you're twenty-five.

S.—thank you for lending a major character your middle name. And for everything, really. You live in every line.

The Perfect Find

CHAPTER 1

www.stylezine.com
Just Jenna: Style Secrets from our Intrepid Glambassador!

Q: "I've had a series of terrible BFs, but I just met this awesome guy and I hella-heart him. The issue? I'm six-foot-one and he's 5'10." When I'm in stilettos he looks like Kevin Hart and I feel like Lurch. Are kitten heels the worst?"—@ LongTallSally1981

A: Yes, sugar, kitten heels are the worst. Only appropriate if you're Michelle Obama or Carla Bruni, you're a smidge taller than your president husband, and you absolutely cannot dwarf him in front of the world. The Obama-Bruni Clause. Excuse me while I have this notarized…

Here's the thing. You seem charmed by the new man. Focus on the thrill of new love. It hardly ever comes in the package we envisioned. Instead of hiding an imagined flaw, enhance it. He knows you're tall and loves it. You should love it, too. Rock the most obscene heel you have and watch him gaze up at you like he's just aching to climb your mountain. I'd suggest Guiseppe Zanotti's Grommet Ankle-Buckle Heel. It's so S&M fierce. Like something out of the Red Room. Raowr.

Jenna Jones clicked the "publish" button, sat back in her new chair at her new desk at StyleZine.com—and grinned. She whipped her compact out of her makeup bag and freshened her lip gloss. It was the

Friday of her first week on the job, and she was due in her boss's office in five minutes. As she fluffed up her Flashdance-style curls, she felt relieved. Her stomach might've been in knots, but at least she looked perky.

She crossed the bare-bones, industrial loft space filled with cubicles. One wall was tiger-striped, the floor was made of steel, and the only decorations were a few banana yellow chaise lounges and an oversized print of Marc Jacobs in drag. Jenna's look that day was "Cerebral Charlie's Angel" (since elementary school, she had a near-OCD level need to name every outfit in her orbit): a vintage Seventies denim wrap skirt, an oxford rolled up at the sleeves, and sky-high cork stilettos. Getting dressed that morning, she almost felt confident—like the woman she used to be, before her life fell apart. Before she fled to her childhood home in rural Virginia.

She was trying her hardest to fit in at StyleZine, an online fashion mag devoted to street style, but Jenna missed the print world, where she felt safe. She ached for her glitzy life at *Darling* magazine, where she worked as the fashion director for ages until her quasi-nervous breakdown. She mourned the loss of her healthy clothing allowance, massive photo shoot budgets, and the pony skin rug in her office (God, that rug was so good). Sexy *Cosmo* girls, icy *Vogue* bitches, fiercely toned *Self* chicks—it was all she knew.

But that world, with its Columbia School of Journalism degree-wielding socialites and high-glam aesthetic was old school and barely breathing. To be a fashion expert these days, all you had to do was *decide* you were one. Any wily twenty-year-old with a covetable look, a WordPress account and enough followers could be a powerful style insider. They'd displaced major editors from the front row at Gucci!

She arrived at her boss's office and Terry, an associate editor, hurried over to intercept her.

"Jenna, I was supposed to tell you that Darcy's gonna be late. It's a thousand percent my bad," Terry said. She was the eyes and ears of the office; a cheerful gossip who made it her business to know everyone's business, and who always said exactly what she was thinking, blithely and with no filter. The combination made her a social magnet, and *the* person to have as an ally. Jenna needed a friend in the office, but so far, everyone regarded her with a polite, slightly patronizing wariness.

She was determined to befriend that girl, if it killed her.

"No problem," said Jenna. Terry was wearing a backless cherry red bodysuit, purple throwback Reebok high-tops and black lipstick. The part of her strawberry blonde hair that wasn't shaved was scraped up into a tight topknot. Jenna mentally labeled the outfit "Athleisure Lolita."

"Your bodysuit is gorge," Jenna continued. "Kenzo? I've always been a fan of Kenzo."

Stop being so gushy, Jenna thought. *Twenty-something fashion girls can smell fear. I should know; I once was one.*

"Yeah. Kenzo's cute, but way too expensive." Terry was multi-tasking, scrolling through her phone while chatting. "I mean, whatever, it's a *leotard.* But they gave it to me for free. All I had to do was IG a selfie in it for #OOTD. You know how that whole thing goes."

"Absolutely," said Jenna. She did not know how that whole thing went, and had never heard of #OOTD.

"Speaking of #OOTD, did you take a pic of your outfit today? You should. It's a totally new look for a StyleZine staffer. You're giving 'established grownup realness.' You're so pulled-together." Terry said this with the slightest hint of condescension. It was not lost on Jenna that in an office of artfully mismatched millennials doing a punky-funky-urban thing, she stuck out as slightly too…sophisticated. "Carolina Herrera?"

"Good eye!" Her outfit wasn't Carolina Herrera. It wasn't even Old Navy. But before Terry asked any more questions, she decided to change the subject. "I meant to tell you that your Instagram is truly breathtaking."

Jenna had done her new-job research, scrolling through the Insta-accounts of all of StyleZine's editors, each of whom had a zillion followers.

"Seriously? Thanks."

"You have this one shot in a furry white vest, and oh!" Jenna clutched her heart. "With your white-blonde hair and the animal print leggings? It reminded me of an Alaskan cover shoot I did with Karolina Kurkova in 2000. There were artificial igloos and white tigers. So dazzling! You're twins."

"Never heard of her."

"Karolina? She was a Czech supermodel."

"Ohhh yeah, I sort of remember that Eastern Bloc era. Way back in, like, second grade when I used to cut up mom's fashion magazines to make collages. All the models were like slumped and pale, and looked mad bummed." She giggled. "Chernobyl chic."

"Chernobyl chic, so funny," said Jenna. Her mom's magazines? Second grade?

Terry's phone buzzed, and she looked down at it and groaned. "Ugh, it's Kevin, *fuck my life.* He's so obvious, with his black nail polish and generic polysexuality. Dude, you're a former high school lacrosse player from Myrtle Beach; you're not dangerous. Whatevs, I'm breaking up with him after the Watch the Throne concert."

Jenna cleared her throat and tried another angle. "So, I was really impressed with the quality of your photos. They look professional."

"I'm the queen of filters," said Terry. "What's your Instagram?"

"I don't have one. I mean, not yet."

Terry's jaw dropped. "It's 2012! You're not on the 'Gram? I don't know if that's punk rock or completely dysfunctional."

"Actually, I'm just a terrible photographer." The truth? During Jenna's tear-stained sabbatical, she'd rejected technology and fully missed the social media revolution. "I've never even taken a selfie!"

"Well, it's an art. Don't let anyone tell you different."

"Question. If someone else takes the pic for you, is it called a 'self-helpie?' You know, because you got help?'"

As soon as the attempt at a joke left her mouth, she knew how dumb she sounded.

"Umm…no," said Terry slowly, like she was talking to a child.

"Of course, I know," tittered Jenna. "Duh."

Why was her personality coming off so weird in this place? All week, she'd been wearing her past like armor, praying that no one could sense that she was an expensive-looking fake. Even her outfit was fake—which, for someone who was supposed to be an arbiter of style, was unthinkable. Carolina Herrera? Please.

I am a forty-year-old woman in a $4.99 shirt from Wet Seal because I sold all my designer clothes to move back here, and I have exactly enough in my account to cover this month's rent, and right now I'd consider American Eagle an extravagance. I'm a former glamour girl hoping that no one notices the vague stain on my skirt—a stain I don't even know the origins of, since I got it at a stoop sale in my new 'hood, a sketched-out Brooklyn block where I share real estate with a KFC and beauty salon called Snip It Real Good. I am a grown woman wearing 1974-era heels I stole from my mother's closet.

Terry shot Jenna a pitying look, then whispered, "Just so I'm clear… you were kidding about the self-helpie thing, right?"

"Dumb joke."

"Dude! You're, like, awkward squared!" She said this brightly, without a trace of meanness. "It's always weird being the new girl. Just relax."

"Thank you," said Jenna, smiling weakly. "I haven't had coffee yet. I should never attempt to be funny before noon."

Terry lowered her voice. "Are you nervous because you're working for Darcy? Don't be. I mean, we're all terrified of her, but you're, like, contemporaries, so she'll probably go easy on you."

Darcy was the CEO of Belladonna Media, the digital media company that owned StyleZine and eight other successful women's online magazines. She was widely known to be an unrepentant bitch.

"She's so frightening," continued Terry, in a low whisper. "She banned me from work for a week last month, no pay, because I had some bad sushi at Chuko and my face broke out. She said my skin was making her gag."

"That's Darcy," said Jenna, rolling her eyes. "But I'm not scared of her. I've known her since we were editorial assistants. When I look at her, I see a twenty-five-year-old dressed like the frontwoman of a ska/hip hop fusion band."

"I was so much flyer than Gwen Stefani," said a withering, raspy voice behind Jenna.

Terry's face blanched. Jenna turned around and saw Darcy, standing with her hands on her hips.

"Hey, Darcy!" said Jenna.

"Well, if it isn't the patron saint of wanna-be fashionistas from flyover states," said the elfin CEO. She clocked in at only five feet, but her presence was massive. With her enormous, always-appraising (and never quite impressed) hazel-brown eyes, perfect miniature body, and smoky voice that always sounded like she just woke up, she was one of those mesmerizing women that men couldn't get enough of without understanding why.

She focused her attention on Terry. "We need to talk, lover. Your post on the blonde in the Giambattista Valli ethnic print swing blouse? Incredible style, but she looks like Mayor Bloomberg. No ugly girls. We need our readers lusting to look like these broads, or else we lose traffic, advertisers, and our jobs. Wake up!" She clapped in her face, twice. "Mitchell's such a clued-in photo editor, what was he thinking? That husky queen needs to spend less time photographing himself in front of gelato shops," this was a reference to his fledgling food blog, "and focus on the job that pays his goddamned bills. Fucking gelato. That's why he's built like a 9 volt Duracell battery."

"I...I'm sorry, Darcy, I'll delete the post."

"Damned right. Leave us."

Terry scrambled away, and Darcy shot Jenna an exasperated look. "Children."

Jenna fake-smiled and nodded, almost blown away by that diatribe—but not really. She was used to Darcy's acerbic persona. Actually, given her history with the CEO, it was bizarre that they were even in the same room and on speaking terms, let alone working together.

It had all started with a man. When Jenna was twenty-three she dated an Arista Records exec named Marcus. For a small town girl new to the big city, dating a guy that was a major industry player was magical! For months, she ignored the fact that Marcus' phone rang at weird times, and that he was only available at the most random hours (dinner at either 5 or 11?). But he was a great kisser and he knew Method Man personally, so she was super-into him.

On Valentine's Day, Jenna decided to surprise him at his Brooklyn apartment with a homemade cake. But he didn't answer the door—a tiny, furious chick with a chic pixie-cut did. It was Marcus' real girlfriend. His fiancée, a twenty-four-year old *Mademoiselle* editorial assistant named Darcy Vale.

She grabbed the cake and slammed it in Jenna's face. Hard. Not only was Jenna knocked out, she had an icing-smeared cut on her lip that required three stitches.

Both women were soon-to-be powerful in media (and powerful *black* women in media), so their social circles intersected a thousand different ways. The two were at the same parties, fashion shows, and weddings. There was no avoiding her as they ascended in the industry, and Darcy tortured Jenna every chance she could.

"So, how was your first week?" asked Darcy, striding into her office, with Jenna following behind.

"It's been fun," said Jenna, fussing with her hair again. The curls, like everything else about her, were new. In Virginia, she'd been too Xanax-zonked to deal with relaxers, so she let her natural hair happen. "Thanks again for the opportunity."

"It wasn't a favor. I'm a businesswoman and, the truth is, I need you. StyleZine has some of the sharpest fashion brains in the industry, but they're kids. They're lacking connections, real access. I needed an experienced OG editor to attract flashy advertisers and media attention. *Darling's* Fashion Director? The good-cop judge on ABC's cheesiest hit, *America's Modeling Competition*? You're perfect." She tousled her honey-highlighted Halle spikes. "Though I don't know why I trust you after you stole that *Harper's Bazaar* position from me, fifteen years ago."

"I didn't steal it," Jenna said, patiently. "You got fired and I got hired."

"You'd been campaigning for the position for months. But it's all good. Forever ago, right?" Darcy smiled, slightly menacingly. "Where are you living now? Certainly not the West Village townhouse; I read somewhere that Brian's still there."

Jenna flinched when she heard his name. "I moved to a one-bedroom on Reade."

"Reade in Tribeca? Those rents are astronomical; Brian must've hooked it up for you. You can't afford it on your salary. God, I'm so tickled to have gotten an establishment editor basically for free."

She'll never let me forget that I was desperate enough to accept a humiliating pay cut. Anything for a second chance.

"No, Reade in Brooklyn," Jenna said, trying to temper her irritation. "It's an up-and-coming neighborhood."

"Charming." Darcy crinkled her adorable nose. "So, how was Virginia?"

She pasted a cheery smile. "Cathartic. I loved taking the time to unplug."

"Ha! That's what every out-of-work editor says when she's spending the day doing Kegels and obsessively updating her LinkedIn profile."

Jenna ignored this, returning to her rehearsed spiel. "Also, the style theory class I taught at the community college really gave me a fresh insight to . . ."

"Whatever. Just know I was sympathetic to your situation," Darcy interrupted. "You're better off without Brian. All that jet-setting without you. Those rumors! You can't trust a self-made millionaire. Their dicks are too hard for the lifestyle. Next time, get a man with family inheritance." She winked. "The money's less sexy to them."

Jenna stared at her for a beat, too shocked at her audacity to speak.

"Darcy, I respect you. And I'm thrilled to be here. But I'd appreciate it if you stop mentioning my ex-fiancée."

Darcy raised her eyebrows. "You've gotten feisty in your old age. I like it."

"Not feisty. Direct."

"Okay." She eyed her old rival. "Let's get something straight. I won't forget how you dropped every ounce of professionalism and skipped town over personal drama. You have an eight-month contract—I expect you to triple StyleZine's readership in that time. Fail, and you're fired. Because if you fuck me, you know I'll fuck you harder."

Jenna looked at her, galled. This was a girl who, at a Def Jam assistant's house party in 1997, made besties with a famed video vixen—and then convinced the vixen's rapper boyfriend to pay her rent for a year. A woman who, in 2003, purposely dated a photographer who'd snapped nude pics of her *Seventeen* publisher, and then secretly sold copies to the gossip blogs—resulting in her boss' dismissal and Darcy's promotion to her spot. A shark who, after predicting in 2007 that magazines were doomed, lured tycoon businessman Louis Belladonna away from his wife, pillaged his bank account to launch Belladonna Media, transformed two style blogs into an eight-website beauty and fashion conglomerate…and then divorced him.

Jenna had her number. So, there was no way in hell she'd allow Darcy to threaten her.

"You've already made it clear that I need to deliver. I'm here to write my 'Just Jenna' advice column and develop a fashion web series. Let me do my job, Darcy, and we both know I'll make this site more successful than ever."

"I'm *loving* this new you," said Darcy. "I wish you'd always been this feisty. Sparring with you would've been so much more satisfying."

"Sparring?" Jenna laughed. "In '99, you impersonated Karl Lagerfield's publicist and emailed me a fake itinerary for the Chanel press trip! Ten fashion editors were flown to Ibiza for the weekend, and I ended up at a sweatshop in Gowanus."

"Which inspired your 'ugly beauty' *Darling* shoot at the Gowanus Canal with ballerinas wearing tattered Vivienne Westwood. You're welcome."

"Those were the good old days," said Jenna.

"These are the good old days," said Darcy, eyeing her Cartier tank watch. "I'm late for lunch at Brasserie."

She stood and headed for the door, shouting directives at Jenna as she went. "I need three more Just Jenna posts by 5. And come up with ideas for your web series—the new videographer is starting on Monday. And get your social media footprint together. Our editors are digital stars; you need to be one, too. Figure it out."

It was then that Jenna truly started to panic. Social media footprint? What did that even mean?

CHAPTER 2

Jenna had shut the world out in Virginia. It was just her, hiding out in her parents' house in a holy flannel shirt and circa-1989 Bart Simpson boxers ("Trailer Park Hopelessness"), developing a smoking habit and binge-watching "Game of Thrones." She'd been groggy with isolation and languishing in her childhood bedroom, which was overflowing with trash bags full of her designer clothes, handbags and shoes—artifacts from a past life. There was no waxing, no mani/pedis, no sex, and she only used the Internet to check the weather. The last thing on her mind was social media. But now, it was time to figure it out.

Jenna flipped open the laptop perched on her desk in her tiny office (as StyleZine's Elder Stateswoman, she was awarded a former custodial closet instead of a cubicle. Thrilled to have a door, she accepted). Since the idea of wading through Twitter incinerated her brain, she pulled up Facebook. From 2010 to 2012, the site had gone from a chatty family reunion to an orgy of oversharing.

She had so many questions. GIFs—did no one think they were disturbing, like bad acid trip hallucinations? Who created those spiritual epithets written in spunky fonts over pictures of sunsets? Was there an approved list of hashtags somewhere? Pausing to photograph your pecan-encrusted French toast before eating it—was this the digital version of saying grace? Kanye, Kim, and kale—did nothing else matter? Jenna felt like she'd just rocketed from the Paleolithic era in a Delorean.

Already overwhelmed, she swiveled her chair around to stare at the wall behind her desk. She hadn't yet decorated, save for one important thing—her beloved vintage movie poster of Nina Mae McKinney in the 1928 musical *Hallelujah*. Forgotten today, Nina Mae McKinney was the most beautiful black woman in Hollywood before Halle, Dorothy, or Lena ever drew a breath. Just a small-town Southern girl who was plucked out of the chorus line to star in the first black musical, ever—and then Charlestoned her way through Europe, romancing royals and drinking bathtub gin. She was Jenna's spirit animal. The poster had hung in every office she'd ever had.

Who would she be today? thought Jenna. *Probably Beyoncé, since Nina was a triple threat, too. Is Beyoncé a great actress, though? She was glorious in Dreamgirls, but she looked like she was nursing an ulcer as Etta James in Cadillac Records…*

Just then, her iPhone vibrated on top of her desk. Swiveling around, she grabbed it—and when she saw who it was, all breath left her body.

Brian Stein. Her former Jewish Adonis. Why would he be calling? What did they have to talk about?

Paralyzed, Jenna stared as the phone vibrated five times. And then, a millisecond before the call went to voice mail, she answered. "Jenna?"

"Is this Stromboli's Pizzeria again? I didn't order; you have the wrong number."

"Funny."

"Hi." She held her breath.

"Hi. I can't believe I'm actually hearing your voice."

"Yeah. Weird. Can I help you?"

"I assume a 'welcome back' is in order? I was surprised to hear that you were back in the city. I thought you would've called me."

"Honestly, I didn't think it would affect your life in any way."

"I know we've been through hell, JJ, but you can't pretend we're not connected. We were together for twenty years. Can't we be friends?"

"*You* left *me*."

"No, I told you I was opposed to your vision for our future."

"You told me? I wasn't your secretary, Brian. We were two people in a relationship!"

"You weren't happy either."

"I wasn't happy because the love of my life—my first and only love, since I was a freshman at Georgetown—wasted my sexiest years, pretended he wanted to marry me, and then changed his mind about being a husband and a father. That was thrilling news for a woman with thirty-eight-year-old eggs."

"Look, I just want us to be on good terms. Are you open to grabbing coffee? I'll send a car to your office."

"Brian, I wish you well. But I'm not interested in sipping lattes with you and pretending you didn't ruin my life."

"Fine, JJ." He sighed. "There was another reason for my call. I…I guess I wanted you to hear this from me. I've been seeing someone, seriously."

"Oh?" Jenna clutched her stomach and shut her eyes. She knew this moment would come, but she wasn't ready. And she'd wanted to have a boyfriend first.

"You might know her. Lily. She works for *Salon*."

"*Lily L'Amour?* You're seeing the relationship columnist at *Salon*? You couldn't find someone in a different industry? And her name isn't Lily, by the way. It's Celeste Wexler."

"I know."

"Anna must be thrilled you have a Jewish girlfriend."

"You know my mom adores you. Won't even look Lily in the eyes, she's so loyal to you. The first and last time I took Lily home, she had an episode of *America's Modeling Competition* playing on DVR."

This gave Jenna a surge of ex-girlfriend satisfaction. "Well, I'm happy you're happy."

"You were gone. You didn't even give us a chance to figure it out."

"Figure what out? You threw yourself into your work, into being the famous real estate developer, the man I helped make. You hadn't touched me in over a year." She swallowed. "I'm still wondering who you were touching."

"Holy Christ. I'm not dignifying that with a response."

"You never have." She slumped down in her chair, hit by a tidal wave of sadness. "We'd planned a whole life together. You backed out."

"I didn't want what you wanted. But I didn't want to lose you."

"And the award for most classically male declaration of selfishness goes to..."

"You imploded," said Brian. "You sold my Warhol and my Koons on the stoop for five dollars. You fought with me in the street, accusing me of cheating with everyone from our dry cleaner's daughter to the gay guy who installs sewage systems in my residential communities. The gay guy?"

"Well, you'd become so secretive! And you're obsessed with fancy exfoliants. Plus, you had that man-crush on George Clooney..."

"I'm a wealthy guy who lives in suits. Clooney is the best-dressed man in the world. Damned right I have a man-crush on him." He paused. "You left without saying goodbye. It was very difficult."

"Difficult? *Zumba* is difficult!"

"I called, I emailed—and nothing. I waited for you," he said. "But I couldn't stay alone forever."

"Of course not. Look, I wish you and Celeste the best. I will check *Salon* every month to see if she mentions your left-leaning penis in her column." She took a deep breath. "I'm finally over you, Brian. And I just want you to be happy."

"Thank you. Even though you just insulted my penis." He paused. "I'll let you go, I'm catching a flight to the country."

He means the East Hampton house that I decorated. I art-directed our lives, and he financed it. We were sure to crumble under the weight of all that pretty.

"Just…congratulations on the job. And JJ? If Darcy Vale gives you any trouble, I'll buy her company and sell it to OWN."

"I can handle Darcy."

"Hmm. I recall a younger you crying in my arms after she caked you," said Brian, with a light chuckle. "We broke up one time, and you ended up with her fiancé. Of all the men in Manhattan."

"Yeah, well that was a long time ago."

"I hope you change your mind about coffee."

"I hope you change your mind about hoping I change my mind."

Jenna hung up and stared into space. Since stepping into the office this morning, she'd gone from zingy excitement about her comeback, to feeling like an out-of-step dinosaur, to stomach-churning hurt. She hated that Brian could still affect her. She got up, shut her office door, and sat on top of her desk. And bawled.

"*Lily L'Amour?* With her silly, pedantic Carrie Bradshaw-lite column that reads like *Twilight* fan fiction crossed with *Are You There God It's Me Margaret?* This is the woman that my fiancé is deeply in love with? He went from me to that? You guys go on without me, I'll just be here. Dead."

It was later that evening, and Jenna was lying on her back on an enormous, all-white bed in an all-white suite at the Highline Hotel on 20th Street. The hotel's creative director, Elodie Franklin, was Jenna's best friend since Georgetown—and tonight, she was throwing a book launch in the hotel's Refectory. The fete started in fifteen minutes, and the girls were having pre-game champagne.

"If you die over Brian Stein, I'll kill you." Elodie was perched at the vanity, painstakingly applying a dramatic swoop of black liquid liner. She'd been raised on a hippie commune in Berkeley by a Korean mother and black father (she looked so much like a certain music mogul divorcee that she'd been known to sign autographs on Kimora's behalf). As a kid, when anyone on the commune had an issue, they all sat in a circle, practiced their primal screams and kept it moving. She abhorred delving too deeply in emotions. Her style was to barrel straight to the point, boundary-free; whether it was during an argument or while seducing one of her many grateful conquests. A stunner, she stood at least 5'11 in her usual "Medieval Whore Meets Biker Chick" look: a gauzy maxi-dress that exposed her massive cleavage, a long braid tossed over one shoulder, and motorcycle boots.

"You're heartless," said Billie Burke-Lane, Jenna's other closest friend. She was on the floor in Downward Dog. As an overscheduled wife and mother, yoga was the only thing that calmed her, even when done in the middle of a conversation.

"I'm not heartless. I adore my Chihuahuas," said Elodie.

"You are. Jenna just found out that Brian is dating the genius who dreams up gems like, '10 Ways to Relate to His Penis Personality.' Show some compassion," said Billie.

A busty cutie with a swingy, chestnut blowout, she met Jenna in the Condé Nast cafeteria in 2001, where they'd bonded over being black editors at mainstream magazines. At the time, Billie had been *Du Jour's* beauty director, but when the magazine folded, she joined M. Cosmetics as V.P. of Global Communications. Of Jenna's two friends, she was the nurturing mama bear who worshipped at the altar of openness and true love. She tried to make time for her single friends and their shenanigans— but her true focus was staying sane so she could get home to her five-year-old daughter, May, and her husband, Jay, an award-winning poet who taught Voices of the Diaspora at Fordham University.

Billie and Elodie were bound together because they both loved Jenna, but they bickered like a couple in the first third of a rom-com.

"Billie, I refuse to take you seriously while you're upside down," said Elodie. "Also, I'm insulted that you're not staying for my party."

"I'm only here to support Jenna in her time of woe. I'm jetlagged from that sales conference in Hong Kong. I don't have the energy to celebrate a photography book devoted to dogs dressed in lingerie. I just want to go home and watch *Veep* in my panties."

At the Highline Hotel, Elodie oversaw artsy-fartsy charity soirees or fashion industry events—but her real moneymakers were parties promoting pet projects for A-listers who wanted to be famous for something else. Tonight's fete was for a Guess model-turned-photographer—and her celebrity chef husband had paid Elodie an obscene amount to make her conceptual coffee table book seem legit.

Elodie spun around her padded bench and faced Jenna.

"You've said Brian's dead to you. Why do you care who he sleeps with?"

"I'm…just scandalized by his choice in women." Her stomach was churning. "Brian has impeccable taste. He has decanters prettier than her! I felt like I had to be flawless for this man, and now he's with a chick who looks like Chelsea Handler?"

"Honestly," continued Elodie with a chuckle, "I can't even see Brian with a white woman. Remember how black he was at school? I love when he tries to go all fake Trump with me. It's like, please don't make me tell the *Wall Street Journal* that you taught my dorm how to do the Roger Rabbit."

"When did he become a sociopath?" wondered Jenna.

"He's not a sociopath," said Billie, now sitting cross-legged on the plush rug. "Just the nightmare New York man."

Elodie nodded. "The kind who makes so much money that he thinks you should ignore your bothersome needs and just be pleased as fuck to be in his orbit."

"But Brian really did love you," said Billie, who always hoped they'd make it through their rough patch. "He was so committed, for so long. But then he just…wasn't."

"And I lost it," said Jenna. "Do you realize that this is my first social event since Le Petit Scandale? I basically had a meltdown in front of Manhattan. All those public fights Brian and I had. Then there was the bleak Dorothy Parker poem I posted on Facebook…"

"'Guns aren't lawful; nooses give; gas smells awful; might as well live.'" Elodie grimaced. "No wonder you swore off social media."

Billie glared at her.

"And then *Darling* sent me on mental health leave, and promoted my number two the next day. I'm not even sure that's legal. I left the Condé Nast building sobbing through the lobby during lunchtime, when the traffic's highest. I'm pretty sure Anna Wintour did a double take."

No one person's bigger than Darling, her editor-in-chief had said. *You were gone, and Bertie stepped up. Frankly, we needed some new energy, anyway.*

"The gossip blogs were terrible," she said. "*Gawker, Page 6,* the blind items. A disgrace. Seriously, I've spent the past two days psyching myself up to show my face at this party."

"You're talking like you were Amanda Bynes," said Elodie. "It was low-level media gossip. Blew over in five minutes. Plus, it gave you an edge."

"Agreed," said Billie. "If you're going to fall apart, make it interesting. Look at Elizabeth Taylor." Billie adored La Liz. "When her life imploded, she binged on fried chicken, became a blowzy alcoholic, wore plus-size Halston and married a Republican. Divine."

Jenna suddenly sat up on the bed, grabbing her glass of champagne from the nightstand. "You know what? No more Brian talk. I'm back, I have this fab new job, and I'm no longer a depressed Zoloftian! I need to get mega-drunk and forget that entire conversation."

"Cheers to your comeback," exclaimed Elodie, lifting up her glass. "Even if you have to work with fashion's answer to Abbie Lee Miller."

"Cheers," said Billie, clinking her glass with the others. "Plus, you cannot waste a dress that good, weeping in a hotel room."

For the first time in ages, Jenna was feeling kind of cute. She wore a clingy, knee-length, white dress with lingerie detailing, which she'd swiped from the fashion closet at work ("South Beach Goldigger")—and sky-high orange stilettos, borrowed from Billie.

"You know what I'd love?" asked Jenna.

"Ombre highlights?" asked Billie, their resident beauty expert. "They'd be everything with your new hair."

"Cute! But no. Sex. It's been *years*. This morning I tried to masturbate and I swear my vagina laughed at me."

"Oh sweetie," said Billie, sadly.

"But I just got my first Brazilian wax in forever, and I'm feeling like this is a step in a lustier direction."

"A bald vag is necessary to have a restorative one-night stand, which is what you need," agreed Elodie.

"Am I ready, though? I doubt I even remember how to properly administer a blowjob."

"Please, it's like riding a bike." Elodie tugged at her dress, exposing more of her F-cup cleavage. "Running to the event now. See you downstairs, Jenna. Tonight, I'm setting you up!"

"Find her a guy you haven't slept with," Billie called out to Elodie, as she swept out the door.

"In this crowd, that might be challenging!" hollered Elodie.

Then, Billie climbed on the bed and handed a slightly worried-looking Jenna a siren-red lipstick. "Like Elizabeth Taylor said, 'Pour yourself a drink, put on some lipstick, and pull yourself together.' Now go. You can't be late for your coming out party."

CHAPTER 3

The Refectory had once been a dorm for monks, and looked it. Elodie had taken advantage of the gothic, cathedral-esque space by going for an *Eyes Wide Shut* vibe with the decor. Billowing, sheer white curtains sectioned off six separate areas—each with its own bar. Crimson candles dripped on to every surface, massive gold chandeliers hung from the arched ceilings; and overstuffed purple velvet chaises were arranged in darkened, sexy corners. As was custom with any event where models were the centerpiece, there were men everywhere.

The crowd was a sampling from every scene, a perfect storm of NYC nightlife. The Weeknd and Drake were blaring—but no one was dancing, except for the guest of honor's fellow Victoria's Secret models. Posed in clusters throughout were their boy-model counterparts, dressed in lumberjack shirts and reeking of Parliaments and Bushwick boredom. Holding court at the bar were the ever-important Suits, who always kept the scene going by financing most of Elodie's celebrity pet projects. Hovering above the crowd was a handful of gorgeous NBA and NFL stars, who were a must at these things, because both the models and the Suits appreciated them. And then there were a few scorchingly chic, high-priced hookers (these were for the Suits too charmless to score a model). Weaving throughout were bespectacled, indie-cute journalists on the arts/lifestyle beat, and young fashion girls, who were as sexy as the models, but short and poor.

Jenna hadn't been in the room for two seconds before her best friend grabbed her arm.

"I found you a man," said Elodie, who'd spent the last twenty minutes shirking her event-planning duties to play matchmaker. "All I know is he went to Yale and he's a radiologist. He's walking toward us now.'"

"Wait! I'm not ready…"

"You haven't had sex since the Bush administration. You're ready." She shoved a glass of champagne at Jenna. "Dialo Banin! This is Jenna Jones. Jenna, this good man has been dying to meet you. Talk amongst yourselves, while I go bounce a few VH1 reality show whores."

With that rushed introduction, Elodie dashed off into the crowd. Dialo stood in front of Jenna, affixing her with a brilliant white smile. He was wearing an achingly expensive suit, a tangerine day scarf arranged just so, and aviators. Indoors. At night.

"So…what were your other two wishes?"

"I'm sorry?"

"Where's your sense of humor, hon?" he asked, smiling. "It was an ice-breaker."

"Oh! Well, ice broken." Coming from this man, with his florid accent, in that getup, the "wishes" line sounded like a come-on that Truman Capote would've delivered at a dude disco in Vegas.

"Would you like to sit down?"

"I'd love to," she said, making a mental note to destroy Elodie for this. Dialo touched her elbow and led her over to an itty-bitty reserved cocktail table flanked by two high-backed, wrought iron chairs. He sat back in his chair, stretching out his legs. There was now no room for her under the table, so she wrapped her ankles around her chair legs, like a schoolgirl. Nervous, she folded her hands in her lap, and then accidentally lasered-in on Dialo's burgundy velvet YSL slippers.

Jenna understood exactly who Dialo was. He was one of those fake-flashy Euro neo-dandies who hung "WC" signs on the bathroom doors in their Murray Hill rentals.

"I have to admit, I'm not a book enthusiast. But I'm glad I came," he said, stroking his chin. "You're lucky to be here."

"I know, it's a great party."

"No, I mean you're lucky to be *here*. With me. I don't usually date black women. But when I Googled you on my phone, I had to make an exception."

"Huh. But you're black. Why don't you..." She stopped talking, because she noticed that Dialo wasn't even looking at her. He peered over her shoulder. She darted her eyes in that direction, and saw a group of twenty-year-olds in tiny dresses—the knockoff version of hers.

An hour before, Jenna had felt a degree of excitement while getting dressed for her first night out since returning to New York. She'd almost felt like a dewy-eyed recent college grad, heading out for a naughty night of club-hopping and hopefully getting pawed by a baby Leo DiCaprio in VIP. But her options were no longer limitless. She was decades older, and being ignored by a fancy-pants douche she wasn't even attracted to.

"I'm black," he continued, "but not American black like you. I'm from Ghana via London. And relax, I just find white women to be more easygoing."

"Ohhh, you're one of those." Jenna swirled her straw in her drink, trying to figure out how to lose this bozo. "But I'm clearly black, so why are you here?"

"I do enjoy some biracial women, which is what I figured you were from your pictures. So you get a pass, love." He guffawed.

"Nope, not biracial. I'm one hundred percent all-American black. So black that my middle name is Keisha."

Dialo grimaced. "Anyway, when I found out you used to be a famous fashion editor, I was impressed. I have a superb publicist, should you need one. He's so stylish. He hooked me up with this Matthew Williamson scarf."

"That's a woman's piece, you know."

"But it works with a strong seamed jacket."

"Indeed." Jenna vowed to kill Elodie. "So, should a radiologist have a publicist? Isn't that breaking some sort of Hippocratic oath?"

"I mostly have A-list clients, so…" he trailed off. "I must say, you look just like a girl I went to Yale with. But surely you're a good ten years younger than me, little lady."

Jenna grinned, deciding to fuck with him a little.

"Doubt it. I'm forty-five." She added on five years, just to watch his head explode. "How old are you?"

"Forty-five? I'm forty-three!"

"So, we're contemporaries."

"But I thought…wow, forty-five? I wouldn't have guessed."

His entire body language changed. He shook his head, as if rejecting the entire notion. And then actually looked at his watch. She signaled a waitress. "Sweetie, could we get some napkins?"

"Why do you need napkins?" Then Dialo lowered his voice and asked Jenna, "Am I making you wet?"

Jenna finished the rest of her champagne and then stood up, slowly rearranging her dress. As she did, she allowed her bag to tip the remaining splash of his cocktail onto one of his velvet slippers.

As Dialo squealed like Babe, she hurried away, grabbing two glasses of champagne from a cater waiter's tray. He was vile. But the worst part? He wasn't at all unique. He was the classic New York mover-and-shaker. A doctor with a publicist. Straight, but so fey you could smell the Kiehl's eye cream.

Jenna stormed through the party, looking everywhere for Elodie. Since she was nowhere to be found, she planted herself next to a bar and downed both glasses. Just then a group of guys swept by her, all Suits. She'd known them peripherally for years—and tonight, they were surrounded by six hotties in their twenties (in outfits Jenna would later describe as being a cross between "Atlanta Prom" and "Who Gives a Fuck"). The guys gave Jenna air-kisses, and the May-December group went on their way.

"What is this?" she murmured out loud to no one, shaking her head in frustration. The room swayed a little bit. Steadying herself by grabbing the edge of the bar, she asked the willowy bartender, "If you have a Brazilian and no one sees it, does it exist? You know, like the tree in the forest thing?"

The girl giggled. "What's wrong, doll?"

"Can I get another glass of Prosecco?" The chick slid her one, Jenna's fourth, and she threw it back. She was well on the road to sloshed. "What's up with the twenty-year-old girls? These men are *my* age. The guys get older, the girls get younger, and where does that leave me? I was with *one man* my whole life. I'm forty and basically dating for the first time. I have no idea how to naviglate... nafligate...navigate this world."

Finishing her drink, she saw one of her Suit friends catch her eye and then point at his model's ass behind her back. He leered. Jenna shot him her middle finger.

"Honey," said the waitress, "why don't you go sit down for a little bit?"

"*Speshtacular* idea."

Jenna spotted an empty chaise in a dark corner, half-hidden by one of the swaying curtains. She managed to weave her way through the crowd and plunk herself down on the little couch. She must've dozed off, because the next thing she knew, someone tapped her shoulder.

"You okay?'

Jenna sat up straight, jerking her head up so fast that her hair got caught in her lip gloss. A man sat next to her. A kid, really—he looked barely out of his teens, wearing Jordans, distressed jeans and a black tee that shouted "Blame Society" in red typeface. A busy swirl of tattoos erupted from his shirtsleeve and covered his arm, stopping at his wrist. His look was effortlessly crisp, in a Red Hook hipster-meets-hip hop way. Lanky and tall with I-play-basketball-all-weekend biceps, he looked like a person who was well aware that he was, by far, the coolest sophomore at NYU.

He eyed her with furrowed concentration. "You okay?" he repeated.

"Yes! I'm fine. I'm great great great."

"Yeah, you sound it." He smiled. "How many drinks?"

"Four. No, five. Are you as drunk as me?"

He nodded, lifting up his glass. "And high. On too many things."

"But you're like, eighteen. Are you even legal? What are you doing here?"

"I'm twenty-two! I have a seriously elite college degree from USC Film School."

"USC Film? Color me impressed! If I wasn't in fashion, I'd be in film. In high school, I thought about being a film historian, but my mother was like, what the hell is a film historian, so I never…" Aware that she was rambling, she stopped herself. "She has a very strong personality. Anyway, that's fantastic."

"Not even. None of us can get jobs. The acceptance rate at USC Film is lower than Harvard Law. We worked our asses off for no reason. I'm here to pick up my boy, one of the waiters. Yo, this guy's one of the illest cinematographers of my generation, and he's serving moscato to a Basketball Wife."

"Yikes, Elodie's gonna be furious. She didn't want any reality people in here."

"They're here. I was just over in the fake butt section." He shuddered. "I haaate plastic surgery. Hard, balloon breasts. And what's that thing women do when they suck the fat out of their thighs?"

"Liposuction."

"Terrible. I like for women to have…" He paused, making grabby gestures in the air. "Smush."

Jenna got comfy, curling up against the back of the couch. "I've always wanted smush, but I'm too skinny. I've had curve-envy my whole life."

"You have smush somewhere. Besides, you're not skinny, you're… svelte. Sinuous."

"You like S words."

"Yeah, I had a lisp in kindergarten, so I like to stunt with my superior 'S' game."

"Awww!"

"I'm cutting myself off." He put his glass down on the cocktail table, shaking his head. "The lisp? Information not to disclose upon meeting a staggeringly pretty girl."

"You think I'm staggeringly pretty?"

He nodded. "Absolutely. You're, like, next-level fancy. Incapable of having a tacky moment. I was just at a party with girls filming twerk videos on Vine, so I can say this with authority."

"Twerk videos on Vine?" Jenna paused, and then frowned. "Actually, I don't even know what or where Vine is."

"You've never heard of Vine?"

She shrugged apologetically. "I've been away."

"See? I feel like you're a different breed of woman. Like you're from a planet of angelic goddesses who are, like, made of the sugary oozy stuff inside Cadbury eggs and speak in Ezra Pound stanzas. And own tiny condos inside of rainbows."

Jenna's mouth opened, and then she howled with unselfconscious laughter. "I'm what? You're so weird!"

"I know," he said, looking bashful. "I read too much science fiction."

"So do I. And weird is good. I love it."

"As long as you love it," he said. And then he grinned at her. Jenna's heart almost stopped. His smile tore through her like lightening. She felt it in her thighs.

Jesus, that mouth. Those puffy, bitable lips…

"You know what else you look like?"

"Tell me," she said.

He folded his arms across his chest and studied her, long and indulgently. Jenna's stomach flip-flopped—she was mesmerized. His eyes were arresting, almond-shaped and beyond black, like ink dipped in water. God, he was beautiful. Finally, his mouth curled into a secret smile, and Jenna smiled back, and then they were two strangers smiling giddily at each other, for no reason.

"You look like you need to be kissed. Badly."

"Worse than you know. How could you tell?"

"'Cause you're staring at my mouth with laser-like focus."

"Cocky."

"Self-aware."

"Well, it's true. Your mouth is really…good." Was it the alcohol, or was he the most fuckable person she'd ever seen? Jenna bit her bottom lip, her mind racing. She could feel her cheeks getting hot. She wanted to rip this kid's clothes off.

Was she drunk enough to do this?

"Do you want to kiss me?" she asked.

"Is that rhetorical?"

She shook her head, scooting a bit closer to him.

"If you knew what I wanted to do," he said, "you'd call security."

"Kiss me, then. We're both wasted. That means we won't muh-member…I mean, remember any of this tomorrow."

"Oh, I'll muh-member."

They both peered over the back of the couch to see how conspicuous they were. They were facing a corner, and the almost-sheer panel billowing from the ceiling was half-shielding them. Everyone was busy doing whatever people do at parties for dog books. Plus, it was really dark.

"No one's looking," she said. "So give me your best kiss. Your A-plus kiss."

"I'll give you the B-plus one. 'Cause I'm a gentleman."

"Lana Turner said a gentleman is a patient wolf," she whispered, tipping her face up to his.

"Lana Turner was correct." He leaned in, his lips almost touching hers. "So…now?"

"Now."

He brushed his lips across hers, barely grazing her. A thousand tingles shot through her body. He kissed her again, his lips soft, but firm. Then things got serious. He slid his hand into her hair, angled his mouth over hers and kissed her deeply, languidly.

A moan escaped her lips—she was totally caught off guard by how electric it felt. He pinned her against the chaise, tonguing her mouth with such sensuous rawness, it was like he was inside of her—and it was so achingly good that she forgot where she was, hiking her leg up around his waist, the hem of her dress sliding all the way to her hips. Holding her still by her hair, he kept at it, unraveling her, all giving, no taking—so that all she could do was grip his sides and drown—until an unimpressed waiter bumped into Jenna while collecting their drinks. Jolted, they drew apart and just looked at each other. Stunned.

"*Fuck,*" whimpered Jenna. Her eyes were half-closed.

"Your turn," he said, his fist still tangled in her hair. "I want your B-plus."

"I'll give you my B," she murmured. "I don't want to destroy you."

"Cocky."

"Self-aware."

Jenna pushed him back and climbed onto his lap, straddling him. Holding the top of the couch for balance, she kissed him with total voraciousness, letting loose all the lust and sexual frustration she'd had for years. He matched her intensity, bruising her lips with his and gripping her where her ass met her thighs.

"Smush," he growled into her mouth. "Told you."

"I…I can't believe I'm making out in the middle of a party," said Jenna, breaking their kiss. "I'm too old for this, we have to stop!"

"Yeah, definitely," he said, planting hot, open-mouthed kisses down her neck.

"I swear to God," she panted, "I think I love you."

"I know I love you," he murmured against her throat. Then, he looked up at her. "Wait, what's your name?"

"Jenna Jones!"

They both looked up in surprise at Elodie and her intern, Misty, who was struggling not to laugh.

They tore away from each other, landing on opposites sides of the couch.

"Kimora Lee Simmons?" He looked confused.

Elodie rolled her eyes. "Jenna, what the hell are you doing?"

"You said I needed a one-night stand!"

"Yes, but I never said you should have it at my event. On a loveseat I rented for six thousand dollars! You could have gotten a room. This is a hotel, there are dozens in this bitch!"

"But…it just felt urgent. I'm bald! I couldn't waste it!"

"Bald? You're not…" He stopped himself, chuckling. "Oh."

Elodie looked from him to Jenna, her long braid swinging.

"Who the hell is this kid? What happened to Dialo?"

"He had on velvet YSL slippers, Elodie. He was the living worst. I hate him."

He shot off the chaise in a drunken rage, unsteady on his feet.

"Velvet slippers? Was he mean to you? Prissy little bitch!"

"Pipe down, junior," said Elodie, grabbing his arm. She paused, squeezed his bicep, then looked him up and down. "Okay I get it, you're pretty or whatever. But this is not an under-eighteen situation. Your being here could get me arrested."

"Why does everyone keep saying I'm a teenager? I'm a grown-ass man, son."

"Sweetie, if you have to declare it…"

"Don't talk to my boyfriend like that," shouted Jenna, who stood up too quickly. She plopped back down on the chaise.

"Boyfriend?" He beamed at her, happily. "I'm Eric, by the way."

"*Erique. Ma Cherie.*" She made a heart shape with her fingers.

"Okay, that? Will be too hilarious tomorrow," said Elodie, stifling giggles. "Misty, escort Jenna's boyfriend over to the model section. Jenna, my love, you're coming to my suite. You need water and a bed. I should've kept my eye on you."

Just then, Jenna's eyes closed and she toppled over, face-first.

"Maaan, look! She passed out before I could get her number," said Eric, his face the picture of disappointment. He gestured toward Elodie. "I sort of feel like you're in charge. Can you give it to me?"

Elodie, who had sunk to her knees in front of the couch, had no time for this. "I'm sure Jenna had a meaningful experience with you tonight. But she's unconscious, so the moment's passed. Deuces, hot stuff."

Eric walked away, dejected. And then Elodie whisked Jenna away to her hotel room, where she spent the night with her head in the toilet. Her Alaia was ruined, she'd behaved like an adolescent, but the next morning, she felt triumphant.

Brian wasn't the only one who could move on.

CHAPTER 4

Rodarte, Helmut Lang, Peter Som, Marchesa, Diane von Furstenberg. Jenna was at her desk, trying to sift through the massive stack of New York Fashion Week invites (and missing the days when she had an assistant). The shows were coming up in less than a week, and it was her first appearance at the New York collections in four seasons. She missed this! Many top fashion editors complained about the rapid-fire show schedules, overpriced snack food, impossible cab situation, and extreme weather (always a thunderstorm, heat wave, or snow)—but Jenna still adored the spectacle too much to become jaded. For her, the bi-yearly New York collections were the most magical time of the year.

But the RSVPs were taking forever because she kept stopping to swipe concealer over her hickie. It was Monday, and it still hadn't faded. Fishing for her compact in her purse, the memory of the kiss washed over her. She stopped, smiling to herself.

So delicious.

That makeout session was, hands down, the silliest moment of her adult life. She'd never hooked up with a stranger—a baby, no less—and certainly not in public. A card-carrying career slut would call it pedestrian (after all, scores of sixteen-year-olds were dry-humping at parties all over Manhattan that night) but to Jenna, it had been empowering. It had been a restorative erotic charge.

Thank God he was a total stranger. If I had to see him again, I'd die.

Just then, Terry rushed up to her doorway.

"Jenna, Darcy wanted me to tell you she's swinging by in two seconds to talk about your videos."

Jenna never understood why Darcy made Terry run ahead of her, blowing the horn, before she made an entrance. The woman was egotistical beyond hope.

"Thanks, Terry. I see her coming up behind you."

Terry grimaced with anxiety. "Cool, I'm outta here." She scrambled away.

Jenna looked down at her desk, gathering the invites to make them look more presentable. When she looked back up, she froze solid. She blinked twice, thinking she was hallucinating. Latent optical side effects from violent vomiting on Friday night? But no. This was real.

It was Darcy. And him. Him. The barely-legal hottie.

In under two seconds, a thousand questions flew through her mind. *How did Darcy find out? Am I in trouble for acting so slutty in public? Will I get fired from StyleZine in disgrace? When is the next Amtrak back to Facquier County, Virginia?*

His face was a mask of bare-naked shock, his mouth forming a tiny "O." Jenna's sharp intake of breath was audible. But within seconds, they'd both recovered. Jenna threw on her brightest TV personality smile. Eric thrust his hands into his pockets and leaned into her doorway, attempting to look composed. He all but whistled.

"What the hell is wrong with you two?" said Darcy, looking from Eric to Jenna.

"Nothing. Nothing at all." Jenna was talking too fast.

"This is our new videographer, Eric. He'll be shooting all of the videos for our YouTube channel. His priority will be your web series. I expect you two to make magic together." Darcy looked at Eric, who's cool had dissolved, and was now staring at the floor, biting his lip, barely holding back nervous laughter.

"What's so funny?" asked Darcy. "Oh I get it. You recognize her."

"No! If I met this woman, I'd definitely remember."

Darcy smiled, which was always a panicky experience for all involved. It usually meant she was about to drop a bomb.

"Well, you have met."

Jenna began to sweat. "No we haven't! He's a complete stranger."

"Jenna. You don't remember my son?"

"Your...son?" she squeaked. Her brain was too overwhelmed to produce an intelligent response. Weakly, she looked up at Eric. "Darcy's your..."

"My mother," he said apologetically.

"You two met at Raymond and Joanne Chase's wedding, like twelve years ago," said Darcy. "Eric was little, he had braces..."

"And a lisp." He glanced at Jenna. She almost choked on her Altoid.

"And the only reason I took him to that clusterfuck of New Money Blacks was because the New York Times' style section was shooting us right after. A Mother's Day spread with notable moms and their kids. Remember that, E? You were running past Jenna's table, a bad ass kid, always. You knocked red wine all over her dress. Which improved it, I must say. DKNY was already over by 2000."

"That was you?" Eric shook his head. "This is too embarrassing."

"That was me," said Jenna, nodding in slow motion. She remembered that wedding, the ruined dress, and the mischievous boy. He was adorable, a tiny milk chocolate drop with a handheld camera, interviewing pretty women about their Oscar picks. He'd announced to her table, "James Cameron's terrible. Wanna see the biopic I made about Busta Rhymes? All my friendth are in it!" She and Billie had giggled about him for weeks.

"Of course," continued Darcy, "everyone knew my feelings about you, so they thought I ordered my kid to destroy your dress."

"Wait, you know each other, outside of work?" It was dawning on Eric that his mother and Jenna had a history. "You're friends?"

"Well…"

"Definitely not friends," interrupted Darcy. "We came up in the industry together. Remember my fiancé, Marcus? Ever wonder why I kicked him out? Well, this sweet-faced jezebel ruined our happy home."

"I had no idea they were together," Jenna blurted out, the words running into each other. She was mortified to her core. Now he knew that she and his mother had slept with the same guy.

Eric side-eyed his mom, and then glanced at Jenna, who pasted on her maniacal fake smile.

"You two shared a dude. Like, in the Bad Boy era." He massaged a temple. "I'm nauseous."

"Oh, grow up." Darcy raised a brow in Jenna's direction. "My son can't deal with the fact that I'm a multi-layered woman. By the way, this isn't a nepotism thing. I gave Eric the summer to pursue his Scorcese shit and if he didn't land something with a real salary, he had to got a real job. The only place that was hiring was here. I made this kid do eight test shoots." She put her hands on her hips. "We all know there's no stability in the arts right now. Tell him, Jenna. He needs to drop his moviemaking fantasies."

"I don't think," started Jenna, unsteadily, "that I could discourage someone with talent from following their dreams."

Eric's mouth curved into a crooked half-smile. Jenna swallowed.

Was it possible that he was even cuter in the light of day? Standing there tall and cool in his just-rumpled-enough cargos and perfectly cut tee (perfectly cut arms, too) looking like he just returned from Iraq, but did a quick drive-by at Alexander Wang? Why did he have to have style, too?

"You wouldn't discourage him?" Darcy chuckled with condescension. "Spoken like a childless woman."

Jenna flinched.

"I have to run. People, I'm giving you carte blanche to make the series whatever you want. Just make it a winning idea. It better go viral. I need a rough cut of the first video by end of day Wednesday."

With that, Darcy disappeared. And then Eric and Jenna were left to deal with each other, alone. Again.

Eric sat across the desk from her, tapping his fingers on the arms of the chair. Jenna stared at her hands, which were clasped so tightly that her fingers were turning white. She was unable to look at him.

"So," he said, his voice breezy. "Miss me?"

"Listen," she said, flipping her head up, her curls tumbling everywhere. She lowered her voice to a whispery hiss. "I want you to know that I barely remember anything. I was wasted. It's a total blur." Feeling like her face was on fire, Jenna put her hands on her cheeks. "Christ, I'm mortified."

"If you don't remember anything, why are you mortified?"

"This isn't funny. This is terrible."

"I'm not laughing. But I do need to know one thing."

"What?"

"You still love me, or nah?" He grinned.

"Please don't make this worse. What happened? No one can ever know. This job is too important to my career right now." Jenna took a deep breath. "You're the boss' son. Darcy loves to hate me and she'd murder me over this. Plus, besides her, we're the only two black people at Belladonna Media. This is your first job, so you don't know, but in white office culture, we're watched more closely than everyone else. Especially in fashion. We can't slip."

"You think this is my first experience being the only black guy in the room?"

"My point is, we cannot give anyone a reason to think we know each other outside of work. No one will ever take me seriously again. Especially after…"

"After what?

"Nothing." Jenna shook her head, unable to believe this situation. "By the way, what kind of guy takes advantage of a drunk woman at a party?"

"First of all, I was drunker than you. I woke up with a hangover worse than *Hangover 3*. Secondly? You ordered me to kiss you. And then climbed on top of me..."

"Please," she wailed. "Don't say anything else."

"You wanted to have your way with me and you did. You're just as bad as me."

"If you'd told me who your mother was, this could've been avoided."

"Yeah. 'Cause that's normal, mentioning your mommy mid-kiss," he said. "Besides, you know her pretty well, right?"

"Right."

"If Darcy Vale was your mother, would you lead with that?"

"Fair enough."

"I can't believe you're her...peer."

"I can't believe you're her son." She sat back in her chair, overwhelmed. "What must your childhood have been like? That woman as a mother?"

"My mom is...hmm, how do I describe her?" He chewed the inside of his mouth. "On the scale of shitty mothers, from Hamlet's mom to Delora on *The Wire*, I'd say she hovers right in the middle. For my sanity, I can't engage. Especially here. The day I do, I might lose it and commit momicide."

"She'd commit Jenna-cide if she knew about this."

"Jenna-cide! Nice."

"This is very bad. I don't have a great history with her."

"So I hear," he said, making a face. "You and her were with the same dude, who I don't remember because I had more 'uncles' than fucks to give. And then I made out with you, which means I basically kissed my mother. Yo, that shit is mad disturbing. I'm inconsolable."

"*You're* inconsolable?"

"Irreparably." Then he settled down into his chair. He looked around her office, taking in her surroundings. He stopped at the vintage Nina Mae McKinney movie poster above her head. Then he looked back at Jenna. "I can get over it, though. *Ma Cherie*."

He blinked innocently at Jenna, who was distracted by his obscenely long lashes. A shadow of a smile passed his face, and God help her, she noticed a tiny dimple under one of his cheekbones. Seriously? It was almost obnoxious. Eric knew exactly what he looked like—and even worse, the effect he was having on her. Jenna glanced away from him, pretending to pick lint off of her skirt.

How am I going to sit two feet from him? I can't even look him in the face.

"Why are you getting so worked up?" he asked. "If this can't be funny, we're fucked."

"You don't understand. This is my career, my life!"

"I'm just saying," started Eric, "you're blowing this out of proportion. We made out at a party. It happens. You don't even want to know what I did with a RAC in the bathroom of Lit Lounge."

"RAC?"

"Random Asian Chick."

"You did not just say that."

Of course he did. Their makeout session was probably one of fifteen he'd had on Friday night. He barely remembered it—but secretly, it had been a sexually empowering moment for her. Jenna felt ridiculous. And old.

"I can't do this," she said.

"Look, neither one of us expected to see each other, today. I know it's mad awkward, but so?" He shrugged. "It'll never be boring."

"You actually look excited. Are you enjoying this?"

"A little."

"How do I know you're mature enough to keep it a secret?"

"I have an emotional maturity that belies my age," he said, totally deadpan.

Jenna just looked at him.

"I'm not a *zygote*, Jenna. Give me some credit."

Trying to project assertiveness, she chucked up her chin and looked him directly in his eyes. Huge mistake. An instant sensory replay went through her mind—Eric biting her lip, sucking her neck—and her stomach flip-flopped.

She cleared her throat. "I…I should tell Darcy that we can't do this together."

"Okay," he said. "You're gonna tell her why?"

"I'll figure something out."

He watched Jenna with barely-hidden amusement as she fidgeted and blushed and tried to convey a sense of authority.

"What?" asked Jenna.

"It was that good, wasn't it?"

"Oh my God."

"I'm kidding. I'm sorry; you just make it so easy. Look, at least work with me before you decide you don't want to."

Jenna shook her head and moved papers around her desk, mumbling to herself. "I shouldn't have come back, I knew it was a mistake, I should never have come here…"

He leaned forward and put his hands on top of her papers. "Hey. Jenna, it's cool. I'm not gonna, like, defile you in the hallway. I don't even wanna be here. I can't overstate how unhyped I am to be here. My short film won the Jack Nicholson Directing Award at the toughest film school in the country. *Variety* named me 'One to Watch' in their college special. And now my job is to roam around Lower Manhattan with a camera asking fake Miley Cyruses for interviews about their bra tops and neon Doc Martens? I'm an artist. I'm offended."

Jenna frowned. First he made her feel like a fool for getting worked up over their little tryst, and now he was denigrating the place where she was grateful to be working?

Suddenly, she was irrationally mad at him. She was mad that he kissed her so good, mad that he knew it, mad at his smirky attitude, and mad that there was no escaping working with him.

"We're all artists in this industry. And most people hate their jobs. Welcome to life."

"Welcome to life, though?"

"You were basically just gifted a job by your mom!"

"With all due respect, ma'am, you know nothing about me or my relationship with that mini supervillain."

"Please don't call me ma'am."

"It seemed age-appropriate."

"Excuse me?"

"You can be rude," he said, "but I'm supposed to kiss your ass?"

No one had ever spoken to her like that at work. "You can't talk to me that way! I'm...you're superior."

"Superior? We're partners on a project."

Totally flustered, she tried to regain some semblance of control over the conversation. Jenna threw back her shoulders and went there.

"Don't you know who I am?"

Eric's face lit up at the boldness of the question. "Am I supposed to know who you are?"

Then Jenna said something she never thought would pass her lips.

"Google me."

"Oh word? I'll do that." He nodded, like he respected her sudden burst of swagger. "You know, when I woke up this morning, I thought I knew what my biggest problems in life were. I had no idea that I'd end up working for a woman who can't decide if I'm a career-ender or her boyfriend."

"*Stop talking about it*," she hissed through gritted teeth. She pointed to her door. "You have to go."

"Shouldn't we be brainstorming? We only have three days!"

"We'll brainstorm separately for now."

"Come on, we're better together."

"Go!"

"Fine." In the doorway, he turned around. "My bad for the hickey. I don't think anyone else'll notice, do you?"

Then he shot her that crooked smile, and she stood up and closed the door behind him.

The next five hours were hell. Jenna had never had a panic attack, but if it felt like the walls were closing in and your life had become a telenovela, then she'd had several since Eric left her office. Too terrified of running into him, she'd stayed chained to her desk, quietly banging out her next six "Just Jenna" posts. Jenna never had to pee so badly in her life, but she held it until she took lunch at two thirty—at which point she scurried down the hallway to the elevators with her head down, careful not to meet anyone's eyes.

In the abstract, Jenna knew she was being ridiculous. But she'd just returned to civilization, and was already on edge. Her week-old job, her apartment, her social life—nothing felt settled. It was still an effort to feel like herself in normal social situations, let alone one as ridiculous as this.

After a forty-five minute "lunch" where she scarfed down a street pretzel and then hid in the Hollywood history section of the Astor Place Barnes and Noble (always her safe place), Jenna realized that she was being insane, and headed back to StyleZine. She couldn't run. The reality was that she was stuck in the office with Eric, and though it wasn't ideal, she was a pro and would make it work. That morning, she'd been flustered and reactive because of the shock. But now, Jenna would just channel the good-natured, yet decisive and firm top editrix she used to be. True, it might be challenging to command respect from someone who'd had her ass in his hands only two nights before—but she could do this.

This time, when Jenna exited the elevators, she pasted on a smile (for no one, since the staff was busy at their desks), and strode breezily to her office—where she saw a white box from Cupcake Café on her desk, wrapped in a bright red bow.

She excitedly sat down and tore open the box. It was an enormous red velvet cupcake. Turning the box upside down, she looked for a gift card and didn't see one. At first, she assumed it was a fashion PR gift. Ever since her first day last Monday, she'd been getting a steady stream of "welcome back" flowers, champagne, and high-end gift cards from colleagues.

But now that she thought about it, being gifted a cupcake by an industry acquaintance seemed odd. All those calories? Fashion people didn't eat. She wondered who it could be from.

And then it hit her.

Jenna grabbed her office phone, typed in "E" and an "R," and Eric Combs' number popped onto her screen. It rang twice, and then he picked up.

"I need to see you in my office."

"Nothing good ever came out of that sentence."

"Now, please."

She hung up, and positioned herself in the most poised, professional manner possible. When Eric came in—this time, clutching a handheld camera—she was prepared.

"I feel like I'm in trouble," he said, from her doorway.

"Have a seat," she said, calmly and firmly.

He did.

"Why do you have a camera?"

"I always have my camera. My hand feels itchy without it."

Jenna nodded, her face the picture of control. She handed him the opened cupcake box. "I can't accept any gifts from you. I'm not entirely sure what your motivations were, but if this was an attempt to…keep things going? To flirt? Please understand that I am not available. Are we clear?"

Eric nodded, his brow furrowed. As soon as he opened his mouth to protest, the gift card caught his eye. It had fallen to the floor next to Jenna's desk—and she obviously hadn't seen it. It read "Cupcake Café" in sparkly cursive on the outside, and on the inside he could faintly make out a note and a signature.

Proof that he didn't do it.

"I did it," he lied.

Jenna clasped her hands together, trying to stay composed. "Eric, why are you making this so hard? What the hell were you thinking?"

"You really wanna know?"

"No," she said quickly. "I just want you to stop. No snappy comebacks, no gifts. Be professional, and stop."

"Okay."

"Thank you." Jenna sat primly, with her hands folded. Eric sat across from her, looking sad and dejected.

Jenna threw her hands up with exasperation. "Fine! Tell me why you did this."

Eric exhaled slowly. "I'm haunted by you."

"What?"

"You're the only thought in my brain. That night, the way you looked, the way you tasted…" He stopped, looking soulfully into her eyes. "I could've kissed you, only kissed you, till this morning."

Jenna's mouth dropped open.

"I know you're somebody and I'm nobody, but I don't care. I'm obsessed with you. And the most memorable way I could think to communicate this was through…a giant red cupcake."

The absurdity of this statement went right over Jenna's head. Once she caught her breath, she said, "I can't even express how dangerous every last one of those words were. You've just crossed every line of corporate conduct. I won't tolerate it."

Eric shrugged. "You asked."

"Please understand that if you address me that way again, I'm calling HR."

"No, it's cool. I get it," he said, and then gestured to the floor. "Will you at least read the card? It's right there, on the floor."

Glaring at him, she snatched up the tiny white card. She opened it and read the message scrawled in slanted black cursive:

Dear Jenna,
Congrats on a fabulous first week of work (and, I hear, an even better Friday night). You're back, baby!
Love, Billie

Jenna looked at the note, read it two more times, and then shut it slowly.

"Oh," she said.

"Yeah. Oh."

"I…well, I just…thought…"

"I know exactly what you thought." Eric's voice bristled with real, not-jokey, irritation. "This was all fun and games until you insulted my manhood with a cupcake."

"But…"

"Don't flatter yourself, Mrs. Robinson. First of all, I'd never stoop to woo a middle-aged woman with a fucking pastry. Secondly, if I wanted you, I'm confident I could get you without a prop. And third, the only way we're gonna survive this shit is if you calm down and get what happened out of your head. You can't get all blushy and mean every time we speak. Chill. Please. I beg of you."

Jenna sat very still, unblinking and mortally humiliated.

"This was… a misunderstanding," she finally uttered. "It is out of my head."

"Yeah, okay. That's why you jumped to this cupcake conclusion. You set me up with that 'I'm so obsessed with you' stuff! You deliberately tried to embarrass me!"

"No, you did that all by yourself. You did it big, too. Like 'embarrassment' in all caps. 'Embarrassment' accompanied by pyrotechnics and the Grambling State marching band."

Jenna stood, fiery indignation rushing through her veins.

"This conversation is…"

"Yeah, I know. Over." Eric stood up and tossed the Cupcake Café box onto her desk.

"Good! And…I'm not middle-aged!"

"Stop acting it, then," he said, already out the door.

She plopped down in her chair and buried her face in her hands. After a moment, she swiveled her chair around to face her beloved poster. If she were Nina, what would she do next? Actually, Jenna was positive that the vampy flapper was too sexually savvy and self-possessed to have ever found herself caught in a situation like this.

How did I get here, Nina? Where did I go wrong?

She wanted to evaporate.

"One more thing," said Eric, who'd appeared in her doorway again. Startled, she swiveled back around.

"No, this isn't my dream job, but I'm good and I don't do anything halfway. I won't leave without a product I'm proud of. If it's between creating your web series and shooting girls on Bleecker theorizing boyfriend jeans—there is no choice. So let's stop bullshitting and start impressing the fuck out of each other."

And then he left again. If nothing else, he definitely shared his mother's must-have-the-last-word gene.

www.stylezine.com
Just Jenna! Style Secrets from our Intrepid Glambassador

Q: *"I think high-waisted denim shorts are everything. But this guy I have a crush on says they make my butt look long! Whatever, I know I slay in them. In a Kylie Jenner way. But am I being unwomanly? Should I alter the way I dress to please a man?" -@itsnotmeitsyou1982*

A: *When I was younger, I used to dress differently for my boyfriend than I did at work. I'd rock all my weirdo avant garde pieces to Darling magazine, but my boyfriend liked me in tight, bodycon stuff, so when were together, I'd dress like Chrissy Tiegan going to the MTV Movie Awards. I spent half my life doing costume changes. And here's the thing—we broke up anyway. Now he's with a relentlessly preppy woman who dresses like James Spader in Pretty in Pink.*

Honestly, who knows what men want? Being yourself is easier than guessing. The right guy will love your shorts, because you're in them. By the way, American Apparel makes the hottest ones.

CHAPTER 5

Tim Milagro-Carroll was used to Eric's dual personas. Either he was Mr. Personality, soaking up all the attention in the room, or a brooding, intense son of a bitch. Today, he was broody. Eric had showed up at the well-worn Milagro-Carroll family Murray Hill townhouse for their usual Monday night activity—shouting obscenities at ESPN, smoking weed, and playing video games on Xbox. He'd let himself in with his key, hugged Tim's adopted nine-year-old sisters (the Ecuadorian twins were leaning against a piano, getting singing lessons from Jessie L. Martin), and busted into Tim's spray-paint-splattered, disgusting downstairs bedroom. With a grumbly, "What's good?" Eric collapsed into a director's chair and receded into stormy silence.

Eric met Tim on his first day of fifth grade at Manhattan's Dalton Lower School, that bastion of good breeding on the Upper East Side. Only a week before, he was barely staying awake in his war zone public school in Bed Stuy, Brooklyn—and suddenly, he was not only residing in a ritzy Manhattan zip code, he was thrust into an institution flush with the children of Old Money gazilionnaires. Tim was the only other black boy in their grade, and the pint-sized troublemaker made a B-line for Eric in the cafeteria, making it his mission to school him on how to get away with murder at a posh prep school.

Even though Tim wasn't from real New York money, his theater-royalty parents had cultural capital. He was the oldest of a multi-ethnic, adopted clan of kids whose parents were Carlos Milagro, the famous Filipino Broadway director; and his Irish husband, Jay-Jay Carroll, a Tony Award-winning costume designer. They ran their house as a salon for stage gypsies, which kept them distracted—and gave Tim carte blanche to wreak havoc on the city. He brought Eric along.

They bonded, falling into the roles that would follow them forever— Eric was the golden boy and Tim was the fuck up. Eric skated through adolescence with a bulletproof GPA and enough part-time Foot Locker money saved to buy the sexiest equipment for his Canon C300; Tim barely made it to tenth grade without catching a drug charge and getting caught in a PR-nightmare after an orgy with two Disney Channel stars. Tim gave Eric an edge, Eric gave Tim an alibi—and together, they were tighter than brothers.

They were complete opposites, but had the same sensibility, born of a thousand high-low city kid influences. They were steeped in hip-hop but prep-schooled, jaded but adventurous, privileged but underground, sophisticated but street. They wouldn't step out of the house without vanity sneakers, ironic tees and fitteds, but they could give a compelling argument for why Basquiat was the Junot Diaz of art. On more than a few occasions, Eric had been referred to as a "blipster"—a black hipster—which deeply offended him. So what if he liked Bloc Party and had once co-hosted a street art show at Mighty Tanaka? He was cultured, just like everyone he knew. The moniker should've been Person of Color Who Doesn't Live Under a Rock.

While Eric was horrified to be an adult living in his mother's house, Tim was downright pleased with it. His visual arts degree from Rhode Island School of Design hadn't landed him a job, so he was doing a thousand things at once—tattoo design, managing strippers, and blogging his bedroom wall graffiti. And since Tim's dads were cool about weed, his room was their perfect chill spot. Eric's goal over the next hour was to smoke himself into a coma.

At the moment, Tim was beating Eric at his favorite video game, "Legend of Zelda," while giving his thirteen-year-old brother, Thuong, advice on how to handle a 'video model' he'd been having a direct message relationship with on Twitter. Eric was lost in his own thoughts, which was a challenging feat, since Childish Gambino's latest mixtape was cranked full-throttle and the game was blaring.

"Oh shit," said Thuong, peering at his iPhone. He was Vietnamese but staunchly black-identified.

"What'd she say?" Tim didn't take his eyes off the screen. He was a wiry 5'5", covered in tats, and sporting an authentic Eric B. and Rakim concert tee with a denim vest and orange throwback Pumas. He hadn't left the house once that day, but he was *fresh*.

"She called me Daddy."

"Shit just got real," said Tim. "Now demand a nude. Tits, ass, any unclothed region. She'll friend-zone you if you don't make your intentions clear."

Eric broke his half-hour silence. "Yo, why're you such a consistent degenerate?"

"He speaks!" cheered Thuong.

"Why I gotta be consistent, though?"

"Wait," started the eighth grader, "how do you know you're in the friend zone?"

"When you're dog-sitting for her. Installing her Apple TV. Meeting her for brunch." Tim paused. "Upon further review, nah. If it's brunch at Minetta Tavern on MacDougal, you're good. Bouchout mussels and truffled pork sausage? Bring a condom, dog."

Thuong looked overwhelmed. "The friend zone sounds stressful."

"And it can sneak up on you if you don't establish yourself as a sexual gladiator off the rip. Demand a nude."

Eric looked at him. "You're speaking to a child, son."

Tim took a deep drag off the herbal vaporizer and, holding his breath, pronounced, "Those who teach children should be more honored than those who produce them.'" He exhaled. "Aristotle, bitch."

"Hold up, E, I'm not a child! I have a fake I.D. and three-fourths of a mustache!" Thuong punched Eric in the shoulder. Eric punched him back. "Besides, Cherry thinks I'm a small business developer."

"You realize she's Catfishing you, too, right?" said Eric. "Has this woman expressed any interest in meeting you?"

Thuong hesitated. "No, she's a…model. She has stalkers, she's cautious."

"She's not cautious, she's Catfish. Cherry's a brawny dude in Canarsie, eating Cheez-its and squeezing off a quick one while fantasizing about a Suit who's actually a kid failing eighth grade health."

"You're just a hater," Thuong said, unsure.

"No, E's probably right," agreed Tim. "But so? This is practice. By the time you're in high school you'll be a pimp, like I was."

"Don't be like Tim was," said Eric. "The only reason he never got expelled was because I got myself elected the head of the Disciplinary Action Committee."

"For which I arranged for you to lose your virginity to the chesty call girl I pretended was my English Lit tutor." Tim frantically clicked the "L" button on his joystick, making a winning Master Sword move and ending the round. He whooped, and then continued. "I met her in an AOL chat room. Catfishing wasn't invented yet. Simpler times."

Tim looked at his phone. He was expecting his on-and-off girlfriend of three years, Carlita, to bring them takeout from the Jamaican spot. She was a surly, ambitious exotic dancer from a rough neighborhood with a massive ass and a long black weave. "Yooo, where is Carlita?"

"Downstairs pushing the door that says pull," muttered Eric.

Tim kicked his chair. "Why're you all in your feelings tonight?"

Thuong looked concerned. "Did you and Madison get back together and break up again?"

"Word. You know he's in the throes of some girl shit," snickered Tim. "Emotional ass Eric."

"Yeah! Drake ass Eric."

"Taylor Swift ass mothafucka."

Eric closed his eyes. *Why did I come here?*

"But real talk?" Thuong passed the vaporizer to Eric. "Tim, you only deal with hoes, and I might be DM-ing a fat dude right now. So maybe we'd get emotional, too if we had one of E's girls. You know, ballerinas like Madison."

"Hoes?" Tim was offended.

"You know you're about that hoe life. Own it. It's like E always says..." Thuong, who was totally high, drew a blank. "What do you always say, E?"

"The truth shall set you free," said Eric.

"Do not upset me when I'm hungry! First of all, they're not hoes. They're charming young ladies with *hoeish tendencies*. Secondly, I don't seek them out; it's just that I have commitment issues and I'm not ready for women of substance. I banish you from this room," said Tim, standing up. He punched Thuong in the ribs.

"This was my room when you were in college," said Thuong, who also stood up. At six feet tall, the oversized eighth grader looked like the Jolly Green Giant next to Tim. When he punched him in the stomach, Tim toppled to the ground. They started rolling around on the floor. Eric, who'd witnessed this scene three zillion times, sat unmoved in his director's chair, his thoughts drowning out their foolishness.

If Madison hadn't stayed in L.A. to join the Cornerstone Theater Company, they'd still be together. She was just his type; a delicate beauty who believed herself to be sexually prissy until Eric helped her realize she was well past filthy. He was easily able to pierce through her shyness (on their first date, she broke down while rehashing middle school melodramas, greatly upsetting their Benihana's server), but her complaint about Eric was that he was unreachable. He rarely lost his cool.

And yet, after knowing Jenna Jones for two seconds, he confessed to The Lisp. *He'd said the Cadbury eggs thing.* All his goofy came tumbling out. She was overwhelming! The way she'd looked at him, with that bare-naked, almost-intimidating lust—she was all want. Adult, full-bodied want, without a hint of the coyness of girls his age. No girl had ever told him to kiss her. And when he did, her reaction hit him like a body-slam. She went completely liquid under him, clutching him like she was drowning. Like she'd waited years for that kiss. She played the seductress, but was as vulnerable as a virgin.

And the combination was heady as hell.

Today, in Jenna's office, he pretended that he'd been drunker than he was. He faked like it was a throwaway hookup. It wasn't. In that moment, he would've done anything she wanted. No matter how pornographic or depraved. In public. And without even knowing her name.

But after experiencing her evil twin, he was seized with a barrage of questions: Why did Jenna have to be his mother's old rival? And how was she almost twice his age? And why, why, did she have to be so nuts?

But Eric's kryptonite had always been unreasonable, dramatic women. After all, he was raised by one.

When he was very little, Eric worshipped Darcy. She was like an enigmatic older sister who'd breeze in for a couple of days with age-inappropriate gifts (who gives a toddler a leather flask?) and heavily perfumed kisses, but then disappear for endless stretches. Weeks. Months. It was hard lesson for Eric, craving the mother's milk that should've been his right as a human, but getting it purely at random. As an older kid, he turned it off for good.

At sixteen, Darcy Vale was a brilliant, sexually curious daughter of a policeman and his silent wife from Guyana. She lived with her conservative, fanatically Seventh Day Adventist family in a three-family brownstone in Bedford Stuyvesant, Brooklyn, just two blocks from Gentry Houses—the housing project that was home to twenty-five-year-old Otis Combs and his mother. Everyone knew Otis; he was the kind-hearted, sleepy-eyed drummer who never made it, but should have (the "never made it" was due to a debilitating whiskey addiction, not lack of talent).

Sick of being a virgin, Darcy met the sweet lothario while smoking cigarettes outside of a bodega one night after student council. They shared a bottle of Jim Beam, tumbled into a pile of golden leaves in Stuyvesant Park, and fifteen minutes later, Bishop Loughlin High School's debate team captain was pregnant.

Luther Vale immediately disowned his daughter. Humiliated by the scandal, he sold the brownstone and moved the family to Bayonne, New Jersey. They never spoke to Darcy again—or saw Eric. At sixteen, Darcy Vale was a single mother on her own. Lost. But Darcy was a hustler, a force of nature born with one raging hunger—to conquer the world. She wasn't lost for long. She loved her little boy, but she had high school to finish, college scholarships to score, hyper-competitive magazine jobs to land, cocktail parties to attend, and rappers and/or Wall Streeters to squeeze rent money from. So, Darcy left the raising of Eric to Otis's mom, and then went about the business of assuaging her seething ambition.

Eric barely remembered Darcy ever discussing his dad when he was little, except to drill the message into his head that he wasn't allowed to grow up to be a loser like Otis Combs.

"Your last name is Combs," said Darcy, a freezing morning after a rare night that Eric slept at her tiny studio instead of at Gentry Houses. In a rush, she was walking-dragging her seven-year-old son to school so she could make it to the *Mademoiselle* offices before the rest of the staff. She had to toast the accessories editor's bagel perfectly—at 47 seconds—color-coordinate the bracelet drawer, and write the editor-in-chief's "letter from the editor," all before 9:00 am.

"I know my last name, Mommy," he said, sighing up at her with half exasperation, half cautious pleasure. He hadn't seen her in three weeks, but last night she'd picked her up from his grandma's apartment bearing an assortment of random objects: Hawaiian bread rolls (his favorite), and an authentic ninja sword from his new uncle, a Saudi Arabian wrestler named The Sheik of Tears who was also, as he'd explained to Eric, a real-life genie.

"Your last name's Combs," continued Darcy, "but you're all Vale, do you understand me?"

Darcy halted in the middle of the crowded sidewalk. She squatted down so she was face to face with Eric, a too-intense boy who inherited his father's Trinidadian cheekbones and exotic, inky-black eyes. "You won't grow up and bring shame to the Vale family, got it?"

Eric nodded. *What Vale family?*

"Otis can't get off his mother's couch to play a $40 gig. He's nothing," she whispered. "You're not him, baby. You're me. We win."

"I love my daddy," Eric said, confused and horrified. But Darcy had already stood back up and grabbed his hand, rushing them down Nostrand. He kept chanting it, even though he knew she couldn't hear. "I love my daddy," he choked, tears burning down his icy cheeks.

Eric didn't need to be lectured about Otis' failures. He knew that his dad—with his dreamy, drunken impotence—wasn't like the fantasy dads in Pixar movies. But he loved Otis, because he was there. He taught him how to make homemade curry sauce and draw perfect human toes. He drilled him on the history of 1930s blues. He hung out on the playground with him all weekend. He gave him remedial breakdancing lessons. He showed him the value in being kind to people when it didn't benefit you in the slightest. He gave a damn.

But none of that mattered, because Otis was randomly shot and killed in a Halsey Street bodega when Eric was ten. And then Darcy hauled him off to live in Manhattan. She was due to relocate, anyway.

Like clockwork, Darcy moved every two years, committed to upgrading her life. First, she went to more gentrified blocks in Brooklyn, then she swept Eric off to Soho, then Meatpacking and then, once she married the world's shadiest financier, Luca Belladonna, they landed in a Tribeca penthouse. Eric had felt schizophrenic when he first arrived at Dalton Lower School. Was he a project kid or a louche preppie? The first time a Dalton kid asked where he was from, he flinched and raised his little fists. Back in his section of Brooklyn, if someone asked you that, it's because you'd wandered in the wrong neighborhood—and it was the last thing you heard before you were robbed or jumped.

But after awhile, Eric pushed the memory of his early years into some dark corner, a locked closet where he couldn't feel the howling loss of Otis—and he ran toward becoming something new.

By high school, he knew who he was. He was class president of the High School of Art and Design. A sixteen-year-old who tore through his AP homework and edited his boy's amateur rap video ("You Said There'd Be Sex (Tonight)"), before prowling the city with the kids of tabloid stars and media moguls. He *was* the kid of a media mogul. He was also, to his delight, the Homecoming date of Vanessa Williams' cutest daughter.

Some things never changed, though. Darcy was still an erratic mirage of a mother, perpetually working, traveling or partying, leaving Eric alone with an empty refrigerator and a credit card. She only paid attention to him to trot him out to charity events or awkward, staged mother/son photo ops—or to berate him for putting chinks in her hard-won social armor (*that bow-legged tramp's dad works at a T-Mobile store, kill it immediately, how will she make me look? Wait, you're applying to public high school, you ungrateful shit, after I've slaved to give you this life? If you knew what I did to get you into Dalton you'd wet your fucking bed*).

Eric had no family. But he had that innate (yes, undeniably Vale) I-must-win thing that kept him focused when it would've been easier to take the route of every other rich, ignored Manhattan teen—and overdose on blow while balls-deep inside a call girl. And when he felt lost, he'd escape to the frenetic Milagro-Carroll house and stay for a week. The perfect escape from Darcy's chilly, empty, penthouse of doom.

But now he was a grown man, and right back there. He was too broke to move out, and too proud to allow Darcy to buy him a place. Staying up all night packaging his movie to meet the submission guidelines for every film festival on Earth. Spending cash he didn't have on insane entry fees. Praying that a festival would notice him, so that he could find investors to finance a full-length feature, or an agent to land him work in TV or docs or music videos or porn or anywhere. Wishing that he'd been good at something else, like math, so he could be a trader and live an artless-yet-secure life with bonuses and hooker-decorated parties.

And now he was stuck in an office with a woman who wanted to have him fired for being a good kisser. Obviously, he'd made things worse by teasing Jenna, but he couldn't resist. Watching her squirm and blush behind that desk, knowing that it was because she was thinking of him? It was too sexy. He'd have to stop, though, because if CupcakeGate proved anything, he was driving an already twitchy woman out of her damned mind.

All Eric wanted to do was stay out of trouble, save every cent of his paycheck, and get out of StyleZine. He was desperate for his life to start.

Jenna Jones hates me because she wants me and it freaks her out, he thought to himself. He had to show her he was trustworthy.

Abruptly, Eric shot out of his chair.

"I'm out. I gotta go." He was out the door before either brother had time to get up.

Thuong looked down at Tim, who he had pinned in a headlock.

"Yeah," nodded Tim. "It's definitely about a bitch."

CHAPTER 6

I *was a spaz,* Jenna thought, for the zillionth time that morning. *Eric made me look like a fool over that cupcake because I was a spaz, and now I have to face him in an hour. Shonda Rhimes couldn't even write me out of this plot.*

Jenna was barely awake. She'd had a total of three hours of sleep, obsessing over her StyleZine situation. Luckily, she'd taken the morning off to serve on the jury for the Fashion Institute of Technology's senior collections prelims. It was being held in a massive white box of a loft space on 25th and 10th Avenue, which was filled with thirty rolling racks, each manned by an overwhelmed-looking design student—and peppered with jurors wandering around surveying the projects. The room was lined with floor-to-ceiling windows, allowing white-hot streams of sunlight to flood the space, so the poor kids were not only struggling to explain their prohibitively ethereal collections to their style industry elders, they were blinking blindly into the sun. Oddly, they almost all had Buddy Holly glasses and lavender hair.

Sighing, Jenna approached a rolling rack filled with extravagantly repurposed vintage white and cream nightgowns in silks, satins, and crushed velvets. The designer, a chubby strawberry blonde with hair styled like Rita Hayworth's, bit her bottom lip.

"Hi, Ms. Jones," she said in a fluttery voice.

"Hi! Well, these are lovely. I love how you combined '30s bias cut shapes with flouncy '60s silhouettes."

"Thank you," she whispered. "I guess I really like...the vulnerability and sensuality of undergarments...worn on the outside. You know, the duality of being a powerful woman, but...I don't know, wearing these delicate, flimsy fabrics as armor. I guess?"

Jenna smiled. She recognized her beloved students from Northern Virginia Community College in this girl. Bursting with ideas and compelled to express them, but at the same time, worried that their every thought was garbage. This was what she loved so much about mentoring, being able to lead them through the process, helping them refine their ideas and trust their instincts.

"I'd suggest that you push yourself, though. Play with shapes that might be a bit more unexpected. You know, because we've seen this look before. You were clearly influenced by the Riot Grrrls from the early 90's."

"Riot what?"

Jenna looked at her. "Courtney Love? Hole? Babes in Toyland? The whole 'kinderwhore' style movement, with the slips and Mary Janes?"

I am a thousand years old.

She tucked her clipboard under her arm. "Lesley, so much of fashion is understanding where the influences lie. You should watch Courtney Love's videos for "Doll Parts" and "Violet." Also, find *Baby Doll* on Netflix. It's a 1962 film about a childlike seventeen-year-old who lives with this shady older man, who makes her sleep in a crib and wear these exquisite little girl nightgowns until she's of age and he can marry her. It's totally sick and genius, and you'll be inspired by the costuming. After that, rethink your direction a bit, okay?"

"Yes...I will...I really will. Thank you."

The grateful expression on the designer's face made her morning. And then she remembered the situation awaiting her in the office.

So, she gave Lesley a hug and headed to the refreshments table—where she stalled like crazy, grazing on crudité and sipping Bellinis for the next forty-five minutes.

Jenna was standing in the tiny kitchenette by the cubicles, chugging her second cup of black coffee (she'd had one too many bellinis). Just back from FIT, she'd intended to get a quick shot of caffeine before getting back to work. It was Tuesday. She and Eric were supposed to have a rough cut of their first video to Darcy by end-of-day tomorrow and, due to brain-freezing stress, every idea she came up with was uninspired and unusable. She had to have something prepared in the next hour—plus, she needed to psyche herself up before seeing Eric again.

As she gulped down the second cup, Terry and the assistant market editor, Jinx, swept into the tiny enclave, all hectic energy. Terry was swiping away on her phone, while Jinx, a perpetually frantic Persian-American beauty, was pulling a rolling rack of outfits behind her.

They completely ignored Jenna's presence.

"…and I've done the "where to buy" info for our five outfits of the day, but my headlines are so blah," said Terry, a vision in designer sweatpants and Supra high-tops. Every morning Mitchell, the photo editor, sent her pics of cool-looking girls that he'd curated from all over the world, and she captioned them.

"Let me see," said Jinx, dry-swallowing a diet pill. Her dark, voluptuous beauty was lost on her. She wanted to be a basic white girl. She longed for suburban blonde highlights, loved seasonally-flavored coffee and wore celebrity perfumes. She looked like a mysterious, dark-eyed enchantress— but on the inside, she was Lauren Conrad.

Terry shoved her phone in Jinx's face. "Look at the pic. She has blood-red lips, cowboy boots and a white-collared black dress. I called it 'Daytime

Goth,' but that sucks. Darcy said my captions sound like they were written by someone on the spectrum."

"'Bleak Chic?' I don't know, I can't concentrate!" wailed Jinx. "I'm on deadline and these pills give me tremors. I have to lose five pounds by Thursday so I can wear a crop top to Le Bain without the gays shading me!"

Jenna took a little breath and spoke up. "Hi, guys."

"Oh we didn't see you," said Terry, despite the kitchenette being the size of a linen closet.

"Hi, Jenna," said Jinx. "I've been meaning to ask, what's your Instagram? Darcy wants us to follow you."

"She doesn't have Instagram," said Terry, eyebrows raised.

"Really?" Jinx frowned at Jenna. "Well that's...umm...anyway, I really like your column. So cuuute," she said, dismissing her. She refocused her attention on Terry. "Show me the girl one more time?"

"Maybe I can help," said Jenna.

Terry and Jinx looked at each other, and then the blonde shrugged. "Sure."

Jenna took Terry's phone. She studied the outfit for a moment. "Vampire Pilgrim Walks into a Saloon."

Terry nodded slowly, smiling. "That's actually good."

"It is! How'd you do that?" asked Jinx.

"Don't be so literal," said Jenna. "Push the description as far as it can go. Even if it feels ridiculous. The silliest, most far-out headlines are the most memorable."

"Damn," said Terry, "can you write all my captions?"

Jenna beamed.

"Omigod, maybe you can help me, too," wailed Jinx, who until five minutes ago, had never spoken four words to Jenna. She pulled an outfit off of the rack and thrust it at her. "Our first 'Get the Look' of the day is going up in forty minutes, and Mitchell's shooting me in our version of a

Kristen Stewart outfit. K-Stew, with my huge tits. I have no idea how to pose!"

"Hmmm," said Jenna, thinking. "'Get the Look' is a split screen, with the celeb and editor pics, side-by side. The editor's always in the same arms-by-her-sides pose. You should switch it up, make it editorial."

Jenna shook her hair into her face and slumped her shoulders, crossing her feet at the ankles. Despite the fact that she was wearing a tulip-skirted sundress of Billie's ("Belle of the Barbeque"), she transformed into the sullen, twenty-something movie star. "Do a play on her persona. That whole 'yeah-my-fans-made-me-the-highest-paid-woman-in-Hollywood-but-I-won't-give-them-one-single-smile thing."

"But I look nothing like her. She's a tiny pixie person." Jinx was skeptical.

"I know; it's just a send-up of her mythology. You're being ironic. Wear tons of black eyeliner. Be glum—but with a wink. Have a sense of humor about it. Fashion is fantasy; the reader wants a story!"

"That could work," said Jinx, looking at Jenna with a mixture of vague mistrust and burgeoning interest. "Terry, what do you think?"

I can't believe she's checking in with a woman fifteen years my junior before going with my great idea. I used to run a massive fashion department! Am I seriously this beside-the-point? I really need to adjust my expectations. And a cocktail. I need a cocktail.

"You, posing like Kristen Stewart?" Terry clapped her hands together. "I cannot with the genius!"

Jinx squealed. "Do either of you have black eyeliner? Do we have Spanx in the fashion closet? This might turn out really dope, thanks, Jenna."

"Anytime," exclaimed Jenna, embarrassed by how proud she felt by their approval.

Just then, Jenna noticed Terry peering over her shoulder. She started hopping up and down. "Eric Combs!!"

Jenna whipped around. There he was, walking past the kitchenette. He stopped, tensed up almost imperceptibly—and then relaxed. The picture of cool. She smiled hugely at him, overdoing it. All night long, she'd been praying that she'd come into the office and discover that her mortification over what happened yesterday had been like a twenty-four hour virus. Intense, but short-lived. Sadly, this was wishful thinking.

"Hiyee!" she trilled too loudly, offering up a dumb, fluttery wave.

"Hey, Jenna," he said with careful, benign friendliness. "How are you?"

Before she could answer, Terry pushed past her and launched into his arms.

"Hi, baby," she squealed. "I didn't get to see you on your first day! Can you believe we actually work together? Dude, it's so beyond on."

"What's good, Teezy?" Eric hugged her back.

"You know each other?" asked Jenna, forcing herself to join the conversation.

"I've known Eric since he was shorter than me. And I'm the reason he's here!" She lowered her voice to a conspiratorial whisper. "I told him not to freak out about working for his mom. At least it's a paycheck."

"Terry dated one of my boys back in eighth grade or whatever," he said. "Who're you with now?"

"I'm about to break up with Kevin Watson, and I have Jamal Crebb on standby."

"Jamal Crebb. Power forward at Columbia?"

She sighed, placing her hand over her heart. "Bae."

"Figures," he said, to Jenna and Jinx. "This girl loves a black guy. Look at her hair, she has the side shave. That's code for 'I bone black guys.'"

"So that's what that means?" asked Jinx. "I should do something cool to my hair. My boyfriend doesn't like it anyway."

"But it's so good," said Eric. "It looks like Lara Croft's. I have questions for a dude who doesn't appreciate comic book heroine hair."

She lit up. "You totally have a point."

"Stop looking at Eric like he's a Cinnabon," said Terry. "Sorry, E. This is an office full of women. We're not used to straight male energy. You might get sexually assaulted."

"I don't know, the women I've met seem pretty composed," he said, unable to help himself. "I can't picture anyone here trying to molest me."

Jenna cut her eyes at him.

Just then, Darcy stormed past the kitchenette, and then retraced her steps, stepping into the now-full space. An impressive extravaganza of multi-tasking, she was typing into her iPhone, applying lip gloss, and barking orders into a second phone cradled between her shoulder and ear.

After making the foursome wait for thirty seconds, she tossed both phones and the gloss into her bag.

"Jenna, how was FIT? Did you represent us beautifully?"

"I think so," said Jenna. "You can't imagine the creativity pouring out of those students, and it was a great opportunity to…"

"Perfect. So, Jinx."

"Y-yes?" asked the brunette.

"I had lunch with Alexandra from Commes des Garcon, and she told me you'd RSVP'd to their spring tee-shirt launch? You can't go to that, you're too junior. Besides, you're banned from attending any fashion events until you get your undiagnosed eating disorder under control. At that TopShop lunch, I heard you tunneled a hole through all the mini baguettes in the bread basket, leaving crust carcasses everywhere. StyleZine girls are always the coolest bitches in the room. Do spare me the starving fashion girl cliché."

Jinx blushed and nodded. "Yes. I will."

Out of Darcy's sightline, Eric looked like it was taking everything he had to keep his mouth shut.

"And Jenna. Your last three 'Just Jenna' posts got ridiculous traffic, which I like. What I don't like is that the traffic would've quadrupled if you had promoted them. Please tell me you did it today."

Jenna still hadn't mastered the art of digital promotion—it wasn't a natural reflex for her to write something and then broadcast the link to zillions of strangers. Jenna had dropped the ball, and was about to be outed in front of these girls, who she'd just gotten to consider that she might be a valuable addition to the office. And Eric, who already thought she was ridiculous.

"Hello? Jenna?"

Terry and Jinx glanced at each other, and then down at the floor.

"I…well, I…" Jenna felt like an entry-level assistant, getting confronted by her boss for forgetting to tell her that the London Times called to interview her about an Isaac Mizrahi show. What could she say? "I was…"

"She handled it," said Eric.

Jenna whipped her head in his direction. Darcy asked, "How would you know?"

"You don't have access to our HootSuite account, do you?"

"I don't even know what that is," spat Darcy, impatiently.

"You should. It helps you schedule your social media engagement. I checked it earlier and saw that Jenna has four tweets queued for this afternoon and something on Google Plus. And a Facebook post set for three o'clock. Or is it three-thirty?"

"Umm, three-thirty." Jenna wiped her palms on her skirt. She had no clue what he was talking about. "On Who Sweet, that's it."

"HootSuite," repeated Eric.

"Right!"

"Huh. Good." Darcy eyed her with distracted skepticism, and then started to walk away. "Jenna and Eric, looking forward to the first video."

The two girls scurried behind Darcy, and Jenna and Eric were left standing in the kitchen. Jenna exhaled, slumping back against the counter. She gestured for Eric to come closer.

"I don't know what to say," she whispered, with great difficulty. "Except thank you."

"You don't have to thank me," he said. "You were drowning; it was painful."

"But you could've let me drown. You know, after our... challenging day yesterday."

"Challenging? That's the word we're going with?"

"Fine, I was a tad hysterical."

"I mean, yeah, you were extra. But it was almost cinematic. You made it count."

"Eric," she started grandly, "I would like to tell you...I think you deserve an...I'm sorry...about my behavior yesterday."

Eric looked surprised. "Wow. I bet that hurt."

"You can't imagine."

He folded his arms. "Apology accepted. And I'm sorry for calling you middle-aged."

"And Mrs. Robinson," she added.

"And Mrs. Robinson."

"I'm not a bitch. I'm really not. I'm actually one of the nicest people you'll ever meet. Though that's like saying you're beautiful or hilarious. It's one of those things you should wait for someone else to say about you."

"I don't think you're a bitch," he said, leaning up against the counter next to Jenna—but a good two feet away. There was a Keurig coffee maker and a basket of Twinings tea bags between them. "I think you were freaked out. And I didn't help."

"Who are you today?"

"See? I'm a cool dude, and you were trying to report me to HR."

Jenna crossed her arms. "This is so stressful. I had no idea what you were talking about to Darcy. It sounded like Bantu Swahili."

"Why are you stressed?"

"Okay," she said with a pained sigh. "I'll keep it one hundred."

"Nooo," he said, laughing. "No, you will not keep it one hundred."

"Isn't that what the kids are saying these days?"

"Yeah, but it's keep it one hunnid," he said. "Now tell me what's wrong."

She paused, sizing him up. Eric was so sure of himself, so comfortable—he truly wasn't thrown by their *Three's Company*-level, shit-storm of a situation. Yesterday, this had aggravated her. Today, she was grateful. It was like he refused to give awkwardness between them a chance to set in—which was sort of gallant.

"I was teaching in Virginia for a long time and I just came back to New York." She lowered her voice. "It's my first time working for a website and, I'm a little lost."

"And you're scared if you ask for help, you'll give yourself away."

"Pretty much. Instagramming? Twittering? I'm clueless."

"Twittering? Okay, that's the cutest thing that's ever happened."

Cute? Jenna couldn't remember the last time a man called her cute.

"You seemed to know what you were talking about," she said. "With Hoo Tweet and everything."

"HootSuite."

"HootSuite."

"She just wants you to post links to your stories to get people to sideways click," said Eric.

"Bantu Swahili."

"No one, like, directly enters a URL or a website name into their browser anymore. You find websites and stories from links on different platforms. You know, sideways."

"I see." Jenna let this sink in. Then, she cleared her throat and, with hesitancy, turned toward him. "Do you think...you could help me? Give me a tutorial? I really need your expertise. I need you."

"What was that?"

"I need you," she said through clenched teeth.

Eric radiated satisfaction, but said nothing.

"What?"

"I'm trying this new thing where I don't say the first thing that pops in my head."

"Thank you for that."

"Of course I'll help you. And SpikeMee90 will be your first official follower."

"90? Is that really the year you were born?"

"Yeah, definitely the wrong year, though. Everything good happened before my time, or when I was too young to get it. Thirties gangster flicks. Brando. *Blazing Saddles*. Blaxploitation. Soundgarden. Outkast. But 1994 Outkast, not that 'Hey Ya' shit." He shrugged. "Older is…better. It's richer. Older is sexier."

Older is sexier.

He didn't realize what he'd said until it was out. Eric glanced at Jenna to see if she'd reacted, and caught her eyes. Jenna hesitated longer than was appropriate and then looked away. Without realizing it, she scooted further away from him.

"Wow. Soundgarden," said Jenna, trying to keep the conversation going. "When I was in high school you couldn't be black and into so-called 'white' stuff. Admitting I loved Motley Crue would've meant instant 'Oreo' status."

"You loved Motley Crue? With your fluttery hands and bougie hair flips?"

"Fluttery hands? How did you notice that?"

"I'm a filmmaker. I notice everything."

"Okay filmmaker, if we don't figure out this series, we should both quit now."

"Right. Let's focus." Eric pulled a bag of Skittles out of his pocket, popping a handful in his mouth.

"You need Skittles to focus?"

"No, I just have a low grade oral fixation and a candy addiction. I gotta taste the rainbow at least twice a day." He offered her the bag.

"No thanks." She reconsidered. "Actually yes."

She took a handful and grabbed a napkin. Then, she fished around for the yellows and lined them up on the napkin. Eric watched her do this for a moment, mystified.

"You gotta explain this."

"Everyone knows that lemon's the tastiest flavor. That's the rule."

"Oh *that's* the rule."

Jenna pulled her analog Smythson journal out of her bag, and flipped to her notes from the night before. She scrolled down her list of half-hatched ideas, and stopped on the only one that was viable.

"First of all, do you have any intel? I mean, what does Darcy love? Any particular designers? Art? Models? What could we give her that would blow her mind?"

"The blood of virgins? How would I know?"

"So no intel. Well, here's my idea. You've heard of Isabelle Mirielle's, right? The fancy shoe line all the celebs and It-girls fetishize? They're what Jimmy Choos used to be. Well the designer, Greta Blumen, is an old friend. She's super-mysterious and never does press, but she'll speak to me. Let's go to her studio and interview her. We could get a preview of next season! It'll blow everyone's minds."

"Hmm. Okay." Eric offered Jenna more Skittles.

"What does 'okay' mean?"

"I don't get it."

"What's not to get?" She popped the yellows in her mouth. "I know the hottest shoe designer in the game, why wouldn't girls want an insider's peek into the creation of the stilettos they covet?"

"That's a magazine article," he said, simply.

Eric offered more Skittles to Jenna, and this time, instead of taking a few, she snatched the whole bag out of his hand. "What are you talking about?"

"It's static. You could read that story. It's not visual. It's not clicky."

"Pardon me?"

"No one will click on it! Also, that's one video. What would the series be?"

"A series of interviews between me and fashion VIPs."

Eric ran his hand over his face. "Yo, that's such a flatline."

"It's fabulous!" She poured the bag into her mouth, finishing it off. "I happen to have just a tad more experience than you. Trust me."

"Your boss is expecting this to go viral. This will not go viral."

Jenna, who only had the vaguest understanding of what 'viral' meant, said, "It will go triple viral."

"Does this shoe chick have a dynamic personality, at least?"

"I can pull dazzle out of anyone. I've been doing this for a long time. No shade, I think it would behoove you to sit back, watch, and learn."

"I think you just threw plenty shade."

"How do you know it won't work? You're sitting there eating Skittles and telling me how to do my job. You're a kid. You probably rode to work on a skateboard."

"And what's the make and model of the broom you rode in on?"

"What?"

"We could do this all day. You won't win. And not for nothing, you ate all my Skittles."

Jenna looked down at the empty bag.

They were quiet for a moment, each realizing that they lost their battles to control themselves. Jenna had promised herself that she'd stop the defensive outbursts, but something about Eric stoked this in her. And Eric had truly attempted to curb his innate smartassedness, but Jenna drove him to it. It was clear—they knew how to bring out the worst in each other.

"Look," said Eric, "we had such a promising start to this conversation. We can't do yesterday again. I have banter burnout."

"Me too."

"And you're right—I am green. So, let's do this shoe designer thing."

She smiled triumphantly. "Thank you."

Eric cocked his head. "You always get what you want?"

"More or less."

Eric nodded, thinking to himself. And then with a coolly assured expression, he said, "So do I."

CHAPTER 7

The Isabel Mirielle showroom was inside of an eight-story building on 37th Street, and was typical of all the other buildings in the Garment District—run down, over a century old, and boasting a tacky ground floor wholesale boutique overloaded with polyester, pageant-lite Sweet Sixteen gowns and First Communion dresses. From the outside, you'd never know that the tenement-style buildings housed the factories and showrooms of some of world's most important fashion houses. In fact, the architecture was so dreary that it always felt like it was about to rain—and today it was sunny and almost eighty degrees, a beautiful early-September day.

Eric was standing in front of 210 West 37th with his camera equipment, waiting for Jenna and musing on the vast number of red flags indicating this shoot would be a fail. Thanks to their tumultuous two days, Jenna and Eric waited too long to come up with an idea and now it was rushed. They had zero plan of action. He should've spoken to Greta, himself, to go over the direction—but Jenna got all territorial, insisting that she speak to her directly. And she was only able to get the assistant, because Greta was out of the country until this morning.

Jenna had picked a mysterious person with no digital footprint, so he couldn't do any research on Greta to help him prepare. So basically, neither he, Jenna—or this phantom of a shoe designer—had an idea what they were walking into this morning.

He didn't challenge any of this bullshit because…why should he? Jenna was so smug, so stubborn—so loud and wrong. It was impossible to get through to her when she thought she had the answer. He'd let her find out. Terry told him she'd been a judge on a TV show.

Clearly, Jenna was used to big budget productions with assistants and handlers making the major decisions, and now that she was on her own, she had no idea how guerilla-style, low-budget shoots went. Jenna wasn't aware that she wasn't just the talent—she had to help produce her content. Not just show up and sparkle.

Jenna was a diva. And the worst kind—the kind who thought she was down-to-earth.

That was the thing about her, though. She was totally lacking in self-awareness. She thought she came across as powerful during those temper tantrums—but she just sounded scared. This morning, after he spent twenty exasperating minutes walking her through Instagram, she thought she looked busy and unbothered by declining to share a cab uptown ("Sorry, I just need to finish up this post, I'll meet you."). But all she did was broadcast that she couldn't be alone in a cab with him.

Actually, Eric wasn't comfortable being alone with her, either. Over the past day, he'd discovered that the stress of dealing with Jenna's Jennaness gave him a splitting headache. He'd taken two Excedrin on the ride over, as a preemptive measure. Yes, she could be cool-ish when she wasn't yelling at him—but that's where their conversations always ended up.

I've never regretted kissing a woman in my life, until now, he thought. *I should never have gone to that dog party. I should've just gone to Tim's and watched Key and Peele for fifteen hours. My life would be so easy right now.*

A cab slowed down to a stop in front of him. Squinting against the glare bouncing off of the back window, he saw Jenna inside.

And then she opened the door and stepped out wearing a shrunken red sweatshirt with a sliver of midriff showing, a thousand pearl necklaces and skintight, ass-hugging denim sailor pants. Her curls were pinned up on one side. Pony-skin stilettos. Glossy lips. Movie star shades.

Eric blinked. And then chased every unprofessional thought from his head.

"Hi," said Jenna, walking up to him with a businesslike smile. "Hey. You changed."

"I know, this is my 'Socialite Sailor' look. Red usually reads well for me on camera."

"It's good that you wore solids. I forgot to tell you that prints can throw off the perspective."

"I know that trick. I've been in front of the camera a few times."

"Yeah, I heard you were a fancy TV star. Explains so much," he muttered under his breath. "So. Before we go in, let's shoot the intro. We only have twenty minutes with…"

"…Greta Blumen."

"So we gotta hurry." Eric looked up and down 37th, his brow furrowed. "Stand right here, with Seventh Ave. behind you, so we can get the street traffic."

"Here?" She backed up.

He peered over her head and then looked up at the sun. "No, to the left. We need to catch that light."

Without thinking, Eric held Jenna by the shoulders and gently moved her to the left, and then slightly to the right. He was so lost in setting up the shot, that he didn't realize he was touching her—until he looked down at Jenna's face, and saw her widened eyes. He dropped his hands.

"Perfect," he said. Eric planted his tripod ten paces in front of her, and positioned the camera on top. Peering into his lens, Jenna looked rigid. Her lips were in a tight little line and her arms hung stiffly at her sides. He had to loosen her up.

He lifted up his head. "Did you ever have a pet?"

"A pet? I'm allergic to every animal fur under the sun. But I did have a hairless cat."

"What was its name?"

"Colleen. I've always loved the idea of giving pets inappropriately human names. She was almost going to be Rachel. Or Tameika."

"Pets weren't allowed at the Vale crib, but in sixth grade, I adopted this little Terrier and kept him at my boy, Tim's. His name was Rocky 4." He ducked behind the camera, adjusting the lens. "Anyway, your bag reminds me of Rocky 4's fur."

"Are you comparing my cross-body clutch to a dog? This is high-quality faux chinchilla!"

"Oh, faux real?

Jenna chuckled a little.

"It's a compliment," said Eric. "I loved that dog."

Jenna shook her head. Fluffing her hair and fidgeting, she watched Eric replace a lens, adjust the angle, and do it again. His brow was furrowed in concentration.

"So why do you love this?" she asked. "What made you want to make movies?"

Eric popped his head up again.

"It's just always been there. I guess, when I was a kid, my life felt... messy. I loved that movies had a beginning, middle, and end. Everything works out in the third act. Or maybe it doesn't, but at least you have an answer. And I like making the world look how I want it to look. It feels like I'm god," he said. "It's crazy. Sometimes I have a memory, and it feels mad visceral, and it's a good five minutes before I realize that it's not real; it's a scene from a movie."

She smiled with recognition. "I can relate. I feel the same way, but about what the characters were wearing. Can I ask you what's your short's about?"

"No. Please, noooo," he groaned. "How come?"

"Just thinking about it stresses me out. I'm having a panic attack from the question," he said. "So, what about you? Why'd you want to be in fashion?

"Clothes say everything about who you are before you even open your mouth. Take you, for example. It's clear what you want the world to think about you."

"And what's that?"

"Like you don't try at all, even though you clearly do. Accidentally cool. Off-duty actor caught by the paparazzi."

He looked down at himself. "I don't try. I'm a dude; I just throw some shit on."

"Please! You had on the white and grey Air Yeezy's yesterday. The crispest sneakers Kanye ever designed. With a RZA tee I know you got at VFiles on Lafayette. Is that place still open?"

"Yeah, but, I mean…"

"And today, you're wearing the plaid shirt that's currently in the window at the Soho H&M. Plus, faded Rag & Bone jeans and fancy workboots—what are those, Artful Dodger? Limited Edition J. Crew?" She giggled. "Fall workboots, even though it's eighty degrees. That's a fashion person move. You definitely try."

"How did you do that?" Eric looked down at himself. "I feel so exposed."

Jenna narrowed her eyes, studying him. "I've got it. You're a hybrid of Platinum-Selling Rapper Sitting Courtside and Haute Hipster."

He stepped away from the tripod. "Hipster? Do I look like a person who drinks artisanal craft beer? Am I dressed like a 19th century farmer?"

"No, but you *are* dressed like a 19th century logger."

"It should be noted that you've memorized my entire wardrobe," he said. "Why're you looking so hard?"

"Please, I do this with everyone."

"Yeah okay," he said, with a pleased grin.

Satisfied with the setup and assured that the ice was broken with Jenna, Eric said, "Let's do a run through of your intro. This is your first one, so it's gonna set the tone for the whole series. Remind people who you are. What to expect."

He handed her the StyleZine microphone. She took a deep breath and blew it out hard; scrunched up her nose and released it; and wiggled her shoulders.

"I'm ready." She threw on a big smile. "Hello everyone, it's Jenna Jones, the new editor at large at StyleZine. I'm so excited to bring you my very first video blog! Today, we're at the Isabel Mireille shoe showroom, where…Eric Combs has just looked up from his camera with obvious dissatisfaction."

"Whose voice is that?"

"It's my voice!" She frowned.

"Just be conversational. Casual. YouTube vloggers talk in their bathrooms and kitchens like they're talking to friends. It's about being real."

"I don't sound real?"

"You sound like Siri."

"This used to be so easy! I guess I'm really out of practice."

"It's cool. Just relax."

Jenna started again, but got thrown off when a gust of wind tousled her hair. She smoothed it down, peered into her compact, and started over. Then she got too close to her microphone and smeared her lip gloss, so she had to look into her compact again. At which point she noticed that her blush had faded in the sun, so she pulled some out of her bag and reapplied. On the third take, she yelled, "Cut!" to fidget with the placement of her necklaces.

"Yo, what are you doing?"

"I'm used to having hair and makeup and a stylist before I go on-camera!" She looked into the mirror again, smoothed her undereye concealer, and started over. "Take four. I'm Jenna Jones, and…"

Eric turned off the camera. "You're taking all the spontaneity out of this. You don't wanna overdose on perfect."

"Yes I do."

"No, you wanna be relatable. Besides, there's no art in idealizing beautiful women on film. It's about the vulnerable, feminine moments. You know, when it's windy and a woman's hair gets caught in her lip gloss. When she laughs too loud and and covers her mouth. When she unconsciously smoothes her skirt over her ass 'cause she thinks it's too big, or too small. Imperfections."

"At my age, imperfections are illegal."

"Just stop overthinking it, and do whatever feels natural. Let's do the intro again, and this time don't stop. You're gonna kill it."

It took three more takes and Eric's gentle coaching for Jenna to nail it. Finally, she dropped the stiff bit and came across as authentically her—authoritative, smart, but with the slightly kooky, self-deprecating edge that made her a fan favorite on *America's Modeling Challenge*. When she stumbled over "Isabel Mireille," she didn't stop. Instead, she giggled and said, "Don't mind me, I'm new to fashion." It worked.

This might not be so bad, he thought.

And when Greta's assistant buzzed them upstairs to the warehouse (which was a modest space, the size of a two-bedroom apartment in a Midtown high-rise) Eric felt hopeful. The showroom was gorgeous, an explosion of luxe bohemianism. There were embroidered, crushed velvet scarves draped over everything, exquisitely crafted incense pots, and a psychedelic Turkish rug covering the purposely beat-up wood floor. A Moroccan tiled wall running the length of the room was lined with shoes, from the ceiling to the floor, with a panel of sheer organza floating in front of it. And there were four young women perched on plush, pillowed ottomans around a weathered white table, poring over shoe designs.

"Hi, I'm Rosie," announced Greta Blumen's assistant, striding over to them. She was stocky, with a tangle of orangey hippie hair. She looked hearty, like she could fell a mastadoon with her bare hands.

"Right, we spoke on the phone!" said Jenna.

"Ms. Blumen's in the back," she said, looking past Jenna and zeroing in on Eric. "And, well, I think she's having second thoughts. Can you come back another time?"

"What?" Jenna was stunned. "You can't go talk to her for us?"

"Wellll…she's coming off of an intense week. And she's so unpredictable. I can't afford to get fired right now." She made a move to usher them to the door.

"But Rosie," said Jenna, trying to stave off panic, "you committed to the shoot yesterday, and…"

"Why is she having second thoughts?" asked Eric, addressing Rosie directly.

"She never appears on camera," she said, shyly glancing at him again. "She's having jitters."

"It's natural," said Eric. "She's used to being behind-the-scenes. But she'll be fine."

"How can you be so sure?"

"I know how to get women to loosen up," he said, his dimple flashing.

Rosie looked at him and then she rolled her eyes, blushing. "I bet you do."

He grinned. "What's that mean?"

"Nooothing," she said, all saucy.

"All I was saying," continued Eric, with faux innocence, "was that every director should know how to make his leading lady feel comfortable. Why're you making it a thing, Rosie?"

"I'm not making it a thing!" she giggled. "God!"

Jenna looked from Eric to Rosie and then back at Eric, stunned by what she was witnessing. Rosie's posture had gone from tense to almost comically languid. She was leaning against the wall, lazily stroking a chunk of her gnarled hair.

"Okay. So, look. I don't wanna get you fired. But can you just try to get her for us?"

"I don't think I can convince her to come out."

"You sure?" said Eric, his voice going low. "You seem the kind of girl who knows how to get what she wants."

"I do?"

"Am I wrong?"

"Yeah. I mean no. I mean, yes?" Rosie shook her head, discombobulated. "Umm...I'll be right back.."

The redhead left them in the doorway, and scurried across the room.

Jenna turned toward Eric and stared at him, incredulous.

"What?" he whispered.

Jenna whispered-hissed back, "What the hell was that?"

"One of us had to think quickly."

"That's quick-thinking to you? Eye-fucking her into helping us?"

"I was just using the resources available to me to save our asses."

"That was so cheap, Eric."

"Yeah, but it worked. What was your plan?"

"Who had time to think of one? You'd already gotten her pregnant!"

Just then, Rosie hurried back over to them.

"Good news. Ms. Blumen has agreed to give you guys five minutes."

"Thank God!" exclaimed Jenna.

"Thank you," said Eric to Rosie.

"My pleasure," she purred, tossing her tangles behind one shoulder. Jenna wanted to gag.

"So guys," Rosie continued, "she's in the bathroom, finishing up massaging her pulse points with myrrh oil. But be prepared. She's had a rough couple of weeks."

Just then, they heard a loud, husky voice in a heavy German accent, coming from somewhere behind them.

"Sank you, Rosie, you're dismissed. Jenna! Oh Jenna, my luff!" They spun around, and there was Greta, all frenetic, jittery energy, emerging from the bathroom. She looked like a fortune teller and appeared to be on blow. She was wearing a flowy, ikat-print blouson dress, satin Capezio tango pumps, and a gold headscarf lined in dangling pailettes—with wild black waves tumbling out from beneath. Her getup looked totally natural, like she sprang from the womb a fully-developed woman wearing a gold snake armband and clutching a crystal ball.

Greta did have on a few accessories that didn't go with the outfit—a massive white neck brace and a full cast covering her entire left arm. And crutches.

Jenna and Eric looked at each other.

"Mein leibling!" She limped over to Jenna and gave her a stiff-necked, encumbered hug, and then did the same to Eric. Then, in obvious pain, she put her hands in a prayer pose. "I've been nervous for the shoot all day, because uff my injuries, but Rosie said that my old friend and the cutie looked so sad that it vould be just a disaster to let you down. So, let's go! I'm an open buch."

"Greta? What happened? Your assistant didn't mention anything about you being…injured."

"I was chasing my peacock, Taraji P. Henson, around my garden for exercise, and I slipped on my pile of meditation pebbles. Sprained everything and broke my arm. It was a catastrophe, *but what doesn't kill you makes you stronger.*"

"Oh Greta," managed Jenna, who had forgotten that Greta was prone to peppering her speech with mind-numbingly obvious cliché's.

"My husband was angered that I was so reckless. He threw a fit because we don't haff insurance? Ach! I make him no attention. *Hurt people hurt people.*"

"Well, maybe the brace and cast will give the interview some extra color! Right, Eric?"

Eric had no words.

"Eric?"

"Yeah, absolutely," he said, springing back to life. "So, Greta, are you ready? The shoe wall is a nice place to start."

"Not there. I'm very superstitious, and I just had this place feng shui'd for the seventh time. We haff to be careful not to disrupt the chi."

Eric looked around. "How about in that corner, with the gold couch?"

"Absolutely not, that's where I perch to dream up ideas. I can't share that viss the vorld."

Turns out, Greta was averse to Eric filming anything meaningful or "special" in the showroom; the one place she agreed to shoot was in front of a white closet door. After setting up, he peered in the lens and saw that the setup looked as cheap and amateurish as it felt.

Faced with no other choice, he cued Jenna and Greta to start. "Hello again! I'm here with the famous, but mysterious Greta Blumen, Isabel Mirielle's shoe designer."

Greta leaned on her right crutch and waved hello to the camera, her casted hand whipping back and forth like a bulky white windshield wiper.

"Greta, can you tell us about your inspiration?"

"Too personal! All I can say is that I find joy in taking risks. *I dance like no one's watching.*"

"Well, what's your process? Do you have any rituals?"

"I do, but they're my rituals, leibling. Telling you would be like giving away one's birssday vish." She burst out laughing. "But seriously, *I try to work smarter, not harder.*"

"Can you tell us what's coming up from Isabel Mirielle?"

"I can nacht, but there's somessing for everyone. Because, it's like I always say, *beauty is in the eye of the beholder.*"

"You must have some fabulous new styles you'd like to show our viewers. Just a sneak peek?"

"Nein! After all, *good things come to those who wait.*"

Jenna glanced at Eric, whose expression was an exasperated blend of "Is she for real?" and "I want to kill you."

"Okay…well, we at least have to discuss your famous over-the-knee 'Clara' boot, with the studded, six-inch stiletto heel. Why do you think it made such an impact?"

"Vell, I've thought about this deeply, and you know vhat my theory is?"

Jenna looked hopeful. Finally, some details that would give this dead-end interview some meat!

"What's your theory?"

"*Sex sells.*"

"Cut!" said Eric, turning off the camera. "Greta, you're doing great. I just need to have a word with Jenna. We'll step outside for a second. Don't mind us."

Jenna smiled at Greta, and then followed Eric into the hallway. The second he shut the door, they began whisper-yelling at each other.

"Jenna! What in every kind of fuck?"

"I know!"

"This is why I asked you if she'd be good on camera. She's your friend! You didn't know she was on crack?"

"I haven't seen Greta in years, all I remembered was that she had huge personality. I thought she'd be epic!"

"Epic? This bitch speaks in memes!"

"What's a meme?"

"And I can't believe her minion didn't tell you she was, like, in a full body cast." Eric started pacing. "I mean…I can't…this is a fatal fail, kid."

"Well…why didn't you dissuade me?"

"You're seriously suggesting this is my bad? Nah yo, this was your struggle idea. You picked that madcap medium."

"But you went along with it!"

"Because arguing with you is so demoralizing, Jenna! Has anyone ever told you that? You have no chill!"

"I do have chill!" Jenna wasn't positive what 'having chill' meant, but she had a feeling he was right. "But what are we going to do? We don't have time to shoot anything else. How can we fix it?"

"I'll have to make the best of it, somehow. I'll edit it to death?

"I don't know. I've never had to package anything this shitty."

"This is all my fault," groaned Jenna. "We're so screwed!"

"When you said you needed me yesterday? You really do. And not just as a Twitter tutor. One of the keys to greatness is realizing what you don't know, and then pillaging the people around you that do."

"You're lecturing me on greatness."

"Actually, that was a quote from my academic advisor."

"I don't know what I'm doing." Her forehead was knotted with worry. "The enormity of this just hit me. And I have everything riding on this."

Jenna looked scared, utterly defenseless—which made Eric feel guilty. He had set her up. He'd known that her idea sucked, and could've put a stop to it—but he let her flop to prove a point.

"Jenna, look," he said. "We're both responsible for this fuckery. If we still have jobs after we turn this in, we'll make sure the next one kills. But we have to work together. Cool?"

She nodded. "Together. Cool."

Grimly, they went back into Greta's lair to continue the 'interview,' which she wrapped up in five minutes—but not before pressing a calming alexandrite crystal into Eric's palm and declaring that his Sahasraha chakra seemed pissed off.

In less than a half an hour, the hot mess of a shoot was over. This time, Jenna and Eric shared a cab downtown. They were both pressed to the door on their respective sides, seated far apart, and submerged in brooding silence. The only thing uniting them was the shared feeling that their run at StyleZine might be over before it started.

CHAPTER 8

Forty-five agonizing minutes later, Jenna and Eric were still in the cab. The midday traffic down Sixth Avenue was locked to a standstill on 29th. The temperature had risen to ninety degrees, and the cabbie's AC wasn't working. The air, so clear earlier that morning, had gone humid and oppressive. The cab smelled like kimchee and onion rings.

They were too far from Soho to walk (Eric had too much bulky equipment). The closest train, the F, was rerouted that morning due to a bed bug infestation. Jenna and Eric were stuck in hell. They were starving, wilting, and ready to crawl out of their skin.

Jenna had rolled the arms of her shirt up to her shoulders and was fanning it out from her chest (she'd stolen the slightly cropped, micro-sweatshirt idea from the Marc Jacobs runway, buying a little boy's version from Marshall's and shrinking it in her oven). Her cluster of chunky pearls felt like they were choking her, so she unhooked them—at which point the cheap, Claire's Boutique beads popped off, bouncing to the floor.

Apt metaphor for my life. It's about to fall apart. How much longer can I pretend to be fancy when I'm really a knockoff? How much longer can I act like I can handle this job, when I'm in over my head?

Embarrassed that her necklace was now pooled at her feet, she scooped up the plastic pearls and dumped them in her purse. Then, she glanced over at Eric. He hadn't noticed. He was swiping away on his phone. Clearly exasperated, he suddenly dropped it and, with an angsty groan, he stretched a little, trying to make his 6'2" frame fit in the tiny space. His shirt slid up to expose the briefest glimpse of ridiculously taut abs. Jenna's mouth went dry. His stomach was ridiculous. It could've starred in a weight loss supplement ad.

"I need air," she mumbled, fanning with a *Marie Claire* from her purse. "I can't breathe."

Eric didn't even look up, which was fine, because she wasn't addressing him. They weren't ignoring each other, but neither one of them had spoken to each other the entire time. At random intervals, they would mutter exasperated exclamations under their breath.

Eric: Yooo this heat, son! I'm gonna die in this bitch.

Jenna: I completely sweated out my hair. I am offensive.

Eric: I want Shake Shack. We're near Shake Shack.

Jenna: What are those cars honking at? There's no point, no one's going anywhere!

Eric: Yo, why does this cab smell like the Bloomin' Onion appetizer from Outback?

But soon, they accepted that they were stuck in there—together and indefinitely—and gave up on bemoaning their fate. Jenna laid her head against the windowsill, closing her eyes and trying to breath in some fresh air. But Eric was all antsy, pent-up energy. First he listened to music, bobbing his head to a rap song with a bass so throbbing that Jenna heard it through his Beats by Dre headphones. That ended, and then he zeroed in on his phone, tweeting, playing video games, watching WorldStarHipHop. com—loudly. Eric had the volume turned up on his phone. Every "click" of a key, every sound effect, reverberated through Jenna's head at the eleventh decibel.

Finally, she spoke up.

"Do you mind turning down the phone?"

"My bad."

"Thanks."

Eric went to adjust the volume, but before he could, the unmistakable "ding" of a new text rang out. He checked it, and then sat up straighter and began texting in a flurry. Over the next two minutes, his expression ran the emotional gamut (frowny, hopeful, bummed, smiley).

If it's that important, thought Jenna, *why doesn't he speak to that person on the phone instead of texting?*

Like clockwork, the phone rang. Eric froze, looking at it like he'd never seen it before. Then he glanced at Jenna. It kept ringing. And ringing.

"Aren't you going to answer?"

"It's cool," he said, stalling, "It's rude to talk while we're both trapped here; I don't want to bother you. You seem so serene. A calm you is a happy me."

"Eric, answer the phone!"

"Okay."

He put it to his ear and leaned even closer to his door. In a low voice, almost a whisper, he said, "Hey. No, I can't talk right now. So…I'm sorry too. I will. But right now I gotta go. I…umm…" He lowered his voice even more. "I miss you, too."

Eric turned off the phone, slid it in his pocket and slumped in his seat. Jenna folded her arms and eyed him, a surprised smirk on her face.

"Oh really?"

"I don't wanna talk about it." He rubbed his temples.

"So, who was that goddess among women?"

"Here we go."

"Eric, do you have a girlfriend?"

"An ex-girlfriend. Ex."

"And how long has she been your ex? Were you…together when, you know…"

"No, I don't cheat. I never got the point. Why be in a relationship?" Deeply uncomfortable, he rubbed his sweaty palms on his jeans. "We just broke up."

"How long ago is 'just?'"

"Jenna," he said. "I'm just gonna close my eyes and get a moment of peace before we go back and my mother shits on my entire existence. Okay?"

"Okay," she said, but she was bursting with curiosity. Who was this girl? What did she look like? Did he kiss her the way...

Don't even think about it. Never happened, remember?

Still, she had to know.

"Can you at least tell me her name?" she blurted out. "What does she do?"

"Madison," he said, stiffly. "Ballerina."

"Why did you break up?"

"No offense, but it's none of your business."

"True, but what else are we going to do? We're stuck in here together, we might as well talk. Plus, I give great relationship advice. Though I never could figure out my own."

He raised his brows. "You're in a relationship?"

"No. I'm in that terrible set-up phase between relationships."

"How's that going for you?"

"It's not. Men my age want women your age," she said. "So, tell me more about Madison."

"No."

"Why?"

"'Cause you're mean to me. And I'd like to keep a healthy emotional distance from you."

"Please?"

"Omigooodd," groaned Eric, leaning back against his seat. "Get me outta this cab."

"Why did you break up?"

"Fine," he said, exasperated. "She dances with this company in LA, and she's a sophomore at UCLA, but I'm here. So it would've been a weird long-distance thing."

"Wait. She's a sophomore in college? How old is she?"

"Almost nineteen."

Jenna swiped aside the sweat-soaked curls plastered to her forehead and nodded, trying not to broadcast how she felt—which was shock over the realization that Eric was young enough to conceivably date an eighteen-year-old.

"Well," she started, "sometimes long-distance works. Did you try?"

"I mean, it's complicated. I met her when I was at USC. When I graduated, she wanted to transfer to NYU so we could be together." He frowned, remembering. "I told her to stay on the West Coast. That she shouldn't move across the country for some dude. But then she got mad. Like, very."

Jenna nodded. "Madison wanted you to want her to move here."

"She never said that."

"But that's how she felt. She wanted your feelings to be so intensely passionate for her, that you couldn't fathom any other option."

Eric hit Jenna with a look, like he was engaging a silly little girl. "Intensely passionate? That's a cinematic affectation."

"You don't feel intense passion for Madison?"

"I feel 'hearty like' for her," he said, listlessly. "Seriously, I'm too hot and weak to talk. Let me preserve my energy for editing."

"Do you want her back?"

"I don't know. Yeah?"

"That's so sweet."

Eric rubbed the heels of his hands against his eyes. "Yo, there are so many things I'd rather be doing than sharing this specific moment with you right now."

"So what do you love about her?"

"I said hearty like."

"What do you heartily like about her?"

"She's sweet. Nice."

"Sweet and nice? You could be describing a maltipoo."

"What do you want me to say? That's what I like."

"Does she feed you?"

"Like, does she cook and shit?"

"No, does she feed your soul. Motivate you. Inspire you."

"Is a girlfriend required to do that? I motivate myself." Eric paused. "Look, I don't get all introspective about my relationships. To me, it's straightforward. Just make each other happy and, like, don't not. Complicated situations with complicated women? I'm all the way good on that."

"What do you consider complicated?"

"My boy, Tim's girl, for example. Last week she chased him down Mott with a sword she stole off the wall at a Thai restaurant. And he loved it. What's that about? I like easy-going girls that aren't always trying to get mouthy." He shrugged. "Women I know how to make happy. Uncomplicated girls like Madison."

"Here's a secret, though," said Jenna. "Madison is complicated. We all are. She probably senses that you need her to be simple, so that's what she is."

"You don't even know her."

"Believe me, I do. I was a so-called 'simple girl.' I was ornamental for twenty years. My job was to look pretty, smile, and shut up. Those setups are doomed, because no woman can bury her needs forever. And when she shows herself, the men leave. But you know what? Even the men that date feisty spitfires, like your friend, Tim? They end up running for the hills, too. Because those relationships aren't real either, that's a drama addiction and it fizzles quick. The only ones that make it are equals, like my friends Billie and Jay, who trade power. Sometimes he's the top, and sometimes she is. But that's rare. Maybe you should look into why you feel most comfortable with women that let you get to be you, in all your multi-layered complexity—while their role is to stay un-mouthy."

Eric looked at her. "That was the most judgmental bullshit indictment ever. I'm a great boyfriend. The men coming in and out of my house when I was a kid were complete garbage; I know how *not* to be. You think I thought Madison's role was to shut up and let me shine?"

Jenna hadn't intended to offend him; she was just offering some perspective. Unsolicited, but she wasn't trying to cross the line. All she'd wanted to do was satisfy her intense curiosity about Madison while also engaging Eric in some non-confrontational chit-chat. And now she'd brought them right back to where they always ended up.

"I didn't mean to make you angry."

"You're making me sound like I dismissed Madison as some inconsequential trophy wife. Like it was all about me. It was the opposite. I told her to stay in LA because it was best for her. I care about her, I was being thoughtful."

"I wasn't criticizing you, I was trying…"

"Damn, Jenna. What happened in your life? You're mad bitter about men."

"Bitter?"

Eric was already in a terrible mood from that shoot. He was thrown by the Madison call, and hot. And now Jenna was making damning assumptions about him based on nothing. Yet, her assessment of him struck a nerve. A very small part of him did value that Madison was so agreeable (meek, even) because it made his life easier. But overall, Jenna made him sound self-serving and callous, which hurt him a little—and this was a feeling he loathed. To Eric, hurting a little opened the door to being hurt a lot, which he refused to let happen.

He was pissed at Jenna, but even more irritated with himself letting her opinion matter. So, Eric did what he'd always done when someone punctured his usually impenetrable veneer. He went for the jugular.

"Hell yeah, you're bitter," he told her. "You basically said that all men, no matter what kind of woman they're with, will find a reason to lose interest. See, this is why old dudes date young girls. They're still open and optimistic. No one wants to chill with a woman just waiting for you to fuck up."

Jenna glared at him, fuming. She'd accidentally offended Eric, but now he was deliberately insulting her.

"That was so nasty."

"You dragged me into a conversation I didn't wanna have, only to suggest that I treat my girl like an inflatable doll."

"Your girl? Are you together or not?"

"We're not! And why do you care?"

"I don't," snapped Jenna. "You know, what I really wanted to say is that it's obvious why you like quote-unquote simple women. You grew up with Beowulf. You're looking for the opposite."

"Beowulf?" Eric was so taken aback, he burst out laughing. No one had ever had the balls to say anything like that to his face. "Oh, that's genius. Please, continue."

"Darcy's colored your whole experience with girls. The pathology's so clear. It's why you flirt with everything. You flirted with me, you flirt with the girls in the office. You told Jinx she had Lara Croft hair just to make her swoon."

"I said it to help her self-esteem! That's not flirtation, that's chivalry."

"You even batted your goddamn eyelashes to get us into that interview," she continued. "You're on a constant quest for attention and approval from women, and it's obviously because you didn't get any at home."

He stared at her. The light changed, fifteen cars honked and the cab scooted up three inches. Finally, he responded. "So that's your diagnosis?"

"Pretty much."

"Wanna hear mine?"

"Knock yourself out."

"This evil, jaded thing isn't working for you. Any book parties happening tonight? You should find another twenty-two-year-old to holler at. Fuck all that hurt outta your system."

The second Eric said it, he was sorry. But he was also too pissed to take it back.

Jenna's mouth opened, shut, and then opened again. "I dislike you. Intensely."

"It's more than mutual, Ms. Jones."

"'I can't stay in here with you." Jenna snatched her clutch up and leaned up to the partition, yelling, "Sir? Can you let me out here? I'm going to hop out…"

"Nah, fuck that. I'm getting out, you stay," shouted Eric, knocking on the partition. "Can you open the trunk so I can get my equipment?"

"No! I'm leaving!"

"I don't care which one-a-y'all stays or goes," said the driver, "as long as I get paid, yaheardme?"

Then there was an awkward moment when they were both clamoring to get their doors open, but they were locked, and the driver kept pushing the unlock/lock button, but none of them could get the rhythm right, so Jenna and Eric were left pounding on the doors, cursing in a blind, slapsticky rage.

Jenna's door popped open first. Triumphant, she opened her wallet, whipped out two twenties and threw them at Eric.

The driver watched through the rearview mirror and chuckled, saying, "Aww shit, she makin' it rain!"

Jenna opened her door, hopping out into the cacophonous, congested intersection. As was her luck, the second after she slammed the door, the traffic started moving. She scurried to the sidewalk and watched as the cab spirited Eric off downtown. With a sigh, she wiped the sweat from her forehead and stomped down Sixth Avenue. Nothing good was behind her, and surely nothing good was awaiting her.

"Is this a fucking joke?" raged Darcy, four hours later. She'd just seen Eric's edited, two-minute clip. "Tell me it's a joke."

Jenna and Eric were seated in their boss's office, in ice-cold silence, feeling like wayward children in detention. As Darcy raged, Eric shifted in his chair, looking drained and over it, while Jenna sat at attention, trying to take the well-deserved abuse like a professional.

Her formal posture was at odds with her appearance, though. The walk from 29th Street had done her no favors. By the time she reached the StyleZine building, she was limping from blisters, her mascara was smeared, and her hair had exploded into a puffy halo in the humidity.

"It's boring, pointless nonsense. Jenna, when I gave you free license to do whatever you wanted, it was because I was secure in the fact that you, a seasoned pro, wouldn't churn out a sixth grade visual arts project. And Eric, what's with the disjointed editing? Were you high? And who would pick this dingbat gypsy for your first video? Her accent is unintelligible, and it's not even a chic one, like French or Italian. German? The most *depressing* language. Like, I want to *kill* myself. And the whole time, I'm wondering why she isn't in the ICU at Mount Sinai. Whose idea was this?"

Eric and Jenna said nothing. She didn't want to admit her massive mistake, and he wasn't going to snitch.

"Whose idea was this?"

"Well, I initially…" started Jenna.

"It was mine," he said, simultaneously.

"Nice try, Eric, but no. You have no idea who Greta Blumen is."

"I wanted to give StyleZine an exclusive," said Jenna. "Greta doesn't talk to anyone."

"Precisely. Fraulein Blumen doesn't talk to anyone. Just because she agreed to be on camera didn't mean she was going to talk. Did she say she was going to?"

Jenna couldn't bring herself to say that she hadn't even spoken to her beforehand. When Eric saw her struggling for an answer, he quickly intervened—not because he cared, but because he wanted this to all be over so he could go somewhere and smoke the roach stashed in his wallet.

"Mom…wait, what do I call you at work?"

"Jehovah."

He snickered. "Noted. Look, we did a poor job. We're aware. Next time we won't."

Darcy looked at her son like the top of her head was going to blow off. "Oh really? The only reason you're getting a next time is because it took a lot of thought and effort to hire both of you. I know you can do better. But do not make me sorry I brought you here. You both need me more than I need you, so show up. Do the work. Because Eric, even though I grew you inside my platinum-coated womb…"

He recoiled. *"Platinum-coated?"*

"…I will gleefully toss you out of this building on your ass. And Jenna, may I remind you that you've been charged with tripling our numbers in eight months?"

"You don't need to remind me."

Jenna looked at her hands, and Eric gazed out of the window—both avoiding looking at each other. Darcy eyed both of them. "What's going on with you two?"

"I'm sorry?" Jenna crossed her legs.

"I'm picking up on some negative energy. I know everything that happens at all my websites, but especially my cash cow. Someone overheard you two having a strongly-worded conversation in Jenna's office on Monday. And now, this hack job? You clearly don't feel comfortable working together. You're sitting there all stiff and pissed, like you can't stand the sight of each other. You have no chemistry."

Eric snorted. "You have no idea."

"I can only speak for myself," she said, wanting to smack him with her Rocky 4 purse, "but I feel comfortable! Really, I do."

"Stop bullshitting. Jenna, you're working closely with my child. It probably feels like added pressure. Maybe you feel blocked because you can't relax around the boss's son."

"I don't think..."

"And E, your face went vomit-green when I told you about me and Jenna's history. But the bottom line is, if you two can't handle this project together, tell me now. So I can replace one or both of you."

"No need," said Eric. "We're cool."

Jenna nodded rapidly. "The coolest."

"My mistake was thinking that you were capable of churning out a winning clip in two days. That's on me. Our readership has completely stalled; I got too eager," said Darcy. "Let's pivot. I'll give you a week and a half. In the meantime, overcome this weird awkwardness. Get a rapport going. Build an energy."

Jenna and Eric shifted in their seats.

"Question," he said. "Is it mandatory that we be in the same room while we're building the energy? Or can we just, like, FaceTime?"

"Can the sarcasm," spat Darcy. "I have a migraine throughout my entire body, and I'm late for my Lunchtime Lipo."

"Lunchtime was hours ago."

"It's a brand name, Eric," hissed Jenna, icily. The words were "it's a brand name," but the tone was, "I hope you die violently, you rude little prick."

"See that?" She pointed to Jenna, and then Eric. "Whatever you're doing right now, stop. You're partners. Act like it. Did you get your invites to Terry's birthday drinks on Monday night?"

Darcy wasn't a sentimental person, but she was maniacally obsessed with birthdays and holidays. On these special occasions, she threw voluntary parties for her staff (though the concept of a 'voluntary party' was an oxymoron. Like celebrating under duress).

It never occurred to her that the last thing one of her employees would want to do on their birthday night is spend it in the company of their boss. Especially one they nicknamed The Dream Killer.

"I better see you both there, acting civil," continued Darcy. "Literally, your jobs depend on it. I will see a return on my investment, assholes."

"You will," said Jenna, relieved to get another chance. She was stunned that Darcy had taken their failure as well as she did. "Don't worry."

"I'm not worried. Not in the slightest," she said, her tone calmly threatening. "Jenna, what happened to your hair? You look like the Cowardly Lion. Whatever, not my problem. Dismissed."

CHAPTER 9

*T*he selection here isn't so bad, thought Jenna. *These jeans are actually cute! The rear pocket placement is a little low, which will further flatten my already unplump ass, but the cut is sophisticated. Nice wash.*

Jenna was clothes shopping at Target for the first time. The superstore was positioned in downtown Brooklyn's Atlantic Center mall, kitty-corner to the Barclay Center, at the intersection of every genre of Brooklyn personality: yuppie gentrifiers buying zingy throw pillows for their Restoration Hardware chaise lounges; rowdy, around-the-way teens eating Pizza Hut and making out in the cafe; tattooed hipster moms stalking the kiddie section for organic baby bedding—and Jenna, who in her almost twenty years in fashion, had never worn anything but socks and Maybelline Great Lash mascara from the likes of Target.

She was shopping there because it's all her budget allowed, which would've been depressing if she wasn't sort of getting into it. Over the past half hour, she'd loaded up her cart with three pairs of J brand-esque jeans; two dresses that were perfect Isabel Marant knockoffs; and a chunky, menswear-inspired sweater that, if she squinted, looked like it could've sprung to life from a Matthew Williamson sketch. How had she not known that Target was a delightful Narnia of a retail destination?

It was Saturday morning, and shopping always cleared her head—which she needed, after her abysmal work week. Instead of following

Darcy's direct order to spend more time together, Jenna and Eric did the opposite, avoiding each other completely. The one time they ran into each other, outside of the kitchenette, they did an almost choreographed about-face and took off in the other direction. Jenna couldn't help it. She wanted Eric not to exist.

Which was stupid. She needed him.

Grabbing an electric purple maxi skirt off of a spinning rack, Jenna mused on this. She'd have to be the one to fix it, to apologize. After all, she was the grownup. Yes, Eric calling her hard up and undateable was rude, but Jenna never should've said he had mommy issues. It was inexcusable. No wonder he didn't want anything to do with her.

Jenna was rifling through the next rack, when she heard a familiar pair of voices.

"...because yeah, I'm platinum blonde, but I'm naturally a brunette, so my skin coloring doesn't match my hair. You'd think I'd wear rosy blush, but I really need a coral."

"Do you think my Cleopatra eyeliner is played out? I need an update."

"You can never not do Cleopatra eyeliner. That's your you-drag."

"Me-drag?"

"Your signature look. Like, if someone were to dress up like you, they'd have to wear that eyeliner. Everybody has their me-drag. Mine is athletic techno-slut."

It was Terry and Jinx. Jenna spotted them walking up the main aisle toward the registers, each carrying baskets full of makeup.

Jenna froze. No, no, no. She couldn't let them see her buying a whole wardrobe at Target. Every morning, she used her years of styling expertise to merchandise her outfits in such a way that an American Eagle top looked like Altuzarra. She was supposed to be a Fashion OG, a Major Player! If they saw her, she'd be outed for the broke fraud she was.

She abandoned her cart and ducked behind a pillar. Holding her breath, she tried to make herself small until they passed.

Keep walking, nothing to see here...

"Jenna?"

Her eyes flew open. "Terry!"

She and Jinx looked at each other and burst into giggles.

"I never thought I'd see you at Target!" Jinx looked like a girl who'd just been told the most delicious piece of gossip. "What are you doing here?"

"Oh, I'm...I was picking up some kitchen utensils. I've only been back in New York for a couple of weeks, I still need a lot of household supplies."

"But isn't this your cart of clothes?" asked Terry.

"No!" Jenna laughed. "Why would you think it's mine?"

"That's your furry handbag in the front."

"Oh! Hilarious, yeah. My, um, fifteen-year-old niece needs some back-to-school clothes, so I was just..." Jenna cut herself off, because she realized she was clutching the purple maxi-skirt to her chest like protective armor.

And in that moment, she decided she was sick of hiding the low-budget truth of her life. The veneer hadn't earned her the respect she was going for anyway.

Jenna tossed her skirt into her cart, grabbed her purse and said, Girls, can I treat you to personal pan pizzas at the café?"

Ten minutes later, the three women were enjoying two individual pepperoni pizzas, discussing perception versus reality. "But...you're totes fancy," said Jinx.

"Not anymore," said Jenna.

"You used to work for *Darling*!" exclaimed Terry. "How are you not all designer everything?"

She took a sip of Sprite. "I did have a fabulous wardrobe. But... circumstances changed, and I sold everything because I needed cash to relocate. Now, I'm a financially-challenged 'glambassador' who has the nerve to prescribe fashion advice to StyleZine readers when I bought a pair of fake heels from a site called Fauxboutins. com."

Terry and Jinx stared at her, disbelieving. The Louboutin thing took them over the edge. They never expected that level of tackiness from any of their coworkers, let alone her.

"Do the shoes look legit?" asked Jinx, in hushed tones.

"Girls," said Jenna, moving on, "I'd love it if we could keep this our little secret, okay?"

"Fully," said Terry. She laid her hand—which was adorned with an extravaganza of skeleton and skull-and-crossbones rings—over Jenna's. "This is a circle of trust."

"And don't feel bad about being broke! We all are,'" said Jinx, nibbling gingerly on a small circle of pepperoni.

"Ready for a truthbomb?" asked Terry, helping herself to Jinx's pizza. "This morning I got dressed in the dark. No electricity. It's my roommate's fault. She's sweet, but a butt-slut. Anyway, she's all wrapped up in this illicit thing with the Hasidic dude that runs the check cashing place on our block, and forgot to pay her half of the bill. And I couldn't cover it. That's how financially-challenged I am."

"I'm so poor," said Jinx, "that I make paninis with my flatiron."

"See?" exclaimed Terry. "We're all in the same lane."

Jenna smiled, relief flooding her. Not only had it felt incredible to admit the truth, she loved being able to finally relax around Terry and Jinx. It was sweet of them to try to make her feel less pathetic.

"Yet you both always look incredible. Amazing personal styles."

Terry shrugged. "We write about top designers, but we don't need to wear them to look dope."

"It's easy to get around the money issue." Jinx looked at her blonde friend, her eyes flashing. "Do you think we should…"

"Brilliant minds, Jinx. Oh yes, ma'am, we definitely should."

Jinx hopped up and down in her chair, her thick curtain of black hair swinging around her. "Shopping montage!"

"Focus, babe. How much time do we have before the art thing?"

Jinx checked her phone. "Five hours. Ish."

"Do you have K?"

Jinx pulled a bottle of pills out of her metallic tote and shook it.

"Let's do this, bitches," said Terry. "Jenna, grab your bag. Let's go pay for your Tar-jay finery, and introduce you to the ways of the city's fashionable, cash-poor youth."

Terry and Jinx then took Jenna on what she'd later refer to as the Fashion Hustler's tour. First, they brought her to a townhouse on Eleventh and University Place owned by Laurette DaSilva, a 1970s supermodel who spent her days entertaining Ecuadorian busboys and lolling about her townhouse in a drugged-out fog. Infamously, she traded her exquisite pieces for nothing more than a couple Klonopin pills, which is what happened that afternoon. Then, they settled into a café off Washington Square Park called We Don't Sell Coffee, and whipped out Jinx's iPad, introducing Jenna to the magic of Etsy. There she found a glittering wonderland of brilliantly articulated accessories—handbags, earrings, necklaces—that cost next to nothing. Terry brought her to her girlfriend's Clara Anne Wu's studio on Avenue C, who everyone called the Blue Jean Queen. She destroyed denim—then repaired it, then destroyed it again—to create the sexiest jeans, jackets, and button-downs anyone had ever seen. @BJQ only sold to her besties, and since her step-dad was a partial owner of all the Uno restaurants in Asia and Australia, she was in the position to practically give the pieces away. Finally, to supplement her new finds, they scrolled through Vogue.com to find Jenna's favorite looks from the Fall 2012 shows—and then hit the Fifth Avenue Zara for excellent reproductions. The manager gave Jinx and Terry 40 percent discounts, as long as they agreed to occasionally slip his exceptionally fly register chicks into StyleZine's street style coverage.

By the time they stopped into a Greek diner to grab dinner, Jenna had a delicious new wardrobe. It was younger and fresher, but with a healthy nod to her glamour girl roots. She was bursting with fashion fever—all she wanted to do was rush home and play dress up. And, she'd retail-bonded with Terry and Jinx. It was a lovely day.

"I love inspiring my followers to eat healthy," said Jinx, taking a pic of her salad for the 'Gram. "Umm…Jenna, are you going to eat your cheese fries?"

"No, go ahead," she said, signaling for the check. "I'm calling it a night. I'm obliterated from my week."

Jinx took a fry, emitted an orgasmic moan, and then poured all of them on top of her salad.

"Speaking of your week," started Terry, "are you and E cool? Yesterday he called you 'Ursula the Sea Witch.'"

"Did he say that?" Jenna fake-laughed. "Ohh, that Eric."

Jinx smiled wistfully. "Have you ever noticed his initials are E.C.? Eye Candy?"

"You're such a thirst-bucket," said Terry. "Besides, we all know you have to be an eighteen-year-old *gazelle* to get him. God, he and his ex were hella-dazzling together. But honestly? She wasn't too swift. The only time she spoke up was to recap *Pretty Little Liars*."

"Jenna, I bet when you were eighteen you had it all together," said Jinx.

"Ha! I was clueless. When I was eighteen, I was fourteen." Jenna downed her tea and left cash for the check. Uncomfortable with the turn the conversation was taking, she decided it was time to go. "I should be going, ladies. But thank you so much for my shopping montage. This was a magical day."

Jenna gave them both bear hugs, grabbed her bags and left, blowing the girls kisses.

Ursula the Sea Witch? This standoff had to end. She'd suck it up and take all the blame, so they could get to work. And it had to happen, fast.

CHAPTER 10

At eighteen, Jenna really was fourteen. As a college freshman, Jenna was far less mature than she'd been as a high school freshman. In high school, she knew what to expect. She woke up, ate bacon, and listened to her cooly glamorous, consistently disappointed mother imply that, since no one asked Jenna to parties or on dates, she was officially the social disappointment of Northern Virginia's chapter of the fancy black teen social club, Jack and Jill. Next, she'd berate Jenna's outfit (she went to her all-white, mullets-and-tractors-obsessed rural high school dressed like Jody Watley if she were an alien dropped inside of a Madeleine L'Engle novel). Then, Jenna drove to school, where she was predictably ignored. Afterwards, she escaped to the library—where she'd get lost in a world of Old Hollywood books, science fiction novels, Japanese anime, Harlem Renaissance photography and Grimm's fairy tales. Alone.

She was a friendless outsider, but it was okay. There was almost a comfort in not expecting to be accepted.

She entered Georgetown inexperienced in every way. But in the first week, she found a soulmate in her suitemate—wild, wanton, self-assured Elodie, who bewitched everyone around her, thanks to her I-don't-give-a-fuck attitude, Korean eyes, and black ass. She took one look at Jenna, with her costumes and weird references and bizarre diet of sides and carbs exclusively, and decided she was fantastic. If Elodie thought she was cool, then maybe she was!

She was swept into her orbit. Jenna got slaughtered on Boones Farm at two am and picked up a Parliament Lites habit. She made out with bad boys in sketchy neighborhoods with no ride home. She got abysmal grades for the first time in her life, broke her ankle dancing on a beer-slick table at a Kappa party, and even collapsed, blackout drunk in the middle of M Street. These were all things that her fourteen-year-old self would've known better than to do, but she wanted to feel what everyone else was feeling, no matter how dumb, or immature, or not-careful it was.

Somehow, in the middle of this freshman year messiness, Jenna managed to design a couple of heavily knocked-off-from-*Club-MTV* outfits for the Black Student Association Spring Talent Show. She had a feeling her biker shorts and poet shirts would win, and as she waited backstage with her mannequins, she began practicing an acceptance speech in her head. Lost in her thoughts, she barely noticed the tall white guy stop in front of her.

"What's your talent?" The dude had on enormous, paint-splattered acid wash jeans and flip-up glasses.

"Designing." She showed off her mannequins.

"Downtown Julie Brown knockoffs? Yeah, that's talent."

"Excuse me? What's your talent? You do know this is a BSA show, right?"

"I'm an R&B singer," he said. He had sly, feline-shaped emerald eyes and his mussed, Cobain-esque hair was streaked with amber. He had the face of a pin-up, like he belonged on the cover of *Tiger Beat*—not dressed like a male Left Eye.

"You're an R&B singer?"

"Yeah, like a one-man Jodeci. I live and breathe R&B. It doesn't matter that I'm white. I can still flow."

Jenna folded her arms. "Okay, David Silver. Flow."

He held down his ear, Mariah Carey-style, and started humming to find his pitch. Jenna could barely hold back giggles.

Then he started crooning off the top of his head, in an impressive alto.

Mmm…ooooh yeah, oh yeah…
Microphone check one two one two
Shorty tryna diss the funky fly Jew
Vanilla Xtract's the moniker
You'll fall in love, I'm warning ya
I'll make you jump around like House of Pain
But first, baby girl, tell me what's your name?

Jenna burst out laughing. "Vanilla Xtract? I'm Jenna Jones. And that was ridiculous."

He shook her hand. "Hi JJ. My real name's Brian Stein. And if I win, I'm taking you to The Tombs after the show."

"If you don't win?"

"Then you're taking me to The Tombs."

Brian won. What Jenna didn't know was that he could dance, which, for a white R&B singer in the early nineties, was three-fourths of the battle. He walked away from the show with the unofficial title of Georgetown's funkiest Econ/Accounting major—and the girl. They went to The Tombs, GU's legendary bar that inspired *St. Elmo's Fire*, sat and talked, laughed, and flirted for hours. She found out that Vanilla Xtract was also, shockingly, one of the smartest people she'd ever met. The eldest of six thugged-out brothers from North Philly—a Jewish kid in a Dominican neighborhood who went to a black school—he was an outsider, just like Jenna. But unlike Jenna, he seemed self-possessed. Sure, he grew up in sketchy circumstances, with a wacky waitress mom, in a shabby house full of aspiring career criminals (most with different dads, none of whom were around), but he deflected every hit to his confidence. He saw his background as fuel to his fire, the reason he fought, the thing that would propel him to greatness.

Jenna, who second-guessed herself at every turn, was in awe. "I was so serious in high school," Jenna told him, over Heinekens. "A smarty. But here, I've been acting like the brainless cheerleaders I thought were so silly. College is overwhelming. I don't know how to be."

"Be silly and a smarty. I'm both. I know how dumb I looked, a white R&B singer in a black talent show. But I like black music, so I did it. And won," he said. "Be whoever you want, just never half-ass. And always have a plan. The plan is key."

Jenna smiled. "You're so together."

"I have goals, you know. For my life. I'm sure you do, too." He grabbed two Tombs napkins from the bar, and pulled out a pen. "You know what we should do? Make a list of everything we want, and then check in with each other fifteen years from now, to make sure we did them."

They wrote out their bullet points and then read them out loud. On Jenna's napkin, she wrote: *I want to be a famous fashion editor like Grace Coddington, live in New York, work at Darling, and have a husband and family.*

On Brian's napkin, he scrawled: *I want to be a more important real estate developer than Donald Trump, a millionaire before I'm thirty, build my mom a house on Park Avenue, have a wife and family…and you. I want you.*

They went back to his dorm. And in his bed, in the dark, as a March snowstorm raged outside, he slowly took her clothes off.

"I've never done this," she whispered.

"I have. You're safe. You'll always be safe with me."

Then Brian made love to her, carefully and memorably. By the next morning, he'd taken up permanent residence in her heart. From then on, there was no Brian without Jenna. They moved in together. They arranged their class schedules so they could walk to campus together. Their names even ran together: BriandJenna. Together, they were Georgetown's most type-A couple—at barely twenty, he was already calling her his "power wife." Brian was president of the student council, and she was The Hoya's first black style writer. She was his motivation, and he was her leader—the go-get-em voice in her head, her internal compass when she was lost.

Elodie, who loved Brian like a brother, always felt he was too bossy and controlling. Which he was. But back then, Jenna ate it up; it was what she needed. It was Brian's strength that gave her the balls to stand up to her parents—both of whom wanted her to go to med school, like them—and move with him and Elodie to New York.

New York in the mid-Nineties was a whirlwind. The economy was booming, and two of Manhattan's greatest moneymaking industries were publishing and real estate. Magazines had budgets to fly editors to Ibiza and Marrakech for wildly decadent shoots, venture capitalists were pouring billions into new structures—and Brian and Jenna found themselves in the forefront. They were indestructible—except for the five months they took a break while Brian oversaw a new property development on the West Coast (he decided they should give themselves "healthy space" to grow in each other's absence, but Jenna interpreted this to mean that Brian just wanted space from her, so, disastrously, she ended up in Darcy's fiancé's arms). Within six years, they'd checked everything off of their list but the family part. Who had time to think about marriage and babies? They were late to Donatella's birthday dinner at Moomba!

Jenna was building a name in fashion, and Brian was…building. By twenty-seven, he'd garnered breathless industry praise for building a massive residential development in commuter Nyack, which soon became the go-to luxury houses for Upper West Side families desperate for backyards. By thirty-three, he'd built seventeen buildings from Harlem to Battery Park, and was one of the few developers credited with turning Dumbo, the bleak industrial section of waterfront Brooklyn, into a destination. But he wasn't just the hotshot young developer—he also had astounding financial prowess. He was a savvy, daredevil investor, and had long been a multi-millionaire by his thirtieth birthday. That was the year he built their much-photographed West Village townhouse.

The first night they spent there, Brian, high on power, love, and himself, made Jenna come six times—one in each of the bedrooms. Soon, they had homes in East Hampton and Mustique. Four years later, there was a jet. Their lives were complicated, glamorous, demanding. She'd be in Paris for the couture shows, he'd be in L.A. for a meeting with contractors, but then they'd meet somewhere in the middle for a charity dinner or costume ball. They were one of Manhattan's most invited couples. A biracial Barbie and Ken. In public, they were peerless.

But "in public" began to be the only place they shone. At home, the silences were loud and long. She couldn't pinpoint when it happened, but they stopped being BriandJenna. The spark in his eye that was once for her, was now reserved exclusively for money. The pursuit of it, growing what he already had, building grander, flashier properties. Flossing. Unless she was playing her "power wife" role at a black tie, Jenna couldn't get his attention. Nothing she said or did seemed to interest him—and it only got worse after the economy crashed.

The more anxious Brian became about the bleak state of real estate, the more distant he was—and the more desperate she got. She only talked about things she knew he found interesting. Jenna, who wasn't clear on how her 401K worked, quoted the *Financial Times* in casual conversation. She abandoned her style in favor of little outfits she thought he'd find sexy. She even stopped watching her favorite show, *24*, because Kiefer Sutherland's tense, holy-shit-I-have-five-minutes-to-save-the-world performance only exacerbated Brian's stress level. Brian and Jenna used to be each other's greatest passion. Their top priority. Overnight, he was their top priority.

It was in this precarious place that, at 36, Jenna woke up one morning and decided she was ready for the final goal on their checklist from so long ago. She wanted to be Brian's wife. She wanted a baby. No, she ached for one. Like most ambitious New York women, the thought hadn't even occurred to her, until it did—and when it did, the babylust was so strong, it decimated every other thought. When she brought it up to Brian, he distractedly agreed that it was time for them to officially become the Jones-Steins. He proposed to her in public at the 2008 Met Gala. Andre Leon Talley and Zac Posen stood on their chairs and drunkenly warbled CeCe Peniston's "*Finally*." It was more spectacle than sentiment, but Jenna didn't care. She was thrilled.

It soon became clear that Brian was deeply disinterested in discussing a wedding. He never committed to a date and, a year later, they had no plan. In denial, Jenna threw herself into planning for her fantasy nuptials. She knew she was driving him insane with details and pushing him further away—but she thought she could want it enough for the both of them.

In private, she also started planning for the baby they'd have after the wedding. She met with fertility doctors to make sure her eggs were still viable (they were). She amassed a collection of fertility diet books, maternity clothes, and lists of baby names. She subscribed to parenting magazines, making sure they went to *Darling* instead of their home. She smiled and cooed when Billie had May—who she loved instantly and beyond words—but her stomach was in knots over it. Billie and Jenna had planned to get pregnant together. Now, it was looking like it would never happen for her, at all.

Then Brian stopped sleeping with her.

For someone who had been subject to the mercurial sexuality of her man—always the one seduced, pursued, dominated—this left her totally defanged. That had been their dynamic. Professionally, she was a powerful force, but in bed, she was happily submissive. She understood it was her job to be whatever he needed—if he wanted to take his time, she was Slow Mo Flo. If he wanted it fast, she was Quickie Chickie. He fucked her how and when he wanted to. Brian's hold on Jenna was so overwhelming that when he took it away, she felt buried. Pointless.

And then there was that last, terrible dinner, one sweltering night in June. They were both home on the same night, and Jenna, in a desperate attempt to pretend they weren't miserable, had dinner catered.

"Let's stay in the city this weekend. Prospect Park is starting a series where they screen an old movie every Saturday night, like a drive in. I think this one is *Rebel Without a Cause*. We could take a picnic." She pasted on a smile. "My perfect dream date."

"That's your dream date? We rode camels to a midnight dinner party in Brunei. I'm confused."

She remembered that dinner. It had been a breathtaking night.

But Brian forgot that she was allergic to all animal fur. She spent the entire dinner tittering with ambassadors' wives, trying to pretend that her thighs hadn't turned to Hubba Bubba. She never mentioned it to Brian, and the photos that appeared on *Town & Country's* international party pages were stunning. Which was what mattered.

"Brian, I'm trying. I'm wearing this dress because you saw it on a billboard and mentioned liking it. I don't complain—not even about you not coming home for three days. All I want is one night, doing something small and special."

"I'm so tired of hearing about what you want," said Brian.

"I assume you're talking about the wedding," she said. "You said you wanted to marry me. And have a family. You said it the night we met."

"The night I was dressed like every member of Color Me Badd?"

"You've always said it."

"A lot has changed. People change."

"They do, don't they?" Jenna picked up a forkful of risotto, and then put it down. "Am I even real to you? Or just another thing you own?"

"I could ask you the same question. When did I stop mattering to you? All you care about is getting married. And a baby that doesn't exist. I overheard you asking the handyman to switch paints because Benjamin Moore doesn't have a non-toxic option for babies. What fucking babies?" He slammed his fist down on the table. "Honestly, I don't know what you have to complain about. You have a cleaning lady, a chef, a driver. What else do you want?"

"I've dated you almost half of my life. I don't want to just be your girlfriend."

He ran a hand through his hair and exhaled. "I love you. But you want too much."

Jenna nodded. She knew how he felt, she just wanted to hear him say it. "The houses, the money, the cars? I'd give it up just to matter to you again."

He laughed. "Cute line, but it's such a lie. You'd never give this up. No woman would."

Calmly, she stood up. And with every ounce of strength she could muster, punched him in the mouth. Her knuckles were bruised for a week.

"Who the hell do you think you're talking to? I loved you when you couldn't scrape together five dollars for Taco Bell. I loved you when I financed our lives in college, working at *Contempo fucking Casuals*. I never cared about the money. You did. Watch me give it up, you smug bastard."

Jenna abandoned almost twenty years of intertwined histories, family and friends. She walked away from the money, the houses, the invitations. She separated herself from his mom, Anna, who she'd lain in a hospital bed with for three days during her mastectomy, and loved just a smidge more than her own mother.

She left Brian because she still loved him, and she could feel herself dying from it, like a disease.

CHAPTER 11

Darcy had her assistant pick the coolest place she knew for Terry's birthday drinks, which ended up being Carolina, a rustic, tavern-esque "drinkery" on Avenue B. Thanks to the amber lighting (which made everyone look like a supermodel), the well-hidden, canoodle-friendly enclaves carved into the exposed brick walls, and the most inspired cocktails in the East Village, Carolina was known for being one of the downtown's most reliable first date spots.

It was an odd choice for a work fete, but by everyone's third drink, no one knew where they were, anyway. The owner had pushed four long cocktail tables together for the StyleZine crew and, within forty-five minutes, half of the staff was sloshed, inhaling parmesan fries and Instagramming everything.

Jenna had been sipping her strawberry mint julep—one of Carolina's specialties—since she'd gotten there five minutes before. She was pretending to listen to Jinx bemoan her fifth breakup with her douchey boyfriend, Peneen, but she was actually scanning the crowded room for Darcy. And there she was, stationed in front of the Employee's Only door, chatting up Carolina's owner, a swarthy guy with a barbershop quartet mustache and a straw hat. Jenna had been at enough parties with her to know that whether that dude was gay, straight, or taken, it didn't matter—he would very shortly be on the receiving end of a Blowjob l'Darcy.

Jenna had two goals for the night. As Darcy had ordered in their post-Greta Blumen meeting, Jenna intended to be cordial with Eric, to show her boss that everything was fine. And more importantly, she actually wanted to make everything fine between them. The pressure was closing in on Jenna; now she couldn't even think about Eric or the series without panicking.

Eric was at the bar standing next to Terry, who was perched on a barstool wearing a tutu and a kitten-eared headband. The two friends were lost in conversation. Jenna wondered what they were talking about. Even more, she wondered when Terry would beat it, so she could chat with him.

"...and I know he's super-busy with his urban beekeeping hobby," slurred Jinx, "but he never focuses on me. He's even distracted during sex! He holds the remote the whole time because he's OCD and scared we'll lose it in the bed."

"How can he perform to his best ability with only one hand?" Jenna was mystified.

"Why won't he tell me what he's feeling?"

"'Cause he barely knows what he's feeling. Men have such basic emotional lives. Half the time they're just trying to figure out when's the next time they can jerk off or get to the nearest Chik-Fil-A." Jenna sipped her cocktail. "Have you shared your concerns with him?"

"Naggy girls are buzzkills," she said sadly. "I'm just hoping he wakes up and comes back to me."

"Sweetie! Why wait for him to decide the status of your relationship?" Their waiter looked at Jenna with raised eyebrows. She lowered her voice. "You're a powerful woman. You be the decider."

"You be the decider! That's so real," said Jinx, reaching for her phone. "Must tweet immediately."

Where is all of this steely-eyed clarity about relationships coming from? thought Jenna. *Why couldn't I ever apply this to my life with Brian?*

She glanced over at the bar again, and saw Terry kiss Eric on the cheek and walk away. Her opening. "Want anything from the bar, Jinx?"

"No, I have to be lucid to sext Peneen. He hates typos."

Jenna, who was relieved that texting didn't exist when she was twenty-four, downed her drink and got up. She fluffed her hair, fussed with her 'this ol' thing' cool-girl outfit (a simple white wife-beater with holy jeans, a silver snake bangle, and neon red lips), and headed for the bar. But just before she got there, Terry ran up to Eric with a girl. A mocha-skinned cutie wearing a red-and-white striped tube top. She shot him a dirty smile, dripping with the promise of coke-fueled threesomes, and then shook his hand.

Oh great, she thought. *Is he getting set up right now?*

Quickly, she claimed the only barstool available, which was two people down from him. The bar was so congested that he hadn't even seen her.

"Eric!" squealed Terry, whose pointy kitten ears made her look like Josie and the Pussycats. "This is the girl from my SoulCycle class I wanted you to meet. Jeanine, this is Eric. Fall in love. " With that, she danced away to Rihanna's "Birthday Cake."

Jenna felt like a spy. It was so tacky to eavesdrop, but she had to hear this.

"I've heard so much about you," purred Tube Top. "All true, I see."

"I've heard a lot about you, too. So what do you do?"

"I'm a model. And an actress. And a waitress. I'm many things, boo."

"Clearly. Can I get you a drink?"

"No, I'm detoxing. I need to be in perf shape for my Nickelodeon audition."

"Nickelodeon? Hold on, how old are you?"

"Twenty, but I can play as young as thirteen. My agent says I have one of those dollbaby faces. Like Selena Gomez. Like, dirty old men wanna hit it, but I look as pure as the given snow."

"Driven."

"Huh?"

"Nothing."

"So yeah, I can do tween. Wanna hear lines from my audition script? I'm playing the vain girl in the class who gets the wittiest lines." She took her voice up fifteen octaves, squealing, "You are what you eat? That's funny, I don't remember eating Kate Upton today!"

"You can say 'eating Kate Upton' on Nickelodeon?"

"But wait, here's my favorite one: 'Always be yourself. Unless you can be me. Then always be me.' And here's another one..."

Wearily, Eric turned toward the bar to grab his vodka Red Bull. That's when he noticed Jenna. She gave him the thumbs up sign.

"You know what, Jenna...I mean, Jeanine? I'm sorry, there's someone I need to talk to. From work. It's, like, imperative that I catch her before she leaves."

"Imperative?"

"Necessary. Non-negotiable."

"I like your fancy talk."

"You gonna be here for awhile, though?"

She flipped back her hair and nodded. "Okay, I'll find you."

"You better. I didn't give you my number. And it's *imperative* that you have it," she said, and strutted away.

The second she was out of sight, Eric asked the dude next to Jenna if they could switch places. He moved, with a huffy grumble. Silently, Eric sat beside Jenna—arms folded, eyes narrowed, looking rascally.

"So..." he started. "How long you been there?"

"Why?"

"I'm waiting for the commentary."

"From me?" Jenna bit her lip to hide her smirk. "I have no commentary. Except for, wow, they make 'em eager these days."

"I know. She should've asked the wizard for subtlety."

Jenna took a deep breath, preparing herself for the apology she'd rehearsed on the train. "Eric, I hate that we're in this pattern of insulting each other and then apologizing, but I'm deeply sorry for everything I said in the cab. I didn't mean to offend you."

"It's whatever," said Eric, not wanting to get into a thing. "I'm not offended."

"You are offended. And…well, you hurt my feelings, too. You said I needed to 'fuck my hurt away.' That was shitty.com."

"Shitty.com? Who are you right now?" He paused, just now noticing that she looked different than usual. He zeroed in on her bright lips, and then the lacy bra barely visible under her white tank. He swallowed and refocused. "I apologize, too. That was a horrible thing to say. But it's like, you make me horrible."

"You make me horrible, too! See, I think admitting that is a powerful breakthrough. We don't have to be besties to create great work. *The X Files* was genius, and Scully and Mulder hated each other in real life. We just can't ignore each other. I hate the way I've behaved, Eric. I really want this to work."

Eric looked at the contrite woman—a woman whose cuteness was borderline exhausting to ignore—and saw that she was truly tortured by this. He came to a realization. In little more than a week, she'd taken him from blazing lust, to confusion, to exasperation and, finally, blinding anger. She'd set his world spinning, but not on purpose. He got the feeling it didn't have anything to do with him. It seemed like Jenna was flailing. Like life had fucked with her, and now she didn't know which way was up.

"You wanna squash the beef, huh?" he asked.

"In a phrase, yes."

Eric reached out his hand. "Consider it squashed. Truce."

After a moment of surprised hesitation, Jenna shook his hand. She didn't understand why he was suddenly okay with her, but wasn't going to ask any questions.

"Truce," she said, barely believing it.

"Let's make a rule, though. Going forward, let's not get too personal with each other. That's when shit goes wrong."

Jenna nodded. "No personal information. I'll agree to anything if you stop telling people I'm Ursula the Sea Witch."

Eric grimaced. "I'm divorcing Terry."

"You're forgiven," she said, lightly. "So, did you ask her to set you up?"

"Not even! She's just a busybody. I'm good on relationships right now. Too much to do."

"Good for you," she said. "If I had it to do over again, I'd have done my own thing in my twenties."

"Loaded statement. What were you doing, instead?"

She paused. "I thought we said no personal information."

"Fair enough," he said. "Hey, I've been meaning to tell you—that poster behind your desk? So dope."

"Come again?"

"Nina Mae McKinney. I noticed it the first time I came into your office," he said. "Right after I got over the shock that you were in your office."

"You recognize Nina Mae McKinney?" She'd never come across anyone who'd heard of the forgotten silent star. He even said her name right. Nine-a.

"*Hallelujah.* Terrible film. But kind of amazing considering there were like no resources for black filmmakers in, what, 1927?"

"'28." Jenna stared at him. "I can't believe you're aware of Nina Mae McKinney."

"I can't believe you are. Are you a true fan, or do you just like the poster?"

"Well, I mean…I just…" she sputtered. Her obsessions were so obscure, she wasn't used to talking about them. "I adore the silent film era."

"I know," he said lustily. "Early Hollywood's so fascinating to me because everyone you're watching is, like, dead. It's time traveling. You can experience what it was like to chill in a 1920s speakeasy! You watch *Hallelujah*, none of those actors could imagine that people in 2012 would be spying on their shit, making them immortal. It's almost a hundred years ago. Yo, imagine if motherfuckers in the '20s could've watched films from the early 1800s?"

Jenna nodded. She was thoroughly entertained by Eric's impassioned speech. It was delightful hearing a man speak about something other than his brand, his investments, his BBS cuff links.

"Don't get me started on Expressionist cinema from the Nineteen-teens…"

Jenna interrupted him with incredulous laughter.

"What's funny?"

"The universe is playing a colossal joke on me. I've always wanted to have a casual conversation about Expressionist cinema… but no one cares. What are the chances that you're the person who does?"

"See? I came into your life for a reason. A failed web series and film geek banter." Just then, something caught his eye above Jenna's head. He nodded in that direction. "Look at Jehovah."

Jenna looked to the left. Darcy was following the owner toward the exit, pointing at them and pantomiming applause. Jenna waved tensely.

"Mission accomplished," she breathed. "Darcy saw us being friendly."

"Oh. Is the conversation over now?"

"Well…it is late."

Her drink came. They both sipped in silence. "Don't go yet," said Eric.

"I want to go."

"Do you really?"

Jenna couldn't think of a proper response. After a moment, she said, "You know, these drinks are too strong. No more for me."

"Me either," said Eric, pushing his away. "I wanna say something about it being dangerous, us drinking together. But I'll be a gentleman."

"I know your version of gentleman."

"Yeah. You do," he said, fixing her with his intense eyes.

Jenna was caught, entangled in Eric's gaze (that face, when would she be immune to it?).She felt ridiculous—how could he get to her with one glance? She was no better than Greta Blumen's assistant. Or Jinx, who turned raspberry-red if he stood too close to her.

After a beat she laughed, breaking the tension. "You're so bad."

"Why?"

"You wanted to kill me five minutes ago, and now the face, the look? You can't help yourself!" She tsk'd at him, shaking her head. "You do it for sport, don't you?"

"I know, I'm the worst," he said, his expression mischievous. "But I'm harmless."

"We both know you're not. But it's okay. You're young, you're single, and you have chicks in tube tops throwing themselves at you. Rock out. Just use protection."

"Protection. I'll remember that."

They looked at each other and laughed.

"So," said Jenna. "Are you ever going to tell me what your film's about?"

"No personal information."

"It's public! Everyone at USC saw it."

"But for some reason I'm nervous to tell you." He took another gulp of his drink. "Promise you won't laugh?"

"I'd never."

"Okay. It's called *Tyler on Perry Street*. It's about this black angel named Tyler who lives in Hollywood Heaven, and the only way he can get his wings is if he liberates black movies from stereotypical characters. So he shows up to bartend at a Christmas house party in the West Village, on Perry Street, and it's populated by Tyler Perry-esque personalities. The evil, light-skinned educated woman, the abusive, non-child-support-paying man, the God-fearing blue-collar worker, the angry black woman. And he puts a truth serum in their drinks and, well, you find out that they're the most exaggeratingly interesting people who ever existed."

Jenna threw her head back, howling with laughter.

"You said you wouldn't laugh!"

"*Tyler on Perry Street*? You're a genius!"

For the first time since she'd known Eric, he looked bashful.

"Thank you. I really…it means a lot."

"Darcy must be proud."

"She refuses to watch it. She thinks it's stupid to take on the most powerful black man in Hollywood."

There was so much Jenna wanted to say, but didn't. What kind of mother was she?

"Well, has your dad seen it?"

"I wish."

"Why not? He would love it, I'm sure."

"He was shot when I was a kid."

Jenna clutched her drink to her chest. "Oh no…I'm so sorry. I shouldn't have pushed. Please forget I asked. No personal information."

"No, it's cool. For some reason, it seems okay to tell you." He picked up his glass and swished the drink around. "I never found out why it happened, but he was a street dude, it could've been anything. That day, I was at his apartment for a tuba lesson," he said with a chuckle. "Don't ask me how he afforded a tuba, but he wanted to teach me, so I wanted to learn. Jenna, this man could play anything. Literally could pick up any instrument and play the hell out of it."

Jenna nodded, listening.

"So, I'd made these vanilla smoothies for us—he showed me how, just vanilla ice cream and Sprite and nutmeg. He called them Caucasian shakes. And I was sitting there, just me and the Caucasian shakes. Waited all day.

And all night. I drank the whole blender, made another, drank that, drank another, and then threw up everywhere. I knew something was wrong." He paused. "I was sitting on the kitchen floor surrounded by vomit when the police came. Praying. Which is hilarious because I never belonged to any religion. Who was I praying to? I was ten, who knows what I was thinking.

"When I saw the police at the door, it felt like what it must be like right before you jump off a building. Like, this is the last time I'll feel my feet on the ground. Everything after this will be out-of-control until I crash and feel nothing." He considered this, and then drank the last of his vodka. "It's taken a long time, but I'm finally there. I feel nothing."

Jenna gripped her glass, dumbstruck by how crushed she was for him. Not only for him now; but for the little boy version of him—the one she remembered bouncing around that wedding, who seemed like the happiest, most self-confident kid on the planet, without a hint of darkness.

"I'm so sorry," she said, resting her hand on his arm. He looked down at it and back at her. "No child should have to go through that. Did Darcy help? Did she get you counseling…"

"Counseling? We're West Indian." He smiled faintly. "No, we moved to the city and she rewrote our history. She told me to forget him, the projects, all of it. When you're a kid, you listen to your mom."

Jenna was so horrified by Darcy's mishandling of her son's grief, that she was struck silent.

"I guess…I just wanna make sure his last name means something."

"It will. It already does."

"We'll see," he said, now visibly uncomfortable. "What made me tell you all that? I changed my mind about the drink. I need another one."

"I don't blame you."

"Did your grow up with your dad?" he asked, flagging down the bartender.

"Yes. And he was perfect on the outside. A PhD; an OBGYN. But he spent practically every night of my childhood in an apartment he shared with his mistress an hour away in DC. You know, under the guise of working late at the hospital. Me and my mom pretended not to know. I'm very good at pretending not to notice things."

"Did you ever ask him about it?"

"Never. I was so proud of him as a person, so I never wanted to tarnish that. He was my daddy. My hero, you know?"

"I know all about it."

"Thank you for trusting me with that story. About your father."

"You too," said Eric. "About yours."

"We just broke the 'no personal info' rule. And we're still speaking to each other. Progress, no?"

"Truly. This was the coolest, most honest conversation I've had in forever," he said, almost disbelievingly.

Jenna nodded in agreement, but couldn't say what she really thought—which was that she could've sat there and talked to him for another two hours.

The bartender slid two drinks their way, and they both picked them up.

"To disappearing dads," said Eric.

"And secrets," said Jenna.

"And Nina Mae McKinney."

"And a far superior web series idea that we'll come up with asap."

"Definitely that."

"And to speaking without trying to kill each other."

"And to friendship," said Eric.

"Are we really friends?" Jenna took this in.

"We just spilled our guts to each other. Can't do anything about it now."

"True," she said. "To friendship."

They drank, sliding into contemplative silence. They were both a little shaken by the confidences they'd revealed. It was out-of-character for either

of them to truly show their cards to anyone. But now, they'd each exposed some of their most intimate memories to a person they'd known a week. In the middle of an East Village dive bar, at a twenty-fifth birthday party.

Just then, an obliterated Terry stumbled over. Every fifteen minutes, it seemed that her outfit was evolving into a more ridiculous place. Now, she was wearing kitten ears, a tutu, and three rapper-circa-1988 gold chains.

"What did you think of Jeanine? She's fly, right?"

"Terry. Can't you just let me not wanna be in a relationship in peace?"

"She's so hot! What's the problem?"

"I mean yeah, she's bad, but have you had a conversation with her? She's on Sherri Shepard levels of dumbness."

"Jenna, what did you think?"

"Cute, I guess. If thirst-buckets are your thing," she said, with a dismissive shrug. "Happy Birthday, Terry. I'm heading out."

"Bye babe!" yodeled Terry, grasping Eric's arm for balance.

"You don't want another drink?" asked Eric.

"I really need to get home. But I'll see you bright and early for more brainstorming. Don't get into too much trouble, you guys."

Jenna grabbed her purse and headed up the spiral staircase. Friends. With Eric. This was a development she didn't see coming. All she'd wanted was a functioning, non-abusive working relationship, but now it was blossoming into something else. Which was definitely a surprise. A nice one.

CHAPTER 12

"I know, Auntie Jenna, but what really happens when you die?"

"Well, your body stops working and you…you know, you stop living. It's like you're asleep. But forever."

After work the next day, Jenna was walking hand-in-hand with Billie's charmingly morbid, cheerfully death-obsessed five-year-old, May, through the Grand Army Plaza Greenmarket in Park Slope. Jenna was hanging with May while Billie and Elodie perused the tomato section. Right outside of Prospect Park, the rustic wooden stands of farm-fresh, locally grown produce selection always drew a huge crowd of nutritionally conscious, community-focused Brooklynites. Jenna, Billie, Elodie, and May were the only black people in the vicinity.

"Asleep?" May, a perky-looking moppet with doe eyes and an 80s-style side ponytail, eyed Jenna with skepticism. "Does that mean dead people can dream?"

"Some philosophers believe that death itself is a dream. Or that life is a dream." Jenna caught herself, realizing that she was getting too existential for a five-year-old. May was so intense, so composed, that she sometimes came across like a thirty-five-year-old tax attorney.

"No, sweetie, dead people don't dream," said Jenna. "They just rest quietly. And forever."

"So after I'm dead, what happens to my…thoughts?"

"You mean your spirit? That's a good one, May-May. Theologians and scientists have been trying to figure that out for centuries. No one really knows. But it's highly likely that your beautiful spirit will go to heaven." Jenna had once heard John Lennon or someone say that if you felt in over your head in a conversation, ask the other person to define their terms. "What do you believe, honey?"

"I don't believe in heaven. Or God. I believe in Mother Nature, and oceans, and trees, and the moon. Also wood fairies. I think they live in Cancun. Or the Atlantis Resort in the Bahamas."

Wow, Jenna thought. *Jay and Billie book too many all-inclusive Caribbean family vacations.*

Just then, Billie and Elodie appeared with bags of tomatoes, asparagus and corn on the cob.

"Babe," whispered Jenna to Billie, "are you aware that your daughter's a wiccan?"

"That Mother Nature stuff? Baffling! And the death thing? I don't know whether to be disturbed or thrilled that she's asking the Big Questions before she can properly tie her shoes."

"Be thrilled," said Elodie. "Maybe she'll become an upscale mortician, like Phaedra Parks."

"Mommy, I see Arabella and Waylon from school! Can I go say hi?"

Billie turned around and saw the twins with their mother, Chrissie Proctor, a supporting actress on a ten-year-old network forensics drama. She waved and Chrissie gestured for May to come over. And then, despite her excitement, May cooly walked over to her friends, with the faintest of smiles. It wasn't in her nature to broadcast too much joy.

"This is so good," said Billie, talking mostly to herself. "Chrissie's completely obnoxious—she's a North Slope hippie, she doesn't wear deodorant and pretends she doesn't plop her kids in a corner with Rio on the iPad for hours, like the rest of us. But her oldest son goes to Poly Prep, and she's on the board there. If I get in good with her, maybe May will have a spot for middle school."

"Everything you just said is completely soul-killing," said Elodie.

"Billie, I don't think there's anything wrong with you selling your soul to Chrissie Proctor to get May into private school," Jenna said, who'd been sneaking voyeuristic glances at the TV star. "The New York private school application process is worse than college. I've done the research. I have a whole file, if you need it."

Billie's eyes softened, and she gently grabbed Jenna's hand. Often, she got so involved in the demands and details of raising May, that she'd forget she had everything her friend wanted and didn't have.

Jenna smiled at her, squeezed her hand, and then dropped it.

"Thanks, hon," said Billie. "I might have to take a look at the file. Enough mommy talk, though. While May's schmoozing with Detective Jacinda Brown's offspring, should we catch up on grown-up stuff?"

"I'll go first," said Elodie, sipping on her fresh-squeezed, vegan-organic green tea lemonade. "I feel like I've slept with everyone I'd want to sleep with from our various overlapping social circles, so now I'm online dating."

Billie laughed. "You?"

"Me. And you should see these fools. It's like, you know within five minutes of meeting them why they're forty-five and still single. There's the dude that stalks you on social media prior to meeting you, and shows up for drinks quoting Facebook status updates from 2009. The guy who lives in a penthouse duplex at 70 Pine, but has me meet him at his place for tea for our first date. Cheap bastard. You live in a 3.5 million dollar apartment; I can't even get a Starbucks latte? Or the man who doesn't believe in 'gender roles,' and when you fake-offer to pay for dinner he's like, 'Cool!' Or the Anthony Weiner disciple who, after one date, texts you unsolicited dick pics."

"No woman in the history of nudity," said Jenna, "has ever been sexually aroused by a picture of male genitalia."

"Context-free, too! Just a shot of a hard, disembodied penis."

"I can't believe you're making the effort to go relationship shopping." Billie was baffled. "Didn't they teach you on the commune that monogamy was religious trickery and propaganda?"

Elodie nodded. "Yes, but this is insurance. Turning Forty made me feel a way. I might not be relationship-oriented now, but I'm terrified of waking up at fifty, deciding I'm ready, and realizing that I now look like Sojourner Truth and can no longer get a quality man."

"Sojourner Truth was a handsome woman," said Billie. "Leave her alone."

"Maybe I should consider dating girls."

Billie made a face. "Don't do it to yourself; we're assholes, too."

"Okay, Jenna," said Elodie. "Your turn."

"I'm just counting the days until I'm unemployed again. This video is just not happening. Me and Eric have filmed three different specs and, at best, they're remedial. At worst, they're unintentionally comedic."

"What do you expect?" asked Elodie. "You two treat each other like shit. How do you expect to accomplish anything?"

"No, we're nice to each other now," said Jenna. "It's like, suddenly, we realized how to speak to each other. And it's such a relief. Always being on edge in his presence was exhausting."

"This is great news!" said Billie. "We've secretly been so worried."

"Just be careful," Elodie continued. "Office buddies can turn into office affairs. You're vulnerable, the last thing you need is to trip and fall on the D."

"She'd never," said Billie. "Jenna has more sense than that."

"You feel nothing when you're around him?" asked Elodie.

"God no. A world of nos," said Jenna with a boisterous laugh. "We're beyond platonic. We're like Michael Strahan and Kelly Ripa. Two amiable co-workers whom no one on Earth could imagine intercourse-ing."

"Eww, you painted the picture," said Elodie. "I believe you."

"I like the girls in the office, too. Socially, things are finally good—but aside from my column, I'm bombing. I spend all day and night researching fashion stuff on YouTube, trying to come up with something fresh, and it never happens."

"What you need is a distraction, to reset your brain," said Billie. "And I know how you'll get it. There's a guy I want to set you up with. It has to happen soon, because he's leaving for Prague in two days. But he owns that upscale spirits shop on Gates, Bubbles and Brew? I don't know-him-know-him, but he seems fantastic. I've been watching him, trying to figure out if I should set him up with you or Elodie. I've come to the conclusion that she'll eat him alive, so he's all yours."

Jenna rolled her eyes skyward. "I can't handle a set-up right now. The anticipation, the let-down, the Junior Mints-binge afterwards…"

"How else do you meet men, at our age?" asked Elodie. "We're not out at the clubs. We only work with women and exquisite gays. Our choices are online dating or set-ups."

"But my last set-up was monstrous. Remember YSL slippers?"

"Your mistake was trusting Elodie to identify a dateable man," said Billie. "Her one relationship goal is to find a husband before she starts resembling an abolitionist."

"Fine," said Jenna, "what do you know about this guy?"

"He's fifty. Never been married, no children, but every time I bring May in, he says he's always wanted a daughter as poised as her. So he wants kids. He's super-cultured, but down-to-earth, and he's got a full head of hair."

"I'll take him."

"There's one thing. He's a tad New Brooklyn. He wears converse with Salvation Army high school football tees, and talks about how well his mint and thyme are growing in his community garden. He's on the board of the Brooklyn Bicycle Club. And he lives in Williamsburg. I know, stop looking at me like that. Also, I think I saw him teaching a Tai Chi class in Fort Greene Park."

"Check, please," said Elodie.

"No, he's fantastic! It's just…well, he's nothing like Brian."

Jenna opened her mouth to protest meeting this guy, but then changed her mind. "You know what? I'm going to keep an open mind. I'm in no position to turn down dates."

"You should have one of your famous dinner parties," said Elodie. "But an intimate one. Just us, and maybe a few of your new work people. And Billie can bring your Bubbles and Brew boo!"

"A dinner party? Should I?" Jenna asked the question, but had already decided. Throwing dinner parties used to be her thing. Her cardio, her catharsis, her creative outlet. Maybe it would help clear her head, throwing herself into something besides work. It might be inspiring. She'd only have a day to pull it together, but in her heyday, she'd achieved dinner party brilliance in less time than that. Without giving it a second thought, she was all-in.

Jenna was already mentally planning the seating arrangement when she asked Billie, "Can you find out if he's free tomorrow night?"

CHAPTER 13

Jenna was sitting in her office the next morning, researching her latest post (and also where to cheaply rent upscale-looking serving trays), when Cam from the mailroom knocked on her open door. He was clutching an oversized stunning bouquet of gardenias, calla lilies and tulips.

"These are for you," he said, shoving the arrangement rather gruffly into her hands. Walking away, he mumbled, "Now I'm gonna be smelling like a dryer sheet all day."

She opened the card.

Dear JJ,

I'm still hoping you change your mind about coffee. I need to speak to you. Urgently. It's a matter I can only discuss with you. And for what it's worth, I never wanted you to dress like Chrissy Tiegan. I don't even know who that is. Please call me.

Congrats again,
Brian

Jenna closed the card. She was furious. Her anger overrode her low-grade curiosity about whatever this "matter" was. How dare he? Brian had to be in control of every situation—she wasn't surprised that he'd try to insinuate himself into her life, because it was clear that she was fine without him. It must be driving him crazy, knowing that she was in the city and, for the first time in their lives, not needing or wanting him in the slightest.

I'm the only person you can talk to? Talk to Celeste Lily L'Amour Wexler, you manipulative shit.

Disgustedly, she threw the card away. And then, unable to resist and hating herself for it, she pulled it out of the trash and read it again. Then, she dumped the bouquet into the trash, and tore the card into tiny shreds, cursing under her breath with each rip. This is how Eric found her when he knocked on her open door.

"Whoa. What's up?"

Jenna looked up, and quickly swept all the tiny pieces into her trashcan. They fluttered like snow on top of her gorgeous bouquet. "Hello," she said tensely. "Have a seat. I was just going to call you in for our meeting."

"You seem a little…upset." He sat down, gesturing at the trash. "You okay?"

"Not worth discussing," she said, with a dismissive gesture. Jenna was trying to look steely and disconnected, but when she saw Eric's face, which radiated real concern, she softened. How could she pretend in front of him, after everything they'd shared at Terry's party?

"Pretty flowers. Wrong man. Too late."

"Say no more."

"Thank you," she said, with relief. She scooped a handful of Skittles out of the candy dish on her desk and shoveled it into her mouth. Eric had reminded her how much she loved them.

"So," she chewed, going into businesswoman mode. "Shall we go over our seventeenth terrible idea? I was thinking about what you said about on-screen interviews being static. So, I researched…" She cocked her head, distracted by the busy sleeve of tattoos swirling down his left arm. "Anyway, I researched…"

"You're openly reading my arm?"

"Well, no, I…"

He lifted it up so she could see more clearly.

"Wow. 'Stanley Kubrik is a god.' I like that one. Brilliant director."

"What's your favorite film of his?"

The conversation started spilling out of them. The flowers were forgotten; the series was forgotten. Both Jenna and Eric knew they needed to focus on work, but they'd discovered that they had a real camaraderie. And it was too fun not to indulge in it.

"*The Shining*," said Jenna. "So creepy."

"One of my professors wrote an essay about what makes something creepy versus scary," said Eric. "The brain is wired to understand what's scary so you can protect yourself. A tiger charging at you. Fire. Sharp things. We know not to fuck with that stuff. Creepy is vague. Our brains can't process it as a threat or as something normal. Like that *Twilight Zone* episode where we see the girl watching TV from the back, then she turns around and has no mouth."

"Or the video in *The Ring*," said Jenna. "I have a real-life example! When I was twenty-four, I wrote my first big piece for *Harper's Bazaar* and they ran my picture on the Contributors page. A Patrick Demarchelier photo. Epic."

Eric watched her with a half-smile. He had no idea who Patrick Demarchelier was, but he was thoroughly entertained. Jenna gestured so broadly when she was telling a story. Like she was working it for the seats all the way in the back.

"…and I got an email from a reader, years later. She'd been on vacation in Panama and saw that picture on a billboard."

"The one from *Harper's Bazaar?*"

"Yes. But it was on an ad for a special clip you put on your nose at night to make it smaller! It was a before/after picture, and they'd photo-shopped the 'before' pic to make my nose look bigger. She emailed it to me. Seeing my face with the wrong nose? Now, that's creepy."

Eric threw his head back and laughed a deep "ha-ha-ha" that was neither self-conscious nor dialed-down for the office.

"A gang of Panamanian bandits hijacked your picture for a plastic surgery ad? Is that legal?"

"Hell no!" Jenna shrugged. "But I let it go. Truth be told, I was a little bit proud."

"You still are. I can tell by your delivery."

"Stop noticing me."

"Can't stop, won't stop." He picked up a rubber band ball from her desk and tossed it between his hands. "Hey, can I ask you something?"

"No personal information."

"No longer applies."

"You're right. Shoot."

"When we were shooting Greta Blumen, you said you had everything riding on this job. Why?"

Jenna took a long sip of water, wracking her brain for a way to package the story. Something pithy, tied in a bow, cute. But all that came to her was the ugly truth.

"I begged your mom for this job. Actually, begged is an understatement. I called her from Virginia, groveling. I took a salary that was less than what I was making fifteen years ago, just so she would hire me. My exact words were, 'Please, I'm desperate, I need this, I'll take whatever you offer.'" Jenna chewed her lip. "If I don't do well here, I will have humiliated myself. And I doubt I'll get hired anywhere again."

"Why?"

"This industry is very 'out of sight, out of mind.' And I disappeared for a long time. Plus, I might have burned some important bridges when I left." She realized her voice was shaking a little. "This is my last chance."

Jenna averted her eyes from Eric's. She couldn't believe she'd expressed her fears out loud, at work, and to him.

"Jenna. Look at me."

She did.

"We'll figure out this project. You won't humiliate yourself. You can't, not while you have me. Not *have* me, have me. But you know."

"I know."

"I'll move into my cubicle. I'll slay dragons. I'll do whatever. Just know that I won't stop until you win."

"Why be so committed to helping me?" she asked softly.

"You're one of my people now. I care about what happens to you." He paused, and frowned. "You actually begged my mom?"

"There was no alternative. If I didn't do it, I'd just fade away. I was in a terrible place. Dead inside, afraid of my own shadow. There were weeks where, the only way I kept track of time was because I remembered that every four days I needed to take a shower."

"You're fucking kidding me."

"Rock bottom."

"But…why?" He whispered this, as if the gravity of this news deserved hushed tones.

"Everything I devoted my life to, professionally and personally, was suddenly gone. I had a breakup that was, for all intents and purposes, a divorce. My career was over. Then came the depression, and my daily cocktail of Ambien, Xanax and Prozac. After a while, I got used to feeling horrible. It was easier than figuring out how to start over." She paused. "A couple months ago, I decided that I'd had enough. I would've done anything to get my life back. Begging for this job was just a moment of extreme weakness."

"No, that was extreme strength," he said, looking at her with awe. "You dragged yourself out of a hole, despite having to lean on Darcy Vale to do it. You're tough as shit, Jenna."

She never thought of it that way. All she felt about the past two years was shame. "I generally feel more lame than tough, but I'm getting there." She plucked a bunch of yellow Skittles out of her bowl and arranged them into a smiley face on her desk. She had to change the energy in her office, or she was going to have another nervous breakdown.

Chuckling, she said, "Want to know what's really lame?"

"Everything about Tyga?"

"Yes, but no. I'm being set up, tonight."

"Word?" he said, and then laughed—just a shade too long. "Yo, this is gonna be too epic. I wish I could watch." He paused. "Not in a weird way."

"It won't be epic, it's just a set-up. One must manage one's expectations."

"I can't imagine you on a blind date. You're so, like, so unintentionally funny and…interesting in this very specific way…" He stopped. "This dude isn't gonna know what hit him. Listen, can you meet him in public, like at a bar? I could be your wingman."

"I'm having a dinner party at my house tonight, and my girlfriend Billie's bringing him. I don't even know his name." She disassembled the smiley face, popping the candy into her mouth, one by one. "Why am I nervous? It's so silly."

"He should be nervous. You're smart. You're accomplished. You wear lace bras under see-through tank tops at dive bars."

Jenna gasped. "Stop noticing me!" she repeated, throwing a Skittle at him. Eric ducked, grinning. And then, out of this comfortably jokey moment, she had a crazy thought.

"Hey. Do you want to come?"

"To your party? Like, where you live?"

"Why not? It's going to be small, just my two best friends. And this date guy. Billie suggested I invite a friend from work, and well, you're my friend from work."

"I'm in," he said. "I have to see this."

"Maybe I do need a wingman. Not Billie or Elodie, but a guy who can vouch for me."

"I'm so gifted at wingmanning. Four of my girlfriends are still dating dudes I introduced them to at a house party I threw...*in November of twelfth grade.*"

"Well, that's impressive," said Jenna. "Oh, and bring your friend Tim! He sounds fascinating...two Broadway legend dads?"

"No. Tim's unqualified to attend civilized social gatherings."

"Bring him! I want fresh, young energy."

"Ooookay. But if your house burns down, don't hold me responsible." Eric tried to mask his excitement. He didn't know what he anticipated more, getting a peak into Jenna's personal world—or meeting The Guy.

"I so want to fast-forward six hours," she said, popping the last Skittle in her mouth. "I'm a hell of a hostess. You'll see!"

www.stylezine.com

Just Jenna: Style Secrets from our Intrepid Glambassador

Q: My best friend Megan just got promoted to partner at her law firm, so I'm throwing her a huge party at my fab new apartment. I know it's Megan's celebration, but I sort of feel like it's my night, too. What the hell do I wear? -@ DressDistressInToronto

A: Every time I throw something at my home it feels like it's my debutante ball. So exciting, right? It's your opportunity to flaunt your decorating and hostessing prowess! And what you wear sets the tone. Before choosing an outfit, decide on what kind of night you want to have. Are you throwing the kind of fete where guests end up getting lucky in your bathroom? Rock a tarty tube dress with cut-outs. Planning to introduce hallucinogens after dessert? Wear a far-out, haute hippie ensemble. Itching for an evening of classed-up chicery recalling a Jazz Age Parisian salon (my kind of party)? Go with a flapper-esque cocktail dress. You're creating the ambience, so dress accordingly. Good luck, and congrats to Megan, Esquire!

Check out Nordstrom.com for after-eight dresses made for entertaining.

CHAPTER 14

By 7:30, Jenna had worked herself into a frenzy of anticipation. It had been years since she planned a dinner party, but she realized that she'd retained muscle memory. She also realized that she no longer had a budget. So, in a twenty-four hour period, she called in several favors and abused the one credit card she allowed herself.

Jenna reached out to her old caterer, Jilly Demarco at Jilly's Eats, and planned a gorgeous Frenchy menu: Belgian endive salad, Coq au Vin and potatoes au gratin for dinner, and, for dessert, croquembouche (she'd always been such a loyal client, that Jilly provided her services on credit). Her outfit was perfection—an authentic 1920's tango dress that Philip Lim modernized for her as a 33rd birthday present, complete with satin gloves. She'd donated it to *Darling's* archives, where it was displayed in a glass case in the lobby—but she'd pulled a couple of strings to liberate it for the night. Then, she had Elodie's ex, Guy Donazo, an art director at Grey Advertising, make a custom designed place setting for each guest in lilting, gold filigree calligraphy. She'd even called Hermes' publicist, who she'd always had a great relationship with—and they lent her an extraordinarily rare, vintage private label dinnerware set. She even charged a breathtaking, too-expensive side chair and throw pillows, which she agonized over for forty-five minutes at Roche Bobois. Diptyque Baise candles were burning, and Adele was crooning about setting fire to the rain. Even her help for the night, a pretty Peruvian aspiring actress named Lula, was impeccable (Jenna was paying for her services by referring her to two top agents that Brian had built houses for). Lula was preparing appetizers, wearing a lovely ballerina bun and a simple black DVF dress of Billie's.

She'd thought of everything. Most importantly, she'd made Billie and Elodie swear not to mention her and Eric's make out session. Billie agreed, but Elodie laughed ("Forget? How? The sight is emblazoned on my brain in lights.") So, Jenna in-boxed them contracts she drew up, forbidding them to speak on it—no signature, no admittance.

Jenna might've overextended herself on posh details she couldn't afford, but it felt worth it. Orchestrating this beautiful night was soul-affirming, which was what she needed.

This would be a Pinterest-perfect party. An elegant backdrop for an elegant evening of clever conversation, exquisite food—and possibly meeting her husband.

Jenna perched herself in her new armchair with her hands folded, awaiting her guests. Only a half an hour before the magic began.

As promised, Eric was the first to arrive. As he stood inside her doorway, effortlessly crisp in a navy sweater and dark jeans scrunched around wheat-colored boots, he was trying to quell his mood—which was intense annoyance.

He'd been nervous enough, bringing his most unpredictable friend to Jenna's house. Making it worse? Tim took it upon himself to invite his tacky girlfriend, Carlita, even though Eric expressly asked him not to do this. Carlita was inappropriate at ratchet parties, so he could only imagine how she'd behave in a swanky situation—which was what Eric knew Jenna's dinner party would be. And once he got a look at her beautiful apartment, he realized he'd been correct.

Did it always look so fancy? he wondered. *Or just for tonight?*

He and Tim had grown up surrounded by upper middle class trappings, but their reality as adults was far grungier. They were about seedy underground clubs and after-hours pizza. And he was certain that Carlita had never attended a dinner with place settings. He prayed they both chose benign, non-controversial things to talk about, like the pleasant fall weather.

"Hiiii, Eric! So happy you're here," exclaimed Jenna. She ushered the three of them into her house, beaming. "You must be Tim and Carlita, please come in! Carlita, your bangs are adorable." Carlita was one of those women who, no matter her mood, always looked fed up. The stripper— who was saving her money for dental school—was club-ready in a neon green, microscopic tube dress from Strawberry's. Her nails were covered in newspaper print decals, and her bouncy black weave was freshly cut in Cleopatra bangs. She looked like Princess Tiana reimagined as South Beach's surliest exotic dancer.

Carlita raised her chin at Jenna. "Girl, you did your thing on *Project Runway*. You know Michael Kors?"

Eric squelched his exasperation. "She was a judge on *America's Modeling Competition*."

"Oooh, what's Tyra Banks like?"

"That's *America's Next Top Model*," said Jenna. "But I do know Michael. He'd love you. He'd fall over himself to get you in some camel suede jodhpurs."

And then Carlita did something unusual. She smiled, sort of. Tim, a wiry sprite in an ascot, took Jenna's hand and kissed it.

"*Enchante.*"

"*Enchante*, yourself!"

"It's our distinct pleasure to have been invited to your abode," he said. "Did anyone ever tell you that you give off an Olivia Pope vibe?"

"Kerry Washington? Bless you." She squeezed his hand. "Can I get you all something to drink?"

"You got the drink with the leaves in it?" Carlita looked hopeful.

Eric rubbed a temple.

"A mojito! Excuse me, I'll go give Lula your drink orders."

The second Jenna disappeared, Eric lit into Tim.

"What did I tell you about the ascot? Take it off."

"Carlita, I told you this shit was wack."

"Don't blame your scarf struggle on me, nigga. You wanted to look fancy."

"Me? You're the one who almost wore that fluffy, Easter Sunday dress," said Tim. "E, I was like, are you going to your First Communion? You about to meet Kate Middleton?"

"Just take it off," hissed Eric.

Tim slipped it off his neck and looked around the room. "I gotta say, there's a disconnect between this broad's taste and her neighborhood. This block is a fucking slum. She's living in a studio-plus, but has Hermes dinnerware? Like, it's both confusing and titillating."

Eric's head was pounding. "Just stop talking, Tim. Do not embarrass me tonight. Don't call her Olivia Pope, and don't use Jenna and 'titillating' in the same sentence. Just…be normal."

"I am normal!"

"We normal, E! Chill," said Carlita.

Jenna came back with a breathtaking Lula, who handed out the drinks. Then, she pulled Eric to the side.

"So what do you think?" she asked. Jenna looked like a deb on the morning of her Sweet Sixteen. She grabbed his hand and dragged him over to the table. "So pretty right? Look at the little brown paper bags on each plate…I had the menu written on them and there's a delicious gruyere cheese biscuit inside! Couldn't you die?"

"I'm dead. I love it," he said, looking around. "Everything's dope. And you look…" He stopped himself from going too far. "Pretty. He's lucky."

"Thank you." Jenna smoothed down her dress, and then raised her drink to Eric. "Here's hoping he isn't a troll."

He clinked his glass to hers. "So where is he?"

"He should be here any minute—perfect timing. First hors' d'oeuvres, cocktails and conversation, then the three-course dinner, then aperitifs and dessert. Then everyone leaves and I watch *Clue* in my pajamas." She was standing with Eric, but talking to herself. She started counting things off on her fingers. "Okay, Lula already heated up the appetizers, so those are fresh, and then..."

"You're so intense."

"I'm in hostess mode," she said, wringing her hands. "I just want it to be perfect."

Just then, her front door bell rang and she buzzed up Billie, her husband Jay, and Elodie. Promptly, Elodie stomped over to Eric and gave him a strong, breasty hug.

"Heartbreaker!"

"Kimora Lee Simmons!"

She leaned into his ear and said, "It's hard to recognize you without your arm halfway up Jenna's dress."

"Jenna said she made you sign a contract," whispered Eric.

"You think I'm scared of that girl? I can't act like that night didn't happen. I'm just happy you two are cool now. All her angst over you was making me anxious, and getting worked up about anything besides my mutual funds fucks with my spirituality."

"Hi Eric, I'm Billie!" She edged past Elodie and hugged him, too. "So lovely to meet in person. I've heard tons about you." And then, Billie, who actually did honor Jenna's contract, said, "Um... no I haven't. I don't know anything about anything."

Jay Lane, a ruggedly handsome forty-two-year old, was both a passionate community activist and one of America's leading literary poets.

He'd managed to retain a healthy hint of rough-around-the-edges toughness from his street background. The combination resulted in a complicated intensity that made Fordham's female students come to his Voices of the Diaspora class in smokey eyes and deep-V tees.

He sized Eric up, gave him a pound and said, "The future of American cinema! I did some research on you. I like you, man. You're young, but you have gravitas."

"Gravitas? Wow. I like you, too, professor." If it were possible for Eric to blush, this would've been the moment.

Eric introduced Carlita and Tim to the group, and everyone said their hellos. Then the buzzer rang again, and everyone's head swiveled toward the door. Jenna pressed her buzzer, and seconds later The Guy emerged.

"Hiii," everyone said, in unison.

"Well hello," he said, a little overwhelmed by the cluster of seven people, inspecting him like he was under glass.

"Welcome! I'm Jenna," she said, shaking his hand.

"I'm Jimmy Crockett," he said, and actually tipped his hat. Which was a fedora. An attractive caramel-skinned guy with salt-and-pepper hair, he was wearing, as Billie promised, artfully scuffed Chucks, black skinny jeans (skintight skinny jeans) and a faded, red-and-navy striped, Linus-esque tee that was either vintage or from Urban Outfitters.

Jenna's first thought was, *He's fifty and dresses like this?*

Then, her mind plummeted into the "what if" set-up spiral.

What if this works? Will my friends love him? Will he understand that, after 10pm, I have little to no sexual stamina and will tap out after ten minutes? What will we look like together? At what point will the things I like about him become the things I loathe? Can I love him enough to get to the part where I like him again? IS HE THE ONE?

Jenna shook off her stream-of-consciousness musing, and introduced him to the room. He was polite and gave firm handshakes, looking everyone in the eye. But when he got to Eric, he stopped and pointed at him.

"What have you got, there?"

Eric realized that he was still holding the wine bag he'd picked up from his local liquor store. He had no idea what vintage, type, or brand it was—he just picked out the most special-looking bottle. "Red wine."

"Can I see that?"

Shrugging, Eric pulled the bottle out of the bag. Jimmy inspected the bottle. He nodded. "Beringer Napa Valley. Not bad, young man. Vanilla bean and blackberry undertones. Great starter wine. I prefer something a bit more refined, more savory. You'll have to try the 2005 Guiseppe Mascarello Borolo I brought."

Eric was too taken aback to say anything but, "I'll do that."

"I'm sorry, I own a high-end spirits shoppe"—he said the word with such flourish that it *sounded* like it was spelled the French way—"so wherever I am, I always laser right in on the wine selection." Jimmy chuckled and reached up to slap Eric on the back. "You did a great job, young man."

Jimmy made his way back to Jenna's side, and they launched into a private conversation.

Eric looked at Tim. "Son."

"I believe he was trying to clown you, young man," said Tim. "You want me to get Carlita to beat his ass?"

"I'm supposed to help her close with that pretentious dick?" Eric said, thoroughly disgusted. "Jimmy Crocket. How am I not gonna call him Jiminy Cricket?"

Tim laughed, loving this.

"I need a drink," said Eric.

Everyone was seated in Jenna's living room, while Lula made the rounds with a tray of prosciutto-and-mint wrapped asparagus. They party had broken off into smaller groups, with everyone embroiled in separate conversations. Jenna and Jimmy stood together by the new side chair; Billie, Jay, Tim and Eric were on the couch, and Carlita and Elodie shared a love seat.

As Eric chatted with Billie about the upcoming presidential election, keeping one eye on Jenna and Jimmy. He was supposed to be on matchmaking duty, but it was all he could do not to pelt that asshole with asparagus. But he had a job to do. This night was about helping her bag the second date. So, he excused himself and walked up to the pair.

"...so yes, I've almost completed transforming the basement of Brews & Bottles into a gallery," Jimmy was saying. "Upscale and rustic, but with warmth. Like a man cave in Milan. Actually, 'Milanese Man Cave' isn't a bad name for the space."

"Wonderful idea," said Jenna. "Brooklyn is such a hotbed of talented artists looking for exposure."

"Indeed. For my grand opening, I'm showing my friend's arfe paintings. You know what arfe is, right?"

Jenna groaned inwardly. Jimmy was one of those oh-so-plugged-in New Yorkers who asked if you'd heard of something before just telling you about it—thus putting you on the spot, making you feel like silly if you hadn't.

"Arfe? No, I can't say that I'm familiar."

"They're paintings created using coffee. It's a blend of the words art and café. Arfe is a portmanteau, which is when two words combine to make a new one. Like jazzercise."

Jenna looked like she wanted to cackle and cry at the same time. Eric was intervening at the perfect moment.

"Hey," he said to the pair.

"Hi!" Jenna was so grateful to see him. "Eric, did you know that you and Jimmy are both Guyanese-American?"

"Oh, word?"

"Yes," said Jimmy. "Can you speak patois?"

"No, but I understand it. Everybody's grandma was Guyanese in my neighborhood when I was a kid."

"How often do you visit?"

"I've never been, but I'll get there one day. I hear it's beautiful."

"You've never been? Don't you value your roots? Eric, you haven't lived until you've physically laid down on the ground in the land your people come from."

"I don't know anyone in Guyana," said Eric, mildly. "My people come from Brooklyn, dude. I'm not laying down on Nostrand Ave."

Jimmy looked at him with sadness and pity.

"Sooo Jenna," Eric said, changing the subject, "I don't know what's in these hors d'oeuvres. But I think we need more, they're delicious."

"Indeed," Jimmy said. "What's your recipe?"

"Oh I didn't make them! The one time I tried to cook for a party I stir-fried pork in Pine Sol."

Eric laughed. Jimmy didn't.

"Wait," said Eric. "You can't just leave that there. Explain."

"I reached for what I thought was the Olive Oil, but it was Pine Sol. I swear the bottles looked exactly alike."

"So, you poisoned your guests."

"That girl is poison..." sang Jenna.

"Never trust a big butt and a smile, Jimmy," said Eric.

"I only have one-half of that equation," said Jenna, "so everyone's safe."

Eric and Jenna chuckled to each other. Jimmy watched their two-person skit, generally confused.

"Jenna, you're not living well if you're not cooking well."

"But she sings BBD songs in sequins," said Eric, helpfully. "Who wouldn't find this woman irresistible?"

"I'm hopeless in the kitchen," said Jenna. "And it doesn't help that I have the palette of a kindergartener."

"You may think you do," said Jimmy. "Surely you just haven't been exposed to different cuisines."

"No, I've traveled the world, tried everything. But I always come back to chicken fingers," she said with a self-deprecating laugh.

"Unacceptable. I'll take you to Queens, and introduce you to the Indian, Malaysian, Serbian and Ethiopian restaurants there. You need someone like me to transform you into a proper foodie."

Jenna smiled haltingly. She always wished she were a more adventurous eater, but she just wasn't. She didn't need a man to 'transform' her.

Eric grimaced. This set-up was so awkward. If he didn't want to smack Jimmy with his fedora, he'd feel almost as bad for him as he did for Jenna.

"So," he said, changing the subject again, "you own a liquor store?"

"Upscale spirits shoppe."

"Yeah, you did say that. Jenna, have you been there? You love a good cocktail."

"She should visit my new shoppe, near my condo in Williamsburg. Really, if you live anywhere else in the borough, you're not a real Brooklynite."

"You always speak in absolutes," said Eric. "You have a rule for everything?"

"Without rules, the world slides into chaos, young man," he said, and then turned toward Jenna. "Anyway. I'm in a high rise on the East River. I sit on my terrace with a glass of Bouzeron Aligate and my first edition of Walt Whitman's Crossing Brooklyn Ferry and just vibrate. You must see this book, Jenna. You may think you've read masterpieces, but you haven't had an elevated reading experience until you've laid your hands on this."

"You know, I do remember a Guyanese word," said Eric. "Cunumunu. Excuse me, I'm gonna get a refill."

And then he bailed.

"What does cunumunu mean?" Jenna asked Jimmy.

He looked at her, his lips pressed together tightly. "Fool," he grumbled. "It means fool."

After Eric refilled his drink, he wandered toward Tim. Carlita and Elodie discovered they had a love of cooking, and they'd plopped down on the love seat together. Jenna and Jimmy had joined Billie and Jay, where they began an earnest conversation about wealth and their lack of it.

"How will I ever make enough to own real estate again?" asked Jenna. "I don't even have any investments!"

"Who does?" asked Billie. "We live in the most expensive city in the world."

"Fidelity.com, Jenna," said Jay. "Put a tiny bit into funds every month. The real estate situation is tougher. If you didn't buy years ago, you're almost ass-out."

"Real estate isn't emphasized in the black community," said Jimmy.

"It's true," said Jay. "Hasidic Jews indoctrinate their toddlers in the value of owning the space they live in. They own Brooklyn. Billie, I've been thinking of doing inner city seminars about mortgages, loans, etc. Maybe to at-risk seventh graders."

"Honey, can we get through appetizers, first?" asked Billie. "Jenna, what are you looking at?"

She leaned in close to Billie, whispering, "Listen to Eric and Tim."

They were waving their phones at each other and having the world's most animated debate about… well, it wasn't clear.

"Nah, I won," said Tim.

"I won," said Eric. "You can't beat me at Zelda, fam. You're forgetting how I relieved you of your LeBron P.S. Elites?"

"They're garbage anyway. Check the Jordan 11 Breds." Tim pointed out his spic-and-span clean kicks. "Fire."

"Lightweight fire."

"My followers need to witness this crispiness," said Tim, angling his phone in front of his sneakers for the perfect shot.

"All eighty-nine of your followers," snorted Eric, snapping a pic of his boots. "When you get seven hundred and thirty-two likes off your reflection in a puddle, I'll entertain you."

"Selfie your waves and see who's winning. Waves on swim."

"Your birth mother's half-Mexican. Your waves are disqualified."

Jenna looked at Billie, her eyes wide.

"What are they even talking about?" she whispered. "A video game?"

"Yeah, Prisoner of Zelda's a classic," said Jay. "And incidentally, I'd murder them both."

"We're discussing investments," said Jimmy, "and they're photographing their shoes."

Jay chuckled, listening to them. "It's crazy, the whole world wants to be those two. I just did a reading at the Sorbonne, and the Parisians have a saying, 'Tres Brooklyn.' The sneakers, the slang, the swag; it's so aspirational. Madison Avenue markets directly to the hip-hop generation. They don't know their own power."

"I love youth energy," said Jimmy. "That's why I'm a silent deejay at warehouse parties in Greenpoint."

"I'm sorry," said Billie. "Silent what?"

"It's where the revelers wear special headsets, and I deejay directly into their ears. The whole room is dancing in total silence."

"But why go out?" asked Jenna. "Why not just listen to music alone in your bedroom?"

"Because…there's no one to witness your movement expression," Jimmy said with a healthy amount of 'duh' in his tone. "It's so rad."

"Well, radness is its own reward." Jenna downed her Pinot and wondered if she'd ever had sex again.

On the other side of the room, Carlita and Elodie discussed the organic revolution.

"I'm very organic," said Elodie. "Grass-fed everything. Farm-to-fork."

"I try to cook healthy, but that shit's expensive. Why I gotta pay more for food that has less in it? No nitrates. No gluten. No fat."

"Carlita, you are a motherfucking philosopher."

"My cousin used to say I was like Yoda. Like, I'd just say nothing for mad long and then bust out with a gem. One Thanksgiving, I announced that since my veins were green, it must mean I have Teenage Mutant Ninja Turtle blood."

Elodie laughed. "I took my niece to see the original movie, like twenty years ago. I thought Michelangelo was so sexy."

"He is. I love Michelangelo. And Blasians."

Elodie raised an eyebrow. "Well, aren't you a flirty little nugget." Tossing her hair behind her shoulders, she whispered in Elodie's ear, "Hashtag, me and Tim ain't even that serious and I'm bisexual."

"I see." She raised her chin in the direction of Carlita's long, Times New Roman printed nails. "I thought you lady lovers kept short nails. For obvious reasons."

She waved her fingers in the air, bit her bottom lip and purred, "Press-ons."

Elodie grinned, and then looked around to see if anyone had overheard. That's when she saw Eric across the room, shooting Jimmy murderous glances.

"Hold that thought," she said to Carlita, and went over to Eric. She inserted herself between him and Tim.

"God," said Tim. "If I wasn't taken, I'd say we should go somewhere and molest each other until we bleed."

"You come up to my belly button, sir."

"And that's a problem, why?"

"I need to chat with Eric. Go see about your girlfriend. She misses you."

"My Achilles heel is hypersexual-but-needy women," grumbled Tim, heading off.

Once he was gone, Elodie said, "You don't look happy."

"I hate that dude so very much. He's so many levels of offensive."

"Yeah, I have no patience for aging hipsters. If you're going to dress like One Direction, you can't have grey hair and paunch."

"Tell me I didn't overhear him say he's a silent deejay. How reprehensible is that?"

"It is, but our opinions don't matter. It's about Jenna's."
"But…he's talking over her, he's pretentious. He keeps telling her shit, instead of listening to her. She can't be with a guy like that.

I just want what's best for her."

"You sure that's all it is?" She brought her voice down into an even lower whisper. "You don't realize how you look at her, do you?"

Eric cringed, drawing away from Elodie. He read her expression to see if she was serious. She was.

"It's not even like that. Jenna's my homie. I don't appreciate it when any of my friends get disrespected. That's all."

"Okay, babe," she said, sighing. "Just do me a favor."

"Yeah?"

"If that's the case, fix your face."

CHAPTER 15

s Eric reeled from Elodie's epic misinterpretation, Lula reappeared with a tray of eensy crabcakes nestled in miniature filo cups. "These are so delicate and beautiful," said Billie. "Like tiny party favors."

"I brought some party favors," said Tim. "Anyone want a little Molly before dinner?"

"No," said Eric tensely. "No, we don't want."

"That club drug? Well…I don't know." Jenna wrung her satin-gloved hands.

"I'm dying to try it," said Elodie. "Come on Jenna, don't act like you weren't the E queen of 1995."

"Please, I had one ecstasy incident at Limelight where I spent five hours rubbing my face against a piece of Styrofoam. The rash was abominable." Jenna touched her cheek. "What does tripping on Molly feel like?"

"It elevates the fun. Makes you want to spoon the universe," said Eric. "Not that I'm suggesting we do it."

"And Jenna," started Jimmy, "it's called rolling, not tripping."

Eric whispered to Elodie, "You really expect me not to knock this motherfucker out?"

"Shhh," she said, realizing that Molly might be exactly what this awkward dinner party needed. "I'm making an executive decision. Molly us, Tim."

Tim pulled an envelope out of his pocket and handed a white pill all the guests. Eric noted Jenna's pained, "oh no, what's happening, this wasn't the plan, this wasn't THE PLAN" expression and, even though he was dying to pop a Molly or three, he passed.

Eric saw Jimmy watch him as he turned down the pill. So when Tim offered him one, he passed, too. This made Eric hate him more.

A half an hour later, Jenna was attempting to corral her guests to sit for dinner, but no one was paying attention. With their comically motor-mouthed conversations and smile-y, silly energy, dinner was the last thing on anyone's mind.

"I want to dance, dance, dance," wailed Elodie. "Carlita, wanna dance with me?"

"I always wanna dance!"

They spilled out of the love seat and fast-danced to the slowest song ever, Adele's "Someone Like You."

Tim tuned in and exclaimed, "What's Jenna playing? Adele? That big bitch? Sorry, I'm officially on deejay duty now." He scrolled through iTunes on his phone. "Old school? Should I play some Big? Nah, Kendrick goes harder."

"Kendrick's hard," said Eric, "but he's not harder than Big. Also, you're not on deejay duty." He snatched the phone from Tim.

"I vote for Big," said Jay, who then launched into his favorite Biggie Smalls opening line. "LIVE FROM BEDFORD TUYVESANT, THE LIVEST ONE…"

On cue, Carlita, Elodie, Tim and Jenna's upstairs neighbors (paper thin walls) joined in to yell the next line, "REPRESENTIN' BK TO THE FULLEST!" Then, Tim grabbed his phone back from Eric and cued up the legendary rapper's "Unbelievable" at the highest decibel. Carlita was twerking, her luscious ass shaking in double time. Elodie hopped behind her, and Tim in front of her, the three of them creating a wiggly Carlita sandwich. Jay rapped into one of Jenna's Diptyque candles, pretending it was a microphone. Eric sat on the couch, his face in his hands.

"What am I looking at?" Jenna gasped. "Oh my God, Elodie's slapping Carlita's ass! How did this night go off the rails so fast?"

"Look at my husband, reliving his youth. He's been having an early midlife crisis, all because he has four grey hairs. I think it's distinguished, but he feels like Morgan Freeman." Billie grabbed Jenna's hand and kissed it. "Oh sweetie, I feel sooo gooood. I'm so happy. I love my friends. Let's go play with makeup!"

"I always thought Biggie was too mainstream," said Jimmy, watching the impromptu dance party. "I was more into obscure Seventies funk-jazz ensembles, like Betty Wright's band."

"Of course you were," snapped Jenna. She had lost patience with Jimmy Crockett. She caught Eric's attention, gesturing for him to come over.

"I take full responsibility," he said. "I knew Tim would get everyone too turnt the setting. Look at the professor! Shit's wild, yo; I almost wanna get it on film."

"I need your help," she said, grabbing his arm. "Can you get everybody to the table? My chicken's congealing!"

Jimmy watched this transaction and tipped his fedora over his eye, Robert Mitchum-style. Before Eric could open his mouth, he stood and shouted, "Time to eat!" He walked around the room, trying to herd everyone in the direction of the table. Everyone kept dancing, ignoring the Baby Boomer in Justin Bieber's outfit.

"Not yet!" screeched Elodie.

"Tim, put on some trap music so I can get my life!" said Carlita.

"Everybody chill and come sit down," said Eric, in an authoritative voice. "I'm starving and I heard dinner's delicious, so I'm holding each of you responsible if you keep it from me. Elodie, put on your left shoe. Tim! Unhand Carlita's breasts. Pull it together."

Finally, one by one, they filed over to the table, tittering and perspiring. Eric looked at Jimmy archly; Jimmy folded his small arms across his chest and glared back.

Jenna picked up a glass and tapped it with a spoon. She pasted on her hostess-of-the-year smile. "Everyone, I'm happy you could join me tonight. Have a seat, let's eat!"

Figuring out the seating arrangement blew everyone's minds. Jenna's guests bumped into each other, giggling, and then fell into the wrong chairs, and giggled about that. Carlita knocked into a place setting and Jenna's priceless (borrowed) Hermes plates went crashing to the floor. When everyone finally sat, it took the guests ten minutes to even notice the salads in front of them. Billie and Jay wore goofily euphoric expressions, their hands involved in mysterious business under the table. Carlita peeled off her press-on nails while staring into Elodie's eyes. Tim was lecturing no one on the genius of the cheese biscuits.

And then there was Jenna, sitting between Eric and Jimmy—all three, dead sober.

"These biscuits are so delectable, though," rhapsodized Tim. "They're, like, spiritually fulfilling. If this biscuit were a woman, I'd paint her toenails, and then do the *Magic Mike* 'Pony' dance."

"Channing Tatum looks mad black," said Carlita.

"He does!" exclaimed Billie. "Like he's passing."

"Speaking of Channings who pass," started Elodie, "Carol Channing was secretly black."

Tim frowned. "Who's that?"

"Old musical theater comedienne," said Jimmy.

"The skinny redhead? With the show that reruns on Comedy Network?"

"That's Carol Burnett," said Jay.

"Miss Hannigan's black?"

"Mindy Kaling's black," said Carlita with authority.

Eric sighed.

"Jay," started Billie, "should we call the sitter and see if May went to sleep?"

"No, we should enjoy the dinner and drugs," he said, kissing her cheek.

"They're the cutest married couple I know," Jenna said to Jimmy.

He took a sip of wine, which was from his bottle, as requested. "So what's your story? Have you ever been married?"

Eric pretended to be involved with his salad—but he was hanging on every word of their conversation.

"I was in a very long relationship. Engaged, but we never married. How about you? Marriage? Divorce? Engagement?" Jenna giggled. "Sounds like the over-forty version of the 'Marry, Fuck, Kill' game."

Eric's mind was blown. She'd been engaged? To whom? What happened?

"No," he said. "Never married, divorced, or engaged."

"Oh. Huh."

Suddenly, Jimmy's energy changed from casual to prickly. On-edge. "What does 'huh' mean?"

Before Jenna could respond, he said, "I know what it means." Then he affected a whiny, effeminate voice. "Eww, you're really fifty and you've never been married? You've never even proposed? Oh, you must be a commitment-phobe. You must be emotionally blocked-off. You must be impossible in relationships."

Jenna stared at him, shocked.

"Excuse me, but you asked me if I'd been married," she said, trying to manage the withering read she felt bubbling up inside of her. "Was this not the conversation we were having?"

"No, it's fine," he said, swirling his wine angrily in his glass. "You just had a tone. And I didn't take you for a woman who'd go to such a clichéd place."

That's when Eric snapped.

"*She's* the cliché?"

"I'm sorry?"

"You need to watch your mouth, son," he said.

Jimmy sized him up, and then snorted. "You've been throwing jabs at me all night. Why? And are you really son-ing me? How old are you, anyway? I think it's past your bedtime."

Tim's fork froze halfway up to his mouth.

"What'd you just say?" asked Eric.

"You heard me," said Jimmy.

"Fuck you, American Apparel."

"Eric!" Jenna was flabbergasted.

Jimmy slammed his drink down. "American Apparel?"

"Cool *jeggings,* bro."

"They're skinny jeans, not jeggings."

"They're jeggings," Eric said. "It's a portmanteau, I'd think you'd be elated."

"Do we have a problem here?"

"Not at all," said Jenna, panicking. "Eric, it's fine. Eat your salad. Everyone just settle!"

"Nah, fuck that," said Eric, getting worked up. "I can't let him speak to you like this in your own home. Dude, you're having a temper tantrum because she asked you the same question you asked her? If you feel a way about your past, that's not Jenna's fault. And it is highly suspect that you're mad old and you've never even been engaged. Though you just showed why. This was the audition, asshole! I'm so embarrassed for you, you Williamsburg ass sommelier ass goofy ass fail."

Tim burst out laughing. "Now it's a party!"

Jimmy was sweating and breathing hard. "You're out of line, young man."

"And you're a throbbing forehead vein of a person."

"Is that guy for real?" Jimmy asked Jenna.

"Eric? He is. And I hate to say it, but I tend to agree with him." Realizing she'd lost control of the evening, she tried to end it altogether. "Maybe we should all just call it a night…"

"Maybe he and I should discuss this outside," Jimmy said, standing.

Eric stood, too. "I mean, we can knuckle up if you want. Let's go."

"No one knuckles up at my house!" Jenna hopped up, grabbing Eric's arm. "Jay, do something!"

Jay, who grew up attending parties he had to bring pistols to, was unmoved. "Jimmy, don't front like you're going to fight this kid," he said. "You got three decades on him. It'll end badly for you."

"Nah, E talks real slick, but he has no thug," said Tim. "It'd be over in four seconds."

"Yo, what's wrong with your face?" Eric forgot about Jimmy as he squinted at his best friend. "Why do you have Kanye cheeks?"

They all turned to look at him. His lips and nose had doubled in size, and his cheeks looked like he was storing acorns for the winter. His fingers were Bratwurst-bloated.

Jenna slapped her hand over her mouth.

"My face does feel mad tingly. The fuck?" He flew out of his seat, peering into the antique mirror hanging behind the table. "It's my nut allergy!"

Billie burst into tears. "May said the mangos at that Jamaican resort made her throat itch! What if she has an allergy like this? Lifetime ban on tropical vacations, Jay, we can't risk it, the hospitals are twenty years behind!"

"No more drugs for my wife. Ever," said Jay, hugging her.

"Were there nuts in something?" Eric asked Jenna.

"There were very fine almond slivers in the salad dressing. You didn't see them, Tim?"

"I thought they were skinny pieces of Parmesan! I'm gonna die. Such an un-thug way to die, oh my God…"

Jay sprung to action. "I'm calling an ambulance."

In the commotion, Jimmy grabbed his fedora and stormed out. Jenna hardly noticed. What she did notice was the disappearance of two other guests.

"Where's Carlita and Elodie?" Jenna looked around the room.

She stormed down the hallway to her bedroom, with Eric on her heels. Flinging open the door, she saw Elodie and Carlita intertwined on the beautiful Frette duvet she bought just for the party. Carlita was face-first in Elodie's stomach—inches from her promised land.

"Elodie Franklin! Are you fucking in the middle of my party?"

Elodie giggled and said, "Payback!"

"It was her idea, ma'am," said Carlita.

"Ma'am?" Eric shook his head. "No. 'Ma'am' implies respect. You're about to administer mouth romance on your hostess' bed. Ma'am isn't the thing."

"Sweetie, your boyfriend has swollen up into elephantine proportions," said Jenna. "Jay's taking him to the ER, you should probably go with."

"Can't take him nowhere," she muttered, pulling her dress down and readjusting her panties.

Eric and Jenna looked at each other and shut the door.

Eric stayed to help Jenna clean up. She didn't ask him to, and he didn't offer. But when Carlita and Elodie stumbled out of the door to make more Sapphic mischief, and Billie and Jay dragged Tim into the ambulance—

Eric simply made no move to go. Instead, after Jenna let Lula go early (she was too embarrassed to face her), he grabbed a broom and began sweeping up stray shards of Jenna's dead Hermes plates. Then, he and Jenna did the dishes together—he washed, she dried.

Once everyone had left, Jenna had arranged her glamorous couture gown in its garment bag, and then changed into a pajama top, Equinox shorts and the fuzzy orange slipper socks she'd worn every day in Virginia. Her hair was piled on top of her head in a scrunchie. She looked crazy, but didn't care; she just wanted to relax. Now, she and Eric were plopped side by side on the couch. They were on their third glass of Eric's wine.

"I threw a party that ended with a guest being carted away on a stretcher," Jenna said, dazed. "Wearing an oxygen mask. After narrowly escaping anaphylactic shock. That happened."

"I have so many regrets," said Eric. "I never should've invited Tim. Tim never should've invited Carlita. I never should've gone HAM on Jiminy Cricket."

Jenna laid her head back on the couch, flinging an arm over her eyes. "That was the best part."

"By the way, *fuck* Tim. I do have thug in me," said Eric, having a delayed reaction to Tim's write-off. "Just 'cause I don't lead with it, doesn't mean it's not there."

Jenna took a huge gulp of wine. "Jimmy was so condescending. So rude."

"Why were you even entertaining him, though? You should've bounced him after 'arfe.'"

"He was my guest. I was trying to be a good hostess!" She threw up her arms, and spilled a little wine on her thigh. It dribbled down the inside of her leg. She swiped it up with her finger and licked it off. Eric watched her, and it took him a full ten seconds to return to the conversation.

"I used to throw incredible parties. And I used to be incredible at work." She sighed. "I feel like my best days are behind me."

Eric poured them both more wine. "Why do you keep looking backwards, though?"

"Do I?"

"A lot." He turned toward her. "Can I ask you something? You live in a studio-plus apartment in the hood, next to a building that could pass for the *New Jack City* crack house…"

"Accurate."

"But you hired, like, a servant…"

"Helper!"

"…for the night and had everything catered, and you have this fancy furniture. How'd you pay for all of this?"

Jenna looked around her apartment, feeling both exposed and ashamed. But she was also grateful that Eric was confronting her in this way. She deserved to be called out. And she wanted to deal with it.

"I opened a Barneys charge and blacked out," she confessed. "Why?"

She tucked her hands into the sleeves of her pajama top. "I was trying to be a person I'm not anymore."

"But you have nothing to prove. You're fun and real and … cool, you know? Just being relaxed, regular you. In those socks."

She looked down at her fuzzy orange feet. Until that second, it hadn't occurred to Jenna that she was wearing what she was wearing—in front of Eric. Was she really allowing herself to be seen in gym shorts and a pajama top around a man? With her hair up in a scrunchie? All those years living with Brian, her hanging-around-the-house clothes always matched. And if she was wearing shorts and a top, they were tiny and cute. She tucked her feet under her butt.

"Stop torturing yourself about who you used to be," continued Eric. "This is Jenna Jones, Part Deux. And sequels are always better."

"That is patently untrue!" exclaimed Jenna. *"Aliens? Rambo? Lethal Weapon 2?"*

"So, if I were an '80s action movie, I'd be gold."

"I'm just saying, fuck the past. Get excited about what happens now. And next."

"You're right." She laid her head back on the couch again, thinking. "I was trying to do that tonight. Staying open about meeting someone new. I kind of knew me and Jimmy weren't a match, but I didn't want to write him off. Because you never know. People are weird on first dates."

Eric looked skeptical. "If you feel like someone sucks when you first meet them, they usually suck."

"But would I even be able to recognize a great first date? It's been so long, I can't remember how it feels when it's right with someone."

"How do you want it to feel?"

She thought this over, and then looked over at Eric. Her lips were slightly berry-stained from the wine, her eyes bright with intoxication.

"I've never said this out loud," said Jenna. "So be gentle."

"I gotta hear all parts of this."

"Intellectually, I know what I need. Compatibility, similar world views, kindness, humor, no sociopathic tendencies. But emotionally?" She moaned and put her face in her hands. "No, I can't do this."

"Come on, you can say it."

"Okay, you're a silent movie buff. You've seen that Greta Garbo movie, *Flesh and the Devil?*"

"1926. She plays a lusty, amoral seductress."

"Right!" said Jenna, beaming. It was such a delicious feeling, knowing someone who had the same stuff in his head as she did. "There's this moment in *Flesh and the Devil* when Garbo and her secret lover are in church. During communion, he takes a sip from the chalice. And when it's passed down to her, she stops, caresses it, and then…"

"She turns it around to drink from the same spot his mouth touched." Eric's face broke into a small smile of recognition.

"It's so illicit." Jenna clasped her hand to her heart. "She practically sucks it. In front of everyone. In church."

"Profane as fuck."

"Profane, but pure," she said. "Sacred. That's what I want it to feel like. I don't want these clinical, awkward setups. I don't feel like doing this twenty more times. I can't imagine meeting my soulmate through an interview process. I want to know without words. I want to fall so violently that I risk breaking into a million pieces. I want to love so desperately it's indecent. I want it to be wild and fated and forever. A no-choice connection. Do you know what I mean?"

He glanced at her. "I think so."

"I know that kind of love is an unsustainable fantasy. But I'd kill to have that intensity of feeling for someone." She fingered the sleeves of her pajama top, now feeling self-conscious.

"Don't settle till you have it," said Eric, quietly.

"I won't."

"Promise me."

"I promise."

Then, the air between them went thick. Jenna sat dead-still, her heart pounding. She didn't know if it was the wine, or him, or them—but she felt dizzy. She couldn't look at Eric. And he wouldn't look at her. Her skin flushed hot, and with trembling hands, she lifted a few stray curls off of her neck—and then she sensed Eric tense up. That's when she finally met his eyes. She watched him watch her, mesmerized, as if he wanted to touch her skin back there; to feel it, taste it. It was all over his face. He wanted to taste her everywhere.

Jenna couldn't look away. She squeezed her thighs together, trying to squelch the ache. She stopped breathing, stopped thinking, and allowed herself to slip into whatever electric thing was happening. But in seconds, her brain took over and rejected it completely. She tore her eyes away from his.

Jenna felt exposed. She was shocked that she'd given into that tension even for an instant. Whatever she'd just felt was dangerous, ridiculous and impossible. But secretly, she wanted Eric's mouth on hers again. God, she craved it. The ache was always on the periphery when she was around him. Even when she'd genuinely wanted to murder him. She couldn't get it out of her mind, the way he'd made her feel.

And now Eric knew it.

Oh please. He's always known it.

"I gotta go," he said. "Now."

"Oh. Are you sure?"

"Really sure."

He shot up off the couch and Jenna followed him to the door. "Umm… so how are you getting home? Can I call you a cab? The train is pretty far."

"I'm cool. I'll just walk and smoke."

"Weed? That's so dangerous. What if the cops see you?"

"Don't worry, they won't," he said. "Weed is nothing. Did you smell what the five guys on your corner were smoking?"

"Well, just be safe," she said, opening her door. They hesitated in the doorway, unclear about how they should say goodbye, but they both knew it shouldn't involve touching.

"So I'll see you tomorrow?" said Eric, his hands thrust in his pockets.

"Yep, tomorrow. Have a good night. And thank you."

"For what?"

"For defending my honor. And cleaning. And listening."

He smiled. "Anytime."

Then he was gone. And Jenna stood with her back to her door for ten minutes, clutching her stomach.

For as long as she lived, she'd never figure out what compelled her to go to her window. A part of her just needed air. Another, bigger part hoped she could steal a secret glimpse of Eric walking to the subway. But there was no way he'd still be outside.

Jenna rushed over to the open window so fast that she banged her toe against the coffee table. Yelping, she tore back her curtain—and couldn't believe what she saw.

Eric hadn't gone anywhere. His back was to her, and he was leaning up against the half-dead tree in front of her building. A hazy trail of smoke billowed above him.

"Eric!"

Startled, he turned and peered up at her second-floor window. He looked caught. Guilty.

"Why are you still here?"

"I don't know." He gazed down the street at nothing, and then back up at her. "Why'd you come to the window?"

"I don't know," she said.

He nodded pensively. "Good night, Jenna," he said, and left for good.

CHAPTER 16

The morning after Jenna's soiree from hell, she sat her desk, squinting at Fidelity.com and attempting to figure out the difference between low-risk and moderate-risk investments. She typed her abysmal financial information into Fidelity's user profile—but with every click on her keyboard, her brain screamed: "I'm-in-so-much-trou-ble-I'm-in-so-much-trou-ble…" She couldn't get the details of the night before out of her head. Not her party; she'd come to terms with that epic disaster. It was Eric.

Jenna was too old to try to trick herself into denying the truth. She was lusting after Eric. No, it was more than lust, which was so much worse.

She'd wanted badly for him to stay—and without her saying a word, he just knew. She'd told herself that it was innocent, that she just wanted to hang out with her friend. But before she could get her bearings, they'd had that blistering moment on her couch. He'd had her coming apart at the seams—and he never touched her. What if he had? What if he'd stayed two minutes longer? What if she'd had one more drink? She knew the answer.

Out of the millions of men in New York, out of all the appropriate options, she was attracted to this man—who happened to be the wrong man. She had to figure out a way to hide it. And hide it so well that she'd believe her own lie.

Eric had spent fifteen minutes in his cubicle, preparing himself to be normal when he saw Jenna for their 9:30am meeting. Now, as he walked up to her doorway, he saw that she was the one who wasn't normal. As usual, she was sitting at her desk, squinting into her computer screen. But, she was wearing black horn-rimmed glasses—the kind preferred by 1950's bobbysoxers.

Eric knocked on the door. Jenna looked up, and ripped the glasses off her face. She pasted on the maniacal smile she'd worn when he'd first stepped into her office, with Darcy.

"Hey," he said.

"Hey you! Sit down. Hi!"

It was obvious that she felt weird about last night.

Don't make it weirder, he thought.

"So…hey," he repeated, making it weirder.

Eric had intended to pretend like nothing happened. Because nothing did happen. He hadn't strayed an inch from this proper place in the Friend Zone. But watching her with that dude? It almost broke him. He'd gone over there with the clear-eyed goal of helping her land a boyfriend, and ended up completely cock-blocking. And when it was just the two of them, alone, Eric was hit with a feeling so potent, it levelled him completely.

Elodie was right. He wanted her. Badly. And he'd had no idea; the feeling had snuck up on him. It was like he had no say in it. He did things he'd never done with a girl—and without thought or intention. Attempting to fight for her (beneath him), washing dishes with her (cozy), co-obsessing over an obscure movie with her (nirvana). It all felt like he was doing exactly what he was supposed to be doing.

Everything Eric thought he knew about women, about what he wanted or didn't want, was turned upside down.

"Surprise, I wear glasses!" Jenna gestured to the specs discarded on her desk. "When I'm tired my eyes get blurry. I…I didn't really get a good night's sleep."

"Neither did I. Why were you up?"

"Too much on my mind. Work stuff."

"Right. Me too. Work."

"Right. Anyway, that's why I'm wearing those. They're so doofy."

"No, you look like you're out of a vintage Pepsi ad or something."

"Exactly. Doofy."

"I love them," he said with an embarrassing amount of fervor.

"Thank you."

She slid her specs on top of her head, and then slipped them off again. "But that's just 'cause you're into old things. What was your quote? 'Older is sexier?'"

"Yeah. And it's true."

"I used to agree. But learning from you, I've gained a whole new appreciation for young guys." Jenna caught herself, breaking out in a sweat. "I mean, young people! I mean…you've taught me new ways of doing things."

"I know what you meant," he said, trying to keep a straight face. "But I'll always want what's older."

Jenna rubbed her lips together, nervously, and then said, "Anyway, thank you for complimenting my glasses. They're silly, but…yeah."

There was a moment of hesitant silence. Jenna folded and unfolded her glasses, Eric tapped his fingers on the arms of his chair—and decided he couldn't take the tension. So he made a joke.

"You know, you were right. You're a hell of a hostess. Wanna throw my birthday party next month?"

Jenna smirk-glared at him. Then, the pressure to pretend that they hadn't almost slid into the mess with which they started dissipated a bit.

He smiled. "Too soon?"

"I'm not throwing another party, for a very long time. Maybe May's Sweet Sixteen." Jenna took a deep, sobering breath, and exhaled like she'd been holding it in since the night before. "I have good news. During my insomnia bout, I'm fairly certain that I came up with our series concept."

"Something good came from my insomnia, too!" said Eric. "Before you tell me your idea, I gotta show you something."

He reached in his pocket. The muscles in his bicep worked. He noticed Jenna do a startlingly obvious double take. It always momentarily threw Eric, the way that Jenna unconsciously broadcasted everything she felt. He wondered if she knew how naked she was to him.

"Here," he said, sliding a flash drive across her desk. "Plug it in."

As she stuck the flash drive into her laptop, he said, "I was thinking you needed a trailer for the first video. Just a quick this-why-Jenna-Jones-is-so-dope, to reintroduce you to the audience. So, I did some research on you. I ran through your TV appearances, judging spots, and whatever I could find online. And I came up with this."

Jenna knew Eric was talking, but his voice barely registered because the images she was seeing were so breathtaking, she couldn't process any other information. Out of all the zillions of quips she'd given, ridiculous faces she'd made, and overly earnest on-air exchanges, the vignettes he'd chosen were the ones that were the most her. The intro opened with her as a twenty-two-year old intern saying, "Hi, I'm Jenna Jones and fashion is my passion, but I'm fuh-reeezing," on the set of a *Bazaar* bikini shoot in Alaska with a baby-faced Naomi—the clip had ended up in Jenna's goodbye reel when she left the magazine (and had somehow made it to YouTube). He had a shot of her laughing so hard with Joan Rivers on *Fashion Police* that she toppled out of her chair. The best was a shot that was too raunchy to make *America's Modeling Competition*—it was Jenna in the makeup chair, telling that week's guest judge, Kris Jenner, that her famed reality show should've been called, *The Kardashians: More Butts Than Ashtrays*.

"It's glorious," she gushed. "You've known me for five minutes! How did you capture me so clearly?"

"I studied you all night," he said. "I have a PhD in Jenna Jones now."

She smiled in awe. "You didn't have to do this."

Yes I did, he thought. *I had to. Because seeing you on my screen is the only way I can keep my hands off of you and feel sane.*

"Let me show you my favorite parts," said Eric, trying to keep focused.

He dragged his chair closer and pulled her laptop so it was between them. He leaned in, pressing the forward button on her laptop and scanned the clip's highlights. Out of the corner of his eye, he saw Jenna's eyes traveling up his arm, his shoulder, his profile—and he wished he could crawl inside her mind.

Whatever. He knew exactly what she was thinking.

Eric allowed himself one quick glance at her. Being this close was excruciating. Her perfume, which smelled like honey, vanilla and summertime, made him want to bite her. And the look on her face was maddening. A mixture of "you're my hero" awe and "fuck me up against the wall" lust.

No woman had ever made him feel this out of control.

"Eric," Jenna said softly. "Thank you."

"My pleasure." He suddenly felt a wave of shyness over his little project. It was a love letter.

"So, Miss I'm-fuh-reezing," said Eric, cracking his knuckles, "you ready to tell me your genius idea?"

"Yes! By the way, I'm boycotting Greta Blumen's shoes. I'm wearing some today, but never again."

"I need to see the shoes you almost risked our jobs over," he said, playfully. "Stand up."

Rolling her eyes, Jenna stepped to the side of her desk. She cocked her leg a bit and put her hands on her hips. She was wearing nude stilettos with a faint tone-on-tone print (flesh-toned heels were an old fashion trick; they made your legs look endless).

Eric relaxed, his eyes traveling lazily all the way up her legs and just past the hem of her short skirt. He stopped there—right there—staring blatantly and shamelessly, letting her imagine what was going through his mind, and then his gaze moved up her body, lingered at her breasts, and finally stopped at her face.

Jenna looked giddy. She was high off of his reaction to her.

"Is that a print on your shoe? Or am I just delirious?"

"It's a really faint tonal print," she said, sticking her leg out, torturing him a bit more. "You can tell from that far away?"

"Not really. I think I need to see it up close."

Jenna glanced out the door. The StyleZine floor was a huge rectangle loft space, and her office was in the corner. Darcy's office was across from hers, but she was out at ad meetings all day. A huge conference room was to the right, but it was unoccupied. And far off to the left, out of view, were the maze of cubicles where the rest of the staff sat.

Anyone could walk by at any moment…but probably not.

Jenna took two steps toward Eric, stood in front of him, and planted her foot on the seat of his chair between his legs. Her leg was inches from his mouth. Her skirt slid high up her thighs. His almost undetectable intake of breath was the only sign that she'd affected him in any way—that, and his hands, which gripped the arm of the chair.

"Can you see the print now?"

"Polka dots."

"Right," she whispered, keeping an eye on the door. "This is bad."

"The worst."

"Worse than you think."

"I doubt that vividly."

"There's something I haven't told you."

"Better say it, quick."

"I haven't had sex in three years."

"You haven't had *what* in *what?*"

"I haven't been touched in three years. Not until you." She glanced at the door again. "So me being this close to you again … it's…it's almost too much."

He blinked, taking in this information. Then he reached out an arm and pushed the door closed. Darcy did tell them to lock themselves in her office till they came up with their series.

"Being this close to me," he repeated, "is too much?"

She nodded. She looked like a naughty nun in confession.

"Why are you over here, then?"

"Can't help it."

Jenna knew that what she was doing was inexcusable, unprofessional, unlike her. But the power she felt, standing over Eric like that, knowing she was overwhelming him—it was a rush. And Eric had never wanted to touch a woman so badly. For a fevered five seconds that felt like five hours, Eric negotiated with himself. (*I shut the door and now I can do what I've been dying to do. I can finally…no, wait, not here. I'm not an animal!! I'll just kiss her. That'd be enough. I just need to touch her again…*)

He leaned forward and dipped his head toward her inner thigh, his mouth achingly close to her skin. He heard Jenna's breath quicken, and he looked up. Her eyes were closed, and her cheeks were bright with carnality…or trepidation, or triumph. Or some savagely sexy combination of all three. She couldn't have known what she looked like. She couldn't have known, and expected him to control himself.

He couldn't. Eric planted a hot wet kiss right there, softly biting her— and then her legs buckled and she let out a jagged, desperate little moan. When he heard this, he crashed back to his senses. If he didn't stop right now, he wouldn't stop.

"Move." She didn't.

"Move," he said again. "This is a dangerous game, Jenna."

"Why?"

"'Cause I'm seconds from fucking the shit out of you. Move." This snapped her out of her trance, and blushing, Jenna rushed over to her chair. Eric slumped down into his with a tortured groan, rubbing a hand over his face. Jenna dropped her forehead onto her desk, the loud "thunk" reverberating through the tiny office.

"Jesus, Jenna, you trying to kill me?"

"Did I just...did you really just do that? I can't be trusted around you, Eric. Who am I?"

"A cougar," he joked.

"I've only been forty for three months," she exclaimed, slamming her fist on the desk. "I'm too young to be a cougar!"

"You're too old to be acting this slutty at work."

"Oh, like you're such a damsel in distress," she whispered. "You just gave me a thighgasm in my office."

"What was I supposed to do? I'm a man, Jenna. You serve it to me, I'm eating it." He watched her fan her flushed face, trying to pull herself together. She was trembling. He plucked a bunch of yellow Skittles out of the bowl and handed them to her. "Take these, you'll feel better."

She took them gratefully and chomped in wide-eyed, distressed silence, while fidgeting with the delicate gold bracelet on her arm. She focused on it, in an effort to block out the scorching tingling where Eric's mouth had been. Jenna had weirdly small wrists, so bracelets never fit—and then she stumbled upon this petite one at a Clinton Hill flea market. It had been the perfect find.

The perfect find.

Suddenly, she bolted upright, like there was a puppet string attached to her head from the ceiling.

"Eric," she said with urgency. "I'm scrapping my idea from last night."

"Wait, why?"

"I was hired to take this site to a new level, to bring notoriety in a fresh way. Let's really do that. Your sensibility, my connections... street style... it's too good! Get up!" She grabbed her phone and hopped out of her chair. "Meet me at the elevators in fifteen minutes."

Jenna thought quickly. She'd need a place to quickly produce garments and accessories, so Jenna tracked down her friend who represented Threads Production, an inexpensive, but fairly high quality apparel factory on 39th Street. Her idea would need funding, so she set up a meeting between LVMH, herself, and Darcy for first thing in the morning.

Then she called her first subject, Maggie M. A former supermodel, she was now one of the most in-demand stylists in celebdom (her modeling was short-lived because she didn't have the attention span to diet.). Maggie was both terribly behaved, and one of the best-dressed woman on the planet. She was in town for the collections and the British beauty owed Jenna a few favors. In Maggie's modeling days, Jenna had flown around the world with her half a dozen times, and more often than not, Maggie barely escaped an unplanned pregnancy, arrest, or a coke-induced coma. Each time, Jenna masterminded a way to dig her out of the scrape while keeping her secrets intact.

Maggie's lunatic behavior was tabloid gold. But more importantly, everyone who cared about style hung on her every move. The bodacious blonde had a real body, with a curved tummy and an ample ass, and dressed it to perfection. Her wild, Cher-meets-Kate-Moss fantasy wardrobe (feather headdresses and motorcycle boots) was breathlessly worshipped on blogs.

Jenna's idea was to recruit the most stylish, coolest-looking women around (all shapes, all sizes)—and, in each subject's video, have them come up with an item they dreamed of owning, but could never find. Like, a trench that was warm enough to wear in twenty degree weather. Sexy sweatpants you could rock for cocktails. Chic flats that don't make size eleven feet look like canoes. Or, in Maggie's case, a flowy boho top that made busty girls look ethereal, not expecting.

Acting as their Fairy StyleMother, Jenna would hang out in their bedrooms, rifling through their favorite pieces in their closets, trying on clothes and riffing about their personal style in a gossipy, fun, just-us-girls way—and then give them fifty dollars to have their fantasy item made. Their perfect find. On the site, StyleZine would sell thirty limited edition copies of each piece. Only thirty; first come first serve.

She started with Maggie. And Eric captured her most intimate, girly moments—wiping off lipstick and starting again. Putting on outfits and then changing them, tossing discarded accessories on the bed. Re-parting her hair fourteen times in the mirror, tripping while struggling to put on jeans. Maggie came across not as a beauty icon, but as a friend-in-your-head, a woman who was so funny and cool that her looks were an added bonus. The point? The viewers had to have a piece of her magic.

Readers mobbed the site to be one of the handful to score her Perfect Find. What style follower wouldn't want to own a one-off piece straight from the imagination of a woman whose wardrobe they'd kill to inhabit—and for less cash then they'd spend at brunch? Jenna found the girls and Eric knew how to shoot them. No two videos looked alike. Each one was a collector's edition, an eccentric visual delight. Eric distilled each girl's personality down to an archetype (Retro Vamp, Hot Braniac, Corporate Goddess, Sporty Spice, et.)—and then, he art-directed, edited, and shot each girl in a film style from an era or genre that showcased her persona. The SoCal surfer turned fashion blogger, Coco Lopez, was filmed in sun-drenched, saltwater-sprayed, Endless Summer day glo tones that were so evocative you could smell the coconut oil and Coppertone. The patrician, elegant Indian-Bahamian boutique owner, Sade Ghirmay, was shot like a scene from 1939's The Women—in velvety, Art Deco-esque black and white, as she swanned around her Upper East side penthouse serving her kids breakfast in hot rollers and an ivory satin robe.

No matter who the subject was—the "Chola Girl" barista at the coffee shop on Prince, Jenna's feline lesbian colorist, a girlish CW series starlet—they were all turned into icons by Eric.

When the gays started parodying the clips on YouTube, complete with exaggerated versions of Eric's cinematic style, an overly perky Jenna character in a Glinda the Good Witch dress and a magic wand—and queens coming up with absurd "Perfect Finds" (things like two-foot-long false lashes and ouch-free scrotum tape)—they knew that their little series was pop culture gold.

As a professional team, Jenna and Eric's connection was unmistakable, which baffled the StyleZine staff. They barely knew each other; how did they manage to so brilliantly execute a project on that level? Darcy was particularly stunned. Their energy had literally changed overnight.

Of course, no one knew the truth. Eric and Jenna were high on their chemistry, which amplified their creativity. There was a secret alchemy at work—a director who shot his host while imagining fucking her in fifteen pornographic ways; and a host who knew it, and therefore shimmered with lusty radiance while giggling with a Venezuelan boutique owner about ear cuffs.

The Perfect Find, the web series that breathed new life into the ecommerce industry, that would go on to land StyleZine millions in new advertising and spawn a dozen copycats; the one that quadrupled the site's numbers—was smartly conceived and a stroke of luck. But more than anything else?

It was foreplay.

CHAPTER 17

The next month went by in a blur. After shooting the Maggie video, Jenna and Eric became inseparable. They were best friends, excruciatingly platonic partners in crime. They were uninterested in anything not having to do with them. But no one could know.

The workday was spent figuring out sneaky ways to accidentally-on-purpose run into other. Eric always found a way to be in line at the Starbucks downstairs when Jenna went for her 2 pm coffee run. They never went together, and always left separately. But ten minutes later, they'd appear in the office within seconds of each other, Jenna looking zip-a-dee-doo-daa delighted and Eric acting like Jay Z. After selling out Madison Square Garden.

All day, they'd hope to see each other in the hallway or in the kitchen or somewhere. When they did, if anyone was around, they'd go through this dance of pretending not to be excited about it. But as soon as they parted, they'd text incessantly about that one brief moment.

Eric: Did you part your hair on a different side today just to fuck up my equilibrium?

Jenna: Jesus, your biceps when you were carrying all that camera equipment to the elevator! Are you TRYING to ruin me for all other men?

Like teenagers, they texted all day and talked on the phone all night. Jenna, a person who, a month before, had found technology baffling at worst and distasteful at best, didn't enter a bathroom stall without her iPhone. She'd find excuses to get up from her office just to walk by the vicinity of Eric's cubicle to get a glimpse of him. He'd get a glimpse of her, too, and then he'd have to focus on Chimpanzees and baseball—two things he hated—until he erased the NSFW thoughts from his brain.

Eric and Jenna were in the grips of a full-blow obsession.

The situation drove them to it. If they were two normal adults with a crush, they could've gone to the Cheesecake Factory, seen a movie, boned, and been dating by now. But this wasn't a normal situation—there was Darcy, the job thing, and the age thing. They never saw each other outside of work. They never stood or sat too close, and never touched. After the explosive moment in Jenna's office, they knew that if they so much as grazed each other, it was game over.

They hid in plain sight. Everybody knew Eric and Jenna collaborated on The Perfect Find, which was StyleZine's biggest draw. No one batted an eyelash at their lengthy "meetings" in Jenna's office—they were expected to have a relationship. If anything, the girls in the office assumed that Eric had a hopeless, unrequited thing; and that a much older, quasi media celeb like Jenna would never give him the time of day.

The daily editorial staff meetings were the best because Jenna and Eric got to sit in the same room for twenty minutes. They could text and steal glances while everyone else discussed UTI's and taking Plan B.

Of course, there was always the element of danger—Darcy. Karen O'Quinn, the executive editor, ran the meetings, but their CEO liked to drop in on all of her website's daily meetings. She did it to keep her staff on their toes. No one ever knew when she'd show up and blast them into the Bronx with her withering critiques of their work.

But since The Perfect Find, Darcy had experienced a mild personality transplant. She didn't micromanage as much. She seemed girly, younger. Human. Jinx said she'd even heard faint music playing out of her office— something cheerful, like Bruno Mars. The fact was, Darcy was over the moon at The Perfect Find's raging success, and it showed.

"So congrats to Jenna, who killed the video with the badass Wall Street banker," said Karen O'Quinn. A redhead with round hazel eyes, she wore an oversized white T-shirt belted with a gold rope, and brown suede fringed booties. ("Robin Hood on Estrogen.")

"Every corporate chick will want her soft leather, tie-neck work blouse that's ladylike enough wear under suits, but tough enough to wear with jeans," said Karen.

The sixteen-person editorial staff applauded. Jenna smiled, and did a little chair-curtsey.

"I forgot to tell you guys," said Jenna," Rachel Zoe told me she wanted that blouse for herself."

"I can't believe you know her," said Jinx, whose crush on Eric had deepened and, thus, was caught between jealousy and shero worship of Jenna.

"I've known her since she was Rachel Zoe Rosenzweig, styling B-list music videos," said Jenna, feeling her phone buzz on her lap. She glanced down. "I'm glad it got so many hits."

Jenna Jones
iMessages
October 2, 2012, 12:15 PM

Eric: Don't forget to say you promoted it across all platforms.

"I promoted it across all platforms," she said. Thank god for Eric's social media coaching. She thought in hashtags now.

"Fabulous," said Karen. "You've come so far."

"What about congratulating the homie E on the video?" whined Jinx. "He's the one that brilliantly included cutaway shots of her pushing through a hustle-and-bustle crowd on Wall Street."

"Totally remiss," said Karen. "Great work as usual, 'The Homie E."

Everyone laughed. Eric, who was satisfying his midday candy craving by sucking on a Blow Pop, said, "Thanks, The Homie Karen."

Eric Combs
iMessages
October 2, 2012, 12:19 PM

Jenna: Lucky lollipop.
Eric: Stop staring, it's making me uncomfortable.

"Eric, we need to brainstorm," said Karen. "You have to infuse some Perfect Find magic onto your woman-on-the-street interviews with Terry. They're cute, but they're too easy."

"Easy?" Eric was offended. Bombarding strange chicks, making them sign release forms, and shooting them droning on about their Zara sweaters—he didn't enjoy it. But he worked hard on those clips.

"She means that you, with a camera, are a panty-dropper," said Terry.

"That's not what I meant," said Karen with a bored sigh.

"But it's true," said Terry. "I've literally seen some of those girls grab his phone and type their number in. Tatted up black guys are winning right now."

"We should do a style series on *them*," said Mitchell, the photo editor who Darcy labeled a 'husky queen.'

"So we're clear, those girls do that because they want me to text them their outtakes," said Eric, glancing at Jenna. "For the Gram."

"You emboldened-by-social-media millennials amaze me." She wasn't amazed, she was jealous. Who were these whores? "I've never been that forward with a guy."

Jenna Jones
iMessages
October 2, 2012, 12:25 PM

Eric: Liar.
Jenna: But they don't know that.

"Little do those chicks know he's got a terrible crush," said Terry, punching him in the shoulder. "Ask Jenna."

"Uncalled for." He punched Terry back, lightly. "Jenna, you don't think I have a crush on you, right?"

"I think you have a crush on you," replied Jenna, sweetly.

"Finally, an accurate description of this person," mumbled Mitchell, who was unimpressed by the fuss made over Eric.

"Guys, do I look chubby in these jeans?" Jinx wanted to move on. All this discussion of Eric liking Jenna was hurting her feelings. "I took a selfie today and I looked like Hannah Horvath."

"Jinx, you don't need to lose weight. Your ex was a dickhead for making you think there was anything wrong with you." Eric was fed up with the emotional fallout from her toxic relationship with that roly-poly, bearded brogrammer. "Especially when he looks like furry button. Let him show up here again."

"Thank you, Eric," she said softly, cheeks reddening. Mitchell rolled his eyes. So did Jenna, internally.

"You need a new man," said Terry. "I'm setting you up with my cousin Julian. He's a Tinderoni, but he loves Latinas."

"I'm Persian."

"Close enough."

"Nah, you can't date a Tinder dude," said Eric. "Their right swipe finger is on thirst at all times."

Just then, Darcy walked through the door. She slapped down a folder, her phone, and took a seat next to Karen.

"I am the smartest, savviest, most genius media mogul in Manhattan, and each of you bitches will bow down," she announced to the room with a triumphant gleam. "Want to know why? Because I had the foresight to know that our Homecoming Queen and Eric would create magic together." Darcy looked at both of them. "I just had lunch with the editor-in-chief of *New York* magazine. Their Power 25 issue comes out in early Spring, and they're finalizing their list. Not only did we make the top five, but we're also one of the few getting an interview. With a photo shoot. They're calling it 'Fashion Phenomenon: StyleZine Lands The Perfect Find.'"

The room broke out in whooping applause. Jenna and Eric looked at each other, astonished and delighted, while staff members attacked them with hugs.

"It's my interview, but they're also talking to Jenna, and some of our Perfect Find girls. Eric, I'll fight for you to get a quote, but don't get your hopes up. *New York* is only interested in bold-faced names for the piece." Darcy stood up, posted her hands on her hips and surveyed Jenna and Eric.

"I'm consistently blown away by what you've done with this series. You two really tapped into something." She smiled a real smile. "My dream team."

Eric busted into Jenna's office and sat down hard in the chair across from her.

"Did I hallucinate that shit? My mother has complimented me maybe three times in my life. She's such a tricky asshole, though. It's like the witch luring Hansel and Gretel to her house with candy to fatten them up and eat them. We can't eat the candy, Jenna. But...yooo. Did you see that reaction?"

"Yes! *New York* magazine! Can you believe it?" Jenna hopped up and down in her chair, clapping. "You did that, Eric!"

"No, you!"

"Us."

"I wanna kiss you so bad, it's giving me a headache." He shook his head, trying to process what just happened in the meeting. "I was so embarrassed to be working at StyleZine, so scared the festival committees would *guffaw* when they found out. But The Perfect Find? It has integrity. And the fact that it's getting press… I'm like…I can't even…" He stopped. "I'm speechless."

"Which also deserves press," joked Jenna.

"Don't try to play me, Homecoming Queen."

"I need Darcy to stop calling me that."

Eric paused a beat. "You know what I need?"

"What?"

"To see you. Alone. Tonight."

She flinched. "We so cannot go down this road."

"So what do we do?" He looked at her challengingly. "Keep pretending to be BFFs?"

"We are best friends." Jenna was trying to find a way to get out of this conversation, though, more than anything, she wanted to be alone with him, too.

"Okay, friend. You gonna keep fucking with me?"

"What do you mean?"

"You lean over my laptop and let your skirt slide halfway up your ass," he said. "You take those long sips of Evian and then lick the water off your lips and pretend you don't know I'm seeing the whole thing in '80s soft porn slow-mo. You walk by my cubicle, slow, so I get a glimpse of you and smell your perfume and hear your heels clicking on the goddamned floor—driving me crazy when you know I can't do anything about it but sit there and obsess over you."

"I don't do that."

"Yes you do," he said, laughing a little. "That dress you're wearing with the...what do you call the side of your...."

She glanced down at her chest. "Side boob."

"You're gonna tell me you didn't put that on this morning thinking about me?"

It was unnerving, the way he saw right through her. "It's a dress, Eric."

"You get off on it," he said.

It was true. She did.

"What do you want from me?" asked Jenna.

"Just one date. That's all I need."

"To do what, exactly?"

His expression was wicked. "To ruin you forever."

"Little boy, your confidence is staggering."

"Should I shut the door and remind you why?"

"No! And stop smirking. You know we can't go on a date," she whispered, even though no one could hear them. "Where would we even go?"

"Does it matter? I just need to get you alone outside of this building. We could sit in Thompkins Square Park and commune with the rats and methheads."

Jenna shuddered. "Eww. What would I wear?"

"I'm kidding. Okay, let's focus. We can't go to any of your places, because your places are..."

"...probably her places, too."

"Right." He scrolled through his phone. "Hmm, it's Friday night. I know! Home."

"Home? That'll go over well with Darcy."

"No, not my home. *Home*. It's a random dive-bar-slash-sushi-spot on Ludlow. It's dark, anonymous."

Jenna thought about this and then threw up her hands. "Why am I allowing you to lead me down a path of chaos and destruction?"

Eric's expression was victorious. He had her.

"You realize," said Jenna, "that we both know better than this, right?"

"You both know better than what?"

It was Darcy. She'd just appeared at the door.

"Hiyeee!" said Jenna, too brightly. "Nothing important."

"Hi superstars." Darcy nudged the back of son's chair with her knee. "Of course you're in here. Eric, I hope you're thanking Jenna for letting you monopolize her time. Her guidance is making you look like you know what you're doing."

Jenna frowned. "Other way around, actually."

"Oh, he knows I'm kidding."

"This is why I never eat the candy," muttered Eric.

"Eric's the creative vision behind that whole series," Jenna said mildly, conscious of defending him too stridently. "It wouldn't exist without him."

"To be clear, it wouldn't exist without me. I greenlit the series," said Darcy. "Aren't you glad I've been so supportive of your directing career, Eric? I hope you realize what a gem of a mom you have."

"Appreciate the support. Gem."

Too high on success to pick up on the sarcasm, she said to Jenna, "I'm taking you to lunch. Delicatessen. Meet me in my office in fifteen." Halfway out of the door, Darcy called out, "Eric, stop bothering Jenna. Babysitting you is not in her job description."

Eric and Jenna stared at each other for a good five seconds, a thousand words passing silently between them.

Finally, Jenna whispered, "Are we really doing this?"

"You already said yes."

Jenna sighed dramatically. "Okay, I'll be there, though this goes against my better judgment."

Eric's face broke into a satisfied smile. "Then we better make it worth it."

Darcy and Jenna sat across from each other at Delicatessen, a glossy restaurant on Prince Street, at the perennially cool intersection of the Soho and Nolita neighborhoods. Known for it's upscale comfort food and lowkey celeb-watching, the spot was a favorite of Darcy's because she always got the star table, the plush booth in the far left corner.

They were picking at their lunches, having a surface conversation about Calvin Klein being way past his expiration date, but in all actuality, Jenna was bristling with anxiety. She felt like Darcy could read everything on her face, loud and clear. *I want to fuck your son. I want to fuck your son. I want to...*

"So," started Darcy, stabbing her Cobb salad with her fork and changing the course of the conversation, "you and my kid are like frick and fucking frack, aren't you?"

"What do you mean?" Jenna grabbed a slice of raisin bread out of the bread basket and tore at it.

"Every time I turn around, you two are huddled in your office, chattering like seventh grade girls."

"Eric's so good at what he does. I've been in the business as long as you, and yet I'm learning from him. You should be proud."

"I am," Darcy said, taking a sip of her Chardonnay. "I never noticed how talented he is. It's stunning, knowing that I made him."

"I'm sure," said Jenna, wondering where this capital "N" narcissist was going with this landmine of a conversation.

Darcy scrolled through her phone and landed on a pic. She held it up so Jenna could see. It was Eric around seven years old, dressed in a tiny Knicks uniform and holding a basketball that was triple the size of his head. An irresistible, gap-toothed smile was plastered over his face.

How could that innocent, sweet boy turn into the person who lived in her lustiest fantasies? Feeling pedophile-ish, Jenna smiled politely. "Precious."

"It's like he was in second grade five minutes ago. I still see him as a child." She eyed Jenna. "No doubt you do, too."

Jenna nodded rapidly. "I do. Spilling wine on me at that wedding. That's how I see him."

"Right," said Darcy dryly. "You know, Eric was always popular growing up. Apparently he's fun to be around. I get why you enjoy him."

"Well, everyone does." Jenna was sweating.

"His father was fun to be around, too. Talented, but wasted it. I worry that he'll end up like Otis. Sure, Eric had college success, but he's in the real world now. And his life choices are so foreign to me. His film? If I were trying to break into festivals I'd find out who was on the board and suck and fuck until their dicks were too hard not to let me in. I'd have hustled everyone I knew for cash to hire the hungriest publicist. I would've dropped a MAC truck on the competition. All that matters is the end game."

"He's serious about his artistic integrity, Darcy," she said. "I doubt that sucking and fucking are on his agenda."

She chuckled. "Oh, Homecoming Queen. When you grow up with nothing, integrity gets you nowhere. Do you know how gothic my childhood was? When my dad caught me drinking at fourteen, he sent me to this off-the-grid Catholic reform school for a summer. The nuns ran the place like a lesbian S&M porn horror show," she said calmly. "When he found out I was pregnant, they shipped me back, and the nuns tried to beat Eric out of me. And when I managed to run away, I came home to no home. My family was gone, no return address. I had Eric to spite them. My life was fucked, but I grinded to make opportunities for myself. Eric's life is golden, but he behaves like he's starting from nothing. He grew up with the children of movie execs. Why won't he reach out to them? His mother could pay off those board members. I have no patience for his integrity."

"I had no idea your childhood was so tough." Jenna struggled to find an appropriate response. "And I'm sure it must've been really hard for you raising Eric, having to be the mom and the dad."

"I never thought of it like that." Darcy pushed away her plate. "I was the father figure working my ass off to provide. But I didn't have a wife, so Eric raised himself."

"What does that mean?"

"He was so self-reliant. Why pay for nannies when your kid knows how to use your ATM card to catch a cab home from school, order takeout from Serafina's, and then finish his homework and put his own self to bed? It taught him to be resourceful, that no one saves anyone else in this world. You've only got you." She took another sip of wine and raised an arched brow at Jenna, daring her to judge her.

"Oh," said Jenna, quietly horrified.

"You should see your face," Darcy said, chuckling. "You know, powerful men spend fourteen hours a day lying, cheating, stealing, raping, pillaging—doing whatever it takes to win. Ever asked Brian how he got so rich, so fast? I bet he'd have an interesting answer. Men like him are considered heroes. They're applauded for it. No one expects them to join the PTA, or chaperone field trips, or have Snickerdoodles waiting on the table after school. I built my company from the ground up. I sit in rooms with VP's from Yahoo and YouTube—me, the tiniest woman on Earth— and since my cock is bigger than all of theirs, I leave with every dollar in their wallets. Where's my applause? I don't get any. Because I'm a mother, I get you looking at me like I should be burned at the stake."

"I don't think that."

"Sure." Darcy smiled. "You know, I had a mom who knelt on the floor in her room, praying to God, while my dad tried to give me an abortion by pouring mineral oil down my throat. Eric has a mom who broke her back to give him a life full of opportunities. His lips should be glued to my ass, every day."

"I'm sure he appreciates you," said Jenna, carefully.

"No, he idolizes his dead, deadbeat dad. Ain't that some shit." She threw her shoulders back. "I'm only hard on Eric because I want him to be tough. Cutthroat. Like we were, at that age."

Jenna chuckled at the ridiculousness of this. "I was never cutthroat."

"No?" She laughed. "Of course you were. We're black women in fashion. We're work in an industry that either thinks we're invisible, or ghetto savages who don't know the difference between a peplum and a perineum. Where entry-level PR cunts mistake us for dressers backstage at the shows. Where we have to dress better, write better, and schmooze better than Becky just to be taken seriously."

"I didn't get to where I got by being cuthroat," said Jenna. "I worked hard and I was ambitious. But looking back, I can see that I was charmed. A lot of our peers worked hard but weren't as lucky. The career, my personal life. It all seemed…ordained. Like it could never fall apart. What I wouldn't give for the clueless self-confidence I had at twenty-six."

"Is this the clueless self-confidence that empowered you to steal the *Bazaar* job from me?" Darcy asked, with slight amusement.

"They hired me after you got fired for selling borrowed Gucci pieces to Barneys. Everyone knows it."

"Lies. But it didn't matter, because then I was banished from editorial. I had to start my career all over on the business side, selling ads. Wearing Theory slacks and taking corporate meetings with tampon brands."

"Where you made history. The first black publisher of *Seventeen*, and the youngest."

"It's not what I wanted. I wanted to be a creative. Like you." Darcy took a sip of her wine. "Anyway, I got everything I wanted in the end. I always do. And I'm truly pleased with what you've done at StyleZine. Cheers."

"Cheers," said Jenna, clinking her water glass with her Pinot Noir glass.

"Being a mother makes my teeth hurt," said Darcy, apropos of nothing. "Did you ever think about having kids?"

Jenna didn't know if it was the stress of being confronted about Eric, or the idea that for the first time, Darcy seemed like a real person. But in a move she'd regret forever, she let her guard down.

"I did." Under the table, she ran a hand over her tummy, an unconscious move she did often. The skin there was taut: no stretch marks, no post-pregnancy loose skin. How she would've killed for both. "All I ever wanted was for me and Brian to be married, and be parents. I thought he did, too, but things…changed."

"Brian motherfucking Stein," said Darcy, tisking. "I remember when he proposed! He changed his mind? See, this is why a bitch like me keeps a few goons on the payroll. I'd have had him jumped outside one of his high rises."

Jenna smiled, humorlessly. Had she really just spilled one of the most excruciating parts of her past to Darcy Vale? She wielded insider information like a machete. Certain it would come back to bite her, Jenna took a sip of water and searched for ways to change the subject.

As their waitress plunked the check down on the table, Jenna said, "Thank you for lunch, Darcy. It's been illuminating."

"It's not over," said Darcy, pulling her card out of her wallet. "I asked you to lunch for two reasons. First, to give you talking points for my *New York* magazine interview. Stay on message, which is that, under my direct guidance, we're singlehandedly responsible for breathing new life into the street style genre and revolutionizing fashion ecommerce."

Direct guidance? Inside, Jenna was raging. Darcy had nothing to do with their success!

"The other reason?" she asked.

"My son has a crush on you."

"No, Eric's way too professional to…"

"Don't embarrass yourself, sunshine. You know he does," she said, matter-of-factly. "I'm all for you being a mentor, giving him advice. But the ki-ki'ing will stop. He's a distraction, and I need you present. Plus," she said, "you know how guys his age are. The slightest bit of encouragement; they fall in love. Don't give him any hope. Because then he'll have a broken heart, and The Perfect Find will be compromised—and if you thought 1996 was bad between us, 2012 will blow your wig off. We clear?"

Jenna was clear. Darcy noted her closeness to her son, didn't like it—and without even knowing the half of how inappropriate their relationship was, she wanted it to stop.

Jenna looked Darcy in her eyes, thinking, *in seven hours and forty-one minutes I will be exactly where I'm dying to be: velcroed to your kid. No one will deny me this—the least of all you, you mean girl midget. Fuck you if you think I'm staying away from him.*

Jenna favored her boss with her brightest smile. "I hear you, Darcy. Loud and crystal clear."

www.stylezine.com
Just Jenna: Style Secrets from our Intrepid Glambassador!

Q: "I'm going on a first date with this OKCupid dude, and I don't know what to wear. We've been sexting for a month, so I'm almost certain I'm going to sleep with him. What do I wear that communicates that I'm all for the first date lay, but I'm not a slut?—@LadyBlahBlah1985

A: First of all, kudos to you for finding a guy on OKCupid. (I shuffled through my girlfriend's account once, and was traumatized by the pics of shirtless "brand managers" posing in state school baseball caps in front of bad cars). You're right to nix the hooker getup. On a he'll-be-having-me-for-dessert first date, it's more about the scorching hot details that might not be obvious to him. What's happening under your clothes. You could go sophisticated in a wrap dress, or more casual in jeans and a slinky tee—doesn't matter. Because what he'll remember is that you weren't wearing a bra. Or that later, he discovered you had on a garter belt. If he's already well aware he's bone-bound—make him sweat all dinner long, dying to peel your layers.

For naughty date underthings that'll bring him to his knees, head over to Yandy.com!

CHAPTER 18

Jenna walked into Home at exactly 8:03, and realized she'd been there in two of its former incarnations. In the Nineties it was a gay disco called Oliver's, in the 2000s it was a hip-hop lounge called Fluid, and now it was a so-cool-that-only-the-coolest had heard of it underground sushi bar. It was amazing-looking. In fact, Home was *only* look—there weren't enough stools or liquor options for it to be considered a proper bar, and it only sold sushi downstairs (which only had five tabletops). The only lights were raw red light bulbs hanging from the industrial ceiling, and the deejay was spinning early Nineties hip-hop.

Jenna made her way through the space, which was flush with artsy-looking cool kids in all their indie/street finery—and scanned the bar for him. For the first time since she'd returned to New York, she didn't feel too old for the room. All she felt was electric anticipation.

Eric was somewhere in there; somewhere close. She'd already gone through the stages of disbelief that she was actually going through with this and decided, for tonight, to ignore the red flags. Eric was right. The universe had placed them in front of each other for a reason, and it was their job to figure out why. She'd be damned if she'd been through hell to finally find this kindred spirit and then turn her back on him.

Jenna Jones
iMessages
October 2, 2012, 8:06 PM

Eric: Where are you?
Jenna: I'm here! Where are you?
Eric: Here.
Jenna: Where?
Eric: I see you. You're so gorgeous. Turn around.

She did. He was standing behind her, his expression brighter than Christmas morning.

For a second, Jenna felt awkward. She'd been anticipating this moment, and now she didn't know how to greet him. Should she kiss him on the cheek? Shake his hand? Give him a pound? But then something else took over and she did exactly what she *felt*. Jenna flew into his arms so forcefully that they stumbled backwards against the wall. And they stayed there, hugging like they might never see each other again. They were smashed against each other, every part of their bodies crushed together. Eric's face was buried in Jenna's hair, and she was on her tiptoes, her arms wrapped so tightly around his neck she was almost choking him. It was sensory overload.

"You smell so good it's stupid," he groaned.

"You have like zero percent body fat!" She ran her hands up and down his V-shaped back. "Do you work out?"

"No. Yeah? Is basketball working out? Whatever. You're not wearing a bra."

"It didn't go with this shirt."

"How am I supposed to focus if you're not wearing a bra?"

"Do you have a six pack? It feels like you have a six pack!"

"If you think I do, we can run with that."

Eric squeezed Jenna tighter, lifting her off her feet. Had anything ever felt better? She let out a tiny, satisfied sigh.

"Sexiest sound ever," he said, nuzzling her neck.

"Eric," she whispered, lightheaded.

"What?"

"We should probably let go."

"No," he murmured.

"We have to. This a little embarrassing."

"Okay."

They pulled apart, so that they were still holding each other, but not in a death grip.

"We're not," breathed Jenna, "just going to jump in bed."

"Then stop looking at me like that. Or we won't last two minutes in here."

"We went out on a limb to do this, so let's have a proper date."

"Absolutely. Dinner. Conversation." He kissed her nose. "And then bed."

"Seriously! Let's do this right."

He let go of her. "Let me look at you."

Since she was going to the Lower East Side, Jenna decided to channel mid-80's Madonna ("Desperately Seeking Jenna"): stretchy black skirt; short, black off-the-shoulder sweater; and studded booties.

"God, Jenna."

She beamed at him.

"It's almost like now that you're in front of me, I don't know what to do with you."

"I doubt that very seriously," she said. They decided to skip having a drink at the upstairs bar, and go straight downstairs to the restaurant, where it was quieter. Really, they just wanted to sit down and get as close as they could to each other.

Eric grabbed Jenna's hand—it was easy, natural, like they'd done it a million times—and led her down the stairs. On the way down, he gave two girls hugs, said, "Wassup" to their boyfriends, and introduced them all to Jenna. The girls recognized her and were impressed in an aloof, New York-y way.

Downstairs was the same design, but smaller and darker, lit only by the same raw red light bulbs. There were only a handful of tables, all overpopulated—but one was empty. Eric whispered something to the half-naked hostess and then walked Jenna over to their table. They moved their chairs so they were inches apart, and then sat down. Giddy with closeness, Jenna and Eric held hands on top of the table, just because they finally could.

A purple-lipsticked waitress delivered shots to their table. They clinked them together and downed them. And then Jenna signaled her to bring another round.

Eric looked at her with amusement. "Already?"

"I need to be tipsy. I'm a little nervous."

"Why?"

"Because it's me and you. On a date. What do we do now?"

"I get what you're saying. It is mad weird. Nothing happened in order. Like, we met, hooked up, you said I was your boyfriend, then you hated me, then we became friends, and now we're on our first date."

"Precisely!"

Shyly, Jenna looked down at her hand in his. She couldn't believe that she'd fallen this hard for him. They'd only known each other a month, and he was a baby. But when she was in his arms upstairs, she knew she belonged there. And in this corner with him, she felt more herself than she had in ages. Their situation was bonkers, but their thing? It was real.

"Can I ask you something?"

"Anything."

"Were you telling the truth about never having been in love? Just hearty like?"

"That's a trap. No woman ever wants to hear about her man being in love with anyone else."

"Who says you're my man?"

Eric gazed at her for a beat, and then slid his hand behind her neck. He leaned over as if to kiss her, but then pulled her head back, and planted one on the base of her throat. Jenna melted.

"Tell me I'm not," he said, low, into her ear.

"We'll see," she said. With a saucy smile, she pulled his hand off of her hair and, on the way down, let it graze one of her braless nipples. She dropped his hand on the table.

"You're killing me," said Eric.

"Back to my question," she said. "Have you ever been in love?"

"I never said it out loud, but a couple of times I thought I was. But now I know I wasn't."

"Slick."

"Not slick. Real," he said. "I answered you with complete honesty! Respect my vulnerability."

She smiled. "I respect it. I'm just not used to a man saying exactly how he feels."

"I don't know how else to be," he said, and Jenna believed him.

"Hey," she said. "This might be weird, but I brought you something. It's really small and I know your birthday isn't for another month, but…"

"You brought me a first date gift? I didn't know we were doing this!"

"No, I was unpacking boxes and found something I knew you'd like. Something old."

She handed him a gift bag, and he looked inside.

"Jenna," he whispered, his mouth dropping open. At the bottom of the bag, he saw a boxy, obviously decades-old Polaroid.

"It's a Polaroid 'Impulse,'" said Jenna. "From 1989. The film isn't made anymore, but there's some left in the camera."

"I knew it was an Impulse! I'm a camera tech geek! Yo, I think this is the best day of my life." He looked up at the ceiling. "Jesus, who is this woman?"

"Oh, just some girl who has a PhD in you."

He dragged her chair even closer and kissed her cheek. "Three things. First, no one's ever given me such a thoughtful gift. Second, I can't believe you remembered my birthday. And third?" He stopped and laughed.

"What's so funny?"

"You want me so badly."

"You know, you're really not as cute as you think you are."

"No, seriously. You know I'm a sure thing, right?" He pointed to himself, loving making fun of her. "You didn't have to pull out all the stops."

"Believe me, I know," She leaned in to him, whispering in his ear. "You should see the way you visually molest me in the office."

"You're too much for me sometimes. That thing with your shoe? The walk back to my cubicle was…humbling. I felt like a seventh grader called to the chalkboard with a hard-on."

Jenna laughed.

"I don't even know how to thank you for my gift. I'll think of some memorable ways later."

She looked up at him through her lashes. "Swear?"

He nodded, suddenly dead serious. His gaze was predatory, like he was barely refraining from ripping off her clothes and fucking her to oblivion, right there.

"Yes, ma'am."

Jenna's stomach fluttered. "If I'd never taken this job, I'd have lived my whole life without ever being looked at like that."

"If you'd never taken this job, I would've found you anyway. Somehow." He reached out and twirled one of her ringlets around his finger. He'd been dying to touch her hair.

Their drinks came, along with crackers and a dinner menu. Famished, they demolished the crackers, but ignored the menu.

"My turn to ask a question," said Eric. "Your fiancé. What happened?"

Jenna took a sip of her drink. She knew this moment would come. "We were college sweethearts. We were happy, for a long time. He made an obscene amount of money, and one day that's all that mattered to him. I stopped being sexy to him, or interesting. The only thing we had in common was our past."

"Is he still in your life?" he asked in a quiet, controlled voice. "Do you ever talk to him?"

"No, that chapter is over."

Eric was silent. His expression was stony. And then he said, "I want him dead."

"Wait, what?"

"How was he not dazzled by you? Jenna, please don't ever let me find out who he is. Because me and him will have problems of epic proportions."

"Eric…"

"He didn't think you were sexy? He didn't touch you? I've known you for four weeks and not touching you is unraveling me. Nothing you said interested him? The highlight of my day is listening to you deconstruct the Walter White/Tony Soprano anti-hero archetype while you demolish a croissant. This man had everything I want, what I'd kill for, and didn't care. Not having you will be the death of me, Jenna. So that guy? Him, I'll never understand."

Jenna's eyes widened in an attempt to keep the tears from erupting, but to no avail.

"Oh no," started Eric. "I didn't mean to…I didn't want…"

"Shut up," she said, draping a leg around his under the table.

She grabbed the front of his shirt and pulled him closer. Eric slid one hand up her thigh and under her skirt, while the other one gently wiped the tears from her cheeks. She was dizzy with passion. God help her, she was about to climb on top of him right there at a Lower East Side sushi bar...

"Jenna Jones! I've been trying to get my agent on the phone with you for weeks! I'm perfect for The Perfect Find!"

They whipped their heads around. It was Suki Delgado, the Bronx-born Dominican model. She was currently starring in a Lancome ad and had made the July 2012 cover of British *Marie Claire*. A toffee-skinned stunner, she had almond-shaped eyes and jet-black waves that came to a halt at her heartbreaking little chin.

For drastically different reasons, Eric and Jenna abruptly let go of each other.

"E? You shady motherfucker! Get up and hug me," she demanded. She was clearly bombed. "You haven't returned my Perfect Find calls, either! Why didn't you hit me back? Am I that *never ago* to you?"

"Delgado!" he said, giving her a perfunctory hug. "Doing the 'you look beautiful' thing with you was always redundant."

"Do it anyway!" she shrieked, giggling. She flung a graceful arm around his shoulders, and Eric managed to remove it without seeming rude.

"Jenna, this is Suki Delgado. We went to Art & Design together. She was a dope illustrator, but now she's..."

"A top model," said Jenna, her arms folded across her chest. She was living on the corner of Annoyed Avenue and Panicked Place. "I know, because I discovered her."

"She totally did!" squealed Suki, grabbing Jenna and pulling her out of her seat into a squeezy-tight embrace. "E baby, this woman found me when I was an intern with *Darling's* art department. She booked my first editorial. I lit-trally owe my career to Jenna."

"Oh, that's not true. Girls like you come along, like, never."

This was problematic. All the major players in the fashion industry knew Suki. They were two tweets away from someone at StyleZine finding out that she and Eric were out together. But Jenna was tipsy enough to push this fearsome reality away long enough to find out exactly how close Suki and Eric had been in high school.

"So were you two in the same class?"

"No, but I took him to my Senior Prom! He was only a tenth grader, isn't that hilarious? He always loved older women."

"Adorable."

"Delgado, what are you doing here? You're too famous for this shit. Who're you here with?" Not only was Eric annoyed that his old girlfriend showed up, it had just occurred to him that she could get them into trouble.

"TJ and Jules and Eva," she said, pointing to her table. They all waved at Eric. "I go with TJ now. He's broke, but his dick is big and his dad has that Plaza penthouse and two Oscars, so he might be able to get me into this Tarantino slave movie? What are you two doing out?"

"Working," Jenna blurted out. She looked at Eric and, wordlessly, they decided it was time to go.

"Here? On a Friday night? Wait," exclaimed Suki, the reality of what she was seeing hit her. "Omigod. You two? Seriously? The. Sexiest. Shit. Ever."

This was bad.

"Not sexy. All work. Gotta go." Eric slapped down a fifty and grabbed Jenna's hand.

"This was official StyleZine business," called Jenna, over her shoulder.

"Yeah right," she hollered, as they disappeared up the stairs. "You both reek of pre-bone!"

Outside, they walked down an empty side street hand in hand, lost in thought.

"I know Delgado's a famous model now, but is she that famous?"

"Yep, she is."

"So, StyleZine people know who she is."

"People on Neptune know who she is." They walked half a block. "I know what you're asking honey, and yes. Darcy knows Suki. This could be disastrous."

"Fuck."

"You slept with Suki Delgado when you were in tenth grade?" There was nothing they could do about the supermodel catching them, so Jenna might as well address the second most pressing aspect of that run-in.

"Wellll, when you say 'slept with'...."

"Why am I jealous? It's so petty and weird."

"No, it's cute," said Eric. "Just so you know, the sex wasn't great."

"Come on. You were barely pubescent and she was a nine-foot tall goddess."

"Not then." He paused. "Braces." He paused again. "She was always a maniac, though. She told me to slap her, hard."

"She was like that, even then? I caught her having violent sex with one of our male models on a shoot in Anguila! We had to cover her bruises with Dermablend."

"Yeah, that's Delgado."

"Did you slap her?"

"With all the strength I could muster in my fifteen-year old body." He laughed. "It was insane, but I liked it. I love being with women who surprise me."

"Do I surprise you?"

"Every five minutes."

Jenna stopped, turning to face Eric. She was dying to kiss him, but something held her back. She adored Eric's bravado, his cockiness, but those were also the things she wanted to break down a little. For years, she felt so voiceless in sex, the little woman waiting to be pillaged. She knew how badly he wanted her. Good. This time, she was in charge. She'd revel in this part.

"What would you do to me right now if you could?"

Without hesitation, Eric said, "Make you beg for it."

"Why?"

"You deserve it. You make me feel nuts."

She cocked her head, and then walked backwards until she was up against a flyer-littered brick wall between a closed bodega and an abandoned Laundromat.

"Wanna know what's nuts? How wet I've been all night." Jenna slid her hand up her thigh, over her hip, and under the waistband of her stretchy skirt. She plunged it into her thong.

Eric's mouth opened. In an almost comical gesture, he whipped his head back and forth, looking both ways to make sure no one was coming. It was an empty side street and they were alone.

Leaning against the wall, Jenna plunged her hand deeper inside her panties. Her eyes glazed as she stroked herself. Watching Eric watch her was so erotic—he was mesmerized, rooted to his spot.

But when she started to moan, he snapped out of it and was on her in a flash. He yanked her hand out of her skirt, sucking the wetness off her finger.

"See what you do to me?"

"Yeah, nuts," said Eric. He grabbed her face and gave her the sexiest kiss she'd ever had. It was brain-scrambling, thigh-melting. It grew deeper and hungrier and more chaotic—he sucked her mouth, she bit his bottom lip—until it wasn't enough. Boldly, Eric slipped his hand down between them and into her panties. He gave her a little squeeze and she went weak, her head falling back as his mouth burned hotly on her throat. She was lost in shameless, public ecstasy on the corner of Freeman Alley and Christie. Leaving a trail of delicious kisses along her neck, he cupped her breast and ran his thumb across her nipple. And the assault of sensations was so exquisite that Jenna whimper-whispered his name.

That was too much for Eric. Lightly, he gripped her jaw and held her face still, pausing to relish the fact that he had her like this again. She was trembling for him, hot for him, wet for him. But this time, it meant something.

He kissed her breathless again, until she was reeling. She had to pull herself together. This was too good for her to swoon through—she needed her bearings.

Jenna planted her palms on his chest, pushing him away. It took every ounce of willpower she had to do this. "No," she said, breathing hard.

"Like…literally? Or on some 'no means yes' shit?"

She laughed. "You can't kiss me again until I say."

"Jenna Jones," he said, his voice hoarse. "Are you bipolar?"

"Maybe. But I'm going home. I'm getting in a cab. If you don't mind my mental illness, come over."

Jenna blew him a kiss and left him standing there, caught in the crossfire of a thousand conflicting emotions.

Twenty minutes later, Jenna buzzed Eric up to her apartment. Two seconds later, he was pounding on her door with what sounded like a two-by-four.

"JENNA, OPEN THE DOOR!"

The door was already open, but she'd let him find this out on his own.

"JENNA!"

Then silence. Then the door crashed open and Eric stormed into Jenna's apartment. It was pitch-black. So now, not only was he pissed, he was pissed and disoriented.

"Jenna! Where are…"

Then he felt her behind him. Actually, he smelled her, first—the same irresistible summertime honey-vanilla scent that dismantled him at the office. And then he felt the filmy lace of her bra through the back of his shirt. (When did she put a bra on? he wondered, wildly.)

Without saying a word, she slipped her hands under his shirt, running them up the sinewy muscles of his stomach and chest. He held his breath. Her mouth was on the back of his neck. Then, her hands changed course and plunged downward, stroking his hard-on through his jeans.

"Don't move," she whispered.

Jenna slid in front of him. His eyes adjusted a bit to the darkness, and sort of saw that she was wearing a lace push-up bra and a thong—both so delicate they looked like they'd dissolve at his touch. Her curls were wild. She looked like a bitch goddess from his lustiest fantasies.

Jenna ripped off his shirt, unbuckled his jeans, and got rid of his shoes in one fell swoop. Then she sank to her knees in front of him. Without any hesitation, she took him into her mouth, deep-throating with relish. He let out a shaky, "Fuuuuuck" and plunged his hands into her hair. On and on she licked and sucked, until he couldn't stand it anymore. He pulled her to her feet and tossed her over his shoulder, caveman-style—and with some confused banging, he found her bedroom in the dark.

Eric threw her down on the bed, and all hell broke loose. He unhooked her bra and then ripped the flimsy material of her thong at the top of both thighs, tearing it off of her body. This was exactly what Jenna wanted. Insane, desperate desire. He licked and sucked her nipples, kneading her breasts with one hand, while the other stroked her clit firmly and slowly. Someone taught him this. She loved and hated whoever it was.

"Just d-don't kiss me yet," she moaned, not ready to give in. "Not till I say."

"What are you trying to do to me?" he growled, his mouth full of breast.

"Tell me what you want," she panted, back arched. He had two fingers deep inside her, and she was trying not to come. "I wanna hear it…"

"I want everything," he murmured into her ear. "I wanna suck you, fuck you till you scream, own you…"

It was time.

Weak with outrageous lust, it took all of Jenna's strength to roll on top of Eric. She knew the element of surprise was key, she had to do this quickly or he'd be inside of her and it would all be over. So Jenna grabbed her scarf from under her pillow and tied his wrists to the bedposts. Obviously, like every girl of her generation, she'd learned this from *Basic Instinct.*

"You are not serious!" Eric's eyes were wide with disbelief. Jenna straddled him. He chewed the inside of his mouth, barely containing himself.

"J-Jenna," he started, trying to remain calm. He was six-foot-two. A 120-pound woman had just tied him to her bed. What had become of him? "You gotta let me go. This is cruel and unusual… please…"

"Say it again."

"Which part?"

"Please."

"No."

She shrugged. "You wanted me to beg. Why can't you beg?"

Eric shook his head.

She put the tip of him inside her and with deliberate, sadistic slowness, lowered herself down. And then she lifted herself back up and down again, rocking her hips sinuously, slowly. But she could feel her orgasm approaching…so she stopped, climbing off of him. She took his cock in her hand, pumped it, and then rubbed herself up and down the length of it, covering it in her wetness.

Eric groaned in pleasure, in protest. He was fully tortured. Helpless.

Jenna crawled up the length of him, planting wet kisses along the planes of his stomach, chest, neck. Generously, she rubbed her nipple against his mouth. He sucked hungrily, out of his mind. Her scent, that maddening scent, enveloped him. Smelling her, tasting her—but not being able to touch her, be inside her—sent him careening close to the edge.

I swear to God if I bust before I'm even properly inside this woman I will kill myself, he thought. *I will set myself on fire. I will move to Hoboken. Please God not before I'm even inside her, please God...*

He couldn't take it anymore.

"Please, Jenna," he said. "You win. I don't care about anything. I just want you. Please."

Jenna laid on top of him so their bodies were aligned. They were face to face. This was what she wanted. No pride, no ego—only the purity of desire. He was so beautiful like this, so vulnerable, all hers...

Eric saw her soften.

"Please baby," he whispered, knowing he could kiss her now. He caught her bottom lip with his teeth and drew her mouth to his. The kiss slowed them down, almost paralyzing them with its intensity. It was romantic. He held her captive with it, as if she were the one tied up. And just like that, the power shifted.

"Untie me," Eric ordered, his voice sounding unsteadier than he wanted.

She did, with clumsy fingers. In a swoony daze.

Before Jenna could think, Eric flipped her on her back, hooked his arms behind her knees and slammed into her, to the hilt. The headboard crashed against the wall. She squeezed her eyes shut and cried out with shock and excruciating pleasure. It raged through her in waves.

"Open your eyes," he said.

She did, and he thrust into her again, hard. While deep inside her, he grabbed her wrists and held them above her head.

"Mine," he said, in her ear.

It wasn't a question—far from it—but she answered with cheerleader-level enthusiasm anyway. "Yes, yours," she gasped. "Yours, yours…"

With an anguished groan, he pulled almost all the way out and then drove back into her, grinding against her, sending shock waves radiating through her body. He buried his face in her hair, inhaling her, fucking her hard and steady—almost artlessly, but not quite (he was on the edge of losing control but fought the urge to rail into her, wanting her to feel every stroke). And then Jenna came so ferociously that it stunned her into silence. It was blinding, obliterating. She went still, barely breathing, just letting the orgasm riot through her. It went on and on and just when she thought she couldn't bear any more, Eric plunged into her the final time, crashing her into the pillows—and as he exploded she came again, this time with a ravaged cry.

He collapsed on top of her, his face pillowed in the hollow of her shoulder. They were sweaty, hearts pounding, shaking. Neither expected to be so shattered. They knew it would be good, but not like that.

"Jenna." His voice was muffled, weak.

"Hmm?"

"You're sick. I had no idea."

"Neither did I," she said with a quivery laugh.

"Hashtag fetal position."

They held each other for a moment, trying to recover.

"I like you," said Jenna.

She felt Eric smile against her neck. "Yeah?"

"Yeah. Really, really intensely."

"Well, I love you really intensely. It's the only reason I allowed that bondage shit."

He rolled over on his back and brought her with him. She burrowed into his chest, he kissed the top of her head, and they clung to each other till morning. Give or take a dozen inspired positions, they didn't move for two days.

Jenna thought that if she ever slept with Eric, it would kill the excitement, dissipate the tension. But the opposite happened. It was an ending, but also a door opening. And the two of them plummeted through it, the weight of their obsession propelling them down, down, down.

CHAPTER 19

On Monday morning, Jenna strode into her office exactly on time, greeting everyone she saw with a delighted, "Hiyeeeee!" She all but skipped into her office and sat behind her desk with purpose. She flipped open her laptop, stared into the screen with concentration, and began typing. If anyone of her coworkers saw her, they'd think she was in the middle of writing one of her Just Jenna columns.

In actuality, she was gazing dreamily into a totally blank screen, typing what amounted to: "SKSL;ALKDJA;OEIJTOEPGIJPOG-JOPINGONGNOG." She had one thought on her mind, and it had nothing to do with StyleZine.

She'd slept a total of six hours since Friday, was bruised everywhere, but she'd never felt more vital. Jenna caught a glimpse of the deliriously happy woman in the blank laptop screen and was dumbfounded. Somehow, she'd found a best friend, a lover, and a soulmate—all in the same unlikely person. Eric stilled and stirred her. And they'd spent the entire weekend proving what they'd previously suspected; which was that they were made for each other.

She couldn't remember the last time she'd had so much pure, concentrated fun.

All they did was have sex and laugh, and take baths, and then get really deep (they traded secrets, fantasies, nightmares, hopes for the future), and then have sex and laugh again. Then they'd order takeout and barely eat it because having sex and laughing was more urgent. Since it was Eric and Jenna, most of this happened with Turner Movie Classics on in the background.

It was like she'd left her personality in a cab somewhere years ago, and he'd found it, dusted it off, and delivered it to her doorstep wrapped in a red velvet bow. She felt alive, understood,—and drop-dead sexy.

Jenna didn't know friendship and lust could collide so violently. The orgasms! She'd had amazing ones with Brian, but they were self-conscious. At twenty, thirty, she was too aware of what she was doing. The positions, the hair choreography, her sounds, the aesthetics of her body. She'd curve the small of her back to make her ass look lusher, or poke out her chest. When she laid on her side, she'd always thrust her top hip upwards to create the illusion of Vargas Girl bodaciousness. Her goal was to be his fantasy. But at forty, she lost herself, with no regard for what she looked or sounded like. She just felt. Hard.

Jenna took a sip of her coffee and then paused, a euphoric smile creeping across her face. She heard Eric outside her office.

"I know, but wait… I have to talk about a reshoot with Jenna really quick. Five minutes."

They didn't have to reshoot anything!

Eric burst into her office with his camera.

"I feel like I haven't seen you in ages," she breathed.

He peered out into the hallway. Then he looked at Jenna, put his finger to his mouth, and shut the door.

Eric came around her desk, gripped her by the tops of her arms, pulled her out of her chair and kissed her. For .2 seconds she was too stunned to kiss him back, but then she melted into him. She flung her arms around his neck, and despite it being nine a.m. in Jenna's office, they were making out like it was three a.m. in Jenna's shower. They backed up against her desk, and then, never breaking their kiss, clumsily toppled onto it together, Jenna on top of Eric. Magazines slid to the floor, her framed picture of Diana Vreeland went flying.

They paused to breathe. Eric smoothed Jenna's curls back, holding her face above his.

"Good morning again."

"Good morning, Erique."

Just then, they heard a hard knock on her door and bolted upright. Scrambling off of each other, they jumped into the appropriate chairs.

"We'll be right out," called Jenna. "Umm…just reviewing a clip!"

"My bad," called Jinx. "I'll stop by later."

Behind her desk, Jenna held her hand over her heart and closed her eyes. "That almost gave me a stroke," she said. She whipped out a compact and peered into it, fixing her kiss-smeared lipstick. "Eric, I'm nervous. Do you think they'll notice something's different about us? Do I look normal?"

"You look well-fucked." Eric allowed himself a lazy grin. He leaned back in his chair. The truth was, everything about her looked different. At least, to him.

"What are you staring at? Not another hickey? Hold on, I have concealer somewhere."

"No, it's not that. Jenna, I…I don't know how to do this. How do I go out there and pretend that I don't worship you?"

She beamed. "You worship me?"

Eric nodded. "A lot."

"I know the feeling," she said. "You're my new religion."

"Amen." He leaned over the desk, kissed her, and said, "Open the door so we don't look guilty."

She launched out of her seat, flung the door open, and looked out into the hallway. Inside her office, Jenna and Eric were in the throes of afterglow—but out there, it was business as usual. Girls were hanging out by Jinx's cubicle, listening to her discuss in near-weepy detail her Friday night run-in with her ex. Darcy was storming down the hallway on her cell, mid-rant, and gave Jenna a head nod. Jenna waved, feeling totally naked.

Darcy had warned her to stop being so chummy with her son, and she'd just had nonstop sex with him for two days. Eric needed to get out of her office. But…maybe he could stay for five more minutes. How would she know they that weren't having a professional conversation? *And what can she do about it anyway*, thought Jenna. *Fire me? I'm bringing her too much traffic with The Perfect Find. If I want to be office besties with Eric, Darcy can pout about it, but what could she really do?*

Jenna was playing with fire. And it was so exhilarating.

"Just stay for two more seconds and then walk out nonchalantly," she whispered, tip toeing to her desk.

"Two seconds," agreed Eric. "You know, I had an epiphany this weekend. Well, I had a lot of epiphanies, but one of the main ones? I'm addicted to watching you come."

"You're what? Oh my God." She covered her face with her hands.

"No, it's incredible. You know how old people in Brooklyn pull out plastic chairs in front of their buildings at night, to watch the sunset? I could literally pull out a plastic chair to watch you have an orgasm. Like go get popcorn and sit back and enjoy the majesty of it. You turn like thirteen different shades of pink and tremble like, I don't know, a little bunny. And then you look at me like I'm Superman."

Both embarrassed and flattered, Jenna dropped her head onto the desk and tried to muffle her giggles. When they'd subsided, she looked up and said, "Eric Combs, you're insane. And very sweet. And now I'll be self-conscious forever." She shook her head. "I had an epiphany, too. I always assumed that the older woman/ younger man sex dynamic would be an inexperienced guy with the woman as teacher. Like a 'yes mommy' kind of thing."

"I do have scarf burns on my wrists."

"I'm a little embarrassed by that, in the light of day."

"*You're* embarrassed?"

"Anyway," continued Jenna, "that's not how we are. You're only twenty-two; why can you locate a G-Spot when men twice your age can't find it?"

"Umm, I think that was a happy accident," he said, with barely-disguised pride.

"At your age I had no idea what I was doing." She put her chin in her hand. "When did you lose your virginity?"

"This is an awkward line of questioning." He grimaced. "I was too young. My thirteenth birthday. But it was all Tim's fault."

"Thirteen! I was nineteen!" Jenna was floored. "Wow, when you were thirteen, I was twenty-nine. Older than you are now."

"When you were nineteen, I was three. What if in college, a psychic had told you that your…wait, what am I?"

"My kindred spirit?"

"What if a psychic told you that your kindred spirit was a toddler enrolled in Sunny Sunflower's? You just had to wait for him to grow up?"

"I would've dated shallowly for a couple decades, and then found you the second you turned eighteen. Wearing a microscopic, short Burberry trench and La Perla lingerie underneath."

"That's so you. Also, I hadn't even heard of a G-spot at eighteen, so you would've gotten your cougar fantasy."

"What if we were the same age?" wondered Jenna. "What if we'd gone to high school together?"

Eric exhaled. "You and me in high school? I can't imagine feeling like this, then. It would've saved me years of runner-ups. You never would've met *him*." He half-smiled. "To get to love you through your twenties, your thirties, through everything? I'm sad I didn't get to do that."

"Don't be sad." Jenna rubbed her foot against his leg, under her table. "If we'd met when I was younger, it wouldn't have happened this way. I hid myself."

"I would've seen you."

"I wouldn't have let you."

"You wouldn't have had a choice." Eric's eyes blazed. "I could be fifty, you could be thirty. We could both be eighteen. Our ages don't matter. I can think of ten strong reasons why a woman like you should be outside of my reach, and yet…"

"And yet here I am."

"When we met didn't matter. We're inevitable."

They sat, the space between them in the tiny office charged—that word, "inevitable," hanging in the air.

This is how Terry found them seconds later, when she knocked on the open door and barged into Jenna's office.

"Oh hey, E. Jenna, I'm writing about swimsuits, and I can't figure out how to speak to thong cut bottoms without sexualizing…" She stopped, looking from Jenna to Eric. "You two look weird."

Jenna flinched. "Weird?"

"We look weird? You're wearing neon suspenders."

"No, you look wired or something. Like you've been doing blow." She lowered her voice. "You have some?"

"Should you really be talking about coke with Darcy's office right across the hall?"

Eric snorted. "Seriously? Her dealer lived in one of our upstairs bedrooms for nine months when I was twelve."

Jenna and Terry gasped.

"Her what? I knew she was a cokehead. No one's that intense at 9am, and she never eats! Tell us more! What are her Netflix favorites? Does she…"

"Terry," interrupted Jenna, "let me wrap up this meeting, and then I'll help you with your copy."

"Cool." She headed out the door, but not before saying, "You guys really look weird. Like you were out all night and just rolled into the office. Was there a party I missed?"

"If this woman ever let me go anywhere with her, you'd definitely hear about it."

"I'll stop by in a sec, Terry."

The blonde blew them both a kiss and disappeared. Jenna and Eric both slumped down in their chairs.

"Did I really say that thing about the dealer? I just broke like fifteen personal office codes of conduct," he said. "I should go now, right?"

"Probably," Jenna whispered. "But speaking of codes of conduct, let's make some rules about how this is going to go." She leaned forward, clasping her hands together, trying to look official. "Because everything's changed, and we can't afford to get messy."

"Right, the way we act in here is make-or-break."

"Rule one. If you aren't holding your camera, if it isn't obvious we're working, we'll limit our conversations to no longer than five minutes."

"Five? Word?" He groaned. "Okay, five."

"If we really need to talk, we'll sneak outside of the office. Separately. Or…I know! Our fashion closet is getting full, so the janitor gave me keys to an empty closet on the 10th floor. I've been keeping pieces in there. Maybe we can meet up there sometimes."

"Make me a key!"

"No way."

"Come on. It's so sneaky. You know you want to."

"Fiiiiine."

"God, you're easy. I have a rule. If everyone wants to think I have a crush on you, let them. Just reinforce that I'm like a little brother to you."

"Okay, brotha," said Jenna. "Also, we should never, ever have sex in the office. Too risky."

"That rule's dumb. Isn't office sex one of the perks of sleeping with your coworker? Don't you watch network TV?"

"We can't," said Jenna. "Too risky."

"Fine. What else?"

"That's it. We'll just become brilliant actors and pretend that we're not…whatever we are. Agreed?"

They shook on it. When he was halfway out of the door, Jenna stopped him and he turned to face her.

"Are we crazy? Are we really going to try to pull this off?"

"Could you stop now?" he asked. "Even if you wanted to?"

"Not a chance. You?"

"Never."

It was just the cosign that she needed. Eric had become necessary to her. Her post-Brian brain was telling her to run from feeling this attached to someone, but it was too late. And the sneaking around, the hiding—it might not have been ideal, or respectable, or smart, but it was thrilling.

And she would take him however she could get him.

CHAPTER 20

"And up next," shouted an Australian-accented woman over the loudspeaker, "Miss Koko's four-year-olds in a jazz hip-hop number to 'Moves Like Jagger!'"

The Brooklyn Academy of Music auditorium exploded in applause. It was a blustery Sunday morning in December, and Jenna and Billie were forty minutes into the Maddie's Movers Dance Academy's holiday recital—a show that ranged from preschool age to high school seniors. They were nowhere near May's five-year-old class. The first ten minutes were adorable, but after the endless parade of migraine-inducing neon costumes, onstage meltdowns, and antsy siblings staging a revolution in the aisles, the parents were ready to take a loss on the tuition fees and mainline margaritas at Café Habana up the block.

Even Billie was fighting back yawns. For Jenna, though, the entire spectacle was wannabe-mommy heaven. She was the most enthusiastic audience member, whooping after each number and even playing hand-clapping games with the toddler sitting next to her.

She'd shown up wearing a tee shirt emblazoned with May's be-dimpled face. Above the pic, in hot pink Helvetica, screamed the words "DANCE FOR YOUR LIFE, BABY GIRL!" Jenna had ones made for Billie and Elodie, too. Billie was wearing hers, but Elodie was late, as usual.

"That child makes my uterus ache," said Jenna, pointing onstage to a tiny, light brown girl with curls, doused in a pint of glitter.

"A total doll," said Billie, eyes locked on her phone. She was live-texting the recital with Jay, who was in Philly, teaching a weekend poetry seminar.

Jenna looked around. "I feel like every child here looks just like her, though. Ethnically ambiguous."

"That's because Brooklyn is the interracial couple capital of the world. Jay and I are one of the only fully black families at May's school. At her last birthday party, she had nine kids there, and they were biracial in every combination. Vietnamese-Mexican. Ecuadorian-Indian. Mongolian-Black."

"Not Mongolian-Black."

"Swear. And they actually had the nerve to name their son Genghis-Jermaine."

The "Moves Like Jagger" routine finally drew to a close, and the crowd clapped. Jenna let out an enthusiastic, "Woo-hooo!"

"Time for a brief intermission," screamed the Australian voice.

"Hurry back, because up next, we have Miss Lauren's fabulous five year olds in a Riverdance routine to "We Found Love!"

Just then, Elodie stormed down the left side of the auditorium, wearing a massive faux fur coat, blackout sunglasses, and a Celine bag the size of Rhode Island. Her signature long, ropy braid was twirled into a side bun. She squeezed down Jenna's row and plopped down in the seat next to Billie.

"I'm sorry I'm late," she announced. "I can't accept how freezing it is out there. Like, to whom do I register my displeasure?"

"You okay?" asked Jenna.

"No. I'm hungover, sleep-deprived, and I've plateaued after two weeks on my diet. I have no patience for anything that isn't a bagel."

Billie gestured at Elodie's ensemble. "This is a dance recital, what the hell are you wearing?"

"Diahann Carroll Officiates A Gay Wedding in Aspen," cracked Jenna.

"I haven't been home since my charity event on Friday. I slept with that Morehouse dentist."

"The one you said looked like a flying monkey?" asked Billie.

"Everyone wants to find their Jay Z, but no one's willing to date ugly dudes." She shimmied out of her fur. "I stayed with him in his suite at the Soho House. And he made love to me, which was weird. I don't want soft, meaningful sex with a stranger. Throw me around the room. If there are no rug burns, it didn't happen."

"The title of your autobiography," quipped Billie.

"Put this on." Jenna handed Elodie her May tee shirt.

"I adore May, but Jenna, your Virginia is showing." She slid her sunglasses atop of her head. "So, you've pulled quite the disappearing act over the past couple months. Are you ready to discuss the fact that you're in love with the devil's spawn?"

"Who said anything about love?" Jenna could barely get the sentence out without smiling. "Fine, I'm so in love with him, I can't even think straight."

"Obviously," said Billie. "You have a lit-from-within glow that's usually only achieved with YSL Touche Eclat complexion highlighter."

"You're telling me that this kid is the Teacake to your Janie? The Taye Diggs to your Stella?" Elodie wrinkled her nose. "Come on."

"You've dated younger guys!"

"Correction. I've slept with younger guys. I never said I didn't enjoy the eighteen to twenty-five demo. They're so eager and they still kiss."

"Why do grown men stop kissing?" asked Billie. "It's like, at thirty-two they just decide it's beside the point."

"Anyway, I can do it because I know how to bone and bounce. Do you want a relationship with someone you're so emotionally and financially beyond? He'll feel like your intern."

"You can't help who you fall in love with," said Billie.

"Okay, how about the fact that she works with this kid?"

Jenna groaned. "I know how scandalous it is. It keeps me up at night."

"If you get caught, it'd be so embarrassing. You're a respected, esteemed editor. You've just rebuilt your career. You can't throw everything away for this boy, just 'cause he fucks you silly and looks like Michael B. Jordan. And even if he wasn't on staff with you, he's Darcy Vale's child."

"Darcy is Satan." Billie was glad that Jenna had found love, but worried over who she'd found it with.

"If she finds out you're boning her baby boy with reckless abandon, you'll be finished in New York," said Elodie.

"When you were up for that job at *Harper's Bazaar*," said Billie, "didn't she have someone call the editor-in-chief and tell her you were a kleptomaniac?"

"To this day, Glenda Bailey holds onto her purse whenever I'm in the vicinity." Jenna sighed.

"Back in your seats," wailed the Australian voice. "Get ready for Miss Eladia's five-year-old class performing a Masai dance to 'Titanium.'"

"Shoot me," grumbled Elodie, slipping her sunglasses back over her eyes. "Jenna, while you're doing this Eric thing, why don't I find you some age-appropriate men from my OKCupid account? Adults you might have a future with?"

Jenna understood her friends' concern, but this was annoying. "I'm not using Eric for great sex while I husband-hunt! You think I'd risk everything for an affair? Why is it so hard to believe that I'm in a real relationship with someone eighteen years younger? Men do this constantly."

"Such a double standard," Billie pointed out.

"We live in a patriarchal society," answered Elodie, shrugging. "When a man's with a younger girl, the power balance works. It seems more natural, because culturally, men are supposed to dominate. Hard to pull off that 'it's so big, Daddy' dynamic when your boyfriend's half your age."

Jenna snorted. "Beg to differ with you, sis."

"Billie, did I mention that they barely leave the house, because she can't risk running into anyone who knows Darcy?"

"It's true," admitted Jenna. "My apartment is like our love bubble."

"I just worry," said Billie, "You deserve to be in a normal, non-bizarro world relationship."

"I know," said Jenna. "But being with him is…feel-good overload. I can take every maddening minute of the workweek, not getting a seat on the train, being broke, even the impossibility of our situation—because I know I get Eric at the end of the day. Guys, when he comes over, I barely let him leave the room without me. I cling to him like a pygmy marmoset."

"That's healthy," muttered Elodie.

"I don't know how he does it, because he is so young, but he loves me so perfectly. Like he was born with the Jenna handbook. And I…I can't get enough."

Billie was clutching her heart, moved by Jenna's words. "Then nothing else matters. Figure out the Darcy thing and fight for him. But sweetie," she said, reaching for Jenna's hand, "we're dancing around the obvious. You're ready to settle down. You're looking at the children in here with kidnappy desperation. Promise me you'll talk to Eric about this."

"I really don't think…"

"Who knows, maybe he's mature enough be a young husband and dad! Don't dismiss the idea before you have a heart-to-heart with him."

Jenna knew better than to kill her exciting new relationship with a recent college grad by musing on her biological clock. But Billie's speech had invigorated her. When Billie, Jay and May were together, they looked like belonged to some fabulous little country with their own language and currency. It was the purest thing Jenna had ever seen. If the love was there, why couldn't she have that with Eric?

"I forgot to tell you!" exclaimed Billie. "One of Jay's colleague's at Fordham, James Diaz, is looking for someone to teach a new Fashion

Theory class. You're always talking about how you miss teaching. And this would get you out of StyleZine and you and Eric would be liberated. Well, he'd still be thirteen, but at least you'd be out of the closet."

"Really?" Jenna considered this. "It's too early to leave now, because of my contract—but I'm intrigued."

"Everyone get ready for Miss Sandra's five-year-old jazz class, performing an acrobatic lyrical piece to 'Call Me Maybe!'"

"Oh, that's May's class! My baby!" Billie began shooting pics and texting Jay, as her daughter led her class onto the stage in a rainbow-fringed leotard.

"Go May-May!" shouted Jenna.

"Werk, bitch!" hollered Elodie, to horrified stares from the row ahead of them. And then the Supermommy, the Cougar, and Diahann Carroll screamed so loud they were hoarse the next day.

Hours later, around three in the morning, Jenna and her friends were long asleep—but Eric and Tim, were partying. After waking up at 5am to shoot a funky Asian celeb makeup artist for The Perfect Find, and then editing in all day, and then networking at the Young Filmmakers Association's holiday mixer, Eric should've been too exhausted to go out. But he wasn't; he was exhilarated.

Yes, he woke up at the crack of dawn, but it was to work with his Jenna. Which was heaven. And the networking dinner had been a stale champagne-soaked, rubbery cheese plated geekpalooza, but he got to chill with industry-obsessed kids who spoke his language. Which felt like home. Plus, after the dinner, he sent off his last festival application, to Toronto Film Festival. Eric was on a high and didn't want the day to end.

Only the city's most badly behaved twenty-somethings had heard of Cake, a run-down room tucked underneath a turn-of-the-century bakery in

Bushwick, which was one of New York's sneakiest after-hours spots. There was no paparazzi, no VIP, no banquets, and no pictures allowed—only one sad, cigarette-butted Christmas wreath, some ratty velvet chairs, a bar, a stripper pole and opaque weed smoke. The crowd was schizophrenic in the sexiest possible way, a haven of Cool, where starlets, posh baby socialites, rappers, drug dealers, and the prettiest girls from tough neighborhoods easily comingled. Tonight, Zoe Kravitz was deejay-ing, an underage oil magnate's daughter was swinging on a pole in her bra, and Eric and Tim were floating on a Hennessy haze.

The two of them sat on barstools facing the crowd, bobbing their heads to A$AP Rocky's "Fucking Problems." A$AP Rocky was doing the same thing in a corner surrounded by groupies, while a director filmed B-roll shots for the cornrowed rapper's latest music video.

In front of the bar, Tim's now-serious girlfriend Carlita, was lazily dancing while also grilling Eric about her new favorite subject, Jenna.

"…so when she gonna hang out? And does she know Karl Lagerfield and Alexander Wang, like, personally?" Tonight, she was wearing tangerine lipstick and had switched her jet-black weave to a honey-streaked auburn.

"Stop referencing designers you only know from Rick Ross songs," said Eric, taking two puffs from a blunt and passing it to Tim. He had no idea whose weed it was—someone had passed it down from the other side of the bar.

"You ain't shit and God knows it." She busted out a few body rolls. "Why can't she hook me up with some designer shit? All I want are the Tom Ford shades Amber Rose wore to the VMAs!"

"All you want is Amber Rose," joked Eric.

"Not true," lied Carlita. "I ain't 'bout that bisexual life no more."

"To my endless annoyance," said Tim. "E, Jenna can't get her anything?"

"And you wonder why I never bring her around you street urchins! You don't know how to act."

"Your boy think he fancy 'cause he bagged a TV star," she grumbled to Tim.

"E's always been fancy. Fancy is his default."

"Keep shitting on me like I'm invisible," said Eric.

Tim palmed Carlita's ample ass. "Go take a selfie, bae. Hashtag taken. Me and Eric need to have a board meeting."

"'Kay," she said, kissing him. "Aaaanyways, Eric, I just think it's mad shady that you never bring Jenna around. Tim, talk some sense into this fool, I'm out." Carlita grabbed one of her girls, who was being accosted by a dude with a feather tattooed on his bald head, and headed for the tiny dance floor.

"Carlita's right," said Tim. "How can Jenna think she knows you if she's never really chilled with us?"

"She has chilled with you. You almost died over salad. I think she's good."

"That wasn't real chilling. I had on an ascot. I mean, this. Like, doing shit we always do. My girl's here—where's yours? Why can't she hang with us the way we do with Carlita? Or with our boys in the crib?"

"Because she's forty years old. She has a 401K. She can't go to the club with us. Or anywhere near your bedroom. What would she do? Where would she even sit? She's gonna lay in your bed with Carlita, live-tweeting *Love and Hip Hop* while we watch basketball and smoke?"

"That's not how it goes down." Tim thought about this. "Actually, that's exactly how it goes down. But what do you and Olivia Pope do that's so different?"

"You're not gonna keep calling her Olivia Pope."

"Answer the question."

"We don't do anything. We can't really leave her house."

"See? You're judging me, but you two are shut-ins. Over there like *Grey Gardens.*"

Eric snickered. "You've seen *Grey Gardens?*"

"You haven't? That art direction was insane, bruh."

"Anyway, yeah, we stay home, but it doesn't involve X boxes and shit. She's…classy. It's classy staying home. Staying home, but in French."

Tim snorted. "Whatever."

Eric pulled a pack of cherry Now & Laters from his pocket and tore it open, popping two in his mouth. He handed one to Tim. "I haven't eaten all day. I'm so hungry, I'm not even hungry anymore. I'm so hungry I'm full."

Eric pointed over to A$AP Rocky, who was posted up in a banquette surrounded by a cadre of writhing, multi-ethnic women. His director, an older white gentleman who looked like he'd rather be spooning with his feminist essayist wife in their Upper West Side loft, was filming while standing on a cocktail table.

"This director is such a fail. Look, that girl with the crazy lashes has mannequin hands," said Eric.

"Mannequin hands?"

"Yeah, she's touching him with Barbie hands.. They don't move, they're not fluid. It's like she's doing a stop-and-frisk."

James Cameron went up to every extra on the set of Titanic and gave them a name and a backstory, thought Eric. *And this is why.*

"You stay noticing the most random shit," said Tim. "She's wearing wedges. I hate women in wedges. Put on some fucking heels and grow up."

"You want a girl in silver bra to grow up."

"She's bad, though. In an EBT way. You know I love a slightly deranged project chick."

"Slightly deranged? Your last girl bedazzled her house arrest anklet," said Eric, shaking his head. "I've never met a bougier person more desperate to be street."

"I'm wearing Purple Label twill pants; I have zero desire to be street. I just need my women to be. The sex is better. Fancy bitches just lay there.

The more hood she is—the crazier she is—the better. I wanna consort with a girl who has a toxic relationship with her baby daddy and an undiagnosed personality disorder."

"Carlita's the queen of that, so Merry Christmas."

Tim surveyed the room. "Look at all these lovely international floozies, in town for the holidays. And I'm in a relationship. But whatever yo, I'm committed to Carlita. It's impossible to stay away. I think it's 'cause she's the proud owner of the most flexible legs in the continental U.S. One of the benefits of dating a stripper. It's like fucking one of those bendy pool noodles."

"Why would you wanna fuck one of those?"

"Can Jenna put her legs behind her neck?"

Eric crunched on a Now & Later. "No comment. No."

"No, she can't? Or no, you don't wanna talk about it?"

"No, it's not up for discussion."

"We can't discuss Jenna's legs? They're not holy." Tim was confused. This was how they talked about girls, what made her so different? "Why're you so pussy-whipped, though?"

"I'm man enough to say I'm pussy-whipped," said Eric. "If she showed up here, snapped her fingers and was like, 'E, it's time to go,' I'd ask no questions and dead ass *bounce*, son. I am not ashamed."

Tim shot him a blank stare. "I was not ready for that level of emotional transparency."

"You need therapy."

"Man listen, I gotta tell you, I'm floored that your woman was born in the Seventies. E, your girlfriend graduated high school in the early Nineties. Wutang is not old school to this broad."

"Halle Berry and J. Lo are older than her."

"And they're bad. So is Olivia Pope, don't get me wrong."

"Jenna."

Tim made an impatient noise. "You're acting like Jenna's the love of your life. And yet you're keeping her from me. Me. I'm hurt."

"What motive would I have to do this? Stop being so sensitive, you're ruining my chill."

"I know why. You think that if she sees you around me, it'll expose how juvenile you really are. You can pretend to be all slick in the office, and it's cool, 'cause she doesn't know that we engage in terrible rap battles, and get into actual beef over who'd get to smash Storm if we were X-Men. She doesn't know we can spend an entire afternoon insulting each other's families in the most degrading way. Or that we only stopped cyber-bullying Mr. Bing from AP Biology last year."

"Yo, if you ever tell Jenna any of that, I swear..."

"How'd you get her, anyway? And how are you gonna keep her? You know how old dudes roll in this city. Bentleys and platinum cards. All you have are student loans and a robust sneaker collection. Help me understand."

"It' wasn't about 'getting' her. We just...had to be together. Like, we had no choice. I can't explain it."

Tim burst out laughing. "What do you think this is, *The Notebook*? Whatever, do you. But I can't cosign this Jenna thing until I spend at least an hour of Timmy time with her."

"You will," said Eric, taking two deep puffs and passing the blunt to Tim. "Just...I gotta think of a scenario where it feels natural for the three of us to be in the same room."

"Carlita has to be there."

Eric rolled his eyes. "Y'all are due to break up soon anyway."

Tim gnawed on a fingernail. "I'm entertaining the thought of wifing her permanently. She might be the one. She got me to go to church."

"Church? Word? You burst into flames?"

"I went last Sunday," he said, ignoring Eric's comment. "She goes to one of those super-churches. The reverend drove a Bugatti, like your stepdad use to."

Eric wrinkled his nose at the mention of his ex-stepdad, who he loathed. "All those reverends should be relegated to lives of infinite purposelessness. You're a spiritual leader, not Young Jeezy."

"Point is, if Carlita could introduce my amoral ass to her reverend, then you can do the same with Olivia Pope."

Tim was right. But Eric had no idea how to integrate Jenna into his life. The idea of her, with her balletic hand gestures and prissy curls, sitting between him and Tim at that disreputable club, was both hilarious and impossible.

He couldn't imagine Jenna in Tim's bedroom. Or having patience for his New York party scene. Or hanging with his broke film school friends on somebody's terrible Salvation Army furniture, attacking Kickstarter and drinking away the terror of an elite degree with no prospects. He couldn't see Jenna anywhere in his life but with him.

That wasn't normal, was it?

Whatever, he didn't care. He and Jenna had their own private nirvana and that's all he needed.

"That director needs my help," Eric said, taking one last hit of the blunt and ending the conversation. He headed across the room to introduce himself.

CHAPTER 21

J enna always looked forward to the moment Eric stepped into her apartment. After holding herself back at work, pretending—it was like a sugar addict waiting outside of Krispy Kreme for hours, counting the minutes until it opened, and then having the owner sweep open the door and say, "Have at it! Donut yourself to death!"

But when Jenna buzzed Eric up that Saturday night in late February, he took her breath away. He was standing there with a shiny maroon sleeping bag over one shoulder, and a shopping bag in his hand.

"What are you doing?"

"You know that movie series outside in Prospect Park? They're playing *Butch Cassidy* at midnight. It's not too cold tonight, and it's dark; no one will see us if we sit way in the back, right? I got us a picnic—everything you like, McDonalds fries and assorted croissants and bagels from the bodega. Sides and carbs, no nutritional value. And Skittles, obviously."

She burst into tears.

"What did I do?" He dropped everything on the floor, closed the door and drew her into his arms.

"How did you know? One time I tried to...I mean, I've always wanted to do this! I never even mentioned it! How did you know?"

"I just did," he murmured against her hair. "I know you by heart."

And during the movie, while snuggled up in puffy coats and Eric's sleeping bag, the crisp midnight air thick with the romantic energy of hundreds of Brooklynites on dates—and while Eric was praising Redford's mustache with intense hero worship ("That shit is cold, yo! It looks like it has a pulse. Like it has a Zodiac sign and a verified Twitter account.")—Jenna finally said it.

"I love you."

Eric looked at her, dumbstruck. He felt that she might love him, but he was prepared to never hear her say it. Well, say it again. Sober. It wasn't until she uttered the words that he realized how much he needed to hear them.

"You do?"

"Yes." She palmed his cheek. "I love you."

"Never unsay that. Okay? Never unfeel that." And then he attacked her mouth, throat, and cheeks with a flurry of worshipful, happy kisses.

Eric and Jenna made no sense, but they made perfect sense.

And after months, no one in the office had caught on. Jenna and Eric stuck to their office rules, and had successfully managed to do the impossible—carry out a full-blown relationship under everyone's noses.

There was one rule that they broke.

The no-office-sex thing didn't even last for two days. After Jenna teased the hell out of him in a meeting—sucking her bottom lip in pretend concentration, sliding her foot up his leg under the table, texting him a filthy, Eric-centric fantasy she'd masturbated to that morning—he burst into her office, clapped his hand over her mouth, pushed her up against the wall and finger-fucked her into a piercing, full-body orgasm.

The next day, while he was waiting for an elevator, she yanked him into the unisex hallway bathroom for a sink-quickie so good, so depleting, that he considered calling out sick for the rest of the day. They realized that they couldn't not have sex at StyleZine—the rush was too exquisite. And it was easier than they thought. They both learned that even with the evidence right in front of their eyes, people are ultimately too caught up in their own lives to notice anything that isn't directly pointed out to them.

Terry was a perfect example.

"I'm worried about you, Eric," she blurted out one day.

She was sitting on the side of Eric's desk, scrolling through Buzzfeed on her phone. Eric was leaning far back in his chair, his phone in his hand. Jenna stood across from them in the tiny kitchenette, "getting coffee"—and he had his chair angled so that he could see just a sliver of her. They were in the throes of a text thread about Jenna's *New York* magazine interview today. In an hour, they were shooting Cara Delevingne for The Perfect Find, and a reporter from the magazine was stopping by.

"How am I worrisome?"

"You're, like, so closed off. Last week, I introduced you to the hot, black Look of the Day girl, but you were so…stiff. That street style chick we filmed yesterday with the side-bang was way into you, but you didn't even notice. You used to be so, like, chatty, so charming…"

"I'm no longer charming?"

"…now it's like you don't even care about girls anymore. Like you're unavailable. But I know you're not seeing anyone."

He shrugged. "Maybe I'm just maturing."

They heard a chortle from the kitchen. Eric made a mental note to make Jenna pay for that, later.

"No, I know what the problem is." Terry, a trendy vision in shiny emerald leggings and a studded denim vest, pointed toward the kitchenette. Jenna sipped a latte, appearing to be embroiled in an *ELLE* magazine.

"Jenna Jones is my problem?"

"Dude. Yes. You're madly in love with her. But you won't do anything about it and it's killing your spirit."

Eric exhaled and rubbed a temple. "I'm so tired of running."

"Let it out, E. Talk to me."

"I think about her day and night," he whispered. "Other women don't even register to me. It's really that obvious?"

"Yes! It kills Jinx." She leaned in closer to him. "She watches you watching Jenna in the meetings and then binges Pirate's Booty for an hour."

Eric looked horrified. "There's so much struggle in that sentence, I don't even know how to respond."

"You have to do something. Tell her how you feel."

"First of all, we work together. So...no."

"I mean, it would obvs be a secret."

"But she's so out of my league, its preposterous." Eric shook his head. "Even if it did happen, I feel like she'd boss me around. Older women like to dominate younger guys. She'd make me her little bitch."

Terry giggled. "You might like it."

"The truth is, she intimidates me." Eric's phone buzzed. "Sorry, let me get this, it's...um...Mitchell."

Eric Combs
iMessage
March 1st 11:31am

Jenna: Okay, you're laying it on thick.
Eric: I want you naked in the 10th floor fashion closet in ten minutes.
Jenna: You sure you're not too intimidated?
Eric: Go. And leave on those red heels you're wearing.

"Anyway," he continued, "I don't feel like I'd even have the balls to handle her."

"She's older, but she's still a girl! When have girls ever made you nervous? See, you're not acting like yourself, and..."

Terry stopped talking, because just then, Jenna leaned her head into the cubicle.

"Hi guys," she said.

"Jenna!" exclaimed Eric. "You didn't hear anything I said, right?"

"Every word. And even though I think you're a doll, please know that it'll never happen."

"And please know that I'm painfully aware of that fact. This was all coming from Terry."

"Really, you two have too much time on your hands." She sauntered away, sipping her coffee.

Eric narrowed his eyes at Terry.

"I thought I was being whispery!" she said. "My baaaad."

"Whatever yo, I'll just keep loving her from afar. I'm used to the torture." He got up from his chair. "I gotta eat something before this shoot."

"Cool," she said, sliding off his desk. "But I think Jenna doth protesth too much. Did you see the way she walked away? There was sex in that walk. Just saying."

Minutes later, Eric cracked open the door to the dark stock room and slipped in.

He turned on the dusky light. The closet was chaos, with racks of clothes shoved up against the walls, bins of shoes and jewelry stacked atop each other, and a table full of next season's handbags.

Jenna was standing against the wall wearing only her crimson stilettos. Her legs were apart, and she had one hand on her hip.

"It's such a shame you won't ask me out," she said, "and put yourself out of your misery."

Eric sighed. "I wanna ask you out so bad."

"Why don't you?"

"Incurable shyness."

"Poor baby."

"Come here."

She smiled, and then walked toward him slowly, with feline slinkiness. Then she put her hands on the door on either side of him, and leaned her naked body against the length of his.

"How do you want me?" she whispered into his ear.

"On the table," said Eric.

Jenna walked over to the table, knocked off the bags and climbed on top. Spreading her knees apart, she arched her back, totally exposed. She shot Eric a wicked glance over her shoulder, peering up at him through her lashes.

He came up behind her, grabbed her hips and pulled her to him. "So if I did convince you to be my girl..."

"Oh sweetie, you have no chance." Slowly, Jenna grinded her ass against him.

"Why?"

"You wouldn't know how to fuck me."

Eric fisted his hand in her hair, pulling her head back. He unzipped his fly, and then sank into her—and she was so wet and he penetrated her so deeply that she forgot she was in the office and cried out.

"Say it again."

"You w-wouldn't know how to fuck me."

He thrust into her again, even deeper. She bit her hand to keep from moaning.

"Will you be my teacher, then? If I'm really, really good?" He hit her with another hard thrust on 'good.'

"Only if I can make you my little bitch."

"I already am."

Eric gripped her elbows, lifting her up to her knees. Jenna's head fell back on his shoulder, and he ran his tongue along her neck up to her earlobe. As he drove into her, she matched him thrust for thrust, squeezing her muscles around his dick, massaging it, milking it...weakening him.

"Stop," he groaned.

"No," she breathed.

"Come."

"You."

"No."

"Aww baby, you can't hold it can you?" she whispered. "Only little boys come first."

No more games for Eric. Grabbing her wrists, he planted her palms down on the table, so she was all fours. He gripped her throat with one hand, and with the other, pulsed his middle finger over her clit—and drove into her.

There was no hope for Jenna after that. She broke first, but Eric was a millisecond behind her, their almost-simultaneous orgasm powerful and mightily long.

When it subsided, Jenna collapsed on the table and Eric flopped down on his back next to her. As she tried to catch her breath (quietly, which was a challenge), he pushed her sex-tousled hair aside and kissed her damp neck, just under her ear.

"My favorite spot," he murmured.

"Of all the spots?"

"It's so good. I feel like it has special shamanic properties. Like if I had mono and put my face right here I'd be instantly cured."

"If you ever lose an ounce of weirdness, we're through."

"Same," he said, kissing her deeply. "We gotta go."

"Right. Who first, me or you?"

"Me, I'm already dressed." Eric laid there for thirty more seconds—until he felt pulled-together—and then headed out the door.

Jenna waited ten minutes. Then, she threw on her clothes, putting all the handbags back on the table and hurried downstairs on legs that were jelly-wobbly. It was fine. She'd mastered the art of post-orgasm nonchalance.

Minutes later, in her office, Jenna was reapplying her lipgloss, trying to remove all traces of sex before running to Cara Delevingne's hotel room. She was about to go meet Eric when her phone ring.

Jenna was so taken aback by the name flashing on her screen, that it took her five rings to answer. It was Anna. Anna Stein, Brian's mother. She hadn't spoken to her since she fled for Virginia.

"Anna Banana?"

"Doll! It's me!"

"I know!" She was so excited. "I'm so happy to hear from you. I always want to call, but it seemed inappropriate..."

"You're like my daughter. I will never forgive you for leaving us. Oh my," she said, sucking her teeth. "Listen to me! I stopped taking my mood stabilizers, and it's making me such an ornery jerk-off."

"Why aren't you taking your medicine?"

"Because who cares if I have mood swings? All my boyfriends are dead and the two friends I authentically liked moved to Miami. I don't have a career to throw myself into. Never had one unless you count being a Denny's waitress, where my proudest accomplishment was racking up the most 'Nice tits, toots' tips during Sunday brunch hours. And I'm on my deathbed. Do you have a shrooms dealer, my love? Hashish? Dying would be bearable if I could do it with a proper 1968-era high."

Jenna sighed. Ever since Anna's bout with breast cancer ten years ago, she'd been fatalistic. Several times, she'd been tested for SARS, AIDS, herpes—even scurvy, which no one had gotten in, like, centuries.

"First of all, you might've worked as a waitress, but you're also the most brilliant craftswoman I've ever met. You made every window dressing in my house, and Barneys wanted to carry your embroidered Sevillana scarves. You just never pursued these things. Secondly, you are not on your death bed, Banana."

"This time, I am. I'm gonna die without ever seeing you again."

"Please don't even talk like that, okay?" Jenna felt incredible sadness at being estranged from the woman who'd been her New York mommy for so long. Her own mother had never fully understood her whimsy—but Anna did, because she was a kook, too. She'd fed her, assimilated her into her Former-Hippie-Turned-Park-Avenue-Matrons book club (Erica Jong, Joan Didion and Eastern erotica, only), and regaled her with tales from her days as a beautiful runaway teen, making candles in Manhattan's East Village for Sixties revolutionaries. Toward the end, she gifted her with a wooden chest stuffed with some of Brian's infant clothes and toys, in the hopes that this would bring Jenna pregnancy luck.

"God, I miss you," she said.

"Me too, JJ. Want to go to lunch?"

"I'd love to, but Brian's in a new relationship...I don't think it's right."

"Lily L'amour." She spat this, like she was affronted by the audacity of this woman to exist. "Or is it Celeste? At least she's passably pretty. I couldn't bear it if his rebound relationship was with a troglodyte. Frankly, I'm destroyed that you and Bri cheated me out of my gorgeous, mixed-race grandchildren. Beautiful Baracks and Halles with a Jewish last name. Superhumans!"

"Banana, I'm so sorry, I have to run to a shoot. But let's..."

"I was calling for a reason. Check Forbes.com. They did an interview with Bri where he's talking about his financial wizardry.

But he mentions you. And it's romantic."

Jenna's stomach dipped. "Romantic?"

"Maybe you guys will get back together and give me some mulattos and mulatresses before I die."

"You're not dying. I won't let you."

"Just do me a favor," she said, sighing. "Take care of yourself. And call me sometime."

Jenna smiled. "I will. I love you."

"I love you more."

She sat at her desk, her fingers hovering over her keyboard. What could Brian have said about her that was romantic? And publicly, no less! He was the king of unemotional men. And what about his girlfriend? Jenna was bristling with curiosity—but also scared that reading the piece would send her down a rabbit hole of suppressed Brian baggage. And that wasn't the only reason she couldn't click on Forbes.com.

Tapping into an emotional discipline she didn't know she had, Jenna shut her laptop. She'd check later. Maybe. After all, nothing Brian could say had the power to affect her anymore.

As she walked down the hall, she repeated this to herself over and over again in her head, like a prayer—until she saw Eric and knew it was true.

CHAPTER 22

Jenna, Eric, and a small crew (the bigger The Perfect Find became, the more people it took to pull it off) were assembled in British It-model Cara Delevingne's plush suite at The Standard Hotel. The wild child was in town to shoot a Burberry campaign. With her bushy, dark brows, gritty downtown/underground persona, and rumored cadre of beautiful lesbian lovers, Cara was the supermodel queen of 2012. Where the rest of her peers tried to cultivate a look, she was staunchly anti-glamour and looked fresher than all of them. Cara was the only supermodel backstage at the Paris collections in a Hello Kitty sweater and dirty Adidas.

When *New York* magazine reporter Andrea Granger walked in, she was tapped out on the The Perfect Find story. She and her photographer spent forty-five minutes interviewing and shooting Darcy Vale, who'd only delivered dry, media-conscious quotes. Andrea felt like she was talking to a publicist—she couldn't find the story.

Andrea decided to approach her interview with Jenna differently. Before interviewing her, she'd hang out at the shoot, eavesdropping to gather clues about the creation of this thing. She spotted Jenna across the room at the craft services table, chatting with her partner, Eric Combs. She casually headed in that direction and pretended to serve herself some fruit salad.

They were having a rapid-fire fast conversation.

"I want it to have a late Seventies, early Eighties New York feel," said Eric. "You know, BCBG, punk, early hip hop…"

"Basquiat, Danceteria…" continued Jenna.

"And who's the chick with the white hair? She had a band? She reminds me of Cara."

"Debbie Harry! Blondie. Have you ever seen her in that Fab Five Freddy movie from 1982?"

"*Wild Style*! We need to shoot her somewhere that looks like the East Village in the '80s, like maybe Bushwick? Somewhere with a…"

"Dirty-cool aesthetic."

"Lo-fi. Graffiti."

"Which would be flawless, since her Perfect Find is slim-slouchy jeans that fit somewhere between boyfriend jeans and skinny jeans—the kind you can't find anywhere—and she's attacking them with spray paint."

"Graffiti jeans?"

"Graffiti jeans."

"We read her mind! We're too good at this! Her video's gonna be like the film version of throwback Shelltop Adidas."

"Of course you needed a sneaker reference. Wait, let me find some Grandmaster Flash on iTunes…maybe 'White Lines.' Should I channel my inner Debbie Harry?" Jenna started singing "Rapture."

"If you sing, I'm gonna pop and loc." And then Eric bust out in a quick robot to prove it. "I love this. I want it to look like a vintage 80s *Interview* cover, like, maybe even an old school…"

"Polaroid photo?"

"Exactly." His eyes sparkled.

Then, something odd happened. Jenna took a sip from her plastic cup of water. Without asking, Eric took it from her, turned the cup till it was just so, and drank from it, too.

Andrea didn't know what she'd witnessed—if it meant something, or nothing—but it was unmistakably intimate.

She realized the story wasn't about Darcy Vale breathing life into a stale genre. It was about StyleZine's superstar editor and videographer. A fashion veteran and an unknown kid just out of film school, who were so creatively in sync they were finishing each other's sentences. A pair of black visionaries making genre-elevating work in the notoriously monochromatic fashion industry. A Generation X-er and a millennial who combined their influences to create magic—and as a bonus, were wildly photogenic.

And then there was the way they were looking at each other.

Andrea whispered something in her photographer's ear. He nodded.

She walked up to the two of them. "I'm Andrea Granger, from *New York*. Sorry to interrupt. My intention was to interview Jenna, but I really feel that I should to talk to the both of you. Together and separately."

"Me?" Eric looked at Jenna. "Are you sure?"

"Oh you have to talk to Eric," Jena gushed. "We wouldn't be here if it wasn't for him. He's…"

Andrea held her hand up. "Hold that thought while I turn on my recorder. So, whose idea was this?"

"His."

"Hers."

"Ours," said Jenna, with pride.

Andrea smiled.

A week and a half later, *New York* magazine's Power 25 issue came out. As promised to Darcy, StyleZine was in the top five. Also, as promised, StyleZine was one of the few power players who had their own article. *New York* also awarded the site valuable retail space on the cover.

But the article was not a profile on Darcy. In fact, Darcy had one quote, a throwaway line about StyleZine's impact on ecommerce. The images from Darcy's photo shoot weren't even used.

The whole piece was about Jenna and Eric. Each of their backstories, their passion for the series, their effortless partnership. Andrea explored the cultural impact of trying to broaden the fashion industry's perception of what's chic by profiling deeply fashionable women of all sizes and ethnicities. Andrea detailed Eric's USC success, and reintroduced Jenna to her audience. Jenna sounded like what she was: a seasoned pro who was invigorated by her partner's fresh vision. Eric also sounded exactly like himself; a fledgling filmmaker thrilled at the opportunity to flaunt his skills on such a visible project.

A casual reader would've thought that the lovefest oozing off the pages was just friendly, mutual regard. Jenna's small soliloquy raving about Tyler on Perry Street seemed innocuous. As did Eric's jokey response when Andrea asked him what it was like to shoot so many desirable women: "They're pretty, yeah. But it's easy to forget, with Jenna Jones running around looking like Dorothy Dandridge in leather jeans."

A casual reader might not have even blinked at the trio of black and white photos accompanying the article. The first was of Cara Delevingne in men's Ray Bans, all surly-sexy in an anti-hero stance with lip curled and her fists thrust into her motorcycle jacket. The second was of Cara in a similar pose, but with Jenna vamping next to her in the shades. The third photo was of Jenna and Eric. This time, Eric was wearing the shades. Looking like a black James Dean in a white tee and dark jeans, he held his camera down by his side, while the other arm was flung across Jenna's shoulders. He smiled down at her while she giggled at some private joke.

It was just a candid outtake of a couple of good-looking people caught in a moment of comfortable comraderie. All three pictures were sexy—but for the people who knew Jenna and Eric intimately, that last one was just oblique enough to inspire a double take.

At home, in the Tribeca triplex he'd shared with Jenna, Brian Stein laid awake in bed. It was 1:20 am. He'd read the article five times, and was reading it again. He knew Jenna. He knew that breathless, worshipful tone. The way she spoke about that director—that child—was exactly the way she used to speak about him.

She was fucking that fifth grader. She was in love with that fifth grader.

He stared at the photo and was gutted. He wasn't prepared for this. Stone-faced, he flipped back to the beginning for the twelfth time.

Across the room, Celeste "Lily L'Amour" Wexler was almost finished packing a Lily Pulitzer duffle with the few clothes and toiletries she'd kept at Brian's. She couldn't handle another second competing with Jenna's ghost, a poltergeist in Alexander McQueen thigh-high boots. The Forbes. com piece had been bad enough, despite Brian swearing that he took the interview before they met.

And then there was the thing with his desperately ill mother, Anna. For the past couple of months, Brian had been devastated over Anna's second bout of breast cancer, and nothing Lily did helped. He never even noticed her patience during all those hospital visits, when that horrifically face-lifted harpy reminisced endlessly about Jenna. How Brian and Jenna walked her down the aisle at her second wedding. How Jenna gave her the Pomeranian that she loved more than the man she married. How Jenna should be by her side. It was a Jennabration, each time, and Brian never made an effort to shut Anna up.

And now, he'd dived head first into her *New York* article like it was a Pulitzer Prize masterpiece. Why was he so hung up on her? Hadn't she pulled some completely psychotic, reverse domestic abuse shit and punched him out?

It was too much. Lily loved him, but knew her time was up. After all, she was a relationship columnist.

She tossed her key on the floor, grabbed her bag and left. Fifteen minutes passed before Brian knew she was gone.

Darcy Vale sat at her desk, the magazine open to the page of Jenna and Eric together. She was trembling, and hated it. She was sweating, and hated it. Nothing was worse than feeling a loss of control. Being surprised. Being betrayed. She'd grown StyleZine into the successful brand it was today. She was the visionary who'd staffed the site with the perfect blend of talent, personality and mediagenic hotness. She embraced nepotism and hired Eric. She looked beyond her personal feelings about Jenna, and brought her back. And how did they thank her? They didn't. Neither one of them uttered one word about her. They stole her moment. They made her look...inconsequential.

And their photo was practically pornographic.

She would find a way to fuck that *New York* reporter later. Jenna, too.

In the meantime, she picked up her phone. "Eric."

"Yeah?"

"Get in here."

Five minutes later—too long, so disrespectful—Eric walked up to her office, stopping in the doorway.

"Close the door. Sit down."

He did. "Wassup."

"Wassup? Really? You didn't think to consult me before you took this interview? If I didn't need you for The Perfect Find, I'd fire you on the spot, shared DNA or no."

"That piece has been aggregated on Buzzfeed, on *Vogue's* website, on EW.com. Refinery29. Everywhere. Everybody's talking about StyleZine. Did you hear that Phillip Lim wants to partner with us on a Facebook contest? The most stylish girl wearing his shit gets to do a Perfect Find with us. That's huge." He shrugged. "What exactly did I do wrong?"

Darcy smiled. "You're feeling yourself, aren't you? You got a little press and you feel fly, right?"

"I always feel fly."

"When did you start sleeping with Jenna Jones?"

"Okay, now you're bugging." He started to stand up.

"Don't you fucking move."

"That's what you got from that article? Five months ago you thought I was an aimless, jobless, shiftless Negro. Now, I'm bringing money and publicity to your site. Creating dope work. And you're still mad?" He folded his arms. "Goddamn, woman. Trying to please you is like bench-pressing Earth."

"Are you sleeping with Jenna Jones?"

"No."

Darcy eyed him, her head cocked to one side.

"Jenna is your age. She's like my cool, pretty aunt. She's our Homecoming Queen, like you always say."

"I say that with derision."

"I like Jenna. But even if I *liked* her liked her, I'd never be that unprofessional. I'm offended at the suggestion."

"Oh! He's offended." She leaned forward. "I put everything I had into building this company. I married a billionaire who couldn't get it up to fund this company…"

"Did you really just tell me that? I'm calling Child Protective Services."

"Belladonna Media is my greatest achievement. Everything you do reflects on me. You will not come in here and embarrass me. Don't do it. Not with her. Get the thought out of your head."

"Yeah whatever. Is that it?"

Darcy looked at Eric, so insolent and maddeningly unfazed. So sure of his position in the world—never knowing what it was like to compromise, humble, or degrade himself to survive. Twenty-two years old with a splashy piece in a major publication. He didn't even know how lucky he was.

She wanted to strangle him.

"I want to show you something." She typed onto her laptop keyboard, and swiveled the screen around.

"See that guy? The subject of this Forbes.com profile? That's Brian Stein, the dashing, multi-millionaire real estate developer. He's also the love of Jenna's life. But she left him. You know why? Because she was dying to get married and he wasn't. She was dying for a baby, and he wasn't. She dumped that perfect man because her priorities are a ring and a kid. And you're only a kid, yourself." She leaned back in her chair, looking sad for him. "You're so in over your head with this crush, Eric. She'd never take you seriously."

Eric glanced at the screen, long enough to see Brian's picture and the pull quote: "My proudest achievement? This house. Not the property, but the life I made here. With the woman who made it a home. She decorated it; her touch is everywhere. Everything about me that ever mattered is here, in her details."

After a moment, Eric spoke.

"You're pissed because the *New York* article isn't about you. Which is not my fault. You're weirdly into Jenna's love life. Which is none of my business. And now you're trying to intimidate me with some dude getting misty-eyed over his ex's decorating?" He chuckled a little, standing up. "Meeting adjourned."

Darcy watched him leave, her brow knitted in concentration. Then, she shut her door and made herself a vodka tonic. She didn't yet have proof that he and Jenna were having an affair—but no matter how long it took, she'd get it. And when she did, God help those two for trying to play her.

Eric headed across the loft space toward his desk. But he didn't stop there. He kept going, walking to the elevator bank, riding down to the lobby, and ending up outside. There, he paced back and forth in front of the building, clenching and unclenching his fists, his face a tornado of wild hurt and rage.

Thunderstruck.

Jenna was sitting in her office, reading their article for the zillionth time. She had so many conflicting emotions about it; she couldn't pick which one to run with. She was so proud of Eric. She was so proud of them. She was deeply nervous that she'd gone too far with the public gushing. She was excited that she did what she set out to do at StyleZine, create game-changing work and prove to everyone that she was the same Jenna Jones from *Darling*, maybe even better.

But she was stuck on one part of the interview, and couldn't get past it.

> *New York*: You're a New Yorker, born and bred. Do you aim to be identified as a New York filmmaker, like Lee or Scorcese?
>
> *EC*: I love New York, but I don't know where I'll end up. I obviously want to work in Hollywood. I love the science fiction films coming out of London. I'm at the beginning of my career. I have a lot to experience. I don't want anything holding me back, no ties. These are the hustle years.

No ties.

She read his quote over and over, and each time, she felt smaller and smaller. Eric had become vital to her life, but he hadn't even lived his yet. Sometimes, when they were together, this thought crept into her brain, but she always buried it. Being with him felt too good to tarnish it with… reality. But now the words were in print and she couldn't deny them.

CHAPTER 23

It was the one-week anniversary of their *New York* piece hitting stands, and Jenna and Eric had celebrated by drinking his dad's specialty, rum-spiked Caucasian Shakes, and having lazy, rainy day sex. Now, it was 2am, and they were lying in bed with their limbs intertwined, snacking on a jumbo bag of Skittles. Jenna was naked except for a pair of purple bikini panties. All Eric had on were the USC basketball shorts he kept at Jenna's. Turner Movie Classics was on in the background, playing Hitchcock's *Psycho*, but they were barely watching it. For different reasons, they'd both been on the quiet side all day.

Eric kept trying to make himself go to sleep, but every time he tried to relax, Brian's Forbes.com quote screamed in his head. Whenever his eyes closed, he pictured an ecstatic Jenna riding the Central Park carousel with two flawlessly styled kids. Kids that weren't his. Because, as his evil elf of a mother pointed out, he was just a kid, himself—and he'd never be able to give her what she wanted.

A part of him hoped Darcy had made that up. It was possible. She was so spiteful. His mother was a person who'd spent most of her life obsessing over imagined blows to the rep she'd fought for. Plotting payback.

And Eric wasn't immune to her spite. When he was eleven and got detention for cursing at prep school, Darcy had her fearsome thug of a husband drive over Eric's video camera—back and forth, until it was dust—demolishing two years of footage. Eric was gutted, just like she intended him to be.

He actually prayed that this was one of those times.

"You know what I wish?" she asked, popping three yellow Skittles in her mouth.

"No, what?"

"I wish I could cut off your penis and carry it around with me in my purse."

"You don't even need the rest of me attached to it?" Eric knocked her foot with his. "Would you love me less if I had a really small one?"

"Sort of," she said. "I read something awful in *British Cosmo* once, about a woman whose boyfriend had micro-penis syndrome? It was the size of a mushroom. He'd only have sex with her in the dark. Turns out, he'd been using a dildo on her for seven years and she had no idea."

"But how could she not know?"

"There are some very real-feeling dildos."

Then, they were silent for awhile, both lost in contemplative horror over micro-penis syndrome, the creeping suspense of *Psycho*—and in their own anxious thoughts.

"Eric, can I ask you something?"

He propped his head on his hand, looking down at her. "I don't think dildos have any place in two-person sex. I'd feel so inadequate."

"Do you ever think about our future?" She faced him.

"Oh. *This* conversation." He poured the rest of the Skittles into his mouth, steeling himself for wherever this was going.

"We can't sneak around like this forever," she said. "As thrilled as I am about our *New York* article, it scared me, too. I mean, two more quotes declaring our appreciation for each other's talent, and we might as well have posed naked. And speaking of that picture…"

"I know," he groaned. "So obvious. But only to us. I doubt anyone else would think twice about it."

"We should've been more careful," said Jenna. "What if Darcy picked up on something? Getting away with this lie for seven months has made us lazy. And I hate that we even have to deal with this. The secrecy used to be exciting; now it's just exhausting."

"Agreed. So I'll marry you and end it all."

"You shouldn't even be thinking about marriage. These are your hustle years."

"You caught that, huh? Yes, I said that to the reporter, but I didn't mean…"

"I know what you meant. And it makes sense for you."

"You wouldn't wait for me?"

"Would you want a forty-eight-year-old bride? And what if we wanted…"

A baby, thought Eric. *Just say it. A baby.*

"Wanted what?"

"Nothing," Jenna said. "I just get scared sometimes. I love you in a really big way, and when I imagine our future, I don't see how our paths match up."

"I don't know how it works, either. I just know I want you." He traced the outside of her ear with his finger. "Lustily, repeatedly, and aggressively."

She smiled.

"Yeah, we have epic issues," he said. "But name a couple with a perfect relationship. Besides the Carters."

"Jay and Bey? You think so?"

"They're, like, the dream!"

"I adore them. But they're in show business. It's the Jay/Bey perfection machine. Their jobs are to project aspiration, sex, fairy tale domesticity. In real life, no couple is that flawless."

"Damn. That's black-sphemy, kid."

Jenna laughed a little, but it didn't reach her eyes.

"Please don't stress about us," said Eric.

"But what are we gonna do?" she whispered.

"Whatever we're doing now is good enough for me," he said. "It's everything to me."

"Me too. I live all week for this specific moment. You, with those abs, making bad puns. But when I think about our situation, I get anxious. It's bizarre being a grown woman with a secret boyfriend." She pushed her hair out of her face. "And in the back of my mind is this worry that I have you on borrowed time. Like, I should savor every moment because, given our ages, I don't know how we'll make it."

She paused, folding and re-folding the Skittles bag into a tiny square.

"Gimme that, you're making me nervous." He took it and tossed it into the trash. "Of course we'll make it. I'm yours. Where am I going?"

"I just want the full picture with you," she said, distraught.

Eric knew what she was saying—and what she wasn't saying. But he didn't know how to assuage her fears when he didn't have the answers, himself.

"Jenna," he started, "my life is so up in the air. I have nowhere to live, no money. I don't know what, or when, or how. But I do know who. With the utmost certainty, I know who."

Jenna curled herself into him, squeezing him tight. "Me too. Nothing else makes sense."

Eric could feel the tension in her body, the worry. And he was trying to stave off his own panic. There were too many elements out of his control. If that Suit couldn't keep her, what made Eric think he could? Until that moment in Darcy's office, Eric had been so confident in his place in Jenna's life. All he'd felt was a visceral understanding that they belonged together. But now, he wondered why Jenna even bothered with him. And he felt ridiculous for being so sure of himself.

Eric had to fix this. And since he couldn't change his age, or not be Darcy's son, or be in a place to settle down—and since the idea of Jenna feeling one ounce of anxiety over him was agonizing—he did what he knew he was good at.

Eric held Jenna's face in both hands and kissed her sweetly—shallowly at first, until she started to soften. He caressed her back and stroked her hair; kissing her more deeply until her skin flushed hot. Wanting him, Jenna reached for his waistband, but he caught her hand and held it beside her face on the pillow.

"You're not allowed to do anything."

"Why?"

"I just want you to feel."

"But..."

"Shhh," he whispered. "And don't come until I'm inside you." He traced the planes of her neck with his mouth and tongue, bringing his thigh up between her legs. Languidly, she ran her hands down his strong, beautiful back, loving the feeling of being crushed by him, practically purring under his kisses.

He licked his index finger and thumb, and then softly ran each nipple between them until they were puckered and tender. She squirmed beneath him, even the lightest touch flooding her with tingles. Then, cupping each of her handful-sized breasts, he sucked one leisurely, one then the other—like he had all time in the world, disregarding her soft whimpers.

Gripping his shoulders, Jenna arched her breast into his mouth and rubbed against his leg. Her breath was coming in short gasps, her cheeks were flushed bright crimson. She wanted him desperately, urgently, but Eric said no. From the first time they'd slept together, they established that whoever set the rules first, was boss.

Kissing her neck softly, he flattened his hand under her breast and caressed down along her stomach—passing over her panties, barely allowing the tips of his fingers to graze her—and then stroking down along her inner thigh and then back up again. He stroked her until she trembled in his arms, tormented.

"I can't wait," she breathed. "Please, I can't."

Eric slid two fingers inside of her and she arched her back, moaning. He plunged them into her three more times and then stopped, leaving her aching, throbbing. On the verge.

Then, with deliberate laziness, he left a trail of closed-mouth kisses down her stomach, stopping at the waistband of her panties. Slipping them off, he pushed her thighs back, opened her wide—and closed his mouth over her, sucking thoroughly, deliciously. Jenna gasped, balling the sheets into her fists. The sensation was so vivid that she instinctively tried to inch away.

"God...Eric...Jesus..."

"Who?"

"Too intense," she panted. "Too intense..."

"Good," he said, gripping her thighs firmly, making her take it. He buried his tongue inside her, massaging her clit with his thumb—and that's when Jenna began to fall apart, shuddering uncontrollably, moaning his name. Only then did he cover her with his strong body, kiss her devouringly, and sink inside her. Eric knew she wanted it fast, but he fucked her slow—as slow and deep as he was kissing her—and his measured intensity knocked Jenna into a thundering, white-hot orgasm that seemed to emanate from everywhere at once. In that moment, the only sensation she felt, the only thought in her brain, the source of all the pleasure in the world, was Eric.

And when they both came back down, when Jenna was lying under him, quivering, her cheek pressed against his—Eric whispered, "Nothing else matters does it?"

Still inside of her, he thrust deeper one last time until their bodies were flush together, as if to punctuate the thought. And her nerve endings were so raw, so sensitive, that this sent another wave of electricity tearing through her. She cried out, clawing her fingernails into his back. Finally, she answered his question by shaking her head.

No. Nothing else matters.

When the tears came—inexplicable, frustrating, beyond her control— Eric kissed them away, and Jenna wrapped her arms and legs around him, anchoring his body to hers.

Like if she let go, he'd disappear.

CHAPTER 24

When Jenna received Billie's Evite to May's sixth birthday party, her first thought was how badly she wished Eric could go. After all, if things were different, if they were an "out" couple, he'd be her date. Jenna already knew they worked in work situations and in her apartment. Now she was itching for Eric to see her real-life experiences.

And quietly, she couldn't help but wonder how he'd react to a scenario full of parents and kids. Would he embrace the family thing? Would it bore him—or turn him off completely? Or, hope of hopes, maybe he'd love it! She didn't know.

The plan came to her in the middle of an editorial meeting, while Mitchell was delivering a Dr. Seussian soliloquy about a picture he'd received from a babe with a brown bob in a beaded Balmain blazer. From Birmingham.

Jenna Jones
iMessages
April 16th, 2013, 11:49 AM

Jenna: It can't just be you and me all the time.
Eric: Threesome?

Jenna: Please, I'm a terrible multi-tasker. No, I need you to be my plus-one at May's birthday party!

Eric: You and me, in public? How?

Jenna: Remember how we're shooting a Perfect Find with Elodie in June?

Eric: A detachable 'Clash of the Titans' braid, smh. How does it stick on? This series has taught me that I don't know shit about women.

Jenna: Tiny comb. Anyway, Elodie will be there. So bring your handheld. To the parents, and anyone else who sees us together, it'll look like…

Eric: …we're shooting B-roll for her video.

Jenna: How cunning am I? Also, it's a costume party.

Eric: A costume party at a park in April? Mad random, I already love this kid. What should I get her? What's she into?

Jenna: The afterlife.

Eric: * insert blank-faced emoji here *

Jenna: She's Wednesday Addams with Billie's smile.

May's party fell on the following Saturday. It was a clear, beautiful afternoon perfect for an outdoor celebration. The festivities were being held where most spring/summer Brooklyn kiddie parties went down, at the glorious Brooklyn Bridge Park. A man-made attraction built on a formerly trash-cluttered section of East River beach, the park was an urban oasis. At each pier was a different kid-and-adult friendly attraction: a cute, smallish beach with unsullied (for New York) sand; a preternaturally green grassy knoll perfect for picnics; high-tech volleyball courts; and gourmet taco and gelato stands. Looming above it all was the underside of the mighty Brooklyn Bridge, stretching from the park to the never-not-awesome Lower Manhattan skyline, glittering just beyond the river.

May had chosen to have her party surrounding the park's main attraction—Jane's Carousel, a hopped-up version of the garden variety amusement park ride (the horses were the sizes of Clydesdales, and painted by MOMA artists). The Carousel was surrounded by picnic tables where Billie and Jay had set up hot dogs, hamburgers, and beers for the harried parents.

It was a costume party because May's birthday parties always were. (Halloween was her favorite holiday.) May was Black Swan. Because her friend's parents were mostly fancy Brooklynites in the arts, they took their kids' costumes dead-seriously. The children had no choice in the matter. Little Sebastian wanted to be a Power Ranger? Nope, he'd be the Empire State Building, complete with custom-made taxi-cab shoes.

All of the adults were in over-the-top costumes, too—including Jenna, who was waiting for Eric by a cupcake vendor, hidden away from the picnic tables (they decided to come separately, so they didn't look too couple-y). She was Jennifer Beals from *Flashdance*, which was admittedly uninspired since she basically already had the hair. She wore it half-wet, so it hung as if she was sweaty from dancing like crazy to "Maniac," and added a grey sweatshirt, fuzzy legwarmers, and Capezio jazz shoes. Plus, '80s makeup— rainbow shimmer eyeshadow and bubble gum pink lipstick.

Jenna felt a tap on her shoulder. She turned around to see Eric standing with his camera in one hand, a gift in the other—and no costume.

"Well…hi!" she said.

He gave her a friendly wave. "I'd kiss you, but it's against the rules." He looked at Jenna's get-up, laughing. "What's your costume? Whitney Houston? Why'd you go all out?"

"Look," she said, pointing over to the crowd. "I told you it was a costume party!"

Surveying the complicated get-ups, he grimaced. "Oh no. I thought only the kids were dressing up! But, I mean, I'm low-key the Hulk. I have on a Hulk T-shirt, see?"

"You're not the Hulk, you're Eric in an ironic tee that says 'Hulk Le Incredible.'" She pointed to his snapback. "And why are you wearing a Yankees fitted?"

"Cause it's fresh?"

"I know how to fix this." She reached in her purse for the portable sewing kit she kept with her. "Do those jeans matter to you?"

"No," he said, and then seeing her rip scissors out of her kit, he changed his answer. "Wait…yeah! They matter. A lot."

"Oh please, they were a freebie at a Rick Owens men's fashion event. Plus, they're already a little distressed. Come here, Hulk!"

Because Eric wanted to please her, and because it happened mind-bendingly fast, he allowed Jenna to cut wide slashes in his jeans and tee shirt, rip off his sleeves, and then use them to make a tattered, ripped-up headband—which she tied across his forehead, leaving the remaining material dangling to his shoulder.

When she was done, Jenna stepped back to appraise her project, and burst out laughing.

"What did you do to me?" asked Eric, miserable.

"You look like a member of Full Force!"

"I'm out, yo, I can't go through with this," he said, turning to walk away. Jenna grabbed his arm, giggling.

"No, I'm kidding. You look exactly like the Hulk. And I love you."

Eric looked down at himself, shaking his head. "And I must really love you. Come on, let's do this."

When Jenna and Eric—keeping a benign interpersonal space from each other—walked up to Billie (who was Dionne from *Clueless*, in a yellow plaid miniskirt, matching blazer, and a long micro-braid wig), she was standing with the mothers of two of May's school friends. One was dressed as the World War 2 feminist icon, Rosie the Riveter; the other was Chiquita Banana. From what was visible through their intricate costumes—they were older white women, in their late-forties, who were in svelte, yoga-fied shape.

"Jenna! Hi Eric!" Billie gave them both hugs. "Guys, you remember my good friend, Jenna-fer Beals. And this is her co-worker Eric. Who's dressed as…wait, what are you, Eric? A member of Parliament Funkadelic?"

"Hey Billie," he said, with a sad sigh. "Actually, I'm the Hulk."

Jenna beamed. "Don't you see it?"

"You are *such* a sport," said Billie, patting him on the arm.

"Great to see you again, Jenna. I always love talking to you at Billie's parties," said the woman in the Rosie the Riveter costume, who was wearing denim overalls, and a 1940's updo wrapped with a red kerchief. The forty-eight year-old single mother was a VP of visual merchandising at NBC—and quite intense.

Giving Eric an air-kiss, Rosie said, "You know, you look very familiar."

"I know who you are!" said Chiquita Banana, a Danish wood designer. Her reed-thin body was outfitted in a rainbow-striped flamenco dress, which she accessorized with banana earrings and a basket of real, edible fruit tied to her head. "StyleZine, right? You and Jenna do those fun Perfect Find videos. Loved the *New York* magazine piece."

"Yep, that's me. Great to meet you," he said, bending down to receive her air kiss.

"I'm sorry, this is so rude, but you are too cute," she said with a laugh, nudging Rosie the Riveter.

Eric's exposed chest and arms in his insane ripped tee had not gone unnoticed. He felt more naked than naked. He wanted to hide behind the carousel.

"What he is, is very smart," pointed out Jenna, feeling territorial. She didn't bring him there to be eye candy for horny MILFs.

"Smart?" Rosie the Riveter faced him. "Great, we'd love to get a young person's opinion on the monstrous new Common Core testing system in New York public schools. We were just talking about it."

"Already? Eric just walked in," said Billie.

"But it's so important," said Rosie, scrunching up her rolled denim sleeves past her elbows. "Kindergartners are expected to read like second-graders by the end of the year, or they're left back. And they're all held to the same standards, no matter their learning style. The only reason you should be held back in Kindergarten is if you have severe social issues, not academic ones. Like, if you're a little psychopath."

They all tried not to look at Chiquita Banana, whose daughter Ansel, a complete menace, had brought a safety pin to school and stabbed her classmates in their butt cheeks during Valentine's Day assembly. She told people she was Cupid.

"I have some thoughts about Common Core," said Jenna, hoping to save Eric from having to pontificate on something parent-oriented, not even five minutes into the party.

"Well, I'm dying to hear Eric's perspective," said Chiquita. "He is *far* younger than us and was in school more recently."

"I don't know, man, it sounds like madness," he said. "Whatever happened to valuing creativity? You're producing little robots if you're forcing them to memorize SAT-type shit…I mean, *information*…when they're five. To me, the academic thing should be, like, a journey. Not a destination."

Jenna and Billie raised their eyebrows.

Under pressure, with no real information on the topic—and in the universe's most emasculating outfit—Eric managed to produce an amazing response. Jenna beamed with pride.

Twenty-two, twenty-three, doesn't matter, thought Jenna. *My man can fit in anywhere! He's getting a blowjob the second we leave.*

"A journey, not a destination," said Rosie the Riveter. "If that doesn't nail it, I don't know what does."

"Told you he was smart," said Jenna with a wry smile. "Now ask him about Obama's foreign policy."

"I feel like I'm auditioning for the debate team," said Eric, and everyone laughed. Eric didn't find it so hilarious, though. Why did Jenna keep emphasizing that he was smart? "It's just that I really enjoyed school. Like, I had fun learning stuff. It's not fair that, umm...Baudelaire doesn't get to feel that."

"I agree," said Jenna. "And I hope, when I have a child, that this insane curriculum is overturned."

"And when is that happening, doll?" asked Chiquita Banana. "Do you have a fabulous man in your back pocket? Any plans to procreate?"

"Why does she need a man?" asked Rosie the Riveter. "I didn't. If you want to do it alone, there are ways. In vitro treatments and donor sperm made me a mom."

Jenna let out a twinkly laugh, in the hopes that this would mask how uncomfortable she was. How could she have forgotten how mom-centric—and pushy to the point of rudeness—this crowd was?

"Oh, when it happens, it happens," she said.

"We're in our forties," said Rosie the Riveter. "Too old for 'when it happens, it happens.' Doctors never really tell women the truth about how drastically our fertility decreases with age. You want a baby? Don't wait. Freeze your eggs. Get donor sperm. Adopt."

"Those options cost thousands," said Billie-as-Dionne, just wanting her to shut up. But it was hard for her to look authoritative wearing a bewigged waterfall of synthetic braids. "Not everyone has an NBC salary, sweetie."

Rosie the Riveter reached into the pocket of her denim overalls and handed Jenna her card. "Listen, call me anytime. I can refer you to a brilliant fertility specialist at Mount Sinai."

Jenna caught a quick glance at Eric, who was rubbing a temple and looking like he wanted to be anywhere but there. Her stomach flip-flopped when she imagined what he must be thinking.

Chiquita Banana looked at him. "I'm assuming you don't have kids yet, right?"

"Nooo," he said. "Not me. Not yet. One day...I guess."

Jenna cleared her throat and quickly changed the subject, addressing Chiquita Banana. "So, did you finally move out of your apartment?"

"I did! We're in Prospect Heights now. Are you still in the West Village?"

"No, now I'm a Brooklynite, too."

"And where are you, Eric?" asked Chiquita.

"I live at home. Like, in my mom's condo."

Jenna grimaced. It was the truth, but his answer made him sound like a teenager. "I'm between places right now" would've been just as accurate.

"Adorable," cooed Chiquita Banana. "Your mom!"

"It's only temporary," said Jenna. "You know, just to save money."

"I think it makes great financial sense," said Billie.

"My nephew lives with my sister," said Rosie the Riveter. "He's twenty-five. I get it, the economy's bad. But in their case, I think she just doesn't want to let go of her baby boy. His room still looks like a pre-teen's. So infantilizing."

Precious baby boy? Infantilizing? thought Jenna. *I don't want the love of my life associated with some random loser. Can't we discuss Common Core again?*

"You know, I have a great real estate agent," said Chiquita, "for when you're ready. Want his info?"

"No, it's cool," said Eric, bothered by the antsy expression on Jenna's face. "I'll move out as soon as I save enough."

"Which will be very soon," emphasized Jenna.

Eric raised an eyebrow. "It will?"

"Of course," she said, though they'd never once discussed his living situation. "Eric has such a bright future as a filmmaker. He's got his own Wiki and IMDB pages! He definitely won't be in his mother's house for too long."

"Good for you!" said Rosie. "And if you're looking to build your resume, we need someone to film our upcoming Parent Flash Mob. It happens every year on the last day of school, during lunch. The kids love it."

The kids did not love it. It freaked them out, seeing their moms pop out from under cafeteria tables and shimmy with Principal James to "Living La Vida Loca."

"Interested, Eric?" asked Chiquita. "We can't pay, but it would be a fun little job. Great for your resume."

Jenna bristled at them speaking to Eric like he was a cute kid with a hobby. As if he were a person for whom filming a collection of jazz-handsy elementary school moms—gratis—would be a resume-builder.

Before he could say accept or decline, Jenna said, "Guys, forgive me, but Eric's the lead director on all our productions at StyleZine. I'm almost certain we will have a shoot that day."

Eric was trying to think of a response when a text buzzed through from Tim. Perfect timing—anything to escape the surreal awkwardness of the conversation.

"Sorry, one second," he said, and threw himself into a thread with Tim about their latest Zelda game, while the women carried on around him. After a couple of minutes, Jenna pulled him aside.

"Put your phone away," she whispered.

"I can't. Tim thinks I owe him $150 from our game last night," said Eric, continuing to text. "Why do I do this to myself? Yo I *hate* playing with him."

"You've been on your phone for five minutes; you haven't spoken to anyone."

Eric looked at Jenna. "Can I at least finish my sentence? Damn."

"It's rude! You just started texting mid-conversation."

"Everyone I know starts texting mid-conversation."

'Cause they're kids, thought Jenna. *And now you're acting like one.*

"Why are you being so weird?" hissed Jenna.

"Me?" he whispered back. "I don't even recognize you right now."

"You're actually pouting."

"Forgive me," he said. "I just spent twenty minutes being dissected by middle-aged women dressed like historical pop culture icons. I'm running out of ways to pretend I'm cool in this environment."

"I know, we'll leave soon. But while we're here, just try to stay engaged. For me."

"For you? I'm dressed like a Chippendale dancer for you. I killed that whateverthefuck Core thing for you. The Banana thinks I'm adorable. If you're dissatisfied with my performance, I'm happy to bounce. UNC plays Duke in an hour, and there are three idiots from my eighth grade class waiting for me at Tim's house with Hennessy and Funyons."

"Your performance?"

"Seriously, how many ways are you gonna try to convince them I'm awesome? I feel like a one-legged poodle at a dog show."

"I'm just a proud girlfriend, that's all!"

"You're acting," he whispered, "like a deranged publicist."

"Hey Eric," said Billie, realizing it was almost time for her to set out May's birthday cupcakes. "Can you take a picture of us? We look hilarious, this has to go on Facebook."

"Sure," he said, relieved to end his conversation with Jenna. "Whose phone?"

"Here, use mine," said Jenna, handing it to him.

Eric took it from her, and then entered the password (she'd never bothered to change it after he set it up, way back when she first got her iPhone and didn't even know what an app was). The screen sprung to life, broadcasting a Firefox tab. It was the last thing she was looking at, before it faded to black.

Eric squinted, hoping that he wasn't seeing what he was seeing. Forbes. com. Eric knew what it was before he opened it: "The Business of Being Brian Stein." Without reacting, he clicked the camera icon, raised the phone and took a photo.

She had the fucking thing bookmarked.

CHAPTER 25

Brian.

She still cared. Maybe she'd been in touch with him. Maybe she missed their life, missed being with her someone her age. Someone who didn't live with his mom, someone settled. Loaded. A classy douche who understood proper texting etiquette. Did she still love Brian? How many times had she read that article? Had she been comparing him to Brian the whole time?

Now, this afternoon made sense. He thought Jenna wanted him at the party to liberate them from the office and the bedroom. And he thought it'd be fun, but it was terrible. All that pushy talk about his accomplishments? She wasn't trying to show those old biddies that he was beyond being written off as a hot himbo who was too young to keep up. She was trying to convince herself. She wanted to see if he could be as impressive as her ex. But if this were the game, he'd always come up short.

Eric had told Jimmy Crockett his date with Jenna was a failed audition. Was this his?

His brain was so cloudy with anger and hurt that he checked out of the party. He opted out of the rambling discussion about whose apartment was big enough to conduct rehearsals for that psychotic flash mob. He only spoke when asked a direct question. And because he felt like being a dick—when Chiquita asked him what was wrong, he responded, "fruit allergy."

Eric didn't wake up until a tiny, be-dimpled Black Swan ran over to their cluster, and hugged Billie around the waist.

"This is the best party ever," she said with measured excitement. Where most little girls would've hopped up and down or giggled with joy, the furthest she went was a deadpan high-five with her mom.

"My love!" Jenna bent down and gave May a squeeze. "Happy sixth birthday! Hey, I want you to meet my friend, Eric Combs."

May, who's face was flawlessly made-up to look like an evil, white-faced, black-lipped ballerina, looked at up at Eric with seriousness.

"Hello Hulk," she said, sticking out her hand. She was wearing a black leotard, black tutu, feathery headdress and massive black wings.

"Hello, Black Swan," he said, shaking her hand.

"So, what do you do at work with Auntie Jenna?" May asked.

"See my camera? It sounds…well, it sounds ridiculous when I say it out loud, but generally? I film women talking about their clothes."

"I don't think that sounds rindickalus. Clothes are cool." She turned to Billie. "Mommy, can I talk to Eric about my costume? In front of his camera?"

"Wait, this is to die for," said Jenna, who all but melted into a puddle. "Eric, she wants you to shoot her own StyleZine street style video!"

"Me next!" exclaimed Chiquita Banana.

Eric welcomed this idea. The truth? May was the cutest kid he'd ever seen—and he couldn't get away from his current situation fast enough.

"May Lane," he said, "I feel like this is gonna be the dopest video I've ever shot. Come on, let's go over by the rocks. That Brooklyn Bridge view over the water is sick. Is that okay, Billie?"

"Have at it!" she said. "We'll get you in ten minutes, so we can blow out the candles."

And then a tall Hulk and a tiny swan-demon made their way over to the beach. Without turning around, he knew Jenna was watching them. He was nailing the "…but is he good with kids?" portion of the test.

Minutes later, Eric had positioned tiny May so that she was leaning back against the lovely pile of granite rocks—with small beach, the East River and the Battery Park skyscrapers shimmering behind her. The afternoon sun cast her in a beatific, holy light (especially with the wings), which was a disorienting effect, considering she was dressed like a psychotic swan.

May looked like a fallen deity. Like Angel Gabriel in little girl form. Eric was in love.

He propped his camera up on his shoulder, and aimed it at her. "Okay, so I'm just gonna talk to you a little bit, to warm you up. Cool?"

"Cool!"

Only then did it hit him that he had no idea how to talk to little girls. He hadn't spoken to a six-year-old since he was six. But, he decided they probably weren't that much different than older girls. So he tried to think of things he'd say to his friends.

"So wassup? You look beautiful."

"What does wassup mean?"

"Wassup is another way of saying 'what's up.'"

"Umm, I don't know what's up. I'm having a birthday party, which I like, but last night mommy said I couldn't make a Play-Doh tomb for me to sleep in, which I don't like. So, I don't know wassup. That's a too much confusing question."

"No it isn't." He put the camera down by his side and sat next to her. "If someone asks you wassup, no matter what you have going on, just say, 'Nothing. Chilling.' Keep it simple."

"That's easy."

"So, wassup?"

"Nothing. Chilling. Wassup?"

"Chilling," shrugged Eric. "And now, if you're really cool? You'd give me a pound-bomb."

"What's that?"

"You just pound my fist with yours. Like this." He gathered her fingers into a ball and then pushed it against his. "And then we make a little explosion with our hands, like a bomb. POOF!"

"POOF!" hollered May. "You're funny. Pound-bombs are silly. So are you."

"So I've been told."

"I'm not so silly, but I like silly things sometimes."

"Yeah? You like silly movies?"

"Not really. My favorite movie is the *Prince of Egypt*."

"The Disney movie about Moses?"

"Ancient Egypt is exciting. Because dead people got to be mummies. Even dead cats, if they belonged to a pharaoh. And the men wore eyeliner. I like the Moses story because it shows it's not good manners to make people slaves, or to throw slave babies into a river filled with alligators. Manners are important."

Eric tried not to register his surprise at May's bleak tastes in movies. "So really, out of all the Disney animated flicks, that's your favorite?"

"*Si senor.*"

"That's cool. I like Ancient Egypt, too. I just thought little girls your age skewed more toward Disney princess movies, rather than slave ones."

"I like those, too. I like Tiana, 'cause she looks like us. And *Tangled*, because of her hair. I used to love long hair, when I was four. That's when I always wanted to watch the Barbie show on Netflix. But I wasn't allowed."

"Why?"

"Mommy didn't like that there was no one with brown skin and that Barbie only talked about boys and clothes. But she watches a show called Carrie Bradshaw and there's no brown faces…and boys and clothes is all she talks about."

Eric looked at her in awe. "You might be the smartest person I've ever met."

"Akshally, I'm smarter than regular kindergartners. But I don't tell my friends, 'cause that's bad manners," she said.

"Your manners are epic, kid. I need lessons from you."

"Boys don't know about manners."

"No, we typically don't."

"Do you know what 'wedding' means? Some boys don't know about that, either."

"Yeah, it's when a man and a woman get married. Or, like, two men or two women." Growing up with Tim's two dads had made him sensitive to the legitimacy of same-sex couples. But he didn't know if that was an age-appropriate response. He tried again. "I don't know, I guess it's just when two people…"

"See? Boys don't know what it means," said May. "It's the only part of princess movies that I like. It's what happens at the end of them. There's always a cool song, and she wears a dressy dress and gets to marry a prince."

"Okay, now I think I understand."

"It's fun to see the prince and princess so happy, because you never know, they could die really soon. Everyone dies, you know. And you never know when. So we have to have fun every day."

"Word! Carpe diem."

"Are you married?" asked May. "Maybe to a princess?"

"No, not married. Are you?"

"You really are silly! I've only been six for a day. It's not time yet." She smoothed out her tutu. "I saw you and Auntie Jenna come in together. Are you her true love?"

Eric drew back, wondering if she'd figured it out. He wouldn't be surprised—she seemed like she could call upon the dark arts to steal secrets from her unsuspecting victims.

"No, we're just friends."

May looked like she didn't believe him. "Well, maybe you can marry her. All princesses get husbands. And Auntie Jenna's all by herself. Doesn't it make you sad?"

"Not all princesses need husbands, you know," said Eric, who couldn't believe he was debating this with a baby. "The problem with those movies is that they tell little girls that weddings are the ultimate goal. And then they might rush out just to find someone to marry because they think it's expected—instead of finding the right person. It's smarter to take your time, figure out who you are, make mistakes, and then, when the timing's right, maybe you'll meet someone who makes you want do the Disney wedding."

May nodded, but was unimpressed by Eric's speech.

"So," she said, "do you want the Disney wedding with Auntie Jenna?"

Eric passed his camera from one hand to the other. How had he ended up here? He was barely clothed and being judged by someone who couldn't pronounce "actually." He had nothing to lose, so he told the truth.

"Yeah," he admitted, with a sigh. "I do. But it's not the end of the movie yet."

"Okay."

"That's a secret, Black Swan. Don't tell."

"I'd never ever."

Eric glanced over at Jenna, who was helping Billie unpack May's cupcakes. She waved, flashing an enthusiastic smile. Seeing him with the little girl had made her annoyance vanish. He waved back, but couldn't bring himself to smile.

As May and Eric were wrapping up, Billie, Jay and Jenna came over to watch. When she signed off with the line he fed her—"I'm May Lane, and this was my StyleZine street style look"—the three broke out in applause.

"You killed it, May-May!" exclaimed Jenna. "Should I be worried about my job?"

"We were coming over to tell you that we're blowing out candles now, but we couldn't resist watching," said Billie, giving her daughter a squeeze. "How did it go, May? Did you feel nervous? What's up?"

She shrugged. "Chilling."

Jay, who was dressed as '80s Al Sharpton (complete with a rollerset wig), chuckled. "Nice one, E."

"Look what else Eric taught me." May stuck out her little fist and gave him a pound-bomb.

"My homie, Black Swan," said Eric.

"That," said Jenna, "was beyond adorable."

"Hey Elodie," said Eric, "where have you been?"

Elodie was dressed as Medusa, with a snake fright wig, a green face, and snakeskin contacts. "I was helping Jay take May's guest's tickets at the Carousel. A thankless job. I smoked some w-e-e-d before I came, just so I could deal with the runny noses and temper tantrums, but it just made me tired. Now I wanna take a power nap under that picnic table. Preferable with Chiquita Banana's husband. Did you see him? The one that looks like Idris Elba?"

"So disappointing," said Billie. "I have all these brilliant, beautiful single b-l-a-c-k friends and a Danish b-l-o-n-d-e gets Idris Elba."

"Guys," said Jenna, "I've been waiting all day for us to be alone. Scooch in closer." Everyone huddled together with May in the middle. "We have huge news."

Eric wished she wasn't choosing this moment—when everything was so wrong—to make her announcement.

"Wait," said Billie. "News? The both of you?"

"Yes," squealed Jenna. She was glowing. "And we wanted to share it with you, first, before telling the world. You'll be so happy."

Billie ripped her hand from May's, throwing her arms in the air.

"You're engaged?"

"Wait, I don't..." started Jay, seeing the stricken looks on Eric and Jenna's faces.

"Come on, Jay, this is a huge moment." Billie nudged herself between Jenna and Eric, flinging an arm around them both. "Jenna, you finally had that heart-to-heart, like we talked about! See? It worked out. And we have news, too. I'm two months pregnant! Maybe we'll have babies around the same time, depending on when you start trying!" She kissed him on the cheek. "Eric, she wants this more than anything."

"And so does Eric," said May.

"Wh-what?" Eric could barely find his voice.

"What?" said Jenna.

"Eric said he wanted a Disney wedding with you! Where the prince marries the princess at the end?"

"Eric, that came out of your mouth?" Elodie clapping her hands. "Omigod, you two are giving me a toothache with the sweetness, I can't!"

Jenna looked at him, her face a map of confusion, unfiltered joy and hesitant hope. "You said that? About us?"

The idea took her breath away—but then she got a good look at Eric. He looked like Peter Pan walking the plank. Clearly, it wasn't what he'd said at all.

"No...that's not exactly..." he babbled, his heart pounding in his chest. "We were talking about princess movies and May got carried away."

"Of course," said Jenna, humiliated.

May grimaced. "Oh noo, I forgot to keep the secrret. I'm sorry Eric, that was an axnadent!" And then, understanding that she'd ruined the vibe somehow, Black Swan slipped between her mom's legs and ran to join her friends.

Jenna's body had gone rigid. Somehow, she found the strength to look unbothered, and paste on a tight smile. "Sorry guys. No, we're not...I'm not engaged. But oh Billie, I'm so excited you're pregnant."

Everyone went silent, too stuck in the mire of that terrible moment to say anything. Jenna and Eric were cloaked in a miserable awkwardness; nothing anyone said would've saved them.

Billie let her arms slip from the two of their shoulders. "Excuse me while I drown myself in the East River."

"Billie's had a long day," said Jay, glaring at her. "So, what was your announcement, Jenna?"

She cleared her throat, but her voice sounded weak. "Eric was invited to South by Southwest. The festival."

The congratulations were long and loud—almost too effusive. "The board called him yesterday, and said that they'd already fallen in love with *Tyler on Perry Street*," said Jenna, trying to overcome her dampened enthusiasm. "But after reading the *New York* piece, they knew they had to move before his stock rose and Sundance scooped him up. They actually admitted that."

"Yeah, the dude called me 'talent soup.' Whatever that means." He said this with an empty smile. It had been the greatest call he'd ever received. The call he'd been waiting for since third grade. But in this anticlimactic moment, it was the last thing he wanted to talk about.

"No one deserves it more than you, man," said Jay, shaking his hand. "I'm proud of you."

"Thanks, professor," said Eric.

"Don't forget the little people, heartbreaker," said Elodie, kissing him on the cheek.

Then, in a hurried attempt to fast-forward through the tarnished moment, Billie herded everyone over to the picnic table, to blow out May's candles. Eric and Jenna stood on opposite sides of the table, the space between them seeming to loom oceans-wide.

After the party, Jenna asked Eric to walk with her along Pier 6, which stretched out far beyond May's party area. Neither one felt like talking, but Jenna couldn't go home while things were so abysmal.

They reached the end without speaking, and then leaned back against the railing.

"Want to go first?" asked Jenna.

"Yep," he said. "Why were you selling me so hard to your friends?"

"What do you mean?"

"He lives at home, but he's moving the second he saves money. I know he's just a kid, but it's okay 'cause he has his own Wiki page. He's good enough for y'all. Swear.'"

"Honey, you took that the wrong way."

"Are you embarrassed to be with me?"

"Seriously? You know I'm in awe of you. I'm a you-groupie." She looked at him. "But while we're talking about saving money—are you really betting on video games? A person who's trying to save money doesn't spend it on such silly things."

"Said the woman living in the hood with a fifteen hundred dollar armchair."

"Hilarious." Jenna furrowed her brow. "You didn't seem like you today."

"Neither did you. You were trying to control everything I said, watching to see if I made mistakes. I felt like I was breathing wrong."

"You barely said anything, and then you turned into a jackass.

The fruit allergy thing was particularly memorable." Eric shrugged. "I was over it."

"We weren't ourselves," she said in a small voice.

"No." Eric was silent for a beat. "You're right about me wasting money on video games, though. Maybe I should start reading *Forbes*. You know, to learn how to manage my finances like an adult."

Jenna blinked.

"Maybe Brian Stein needs an intern. He could teach me how to invest, how to use proper cell phone etiquette. How to be a social success around fifty-year-old women. He could send me to Duane Reade to get his mousse. It'd be dope."

"Oh no," groaned Jenna. "My phone. Let me explain…"

"I know technology confuses you. But you should erase your history after Google-fucking your ex." Furious, he shot out of the railing and started pacing. "'Everything I ever loved is in her details.' That's him, Jenna? This clown had you for twenty years and most vividly misses your decorating?"

"Elodie just sent me the link! How could I not read it? But it doesn't mean anything!"

"She *just* sent you the link? You're so bad at this. That shit's been out a month."

"How did you know that?"

"Don't worry about it." He kept pacing. "I bet it feels good, knowing that he's still obsessed with you. How many times did you read it? Did you call him? Have you seen him?"

"No!" Trying not to look as flustered as she felt, she said, "I can't control what he says about me. I heard he'd mentioned me in an article and, of course, I was curious. That's all! I don't want him. I want *you.*"

"But why? He's the antithesis of me. If he's your type, I don't even know why I'm here."

"You're here because I love you!" She paused to catch her breath. "You're here because I want the people I love most to know you. Because I wanted us to tell them about your huge achievement. Because I want you in my life, my actual life."

"Do I look like a fucking idiot to you? This was an audition for the role of your in-real-life boyfriend."

"That's not true! Please don't be upset."

"I'm not upset! *Do I look upset?*"

"Yes! You look like you wanna huff and puff and blow my house down!"

Eric looked up at the sky, trying to calm himself. "I need you to tell me the truth. You want what Billie and Jay have. Like, now."

"Sure, but not…now. Just, you know, in the abstract."

"Don't downplay it. You want it so bad that Billie had a seizure celebrating our fake engagement. You were deflating when the Witches of Eastwick were talking about babies."

Eric wanted to tell her that Darcy had already told him the truth. He'd been obsessing over it since that moment in her office. His own mother had more insight into his relationship than he did. "You talked circles around it the other night, but never said anything real," he continued. "'What does our future look like, Eric? Are we gonna make it, Eric?' It was so hypothetical. Do you know how I felt when I saw how excited you looked over that Disney wedding thing? Like a complete disappointment. Jenna, I just turned twenty-three…I can't give you that life! When were you gonna tell me how unqualified I am to be your man?"

"You're perfect for me," Jenna said quietly.

"Do us both a favor and just say what you want. I wanna hear you say it."

She couldn't. She didn't want to scare him away with her unrealistic daydreams about their future.

Eric waited five seconds, and then twenty, and then gave up.

"You're a coward," he said.

"And you're too young to understand."

"Right," said Eric. "I'm seventeen to eighteen years younger than you, and I live with the antichrist, and I bet on dumbass video games. I met you way too soon and I don't know what we do about that. But I love you. I love you like it's my calling. You don't know, 'cause I don't say it, but there are these times when it hits me so hard, Jenna. Like in the morning when you do that melodramatic, fifteen-minute stretch and try to get up, but then collapse back on the bed like someone shot you. When you pick stuff up off the floor with your toes. When we're in a meeting and your mouth gets tight because you're trying not to laugh at something I said. Your you-ness ruins me." His eyes bore into her. "Whatever happened here today, though? I'm not with it. And I gotta go before it gets worse."

He tried to walk away, but Jenna grabbed his hand. "Eric, are we going to be okay?"

What could he say? They had to be okay. That wasn't in question. He just didn't know how.

He nodded vaguely. And then Jenna released his hand, and let him go.

www.stylezine.com
Just Jenna: Style Secrets from our Intrepid Glambassador!

Q: *"I've always adored fluffy coats and après-ski sweaters and fur-lined boots. My dream is to dress like Julie Christie in Doctor Zhivago. But I live in Taos!! And I adore it. My whole family's here, and I love working with my kindergartners, and the topography moves me. But what about my fashion fantasy?" -@MelissaJustDoingMeLopez*

A: *Sweetie, it might be time to surrender to your reality. It's, like, two thousand degrees in New Mexico—I'm frightened that embracing the Ski Chalet look might give you a heat rash. Also, I can't in good conscience advise you to do what I call "Forcing the Season" (I see this during New York winters when we get a rare day above forty degrees, and women break out their Freakum dresses). The harsh truth is that the temps are too high for your winter style dream. Sure, you might not rock faux-mink earmuffs anytime soon, but you have the privilege of living in a place that you love passionately. Try adding winter-wear elements to your New Mexico wardrobe, like pairing a gauzy sundress with a lightweight, cropped bomber (check out Nordstrom.com or Zara for my favorite season-splicing essentials!).*

PS: *The older I get, the more I wonder if the secret to true happiness is knowing which dreams to let go of.*

CHAPTER 26

T he next evening, Jenna attempted to mask her misery at the New York Academy of Art Tribeca Ball, one of the chicest charity affairs of the spring season. Tonight's theme was "Believe in Luck," and whoever had designed the space had taken this literally. The entire room seemed to have been French-kissed by Tinkerbelle. The ceiling and walls were shot through with a million flickering, tiny white lights. Everything was beige, cream, or ivory, and sprinkled with a fine spray of shimmer—from the waiter's gloves to the satin tablecloths on the dining tables along the perimeter of the room. The guests were a cross-section of New York luminaries. Robert de Niro, Anna Wintour, Zac Posen, Puffy, SJP, and Alec Baldwin mingled with supermodels, fashion editors, brand name socialites, and Wall Street tycoons.

The tickets were upwards of a thousand dollars, but Jenna was invited by Ralph Lauren's PR team. Elodie was invited by one of her clients. When Jenna had received her over-the-top, duchesse satin-wrapped invite, she'd wanted to RSVP no—which she told her best friend the night before.

"Those scene-y, New York-y, fancy-schmancy balls are designed to make civilians feel like shit. The ones I went to with Brian were fun. But if you have your seat paid for through a work connection, you feel like somebody's poor cousin, and then you spend the entire night trying not to get red wine on your borrowed Marchesa gown while being mortified that John Hamm's girlfriend had her publicist tell you to stop staring at him."

"Come again?" Elodie asked.

"It wasn't my finest hour," said Jenna. "Are you bringing anyone?"

"No, I recently saw this psychic who told me to stop with the online dates. According to her, my soulmate is just around the corner. And even weirder? She said he's coming from a sunny state. Do you think she means a sunny state of mind, or literally a state that has a lot of sun?"

"Either way, you're winning," said Jenna. "Nothing wrong with a happy man, or a man with real estate in Malibu. Wait, do you even believe in soulmates?"

"No. But cares? I don't believe in fillers, but I just shot up my laugh lines with Botox."

"Why? You're perfect. The last thing you need is Botox."

"And the last thing you need is to stay in tonight," said Elodie.

"You and Eric just had a tiff."

"It was more than a tiff."

"Jenna, go to the ball. I know you've been sulking at home all day in your trashy cutoffs, eating Nutter Butters and marathoning *Girlfriends.*"

"Purple Rain."

"You need to get out," said Elodie. "It'll be fun. So many couples we know will be there."

Jenna sipped her champagne, remembering this conversation. So many couples we know will be there. Indeed. The room was lousy with couples. Stunning, glamorous women on the arm of rakish, debonair men with grey-flecked temples and fully paid for summer homes in the Hamptons. Married couples with full, rich lives—families, children, college tuitions and robust life insurance plans. If and when the men had affairs, they were respectful. The women allowed their Pilates instructors to give them head, but wasn't that what they were there for? The gala might've been called the

Esteemed Married Couples of Manhattan Ball, because that's exactly who was there.

She adjusted the delicate floral garland in her hair and smoothed her hands over her bias cut, forest green, capped-sleeved Rodarte gown ("Effortlessly Sexy Wood Nymph in Mourning"). She eyed a gorgeous, A-list Asian dermatologist on the dance floor with her stunning Hungarian husband. Deciding she looked unnecessarily smug, Jenna took another sip of champagne and glared daggers at her. *Your guy's foxy, but mine's delicious, and we're not even close to sealing the deal because he was just Prom King, like yesterday. And this fact makes me want to rip those perfect auburn lowlights out of your head, Dr. Jennie. I might look single, but I'm not, I'm taken-taken-taken, just not the way you are, it'll never be the way you are, we'll never be parents like you and that Eastern Bloc bozo and it crushes me, and I feel like you know it, and I hate you, him, and your daughter who's a junior at Sacred Heart and had an emo song on the Billboard charts last month. Fuck the entire Ko-Stanislov family.*

Glowering, Jenna finished off her glass of champagne. She was in hell. She'd texted Eric, called him, sent carrier pigeons—and nothing. She was hardly surprised. He was hurt and stubborn.

Plus, he was right about May's party. Without being conscious of it, she'd wanted to see if Eric measured up—and she'd come off as trying to stage-manage his personality. Alone, in their secret love bubble, they were perfectly in sync! But around other people, their differences were magnified. She'd felt like his mother. And he'd seemed ten years younger than he already was.

The reason why Madonna, J. Lo and Demi Moore can date guys decades younger is because they've already had their children. I hate them, too.

It was an hour into the gala, and she hadn't yet found Elodie in the crowd of hundreds. So she'd been grouchily making the rounds, getting swept into conversations with old colleagues, fashion contacts, designers;

people she hadn't seen in the almost-year she'd been back in New York. And she kept having the similar versions of the same conversations.

"Jenna, is it 2003 or 2013?" Markie Masters had asked her, about five minutes ago. She was a gawky, but chic blonde American who was the head fashion buyer for Nicoletta's, a luxury department store in Milan. "Your complexion is just fantastic. What are your skincare secrets?"

"Well, I don't go to Dr. Jennie."

"And who are you here with? Anyone new? I have to say, the kid in your wildly flattering *New York* article was one hot piece of ass."

"You don't know the half," muttered Jenna. "Nope, not seeing anyone. Not since Brian."

"I'm so sorry about you two," said Markie, who'd often hosted the two at her villa during Milan Fashion Week. "Lily L'Amour. I swear, one day she'll OD on Tory Burch. Well, I hope you get back on the wagon soon. You're such a catch." Katie Couric winked at Markie from two social clusters over, and the redhead waved at the superstar anchor. "Schmoozing calls, but I predict you'll be engaged by the end of the year. Ciao!"

Jenna laughed at this and blew her a kiss. *Yeah right. Like my hot piece of ass will be proposing to me anytime before 2020.*

She plucked another flask of champagne from a roving waiter and relocated to the end of the bar, by the wildly extravagant band. Who paid for this collection of yahoos? The guitarist's butt cleavage was showing and the keyboardist's tux was fifteen sizes too big. Plus, the lead singer's rug was slipping off the side of his head, and he were singing a cabaret-style rendition of "It's Getting Hot in Here," which was awkward, considering that song's superstar producer, Pharell Williams, was twenty feet away.

Suddenly, Jenna noticed a man approaching her from the crowd.

"Hello," said Jenna.

"Are you Jenna Jones?"

He stuck out his hand; she automatically shook it. But she couldn't hear a thing he said over the relentlessly loud band. "What?"

"Are you Jenna Jones?"

"I'm sorry?"

"JENNA JONES?"

"YES!" screamed Jenna. "I'm sorry, I guess standing right by this band is not the place to meet someone. You are?"

"I'm..." he started to speak in a normal voice, and then raised it up ten decibels. "I'm James Diaz! The director of the Fashion Theory program at Fordham! Jay Lane told me all about you!"

"Oh, James Diaz!"

He nodded. He was about six feet tall, with an incredible head of wavy salt-and-pepper hair. He was ruggedly athletic-looking, as if he were a person who might enjoy climbing volcanic mountains or, perhaps herding massive flocks of sheep in his spare time.

"Let's move down there so we don't have to yell!" shouted Jenna.

The two wove through the crowd until they got to a relatively quiet spot at the other end of the bar. Jenna put down her flask of champagne.

"It's a pleasure to meet you," she said, shaking his hand.

"I've been meaning to email you, I've just been so swamped setting up these new courses. I know all about you, I've been following your career. I have to say, when Jay told me you'd been teaching, my first thought was that we had to have you."

"Well, you know I'm at StyleZine now," she started, trying to figure out a way to play this. "And I love it, but God, I miss teaching. I'd love to talk to you about what you have in mind."

"Obviously, this gala is not the place," he said, smiling.

"If you don't mind my asking, are you from Montana? Wisconsin? You sort of look like a cowboy, which begs the question—what's a cowboy doing in fashion?"

"To answer your first question, South Dakota. The Sunshine State."

The Sunshine State?

"And to answer your second, my mom was the most successful seamstress in our town." He shrugged. "I loved what she did. The fabrics intrigued me. The design, the construction. At Parsons, I discovered that I was fascinated by the social history of fashion. And it stuck."

"Yes, it's hard to shake fashion-love," she said, scanning the room for Elodie, James' future wife.

"Impossible," he said. "So yes, let's continue this conversation. You have my information, correct?"

"Correct." Jenna stuck out her hand. "Good to meet you Mr. Diaz."

"James. Until we speak again."

He walked away and Jenna began nibbling on a nail. This might be the thing. James Diaz would be her out. She would leave StyleZine and maybe everything else with Eric would fall into place. Her eight-month contract was almost up, and she'd more than exceeded Darcy's expectations. When Billie first brought him up, it was too early for her to leave her new job with any kind of grace. But now, she'd put in enough time.

She had to tell Eric. Jenna leaned against the mirrored surface of the bar and pulled her phone out of her clutch.

Jenna Jones
iMessages
April 25, 2013, 9:30 PM

Jenna: Call me. Please. Just call me.

She held her phone to her heart, willing him to call her. But, when he didn't after five minutes, she lost hope. So she dropped the phone back in her bag. In an attempt to rid herself of the persistent nausea she'd had since Eric walked away from her on that pier, she searched around in there for her roll of Tums.

That's when a hand reached from behind Jenna and slipped something down on the bar in front of her. Astonished, she dropped the Tums to the floor. Jenna knew who was behind her; she'd recognize that hand anywhere. It was what he placed on the bar that shook her to her core.

As of October 12, 1991, Brian Benjamin Stein wants:
To be a great architect. Better than Frank Lloyd Wright.
To be a millionaire before I'm thirty.
To have homes in three countries.
To build my mom a townhouse on Park Avenue.
To have a wife and kids.
You. I want you.

The napkin from that night at The Tombs had yellowed and was frayed on one side. The original ink had faded, too, but there was new ink. The bottom two bullets were circled in bright red. Speechless, Jenna picked up the napkin and turned around. There was Brian, in a gorgeous tux, his face flushed, naked with more emotion than she ever remembered seeing from him.

"Brian?"

"She's dead."

"Lily?"

"No, my mother. Anna. She just died." He grabbed her hand.

"Come with me."

As Brian hurriedly led Jenna through the party, the gossipy social set shimmered with delight at this very public display of Grand Gesturedom— they'd always wondered what went wrong with that couple, anyway. Elodie, who was flirting with a mysterious cowboy named James Diaz, almost fell into her martini.

Jenna was too shattered by the news to pull away. Or to protest. Or to hear her phone ringing from inside her clutch.

Far across the room, the usually eagle-eyed Darcy Vale had missed the scene with Brian and Jenna. She was busy. With pitch-perfect sadness, she was revealing to Les James, the editor-in-chief of *New York*, that Andrea Granger—the reporter who'd betrayed and diminished her with that StyleZine article—was selling valuable insider tips and story ideas to *Vanity Fair*. Of course, she'd already wrangled a *VF* writer to corroborate the story. On Monday morning, Andrea would be fired in complete disgrace.

Just then, Suki Delgado stumbled over to her. She threw an arm over Darcy's shoulder.

"'Member me?" the model slurred in her ear. Darcy glanced up.

"Of course, I know who you are," she said, offering up her cheek to the bombed bombshell. "Surely you want to discuss The Perfect Find. Sorry, I'm a fan, but we're careful not to shoot too many models. It's more about fashionable real girls, personalities."

"Oh I already talked to Eric about that, and he turned me down. No '*member* me? I took your son to my senior prom."

"Eric went to the prom?"

"So sad," continued Suki, who was too sloshed to pick up on social cues, "that I missed out on being your daughter-in-law. But whatevs. I respect Jenna Jones so much I don't care that she won."

"What did Jenna win?"

"Eric! I saw them out ages ago, and…"

The terrifying look on Darcy's face made Suki clamp her mouth shut. The two editors in mid-conversation with her picked up on the tension, too. Suddenly finding themselves needing to socialize elsewhere, they disappeared into the crowd.

"You know," started Suki, slowly backing away, "I th-think I see Usher over there by Julianne Moore, and he's on my bucket list, sooo…"

The tiny woman—glamorous as ever in a black-and-white striped Elie Saab column gown—grabbed the supermodel's arm, digging her fuschia nails into her skin.

"Suki. Follow. Me. Now."

CHAPTER 27

Jenna was sitting in the back of a parked town car with Brian, her ex-everything, who she hadn't seen in years. And now her beloved Anna was dead. It didn't seem real.

It was definitely real, though. Because Brian was a wreck. Well, his version of a wreck. He sat next to her, his face red and with shaking hands. Jenna had never seen him like this. He was always completely, frustratingly unflappable. But now he was falling apart. "Brian," she started, her voice strangled, "Tell me. What happened?"

"The cancer. It came back fast and aggressive, and it killed her yesterday."

"I'm so sorry. I wish I…"

"I knew how bad it was, the doctors told me it had metastasized everywhere, but I couldn't face it. So I put her in the most elite urgent care facility, hired her a nutritionist and four around-the-clock nurses and a water therapist and a therapist-therapist and arranged for her hairstylist and manicurist to come twice a week. That manicurist saw her more than I did. I couldn't go. I didn't want to remember her bald, seventy-five pounds, and hooked up to fifty IV's. The last time I saw her, she didn't know who I was. I never went back."

"Don't blame yourself, Brian. No one knows how to react when loved ones get sick. There's no manual. You did the best you could."

"No, I didn't," he said, staring into nothing, like he was going over it all in his head. "I wasn't there when she died. I'm never there."

I wasn't there for her, either. She told me she was dying and I didn't believe her.

Jenna pulled Brian into her arms. He resisted, his body stiff—he didn't know how to take it. Brian was never the one who needed soothing (and was definitely not huggy). But right now, it didn't matter. She held him, rocking him like a baby, forcing him to accept her comfort. Finally, he relaxed, slipping his arms around her.

"It'll be okay. It'll be fine," she whispered nonsensically, the way one does with small children. Truthfully, she was trying to calm them both. She refused to cry, this was his moment to grieve. "Anna never would've wanted you to torture yourself this way," she said. "She would've wanted you to drop some LSD in her honor, throw a cocktail party and invite every love of her life."

"I think she did that on her last birthday."

"She was so magical, so Sixties," said Jenna. "Did you know she had an affair with Bob Dylan."

"Why do you know that?"

"'Cause that's a story you pass onto your daughter. I was her de facto daughter," said Jenna. "It was from her candle-making days in the Village, before she followed your dad to Philly. She met him at a Jimi Hendrix show at The Bitter End. Apparently, Jimi and Dylan both wanted her, but Dylan won—because he wrote a song about her. 'Burning the Wick.' He scribbled the lyrics on rolling papers."

"Dylan, huh? Where was he when we were living in a shack so poorly insulated that I slept in a bed filled with puddles when it rained?" Still cocooned in Jenna's arms, he slumped a little. "I never liked Dylan."

After minutes sitting in silence, he drew away from her and leaned back against the seat with a heavy, broken sigh.

"Come home," he said.

"It's not my home anymore."

"It's more yours than mine."

"I can't."

"Please, JJ," said Brian, running a hand through his hair, which was a tousled, rumpled mess. Always so pristine, it was like the stress of the guilt and loss was disassembling him.

Jenna rubbed her temple, a stress-gesture that was classically Eric. It was that phenomenon that happens with lovers, best friends, and siblings—when you're so close, that you start picking up each other's traits through osmosis. She'd absorbed Eric thoroughly.

"Just for an hour," said Brian.

And because she wanted to, Jenna said yes. She was gutted by Anna's death, too. She needed to be around the only person who understood how she was feeling. Even if that person was Brian. For tonight, she could look beyond all the anger, the resentment, the questions.

The first sign that Jenna was in for a surreal night was when they walked up to the door of the gorgeous brownstone on Jane Street, and she reached in her clutch for her house keys.

"Sorry," she said, awkwardly, as Brian opened the door. "This is weird, okay?"

When she walked in, she gasped. Everything was exactly where she left it. Jenna was seized with an urge to touch everything, to walk through all the rooms, to smell them, feel them. So she did, with Brian trailing behind her. She ran her fingers over the turquoise living room wall, over the display of vintage photography and pop art. She caressed the armoire she decoupaged herself, sank into the orange tufted sofa, and bent down in her evening gown to stroke the bright Turkish rugs decorating the white-painted floors. She sat in her office, gazing at the floor-to-ceiling piles of art books—and her former prized possession: a display case of vintage Old Hollywood shoes that Brian had won for her at a Christie's auction. And upstairs, in their old warm, plush bedroom—which was conceived so that every surface had a different, lovely texture—she grazed her fingertips along everything, from the overstuffed velvet armchairs to the shiny, mirrored Art Deco bedside tables.

"Open the drawer," said Brian, gesturing to the table on her side of the bed.

She did, and saw that her three sets of nighttime reading glasses were still nestled inside.

"Why are these still here?" she asked.

He shrugged. "That's where they go."

She gathered up the skirt of her gown with one hand, and sat on the side of fluffy, white king sized bed. Her life had happened in these rooms. Brian had made love to her in all of them. The living room couch was where Brian would wait with a gin and tonic before they went out, while she got ready upstairs. The rooftop is where she spent her 31st birthday, which coincided with the scorching East Coast blackout of 2003 (the entire block stopped by with all the food in their fridges, and they'd barbequed until dawn).

Her office was Jenna's safe haven, where she'd go in the middle of the night to obsess over where Brian had been for two days. And their Moroccan-tiled bathroom, the size of her studio, was where she sat with Elodie in the empty bathtub and, over tears and a bottle of Merlot, decided to leave New York.

The good memories were hazy, faded and sweet. But the bad ones—the ones that left wounds that had just healed—those were sharper.

Brian slipped off his jacket and draped it on the back of a chair. Then, he sat next to Jenna. "What are you thinking?"

"I'm marveling at how familiar everything is. And yet I don't feel connected to it anymore."

It's my stuff, but my energy's been drained from it. I can feel all the other women that have been in these rooms.

"You could've taken your stuff."

"Didn't want it," she said. "Had to go. Fast."

"I understand why you left. I know what I did to you. I made it so it was impossible for you to stay. I didn't realize it then, because… well, I was entangled in some extenuating circumstances."

"What circumstances?"

"This is going to be hard for you to digest, so I just want you to promise to hear me out."

"What happened?"

"I did something unconscionable." He stopped, and undid the top two buttons of his shirt. "I feel like I need a Montecristo cigar to get through this."

"So, who was she?" She took a deep breath and hiked up her dress, scooting back on the bed until she was leaning against the pillows. She folded her legs, steeling herself to finally hear the truth.

"There was no she."

"Of course there was. You were never home. You weren't sleeping with me, so there had to have been someone else."

Brian ran his hand through his hair again, his Malachite green eyes glazed with guilt.

"It's worse than a she."

Jenna grabbed a pillow and cradled it to her chest. "Start talking."

He did. He told her that, by the time he hit his mid-thirties, something switched in him. His moral code started changing. To be a real estate developer with his level of success, you had to be a gangster. A gambler. And no real gambler gets a win, and then walks out of the casino, treats his wife to unlimited breadsticks at Olive Garden, and saves his earnings for retirement. No, he needed more. He hired thuggy scouts who used... intimidating business practices to land him the sexiest lots. His was aware that his assistant spent half the day hopping into town cars with Wall Street players, trading coke for stock tips. At an Amfar gala, Brian once listened as a close colleague spilled info on a Sacramento development he was closing on—and then, in under twenty-four hours, he stole it out from under him. It was so easy. The cash was flowing in; it seemed bottomless.

When you get it easy, you lose it easy.

Everything fell apart. The economy crashed, and most of Brian's properties went into foreclosure. By June of 2007, his net worth had fallen from fifty to twenty million. By December of 2008, he only had five million—most of which wasn't liquid. He only had five million because he'd poured their savings into Bernie Madoff's hedge fund.

With this fatal mistake, his gambler's lust had officially blinded him; making him ignore his 'this is too good to be true' instincts.

He minored in auditing, for Christ's sake, and never bothered to look at the receipts. Men he respected, captains of industry, were investing with Madoff—and that was all the vetting he needed. All the cool kids were doing it.

Brian told Jenna that they were living check to check for years. He told her about the bank seizing the brownstone he built for Anna (back then, he'd said that his mom moved because she wanted to downsize). He came clean about borrowing against credit cards to pay bankruptcy attorneys, about being eight months behind on their mortgage, about the nights he'd spend in hotels, pretending to be traveling for work, too humiliated to come home and face her.

He told her that he'd felt like he was a walking dead man. And how can a dead man love someone properly? He didn't want to sleep with Jenna, that was true. But it wasn't because he was cheating. It was because his manhood had evaporated. He felt like a goddamned eunuch.

Jenna didn't speak until she was certain he was finished.

"Bernie. Madoff."

"Every thought you're having I've already tortured myself with."

"Bernie fucking Madoff was the she?"

Brian's shoulders slumped. "I also had a vague coke problem. Bernie Madoff, coke, and millions blown in the recession. I'm officially a New York City cliché."

"So our entire world was falling apart, but instead of telling the truth, you let me believe that you stopped caring about me? That I was unlovable, unfuckable? Did you ever wonder what that did to me? While you were drowning in self-loathing, did you ever think about how I felt?"

"No," he admitted. "All I cared about was that you were taken care of."

"In the manner to which I'd been accustomed."

"Yes," he said. "I told you it was a lot to digest. But you deserve the truth."

"Years later," she said, her mouth dry.

"I'm sorry I ruined you. Ruined us. It haunts me every day."

Jenna looked at him. The story was so outrageous, so not what she'd expected, that she barely knew how to react. It was like a salacious expose out of *Vanity Fair* magazine (Biracial It-Couple's Financed Felled by the Sketchiest Financial Villain of the Century! Keeping Up With the Stein-Joneses, on Page 67). She should've hated him. If she'd heard this a year ago, she would've taken to her bed for months. But today, she felt the opposite.

Looking at Brian, besieged with shame—and sinking under the devastation of losing Anna—she was reminded that he was just a person. He made massive mistakes, he felt things, he was sorry, and he was trying to find his way, like everyone else. The tragedy was that, if he'd given Jenna the opportunity, she could've convinced him that he was more than what he owned; proved to him that she'd stay, no matter what.

Jenna was angry, but in a surface way that she knew would pass. More than anything, she was relieved to know the truth. But part of her calm was also knowing that those abysmal final years of their relationship could never happen to the person she was now. There's no way she could let a man make her feel so unseen for so long.

Now, she knew what it was like to be seen.

"Brian," she said, pushing the pillow aside and sitting next to him on the edge of the bed. "You didn't ruin me. I ruined me."

"No, I'm completely to blame. Your nervous breakdown, moving to Virginia. Cheating you out of the family we'd always planned. That was all me."

"Yes, you were an asshole. You were careless with me, and selfish. But you didn't cause me to spiral. I did. I gave you so much power that, when you took your love away, I dissolved."

Jenna said this with intensity in her voice. "*I* put myself in that helpless role." Jenna looked at him, her eyes shining. She was over feeling like their breakup happened to her. Because it wasn't true—she'd been the masochist to his sadist. Willingly.

"Brian," she continued, "you backed out of our plans. But you didn't cheat me out of a family. I should've been woman enough to be clear about my terms, instead of suffering quietly for years."

Eric's words—you're a coward—rang in her ears.

"If you didn't want that future with me, I should've had the balls to go out and find that life with someone else. You weren't the only man on Earth."

Brian flinched, caught off guard.

"What happened to us was my fault, too," said Jenna. "But for your part in it, I forgive you."

Brian looked like he was struggling to find words. "Who...are you now? You're so centered, calm. It's like you've gotten an Iyanla Vanzant transplant."

"And try to say that three times fast."

Brian smiled, his expression tinged with regret. For a second she saw a flash of Brian at nineteen, floppy-haired, baby-faced, telling her that he couldn't take her to Uno's Pizzeria because he'd just spent his last dime on bailing two of his junkie brothers out of jail. He didn't even know how he'd eat for the next month. Brian admitted this with such shame. Even then, the idea of not being able to provide made him miserable.

Jenna cleared her throat. "So, have you changed, too?"

"Yes. Want me to prove it?"

"How could you possibly?"

"Woman, you know I have ways. What time is it?" He glanced at his Bulgari watch. It was 11:20 pm. "Let's go somewhere."

She paused. This all felt so familiar. Brian in a tux, Jenna in an evening gown, winding down in their bedroom after a night at a fancy gala. But on every forensics or crime-centric TV show, it was said that when you're abducted, you should never allow yourself to be taken to a second location. The second location is where most victims get killed, or worse.

"I think I should go home," she said, making a move to get up. "But if you ever want to talk about Anna, please call me."

"Jenna."

He never called her by her real name, only JJ. She sat back down, sighing.

"Fine. But where will we even go dressed like this?"

"Somewhere I should've taken you a long time ago," he said, pulling out his phone. He clicked on a number, and then put the phone against his ear.

"Who are you calling?" whispered Jenna.

"Matthieu," he said with a rakish curve of his lip.

Matthieu was Brian's manservant. The Alfred to his Batman. He had the personal cell numbers for every restaurant and boutique owner that mattered. Armed with Brian's credit card information and a salesman's dogged determination—plus, a French-Haitian accent so thick that most vendors couldn't even understand what extravagance they were agreeing to—Matthieu was capable of making anything happen, at any time of the day or night.

"Meet me downstairs in five minutes," he said, leaving the room to speak in private.

And the tiny, miniscule flicker of the thing left inside her that responded to Brian—to him taking the lead, taking control—made her nod "okay." Without asking any questions, she met him in the foyer minutes later. Just like he said.

Jenna knew she should go home. But despite everything, it felt good being with Brian—therapeutic, somehow. In his presence, she had to face the foibles of her past, to reckon with who she used to be. Maybe she had to experience this night to move on with the rest of her life. Maybe it would give her clarity on how to work things out with Eric. Maybe it was just that, in this heightened, emotional moment—Anna's death, Brian's melodramatic story—her defenses slipped, and Jenna Parte Un's voice was louder than Parte Deux's.

God help her, she was going to the second location.

CHAPTER 28

As Brian and Jenna rode in the back of his towncar through Lower Manhattan, they slipped into a hesitant chattiness. They weren't fully comfortable, but they were pleasant, and given everything that Brian just confessed, this was a surprise to them both.

Brian still hadn't told Jenna where they were going, but they were clearly headed toward Brooklyn. Which was odd, because he hated Brooklyn. He thought it was too self-consciously everything (organic, liberal, artsy, urban, etc.). What the hell were they doing?

When the car pulled up at the entrance to Prospect Park, she got it. There was only one thing they could be doing.

Together, they walked on an unpaved path, a path that was familiar to her, and stopped at a sprawling, hilly expanse of grass. It was filled with hundreds of picnic blankets and people, all there for the weekly midnight screening of a classic movie.

It was where she'd asked Brian to take her, during their horrible last dinner together. She'd said it was her dream date, but he'd scoffed, as if it were beneath them. Not only was Brooklyn out of the question, but so were black-and-white movies (and sitting on the cold, hard ground to watch them).

It was also the place Eric had spontaneously taken her—without even knowing she'd been dying to go—where she told him she loved him for the first time. And now, here she was, at the scene of one of her most sublime memories; but she was with Brian, instead of Eric. Her past was colliding with her present.

"Look," said Brian, pointing to a large oak tree set back behind the sea of movie-watchers. In front of the tree was massive, fluffy white blanket with a little table set up next to it, loaded up with an assortment of things she couldn't quite make out. Standing next to the tree was Matthieu, a slip of a mocha-skinned man in a tailored suit and a don't-mind-me-I'm-just-here-to-fulfill-your-every-desire expression. Brian had created their own V.I.P. section in the middle of the park.

He took her hand and wove her through the couples in jeans and hoodies, chilling on well-worn Mexican blankets—all of them turning their heads to gawk at the mystery couple in dramatic black tie. For a moment, the movie wasn't even happening. It was just Jenna and Brian, surrounded by people whispering about who they were, and why they looked like they were about to present one of the lesser awards at the Oscars.

It was paint-by-numbers Brian. He loved making jaws drop. He lived to knock people out with his elegance. His taste. His woman. They made their way over to the blanket, and Jenna got a good look at the folding table—which was filled with raspberries and strawberries (neither of which were in season), cheeses, grapes, toast points, caviar on ice, and three buckets of champagne. There was an Louis Vuitton picnic basket, the size of an airplane carry-on, which was stocked with porcelain tableware, silver cutlery, crystal champagne glasses, a mini French press, and LV linen napkins.

The spread was breathtaking and caught her off guard—but it shouldn't have. Of course Brian couldn't experience the screening like everyone else, in cargo pants, inhaling kettle corn and beer on mismatched beach towels.

I spent most of my adulthood living with this decadence. Why does it seem so over-the-top now?

With an enthusiastic, "Long time no see!" Jenna gave Matthieu a hug that he did not appreciate. (He never encouraged showy forms of affection. He was there to provide a service, and expected everyone to ignore his presence and carry on.) Then, she looked at Brian with a bemused smile.

"You really went all out."

Jenna could practically see Brian's chest puff out. "You always said you wanted me to take you here."

"I know, but it's supposed to be a drive-in type of vibe," said Jenna. "This is mad extravagant!"

"*Mad* extravagant? Are we on MTV Jams?"

"I um…work with a lot of young people," mumbled Jenna. "It's extravagant, JJ, but I know you. You love exquisite details."

"Not so much anymore," she said. "It's gorgeous, but you didn't need to do this for me."

"Fine, then I needed to do it for me."

"A-ha! The truth."

"If I'm going to come out here, sit on the goddamn grass, and watch *Casablanca* surrounded by art directors, self-published novelists, and feminist photographers, I'm going to do it while eating catered hors d'oeuvers. On a waterproof-lined alpaca blanket."

Jenna looked at him blankly. "You had Matthieu bring an alpaca blanket? To a picnic?"

He grinned. "Sit down. Feel it."

Brian held Jenna's hand while she balled up the bottom of her gown and then sank down into the blanket. It *was* luxurious. With much huffing and puffing, Brian sat next to her, his legs stretched front of him.

"You look like the world's most dapper toddler," said Jenna, "being forced to sit down for story time."

"But look how much I've changed. I came to Brooklyn for you! I'm basically *camping* for you."

She laughed. "You consider coming here a sacrifice? That's you, staying exactly the same."

"Well, I'm watching a pre-Eighties movie. Something I'd never do."

"You've never understood my movie thing."

"Why watch a bunch of people who are all dead, deliver corny lines and get caught up in cornball, predictable situations?" He pointed to the screen. "Humphrey Bogart is supposed to be a leading man, but he looks like a butcher."

Jenna sighed. She used to try to explain her film love to Brian, but his boredom was always apparent. It never really bothered her—after all, she couldn't care less about the Giants or, like, wearable tech. It wasn't until Eric that she realized how thrilling it was to share an obsession, to have things in common besides each other.

Just then, Matthieu appeared out of the shadows, draping a pale pink pashmina over Jenna's shoulders. She hopped a little, startled.

"Zere's a chill in ze air, Madame," he said, and disappeared.

"I forgot what he's like," she whispered to Brian, and then continued their conversation. "I don't know what you have against Brooklyn. You know, I live here now."

"I heard," he said. "And I hate that you live in an uninhabitable, dangerous neighborhood. I hate seeing you diminished."

"I love my apartment." And she did. She'd made delicious memories there. "It's the first place I've ever had that's all mine."

"But you're going to argue that it's not low rent compared to us? We had everything."

"And nothing," said Jenna. She drew her knees up to her chest, wrapping her arms around them.

"I want to change that. I regret so much." He paused. "These past couple of years have been…empty."

"I doubt you've spent many nights alone."

"There have been women," he admitted. "Some I've been fond of. Most were transactions. Escorts and gold-diggers make you lonelier than being alone."

"Can't say that I've spent much time with gold-diggers, since I have about four hundred dollars to my name," she said.

"Four hundred dollars?" Brian was scandalized. "Why didn't you ever ask me for help? You have art, I set up bonds in your name. You don't get a medal for being too proud to take what's yours."

"It's not about pride," she said. "I just don't need any help. Especially from you. No offense."

"None taken." He paused. "Well, some taken."

"I've learned how to live very well with little money. I pay my rent, I take the subway instead of cabs, and I hardly ever eat out. Hopefully, when I renegotiate my contract I can make some investments in low-risk funds. I'm fine."

Brian studied Jenna. She was a forty-year-old woman who'd never checked the balance on her checking account, never budgeted, and lived off of a glorified allowance her entire adult life. And now she was discussing her finances with the scrappy capability of a lifelong coupon-counter.

It was like she'd never needed him.

"So, back to the women," said Jenna. "What happened with Lily L'Amour?"

"She left me," Brian said, simply. "Without you, and now without Anna, I feel alone in the world. Now that I'm finally back on my feet—who am I making all this money for? If something happened to me, who would care? I have no purpose."

"I think this is called having a midlife crisis. Can't you just buy a new jet?"

"I'm being serious." He looked at her. "Before, when you wanted to get married and have a baby, I wasn't in a place to do it. Now, I am."

Jenna listened to his words, but they weren't connecting to her brain.

"I'd marry you tomorrow if you'd say yes. I want to be a father. I want your fairy tale."

Her fairy tale. It had been her dream for so long, that even though everything had changed, she wasn't immune to hearing him say the words. The old pull was no longer there, but she got flashes of how it used to feel, like feeling tingles in a phantom limb. Involuntarily, her mind went to the box of Brian's baby clothes that Anna had given her. She wondered where it was.

Jenna was hurt. Not for herself now, but for the girl who'd ruined herself waiting for Brian. All she'd ever wanted was this level of commitment from him.

"You're only feeling this way because you've just suffered a huge loss," said Jenna. "It's your sadness talking."

"No, it isn't," Brian said. "I've missed you for years, I just didn't know what to do about it."

Jenna nodded. She glanced up at the screen, watching an impassioned, conflicted, very married Ingrid Bergman beg her lover Humphrey Bogart to do the thinking for both of them.

And then Matthieu popped out in front of them, scaring the living shit out of Jenna. She was already on edge, but every time he materialized, her nerves frayed like split ends. It was like being tazed every thirty seconds.

"Fromage Francais," he said, wielding a tray of cheese. "You will try ze Boursin or the Brebicet, Madame? I know you enjoy ze soft cheeses."

"Thank you, I'll have the Boursin," said Jenna, dipping a knife into the smushy cheese and spreading it on a toast point. She prayed Matthieu would just relax so she could get her thoughts together.

They sat quiet for a few moments, two old lovers in the dark, bathed in the silvery glow of the screen. Jenna looked at Brian—at his aristocrat-by-way-of-Philly profile –and finally felt bold enough to go there.

"I'll always love you, Brian. But it's not in the same way."

He frowned, scratching his five o'clock shadow. "It's that kid, isn't it?"

"I'm sorry?"

"I read the *New York* magazine interview. You could barely hide it."

"Oh," she said, adjusting her flower garland.

"What are you thinking? He's Darcy's child, do you know how ludicrous that is?"

"Actually no," she said dryly, "it didn't occur to me until this very moment."

"How old is he anyway?"

"It's none of your business. And what does it matter?"

"It matters because he's a sophomore in high school. Are you fucking him or helping him with his World Civ homework?"

She dropped her toast point and made a move to get up—but Brian grabbed her wrist, keeping her in place.

"I'm sorry," he said. "But you have to understand. I wasn't arrogant enough to think you wouldn't find someone else. I just assumed he wouldn't be boy-band age."

Jenna didn't want to talk about Eric with Brian. It felt disrespectful to even bring him into the conversation.

"Tell me you're just getting your groove back."

"No," she said. "I'm in love with him."

"That," he said, "sounds like a bad joke."

"You can't imagine the utter bottomlessness of my disinterest in your opinion."

"You'd honestly choose him over me?"

"It isn't even a choice, Brian."

"Impossible," he said, his face incredulous. "Why?"

Jenna shrugged and peered up at the starless sky. "We're friends."

"We were friends."

"Us?" Jenna chuckled. "We were never friends. You were the boss, and I was your geisha. A feisty one at times, but I was never unclear about my position. My job was to be the person you wanted me to be."

"I take charge. That's who I am. I always thought you liked it. You certainly benefited from it."

She ignored that last comment, because it was a shitty thing to say. "I did like you being my boss. But Brian, I was so young when we met. I'd never even kissed a boy. I knew nothing about guys, or relationships, or myself. You taught me what to like."

Before Brian could respond, Matthieu emerged out of the shadows again, popping in front of them with two bottles of champagne. This time, Jenna yelped.

"Champagne tasting, madame? I have ze 1999 Gaston Chiquet and ze 1993, Dom Perignon. Nectar of ze gods, both a dem!"

"Matthieu, you're going to give me a heart attack!"

"That'll be all for now," said Brian, dismissing him. He disappeared again, with a huffy shrug.

"It just doesn't add up," he continued, unable to get past Jenna's involvement with Eric. "Why him?"

"We're the same," she said. "We're from the same 'soul tribe.' Ever heard that expression?"

Brian scoffed. "It sounds like the name of a Blaxploitation Western flick."

"It's when you meet someone and, no matter who they are, where they come from or what they look like, you know that you're made of the same stuff."

"So, because of this soul tribe member, you're turning down what you've wanted your whole life?"

"No. Even if there was no Eric, I couldn't marry you."

"But it would be perfect," said Brian, overriding what she'd just said. "I've been thinking about this. We could have the wedding in early May, before everyone starts leaving for the summer. A private ceremony with our closest friends on our rooftop. A reception at the MOMA. Remember the year that Amfar had their gala there?"

"The MOMA? I wouldn't want my wedding day to feel like a charity ball."

He ignored her. "You could quit that terrible job. I could bankroll an interior design business for you. Personal styling. Anything."

"I'm no fan of Darcy, but I've been incredibly successful at my job. I'm proud of my work there."

"You're not proud. It must be humiliating being Darcy's employee," he said, brushing her off. "Anyway, after we have the baby, I'd get you a nanny and a wet nurse. And a weekend au pair. All my associates' wives have them. I've done my research."

"Three nannies? Why would I have a baby I never spent time with?"

"Well, we'd have five or six social engagements to attend a week. That's just the reality of our lives together."

Flushing hot with frustration, Jenna slipped off her pashmina and held it in her lap. "Brian, listen to you. You haven't changed. You're still trying to control me, and you can't do that anymore."

"I'm just being thorough. Listen…"

"No, you listen," she said calmly, but sternly. "A while ago, I gave a young girl advice about men. I said she shouldn't wait for a guy to decide what her future would look like. That she should be the decider. I didn't know it then, but I was talking to myself. I waited for you for years. And…" She looked at him. "And now I'm over it."

She listened to her own words, and wondered if she was going to take her own advice. Was she going to wait until Eric was ready to be a father—when she was near fifty and menopausal—to realize her dream? What Jenna needed, he couldn't give her anytime soon. These were facts. There would be no compromise. If they stayed together, one would be forcing the other to commit to their terms. And one of them would lose—most likely, her.

Jenna had her fill of putting her needs second to a man's. And what this might mean for her and Eric, the person she really wanted the fairy tale with, ran her blood cold.

"It's a lovely offer," said Jenna, "but I don't want it anymore."

"Oh, JJ," said Brian, his voice lacking energy, his face slack with disappointment, "I'm not surprised. You just want what every woman wants."

"What's that?"

"What she can't have."

Jenna didn't answer, letting him believe this. His opinion no longer mattered. She handed him her champagne glass, and stood up.

"Goodbye, Brian," said Jenna, knowing that she'd never speak to him again. She walked off into the night, sparkling with a clarity she'd never felt—and at the same time, carrying a dread so overwhelming that she feared it might crush her.

CHAPTER 29

"She's a singer-songwriter," said Eric, "so her video could be a visual representation of the words in her single. It's a top 10 record, so people are familiar with it. She says something about writing haikus in a field of daisies, so I could shoot some pickup of that. There's a line about smoking in an outdoor shower. Maybe I could set that up."

"I don't know," said Karen, who had called an impromptu editorial meeting on Monday morning to decide how to handle Misty Cox's Perfect Find video. The singer was the biggest name they'd ever filmed. The red-headed executive editor usually gave Eric and Jenna carte blanche with the videos—they'd been such a smash. But Misty wasn't just a fashionable "real" person or a model—she was a pop star with an agent, a management team, and record label execs behind her. So, when Karen got the call that Misty was interested, she knew she needed to give it extra attention.

"I don't think we want to show smoking," she said. "It's not politically correct."

"It's just a line in the song, Karen," he said. "It's not literal."

"Well, what are some other lines?"

"Honestly? Those were the best two ones. Let it be known that I find her music to be utter trash."

"I love her," said Jinx. "She's a slutty Taylor Swift."

"Taylor Swift is a slutty Taylor Swift," said Mitchell.

"Word," said Terry. "I love how she maintains her good-girl image when she's boned every dude in *Us Weekly.*"

"No smoking, Eric," said Karen. "I can guarantee that Universal wouldn't go for that."

"Her name is Misty Cox," said Eric, his voice dripping with disdain. "The label sent her out into the world with a porn star name. I doubt they'd trip over a Marlboro Light."

"Do I have to say it again?" asked Karen, surprised at his attitude. Eric always stood up for what he believed in, artistically, but never with such petulance. "Come up with something else."

He shrugged, his body language radiating exasperation. "Whatever you say."

"Why are you in such a bad mood, E?" asked Jinx in her sing-songy whine. She rested her hand on his arm.

"I'm not in a bad mood," he lied. He was in a terrible mood. Jenna was sitting five feet across from him, he hadn't spoken to her all weekend, and he didn't know where they stood. That was the worst part. Not the actual fight at May's party, but having no idea what it meant.

"This is not me in a bad mood," continued Eric. "This is me, trying to make something out of nothing. This is me, trying to figure out how to make a girl who rhymes 'daisy' with 'Bolognese' seem interesting. Yo, she pronounced the 'e' at the end of Bolognese. What do I do with that?"

"Well, this is an important shoot," said Karen. "You need to figure it out soon."

"When have I not figured it out? Given my track record, I feel like I shouldn't be trusted to make the right decisions."

"I agree," said Jinx. "I think we should give him the space to create, right?"

Karen glared at her. "Jinx, either ask him out or take a seat. It's becoming uncomfortable to watch." Jinx gasped with embarrassment. "Jenna, what's your input?"

Like Eric, Jenna was not in a great mood. But instead of getting prickly, she handled the weirdness between them by going mute. Over the past two days, Eric and Jenna had missed each other completely, literally and figuratively. First, Eric ignored her calls, then she missed his when she was with Brian—and when she called him back, it went straight to voice mail.

But she had no idea what she was going to say to him, anyway. The one thing she knew she definitely couldn't say was where she'd been on Saturday night. He'd never understand, and he'd never get over it.

But what I think I might have to tell him is so much worse, thought Jenna.

"Jenna?" Karen addressed her, again.

"Sorry." Jenna, who hadn't devoted two seconds to thinking about Misty Cox's Perfect Find, kept things diplomatic. "I like Eric's idea about bringing some of her lyrics to life. But you're right, it's just about finding the right ones. Which we will."

"Love it," she answered. "I know you two'll come up with something cool. EOD today, please."

An hour later, Jenna still didn't have any usable ideas. Her brain was too cloudy. She couldn't focus on the silly-named Misty Cox without thinking of Eric. And she couldn't think of Eric without getting stuck in a quicksand of confusion. So, she decided she needed a creative palate cleanser—which was focusing on busy work around the office, things she never got around to doing. She'd just gotten a huge shipment of summer pieces—bikinis, sundresses, strappy sandals, sunglasses—and it was time to replace the springy clothes from the fashion closets. Even though StyleZine had interns to work on inventory, Jenna felt like doing it herself. And since the fashion closet on her floor was filled to bursting, she loaded up the clothes on a rolling rack, wheeled them to the elevator, and took them up to the 10th floor closet.

Jenna was knee-deep in color-coding tankinis when she heard a knock on the door.

"Come in, it's open," she yelled.

She looked up from the cluster of bathing suits in her hands. "Hey." It was Eric. He locked the door.

"Hey." Jenna dropped the bathing suits to the floor. "I'm sorry. For everything."

"No, I'm sorry," he said. "I don't know what happened, or who was wrong or why, but I'm sorry."

"It was me," said Jenna, grasping her hands together. "I'm to blame. And I..."

Eric's mouth was on hers before she could complete the thought. They kissed with grasping desperation, like two dying people breathing their souls back into each other. When Eric felt Jenna crumble a little in his arms, he scooped her up and laid her on the table. And there, the whole world fell away.

They'd done this dozens of times, in a dozen different ways, and the details in the little closet—the racks of clothes, the accessories-stuffed bins—had always been the same. But today, one thing was different. And if they'd looked up, they would've noticed. On the ceiling, in the right hand corner, was a small black security camera, the blinking red light signifying that it was recording every minute.

Jenna sat on top of her desk, in a sex haze. She was still breathless. Her heart was still throbbing, her legs still liquid. Eric always did this to her. He dismantled her, and nothing felt more right.

So why, now that she was back in her office, had she fished into her wallet to find Rosie the Riveter's business card?

Call me if you ever want pregnancy advice, she'd said. *Freeze your eggs. Adopt. Get donor sperm. I know a brilliant fertility specialist.*

She held the card in her hand and her phone in the other. Rosie the Riveter, whose real name was Lisa Defozio, had offered to help her. But help her do what? Help her get knocked up by some stranger's sperm she picked up at a bank (didn't she read that homeless junkies donated sperm to pay for their drug habit)? Have a baby that was fertilized in a lab (seemed so cold)? Adopt a stunning Ethiopian girl who looked like Zahara Jolie-Pitt (did she have a baby sister somewhere in Addis Ababa)? These weren't the ways that Jenna had imagined herself becoming a mother, but dammit, they were choices. They opened up a world of possibilities. It was freedom.

Every cell in her body came alive at the thought of being able to go out and get what she wanted, without permission. Without negotiating with someone else.

Someone else.

Then, she crumpled the card in her hand. She couldn't bring herself to call. Because she couldn't entertain these thoughts without accepting that they left Eric out of the equation. She couldn't call Lisa without being willing to give him up. And the thought was unfathomable.

How could she possibly let him go?

Jenna covered her mouth with the back of her hand, feeling queasy. Then, she clutched her stomach, grabbed the trashcan under her desk and threw up.

Sweating and shaking, she sat back up and gripped the edge of the desk for support. There was a terrible lump in her throat, and she was trembling all over. Her stomach lurched again, and she took a couple of deep breaths to calm it down.

God, not now. I can't start stress-hurling now.

This had happened her entire life. Before the SAT's. The night she decided to quit medical school and move to New York. The worst was when she was a twenty-four-year-old assistant editor and her boss went into labor—and, all by herself, she had to present a March fashion spread in a meeting with Oscar de la Renta and Bruce Weber.

Panicking, she knew she had to go home. It was only 1pm, but she had to get out of there.

She grabbed her purse and shot out of her office, slamming the door. Everyone in the cubicles looked up, including Eric. The rest of the staff went back to their business, but when he saw the look on her face—sallow, stricken, with bright pink blotches on her cheeks—he dropped his camera on his desk.

He mouthed, "You okay?"

She couldn't let anyone see her like that, especially not him. So she put her head down, and speed-walked down the hallway.

Eric sat at his desk, fidgeting with worry. He wanted to run after her, but knew it would be so incriminating. He tried to wait a respectable amount of time, but after roughly thirty seconds, he bolted out of his chair, caught an elevator, and was gone. He didn't give a damn what anybody thought. Jenna was in trouble.

In her palatial office, Darcy sat behind her desk, chewing on the business end of a pen. She observed Jenna sprint out of the office, followed shamelessly closely by Eric. She also observed that no one else noticed. Darcy didn't know what she loathed more—that they'd had the balls to carry out this affair, or that she hadn't picked up on it. Because it was so terribly obvious.

She almost wanted to laugh. This was going to be good.

CHAPTER 30

Fighting off persistent waves of nausea, Jenna stood on the corner of Broadway and Bleecker, just outside the StyleZine offices, waiting for the light to change.

Everything will be fine, just calm down, get on the train, and get home. Where you can vomit in peace.

But just as the light changed and she made a move to cross, she saw Eric storm out of their office building. She wasn't ready to confront whatever she was feeling about their situation; she just wanted to go home and think. But before she could make a run for it, he saw her, rushed over, and pulled her into a strong hug. She hung on to him, seeing stars.

"Jesus, Jenna, what's going on?"

"We have to talk. There's so much I need to say to you, but I don't know how, or what…"

"Shhh, we're not doing this here. Come on," he said, hailing a cab. He half-dragged her into the taxi. She slumped against his shoulder, her eyes closed.

"260 West Broadway," he told the driver. "At Beach."

"The American Thread Building? That's where you live?" It was a Downtown Manhattan historical landmark with a zillion luxury condos.

"Yeah, my step-dad signed the condo over to her in the settlement. I think she roofied him first."

Suddenly, Jenna's eyes flew open and she sat up. "Wait, we're going to your place? *Darcy's* place? Are you crazy?"

"It's closest. Jenna, you're green. We have to get you somewhere, fast."

"No! What if Darcy comes home?"

"It's noon, she won't be there 'til at least eight," said Eric. "Just relax. Here, lay down."

As Jenna gingerly laid her head in Eric's lap, trying to keep her breakfast bagel down, she tried to process this information. They were going to Darcy's apartment. His apartment. This had never been an option, for obvious reasons. She'd always wondered what his at-home life looked like, what his bedroom looked like, where his things were, how he moved in those surroundings.

The cab pulled up to the huge 1800s Renaissance Revival building, and Eric got a shaky-legged Jenna to the double doors. He gave the portly doorman a pound and, in his ear, whispered, "What's good, Raul. Forget you ever saw her here, okay? I'll bring you those J's you liked. For your son. I only wore them once." Raul gave the thumbs up sign and grinned. And then, holding Jenna's hand, he led her around the lobby's imposing staircase to the elevators, where they went up to the seventh floor.

When they entered the apartment, it was like stepping into boutique hotel in Milan. It was airy and all-white, punctuated with sleek mahogany floors, doors, and staircases, dazzling objet d'art chandeliers; and sculptural plum and gold furniture. There were no family pictures on the walls, nothing personal at all. The apartment was arrestingly chic—but cold, spare, and uninviting.

Eric led Jenna behind the subway-tiled, white marble countertop kitchen and into a large, loft-like bedroom, with an ultra-modern bathroom. His bedroom. The space itself was lovely. But, as Jenna noted with almost-numb astonishment, it was the room of a kid who'd just come home from college, and had left it untouched since high school.

Eric had two desks that were overrun with film research books, textbooks from Art & Design HS, yearbooks, marble-faced composition pads filled with class notes, and all kinds of school miscellanea. There were wall-to-wall Nike, Adidas and Puma boxes. He had a coat rack full of baseball caps in a corner, and posters of Kobe Bryant taped to the wall. There was a pile of unfolded laundry on a director's chair. An empty pizza box.

For the first time, it truly hit Jenna how young he really was. The bedroom was what broadcasted his youth—not the video games, not the Millennial speak, not the fact that when he bent over, nothing happened to his stomach (not even the eensiest pooch of skin). It looked like the lair of a virgin—of an early teen just graduated from Little League and Power Rangers. It was Theo Huxtable's season-one bedroom. It wasn't the bedroom of a middle-aged woman's life partner.

Eric ran her a hot bath in his sunken tub. While she soaked, he sat on top of the toilet next to the tub, his feet up on the sink. She was too peaky to talk, so he just kept her company as she languished in the water. Closing her eyes, she sunk down as far as she could without drowning—and stayed there until the water went tepid. She willed the universe to deliver an easy solution for her and Eric. Something that made sense, something she could live with. Nothing came.

After almost an hour, she got out of the tub and Eric put her in one of his wife beaters and a pair of boxer shorts. In vain, Eric was trying to figure out how to make her feel better. He'd held her, stroked her hair, given her tea —but she was just sitting there, on top of his desk, leaning back against the wall, looking listless and barely speaking. He felt crushingly inadequate.

He also felt a looming sense of dread.

"Should I get you some DayQuil? Maybe you have the flu."

"No, I'm okay. The bath helped."

"You're not okay, though. What can I do?"

"I don't think you can do anything," she said. "For a really long time. Too long."

"What do you mean?"

"What I want with you, you can't give me right now." Jenna saw Eric stiffen, as if preparing for a blow. "You asked me to admit it on the pier. And I couldn't. Because what I want is unrealistic," she said. "I didn't want to burden you with my silly fantasies. But the truth is, I'd love to marry you. I want a little me-and-you. A baby with your height and….and my taste in accessories. And I know it can't happen, but I think about it every day."

"Why didn't you tell me?" asked Eric. "Nothing you could say would be a burden. It feels like shit when you realize the woman you thought you were making happy is keeping a massive issue from you. I felt ridiculous at that party."

"I'm sorry for that," she whispered.

"Do you…should we…maybe we could, like, could have a baby." Eric could barely form the sentence.

"Are you out of your mind?"

"Why not?" he said, grasping at straws. "People procreate in weird circumstances all the time. Look at my horrible mother. I turned out fucking incredible."

"There's no way, at this stage of your life, that you could be a father."

"I could! I like kids. What if we had one like May, can you imagine?"

"Honey, be serious. You couldn't handle it."

As much as he wished it weren't true—he had to agree with Jenna. He smoked weed constantly, ate pizza for every meal, watched too much PornHub and went out every night he wasn't at her house. These were not dad-ly qualities. His main two focuses were his career and Jenna—the rest of his life was one massive question mark. When he had a kid, he wanted to be established.

He wanted to approach fatherhood with thoughtfulness and dedication. He wanted to be an ABC Family sitcom dad. And until he felt like he'd be great at it, he shouldn't do it.

"No, I couldn't handle it," he said, quietly. "There's no way I could have a baby. How? I can't even fold my laundry."

They lapsed into fraught silence. Eric could feel her slipping away, and couldn't bear it—so he tried to distract them from the heaviness of the conversation.

"I can't believe you're in my room. This is mad surreal. Like in a one-of-these-things-don't-belong way. Like if Joe Biden appeared in one of our editorial meetings."

"Speaking of StyleZine," started Jenna, "we won't be there forever. Let's say something huge comes out of South by Southwest for you. Let's say I get this job at Fordham. If we didn't have the Darcy issue anymore, what would happen to us?"

"We wouldn't have to be a secret." He shrugged. "We'd just be together. We'd just…hang out."

"Just hang out?" Jenna felt on the verge of madwoman laughter. "Eric, when you're with me do you reflect on us at all? Or is this just a fun adventure?"

"Of course I think about us."

"Then where do you see us a year from now?"

He paused. "Umm…can I get back to you?"

"See?" said Jenna. "It's been easy for us to blame Darcy, like we can't fully be together because of her. We act like Darcy's the villain, but…"

"She is the villain."

"She's *a* villain, but she's not *the* villain. Bad timing is."

Eric snorted. "Bad timing never flashed her boob to Dave Getty's dad at his bar mitzvah."

"Is everything a joke to you?" Jenna was suddenly, blindingly angry.

"No, that really happened!"

"You can't just wisecrack your way through life, Eric! At some point you'll have to grow up." She slid off of the desk and started pacing. "I can't do this."

Eric followed her. "Do what?"

"I can't just 'hang out' with the love of my life. It would never be enough."

"Enough for what?" Eric's voice was hectic.

"I'll be forty-one in five minutes. And then forty-two, and forty-three, and you'll still be in your mid-twenties. Who knows when you'll be ready to settle down? You have no idea what it's been like. Being so in love with you that I'm willing to let go of something so vital to me."

"I didn't know being with me was such a sacrifice."

"That's not what I'm saying!"

"Jenna, what are you saying?"

"I think we need to break up."

He stared at her in disbelief. "You can't be serious."

"I am," she said, clutching her stomach. Looking at him was making her dizzy. Her heart, the emotional, unthinking part of her, was desperate to stay—to lock herself in a room with him forever—but her brain knew she couldn't.

"You really want to break up with me?"

"Nothing's worse than the idea of me without you," she said, her voice breaking. "I don't even know how I'm going to survive. You're everything."

"Then...why...what..."

"Eric," she whispered, her heart breaking.

"How am I gonna get through the day? What'll I have to look forward to? What purpose will I have? I mean...who else even knows me?" His face crumbled.

"Don't," she sobbed, moving toward him. He stepped backwards, crying and furious about it. Embarrassed, he swiped away the tears before they had a chance to fall.

"What was the point of falling in love with you if I couldn't keep you?"

"Don't you think I feel the same way? But Eric, I've wanted a baby my whole life."

"Fuck babies. I just want you."

"I want you too, but love isn't always enough."

"What else is there?"

"Life! Let me ask you something. We've been hiding from Darcy, but I still tried to introduce you to my world. You know my best friends. You even know May. But I've never experienced your life outside of me. I've only met Tim once, because I forced you to bring him to my house. All those clubs you go to, the parties, the concerts. Darcy would never be at any of those places, and yet you never asked me to go. You clearly don't see me fitting into your world either."

He threw up his hands. "You're breaking up with me 'cause you wanted to go to a Lil Wayne concert?"

"Eric!"

"No, don't you see how stupid this is? Love is all that matters. You and me."

"That's a very young way of thinking."

"Now I'm immature."

"You're inexperienced."

"Okay, voice of experience. Why don't you explain to me what it takes to sustain an adult relationship. Since your big-girl instincts worked out so well for you before."

"Excuse me?"

"Is this about Brian? Is this your way of getting rid of me to go back to him?"

"You know there's nothing between us!"

"Yeah okay," he said, not fully believing her. He shook his head, trying to understand what was happening. "Was this always the plan? Was it just my job to fuck you till you got your swagger back? Till you felt hot enough to go get the forever guy?"

"Don't do this."

"No, tell me. Who exactly do you want? Break down your after-Eric plan. Is it like, a Wall Street nigga? Engagement in four months, pregnant six months after that? A wedding in the Times, an Upper West Side penthouse and the PTA? Will that make you happy? No, you'll be bored and repressed and stuck with some bullshit ass suit you can't talk to, who'll never see you, who couldn't even begin to know how to make you come till you fucking cry. I'm your air, Jenna. Me. I know where you live." He pushed her in the chest with his index finger, hard, just over her heart. She stumbled backwards.

"Are you done?" she asked.

"Yeah, whatever."

"Look at me, goddamnit, and stop trying to hurt me."

Eric glanced at her, and then focused on some unknown point on the floor.

"You do know where I live, so you know better than that. All those things—the house, the PTA—I wish I could have them with you," said Jenna. "An after-Eric plan? I'm not leaving you to go find someone else."

Eric looked genuinely confused. "Well, where are you gonna get the baby from? CVS?"

Jenna's whole body slumped. She couldn't explain her plan, because she had no idea what it was. "I love you so much, Eric. But you're not ready for what I need."

Eric exhaled, defeated. Jenna watched him turn this over in his head.

"Could I beg you to stay?"

"You could," said Jenna. "And I would. But I'd always feel like something was missing."

"That'd kill me," he said, his voice barely audible. "I wish I could be everything you want."

"You are. Just twenty years too early."

Backing up, Eric sat down on the side of his bed and put his face in his hands. "This doesn't feel real."

He went completely silent for minutes. "Say something," she pleaded.

He looked up. "People search in vain forever to find what we've got. I don't know shit about anything, Jenna, and I might be inexperienced, but I know you'll never love anyone like you love me."

"I won't," she whispered.

"And yet you can leave me so easily for a baby you don't have and a husband you've never met. I'm here, I'm real, and I just lost to a goddamned fantasy. I must've never really had you at all."

There was a blank concentration on Eric's face, like he was already attempting to erase Jenna from his memory. He didn't want this pain. He couldn't take it on. "You should go," he said.

Jenna nodded, eyes cloudy with tears. She couldn't expect him to understand. She started roaming around the room, looking for her clothes. After about ten seconds, the realization of what was happening hit Eric—and he bolted over to her, crushing her against his chest. She locked her arms around him, weeping.

"You are my insides," she rasped. "You have to know that."

"Don't go yet," he said, his voice anguished, choked. "Stay with me. Just for a little while. I can't let you go yet."

They climbed into Eric's bed, the one he'd slept in since he was a child—and they curled up, spooning in the fetal position. Over the next two hours, they lay there lost in unified, but silent despair. As the truth of their disentanglement—that they weren't going to have each other anymore—became real to them, the sting sharpened by the minute. The next day, Jenna would have faint bruises on her arms from how tightly Eric held onto her.

Eric's scars weren't the kind anyone could see.

CHAPTER 31

The next morning, Darcy sent an email to the staff ordering everyone to gather outside her office at noon. She offered no details, just that it was an emergency mini-meeting before the regularly scheduled editorial meeting at two. So, at twelve, the entire staff awaited her in a cluster in the hallway. Their boss never did this; they had no clue what she wanted.

Jenna and Eric stood five people apart. No one could tell they were destroyed. Concealer covered the tiny, angry-red broken capillaries on Jenna's cheeks from hours of weeping. Eric wore a snapback emblazoned with "Brooklyn" pulled low, to hide his swollen, raw eyes.

Everyone around them was buzzing—was this about a new hire? A fire? But Jenna and Eric were so lost in their misery that their surroundings barely registered.

When Darcy finally emerged from her office, she was practically vibrating with intensity.

"So, folks, there's a theft in our midst. Someone's been stealing from the tenth floor fashion closet. I'd put thousands of dollars' worth of jewelry that I borrowed for the gala in there, and it's gone. And little things have been turning up missing. A clutch, a bag of earrings. It could have been someone on the building staff—a cleaning lady, a security guard. But it also could've been one of you. I've seen junior editors steal pieces borrowed for shoots, selling them to stores for profit." She threw her shoulders back, and adjusted her pale pink, peplum blazer. "If you know anything, I urge you to speak up now."

Everyone glanced at each other and then shook their heads—except for Jenna and Eric, who were barely listening.

"Jenna, you're up in that closet constantly. You're sure you haven't seen anyone hanging around up there?"

"On the tenth floor?" asked Jenna foggily, as if awakened too early from an Ambien-laced slumber. "No, I haven't."

"Well, last week, I installed a security camera in the fashion closet so we could catch the thief. Hopefully there's something on the footage."

Jenna snapped out of her daze, every molecule in her body jerking to attention.

A security camera? In the tenth floor fashion closet?

Her heart pounding in her chest, she glanced over at Eric with wide, horrified eyes. He was frozen solid, his face a mask of shock, like he'd just been sucker-punched—which he had, really.

They'd just had sex in there. The day before.

"Jinx, I have a job for you," said Darcy. "The footage streams to a secured website; I'm going to give you my password, and I need you to scan through the past week. See if you can find out what unsavory activity has been going down in there."

"Ooh fun!" Jinx rubbed her hands together and hopped up and down.

Jenna's hand traveled to her throat. Darcy knew. She'd found out about them. This was a trap, her revenge. And now she was sending Jinx to watch Jenna fuck her son.

"Jinx, you can tell us what you find at our two o'clock editorial meeting. You're all excused."

Darcy breezed back into her office. As the photo editors, the writers, the interns, and the sales staff dispersed back to their cubicles, they all wondered if the thief was among them.

Jenna and Eric lingered in the hallway, staring at each other. They would be outed, and in the most lurid, detailed, mortifying way. The moment they'd been dreading was here, and it was about to be worse than they'd imagined. Jenna felt pure panic, like an animal caught in a trap—her feet wouldn't move. Finally, Eric nodded toward her office and stiffly, slowly, she walked in that direction.

Before heading to his own desk, Eric stopped in his mother's doorway. Darcy looked up, and regarded him with unmistakable triumph.

"Anything you want to tell me?" she asked, taking a sip from her rum-spiked latte.

He eyed her with a baffled, confused expression, as if searching for signs of humanity in a table lamp. Finally, he let out a bitter laugh, pulled his brim down even lower and walked away.

Jenna leaned against the inside of her closed office door, rigid with bone-deep mortification. She replayed every second of her and Eric's last sexual encounter in the fashion closet, forcing herself to see exactly what Jinx was going to see—when her phone buzzed.

iMessages
Jenna Jones
April 27, 2013 12:11pm

Eric: She's not the villain?
Jenna: HOW'D SHE KNOW? Where did we slip?
Eric: It doesn't matter. Start packing. This is our last day here.

Jenna stared at the phone until her eyes unfocused. Slowly, she slid down the door until she landed on the floor. There were two more hours until the meeting. Nothing to do now but wait.

At two o'clock, the StyleZine staff filed into the conference room. Jenna and Eric sat next to each other—which they never did—but they had an unspoken need to be a united front. Darcy sat at the head of the table.

Jinx came in dead last, blushing furiously. Casting her eyes downward, she took a seat at the far left hand corner, three empty chairs away from anyone else.

Darcy told Karen that she'd be running the meeting today—and then she proceeded to address every aspect of the site in painstaking detail. Editorial meetings were never longer than twenty minutes, just a quick run-through of the content everyone had planned for the site that day. But today, they were fifty minutes in, and Darcy showed no signs of wrapping it up.

Darcy was unusually animated, uncharacteristically interested in everyone's updates. She wasted time asking needless follow-up questions, micro-managing each of their assignments.

Darcy even took a call a half hour into the meeting. She was torturing Jenna and Eric.

And they took it, because they had no choice. Eric was slumped so far down in his chair he was halfway under the table. His body language was all insolence. Next to him, Jenna sat lightning bolt straight, hands folded like a parochial school student. Overcompensating for her anxiety, she had a brilliantly worded response for every one of her Darcy's time-sucking inquiries.

And poor Jinx was in hell. She was always in the midst of some dramatic personal crisis, but right now she looked to be in the early stages of a panic

TIA WILLIAMS

attack. Hiding behind her thick curtain of wavy black hair, she mumbled all her answers, her face on fire. She stared at her hands and picked at her yellow glitter nail polish.

Their co-workers were thrown off by the obvious tension. Why were the four of them acting like they had personality disorders?

Finally, after an hour, Darcy folded her arms across her chest and said, "Time to figure out this theft business."

Jenna let out a tiny sigh. Here we go.

"Jinx, did you scan through the footage?"

Everyone turned their heads from Darcy to Jinx. Jinx nodded, pursing her lips together.

"Well, what did you see?"

She opened her mouth and closed it, twice. Her cheeks and chest flushed even redder.

"I'm asking you a question."

Jinx shook her head. "I didn't see anything," she said.

"It's obvious you saw something. You're all shaken up." Darcy gestured around the conference room. "Was it one of them?"

Silence.

"You're sweating," said Terry.

"Who was in the room?" Darcy's voice was clipped, severe. "You better answer me, Now."

Jinx glanced across the table, in Jenna and Eric's direction.

Suddenly, everyone's eyes were on them—shocked, disbelieving eyes. Jenna's face felt as hot as Jinx's looked. Eric swiveled his cap to the back and folded his arms across his chest.

"Jenna and Eric are the thieves? You saw them stealing?"

"No!"

"Oh." Darcy looked confused. "Then what were they doing that's got you so verklempt?"

Jinx made a small, miserable noise. She was now blushing to her hairline.

"What were they doing? Solving the economic crisis? Playing Candy Crush? What?"

"Leave her alone," said Eric, under his breath.

"I…I can't say," sputtered Jinx, in a shaky voice.

The first one in the room who got it, Terry slapped her hand over her mouth. "OH EM GEE! They weren't…you saw them…"

"Jinx, you better speak up," said Darcy.

"Leave her alone," repeated Eric, this time loudly. "Jinx, you don't have to answer her."

"Are you her boss?" His mother spat every word. "Jinx? Answer. Me. Now."

"Darcy, that's enough." Jenna glanced at Eric. He squeezed her hand under the table.

Jinx's bottom lip trembled. "They were…they were having…"

"Epileptic seizures? A spot of tea? Having what, goddamnit?"

"We were fucking," said Eric. "I was fucking her. She was fucking me. Fucking."

Jenna closed her eyes.

The meeting erupted into a symphony of gasps and squeals. Mouths dropped open, phones dropped out of hands.

Darcy did her best impression of a CEO and mother who felt so betrayed by her employees, that she was disbelieving. "Are you telling me that my superstar editor and my only child were having intercourse in a stockroom? Jenna, is that true?"

"Yes." Calmly, she folded her hands back in front of her. Now that it was out, she felt humiliated, yes; but also surprisingly serene. The lying, the hiding—for better or worse, it was over. "Yes, it's true."

"I don't believe it," spat Darcy.

"Would you like us to reenact it?" asked Jenna.

Eric snorted.

The room was abuzz with the thrill of discovering the juiciest nugget of gossip, ever. Jenna Jones and Eric? They were having an affair, right under their noses? The staff was so caught up in the news that they forget they were in the presence of Darcy, and exploded into talking-over-each-other exclamations. Terry was vibrating from the thrill of it all.

"I knew she liked him back," screeched Terry. "Eric you're such a sneaky fucking liar! You sluts!"

"Werk!" Mitchell the photo editor hissed at Jenna, before shooting Eric a thumbs up. He had a newfound respect for him.

"Jenna, I'm shocked," whispered a magazine industry-obsessed intern who thought of her in elevated terms, since she was from the old-school-glam print world. "Your clothes always look so pristine, how did you prevent wrinkles? You know, afterwards?"

Darcy banged her fist on the table. "Enough! Look, I'm disgusted. I can't even go on with this meeting. Eric, you were raised better than this. Jenna, I can't even imagine how you were raised. Jinx, you're fired. When your superior tells you to speak, you speak."

Jinx dissolved into silent, shuddering sobs, and just like that, the room went dead silent. Darcy was in one of her unpredictable moods—if she could fire Jinx, any one of them could be next. Suddenly, everyone tried to make themselves as small as possible.

"Darcy, you can't fire Jinx!" exclaimed Jenna. "This has nothing to do with her! This is…"

Just then, there was an explosion on the wall behind Darcy's head. The CEO hopped out of her seat. Eric had picked up Jenna's half empty bottle of Evian and hurled it across the room. Now water was dripping down the wall and puddling on the floor.

"We done here?" Eric stood, knocking his chair over. "Yes? No? Any questions? I'm happy to answer them. Wanna know how many times?

Countless, for months, and in every depraved, filthy way you can think of. Were we just in it for the office fuckfests? Not even a little bit. Jenna's the beginning and end of me. You wanna watch us doing it? Me too, let's screen the footage! No, let's just leak it to the media, maybe we'll get a reality show out of it! Suck my sex tape, biiitch!"

The photo assistant dissolved into giggles, and Karen kicked her chair.

"Eric, pull yourself together. Really, if you're gonna have a meltdown, do it elsewhere."

"Agreed, I'm out." On the way to the door, he stopped at his mother's chair, leaning down to her level. "I hope you enjoyed this, you sick fuck."

Terry's hand flew over her mouth. Mitchell gasped. Half the room was live-texting everyone they knew under the table. "Ignore Eric, I should've been more strident about putting him in time-out as a kid." Darcy cleared her throat. "This meeting is over. Jenna, I need you both in my office in five. Please go get him. And try to keep your clothes on when you do."

Jenna stood up. "Darcy, you are a small, sad, disturbed person. I suggest extensive therapy and an exorcism. Jinx, I'm so sorry. If you...ever need a reference...or anything, you have my number." She swallowed. "My apologies, everyone. My behavior was irresponsible, reckless, and insulting to all of your professionalism. I'm not sure what got into me...but, well, we all make mistakes."

She walked to the door. And the she paused, turning around to face everyone.

"Actually, I'm not sorry. And it wasn't a mistake. Eric was the best time I've ever had. It was..." Her face broke into a wistful smile. "It was fucking fantastic."

Jenna threw back her shoulders and strode out—summoning the ounce of dignity she had left.

Darcy sat her desk, glowering at Jenna and Eric, who were sitting across from her. They sat silently, awaiting their punishment—but their demeanors were polar opposites. Jenna intended to just let Darcy rage so they could all move on with repairing their lives. But Eric was itching for a fight. She'd never seen him so angry. Cartoon steam was practically seeping out of his ears.

"I'll just start off by saying you're both fired."

"Understandably," said Jenna.

"Thankfully," said Eric.

"I hesitated a second before coming to this decision, because The Perfect Find is so important to us. But Eric, you're not the only talented young director in town. And Jenna, there are certainly more of you. If I can figure out how to budget in her clothing and car allowance, Nina Garcia is mine." She gestured at Jenna. "So. Shall we deal with you first, CougarTown?"

"Shoot," said Jenna.

"I could never put my finger on it, but now I know exactly what annoyed me about you. You, with your saccharine persona, making everyone believe you were so squeaky-clean, so sophisticated, so beyond the tacky sluttery that befalls us mere mortals. Meanwhile, you fucked my boyfriend and you fucked my son. My only child."

"Don't pretend that means something to you," said Eric. "That's like saying she fucked your only bonsai tree."

She ignored him. "And you did this after I gifted you with a second chance. Do you just have an obsessive need to sleep with any male that's close to me? Would you like to borrow my ex-husband for the night? My chiropractor? It amazes me, how you've been able to be the Good Girl all these years, when you're really a whore."

Jenna was aghast. With everything she knew about Darcy, she was calling her a whore? But she said nothing.

Eric rubbed his hands over his face. "Listen, Satanic Smurfette. I know this is part of it, that you need us to sit here like you're the Godfather and take your menacing B-movie verbal beat down—which I'm only entertaining because I don't want Jenna to do it alone—but you won't be calling her a whore."

"It's so cute, how you protect her. I like how you said…what was it, that she was 'the beginning and end of you?' So romantic. Was it the beginning or the end of her that you were banging amongst thousands of dollars' worth of designer clothes?"

"If we're fired, can't we just wrap this up and be out?" He looked at Jenna. "Are we on trial? Can I call Gloria Allred? What are we even doing right now?"

"It's your exit interview," said Darcy, "and I'm entitled to this."

"Eric, it's fine." Jenna eyed her former boss. "Darcy, I get why you're upset. But I didn't mean to fall in love with Eric. I just did."

"Fall in love with Eric." Darcy sputtered for a second, struggling with how to respond. In that moment, she completely let down her stone-cold-bitch guard. She couldn't even hide how bewildered she was by the idea of them as a real couple.

"Jenna, this is beyond robbing the cradle. He was…he's my baby. You could be his mother…" She flicked her fingers in her son's direction. "And you! You're twelve. How did you even pull this off?"

He looked at her flatly. "I have a surprising emotional maturity."

"He does," said Jenna.

"Oh I agree. 'Suck my sex tape bitch,' is the height of maturity." She rolled her eyes with her entire body. "You both sound like you're on angel dust right now."

"I don't give a fuck how we sound to you, or anybody," said Eric.

"That's clear. If you did, you'd be humiliated. Running around here like a horny adolescent with a crush on his nympho teacher. Jenna, you never felt it was a wise idea to fight this so-called love you have for my kid?"

"No, she didn't," said Eric.

"I did at first! But then...no, not really."

"Well," said Darcy, "homecoming queens are always the sluttiest."

"Can I ask you a question?" Jenna couldn't resist. "How did you find out about us? How did you know to put a camera on the tenth floor?"

"Because you're messy." She'd never reveal the Suki Delgado connection. "And catching you was easy. This ain't my first time at the rodeo. When co-workers are having an affair, they're definitely screwing in the office. And where would you do it? Jenna's office, or the bathrooms, or in one of the two fashion closets. I installed security cameras in all places, and it took three seconds for you rookies to incriminate yourselves."

"I have a question," said Eric. "Who jumps through hoops to catch their kid having sex? That's pretty vile, even for you."

"I will not let you critique my choices as a parent. Do you know how embarrassed I am? My child embroiled in a sex scandal under my nose."

"It's like a Vale curse, right? I guess we're just doomed to fuck inappropriately and humiliate our parents."

Jenna whipped her head around to look at him.

"What are you talking about?" said Darcy.

"You had your own sex scandal, in high school. Me. And your family disowned you. Do I get disowned now? Good thing I don't depend on you for shit."

"How did you know that?"

"I'm supposed to think you just don't have parents? I know they exist, they're in Jersey. You never even tried to fix it, for my sake." He shook his head. "You're my only family member. Do you know how psychotic that feels?"

Jenna felt like she needed to step in, before this war escalated any further. "Listen, Eric and I are leaving. There's no reason to make the situation more hellish than it already is. Because Darcy, you've already gone way too far with this. Setting a trap for us, humiliating us in front of the staff? Wasn't that enough?"

"Oh no, it's not enough. This was a ballsy move, Jenna, putting your comeback on the line by risking yet another scandal attached to your name. No one's even going to remember all your accomplishments. You'll always be the idiot who ruined her perfect career over personal drama. The chick whose fiancé became romance novel content for a relationship blogger. The desperate cougar who screwed Darcy Vale's son at StyleZine. You think you have nine lives? You think this won't make the gossip blogs? Your former coworkers are texting everyone in media right now." Darcy snickered. "I took a huge gamble on you, Jenna. You should never have fucked with me. I'm so going to enjoy ruining you."

"You're not going to let it get to the blogs," said Eric.

"Why wouldn't I?"

"If you try to ruin her, I'll ruin you."

"There will be no ruining of anyone," Jenna said. "We're real people, this is not *House of Cards*!"

"How would you ruin me, Eric?"

"I'm the only one who could. I know you who you really are."

Eric walked over to the office door, opened it, and leaned in the doorway. "Don't make me embarrass you in front of the entire city," he said, speaking loudly enough for the whole office to hear.

Jenna turned around in her chair and saw that a dozen heads had suddenly popped up over their cubicles.

Darcy gasped. "What are you doing?"

"Jenna has the exact same contact list you do, which means I'm an email away from telling everyone in media how you really got the cash to start Belladonna Inc. It didn't stop at stealing a billionaire from his wife. No, when he was charged with money laundering and bank fraud, which would've left him broke and ruined your funding, you got your lawyer to pin it all on his former business partner. His partner in name only. His wife. You had the mother of his children put in an Italian prison."

Jenna recoiled. "Jesus, Darcy, you did that?"

"No! Well, it was white collar, more like a resort, and she deserved it. Eric Vale Combs, get away from the door."

"Or how about when you asked a security guard at LaGuardia Airport to watch me for five minutes while you ran to get coffee. But you didn't come back to get me until the next morning. Because you were having a threesome with DMX and Foxxy Brown. I spent the night in a police station."

Jenna gasped. "You and Foxxy Brown?"

"Eric, shut up! You're lying because you're mad, and everyone knows it."

"It happened. But my favorite you-anecdote is my dad's funeral."

Darcy shot up out of her chair. "Close the door."

"You made me leave early so I could come home and open the door for your interior designer. I was ten, taking three trains by myself to some cemetery in Queens—and my dad had just been shot, and I could only stay for fifteen minutes. Because you could finally afford a Manhattan apartment, and your goddamned drapes were more urgent. I was his only son, and I didn't get to see him being buried."

Jenna swallowed, the knot in her throat massive.

"I'll expose all your shit, mom. If this story breaks anywhere, if Jenna's hurt in any way, you're done."

He slammed the door so hard the frame shook, and calmly sat back down. The whole office had heard every word. Shaken, Darcy slowly lowered herself back down into her chair.

"You'd sell out your own mother?"

"You just set me up. With relish. Yeah, I'd do it. And when were you a mother?"

"How dare you judge me? After the life I've given you? You've never appreciated me! You deliberately went against my wishes, with this Jenna thing. I wasn't a factor to you at all. I never am. I mean, your first movie is dedicated to Otis, your loser dad. It's the biggest fuck-you ever."

And herein, thought Jenna, *lies the strife.*

"I sacrificed everything to be your mother. I lost my family to be your mother."

"A., you never made one selfless choice when it came to me. And B., no sane mother would pull this kind of stunt on her own kid," said Eric. "Why exactly do you hate me? Is it just because I exist?"

"You're my son. I don't hate you."

"You know what? I sort of believe you. Real hate requires commitment."

"This is all your fault," she seethed at Jenna. "You've poisoned him against me."

"You think this is my fault?" For the first time, she felt sorry for Darcy. "No, it breaks my heart. It's tragic that you missed out on knowing him, and it's tragic that he grew up without a mother. You're broken, Darcy, and what you've both achieved despite that is a miracle. I didn't turn him against you. All I did was love him. You can blow me up on *Page 6,* spread rumors, whatever. I'll be embarrassed for a while, but in the end, I have nothing to be ashamed of. I fell in love and lost my head. Maybe he should've been off-limits, but besides doing my job brilliantly…I don't owe you anything else, Darcy. If I had it to do over again?" She looked over at Eric, whose expression broke her heart. "I'd do it all over again. Emphatically."

Eric met her eyes. "Without hesitation."

"And emphatically, without hesitation, you'd both be fired all over again," snapped Darcy. "And in this economy. Was it worth it?"

Jenna nodded. "It was."

"You're a silly, self-sabotaging fool, Jenna Jones, but at least you stick to your guns. I can respect that," said the CEO. "Hope you keep it in your pants, if you ever get hired again."

Darcy and Jenna shook hands. She stuck her hand in her son's direction, and he eyed it with distaste.

"Oh, we're done. Let's never speak again. I'll be out of the house by tomorrow."

Darcy looked like she'd had the wind knocked out of her. "Where will you go?"

"Anywhere but there."

"Well, whatever you want, Eric. You're an adult now, I...I can't stop you."

He grabbed Jenna's hand and they stood up. The two of them walked out of Darcy's office. They stopped in Jenna's office so she could get her bag and her *Hallelujah* print from the wall. Eric took his camera from his cubicle, leaving behind all the other miscellanea he'd accumulated. And then the staff, too thunderstruck and titillated to do much of anything but wave wistfully, watched with voyeur-behind-a-telescope fascination as the two walked down the hall toward the elevator—hand in hand, unbreakable again, if only for that moment.

Jenna and Eric stood on the sidewalk in front of their building. The past eighteen hours had drained them. And now that everything was over, they weren't sure what to do or say.

"I guess this is it," Jenna began. "The end of an era."

"You're not really moving out, are you?"

"Yeah, I can't live under her roof anymore," said Eric. "After today? That was the most Oedipal, dysfunctional, Dr. Evil-esque shitshow I've ever seen in real life. Poor Jinx."

"Can you imagine what must be going through all their heads? We should start a support group for StyleZine survivors of the Erica scandal."

"Are we Erica? Like Brangelina?"

"Today's been hell, we might as well get a fun celeb couple moniker out of it."

He chuckled. "Cute."

There was a loaded pause. They were no longer a couple; that was a weird thing to say. "So where will you live?"

"No clue."

"Do you have enough money? If…"

"Nah, I'm cool."

"But where will you go? I can help . . ."

"I don't need help." His tone said, this is not your place anymore.

Jenna nodded, backing down.

Then they were silent, sidewalk traffic breezing past them.

"You know, you didn't have to go that far, defending me," said Jenna. "Exposing Darcy to the whole office."

"Yes I did. I can't let anyone hurt you. It's against my religion."

"Even now?"

"Always." He looked past her, down Broadway.

No one will ever love me like this again, she thought.

"So, I guess I'll just wait here for a cab. You're gonna take the train home?"

Jenna nodded.

"But…your big poster."

They both looked down at her *Hallelujah* poster, the vintage print that they bonded over, ages ago.

"It'll break my heart to look at this now," said Jenna. They glanced at each other, and looked away.

"Promise you'll call me when you figure out where you're going to stay?"

"I promise," he said, but he knew he wouldn't. "Will you be okay?"

"I started over before; I can do it again."

There was another awkward pause. Jenna knew it was time for them to part, but the thought of never seeing Eric again was impossible.

"Well," she started, "I should probably go catch the train."

She just stood there.

"Don't make this harder, Jenna. Walk away."

"I know I need to, but I can't."

"Walk away. Or else I'm gonna grab you and take you with me."

Suddenly, she flung her arms around Eric's neck, pressing herself to him, trying to memorize his scent, the way his body felt against hers. She needed to be this close to him again, one last time. But he didn't touch her.

"Go, Jenna."

She shook her head. "Not yet."

"This is what you wanted."

Eric stood there, rigid, trying to resist her. Finally, with a groan of frustration, he pulled her face in front of his and kissed her passionately. He kissed her like he wanted to sear his memory on her brain. Like he wanted her to know he owned her, no matter who came after him. Like he wanted to scar her for life.

He broke it too soon. A few seconds more and they both knew she wouldn't have left. She'd stay with him for the night, another day, a week—but it would've just been postponing the inevitable.

"Goodbye, Jenna," he said, leaning his forehead against hers.

"Goodbye, Eric," she whispered.

And then he vanished into the crowd.

CHAPTER 32

It was a breezy summer's day, almost four years later. Birds were chirping, violets were in-bloom, and Jenna and Billie were drinking lattes on a bench at Hall Playground. The colorful, high-tech playground was near Pratt University's campus and a few blocks from what they now called the Lane-Franklin-Jones Compound. Jenna had moved into the upstairs apartment in Elodie's brownstone, and Billie lived one block away. They were like one big slightly dysfunctional family, splitting babysitting duties and sharing Sunday night dinners (James Diaz, Elodie's newly minted fiancé, usually made ultra-authentic fajitas—with sauce on the side, for Jenna).

"But he's such a wild child," Jenna said to Billie, with barely-hidden pride. She adjusted her cropped gold lame blazer, which was impractical for the playground but so fun ("Cher Does Corporate America"). "There's no way he's walking down the aisle without bursting into the 'Thomas the Train' theme song or something."

"He'll definitely go rogue," said Billie. "But he'll be an adorable ring-bearer! And he'll have his two faux-big sisters right there with him, as flower girls."

On The Compound, May; Billie's frilly youngest daughter, Gracie; and Jenna's wild child son—who everyone referred to as The Baby, since he was the youngest—were practically being raised as siblings. They spent half of their lives in each other's houses.

"We just had May's black taffeta dress made. Gracie's wearing an Elsa costume," said Billie. "It's 2016, I can't believe *Frozen* is still a thing."

What Jenna couldn't believe was that Elodie was going to be a bride. But she was wildly in love, in this shockingly functional, permanent way—and she was doing it on her own terms. No cookie-cutter shenanigans. No rings, no marshmallow dress, no bouquet toss. Just a cool rooftop ceremony, with the bridal party wearing whatever they wanted—and a very grownup reception at an absinthe-soaked cabaret called Moist.

"The Baby's going to look so handsome in his tuxedo sweatshirt and khakis!" Jenna handed Billie her phone. "Look, I took a picture of him in it. Are you dying?"

"Awww!" moaned Billie, enlarging the pic. "I'll never get over how little he looks like you."

"DNA is insane," said Jenna. "Literally, anyone could've been his mother. Oprah, Ariana Grande. Gwyneth. Viola Davis. Anyone."

Jenna watched The Baby chase Gracie, who was wearing enormous sequined wings, around the playground with a toddler-size basketball, trying to convince her to shoot hoops. She was born wielding a magic fairy wand; she wanted no part of little boy games.

Just then, the basketball flew from out of nowhere and smacked Jenna clean between her brows.

"Wooooooopth! I'm outta control, Mommy!" He ran to her and then rubbed her forehead with his pudgy palm.

"Be careful, monkey!" she said, pulling him into her lap and tickling him until he squealed with giggles. She kissed his cheek and he wiggled off her lap, tearing Jenna's iPad out of her bag and cueing up *The Lego Movie*. Then he slipped on his attached toddler-sized Sony headphones, and ran off to watch it by the swings.

"My little miracle," said Jenna with a laugh. "Sometimes I can't believe he's real. It's like I'm looking at a hologram."

"I don't say this enough," started Billie, "but I'm in awe of you. Making the choice to raise a child on your own? While holding down a professorship at Fordham? I think you might be the bravest woman I know."

"Really? I'm so touched," said Jenna, and she was. The past four years had been such a whirlwind; she'd barely taken a second to breathe and reflect.

The day Darcy fired her, she didn't waste one second torturing herself. She emailed James Diaz from the street, asking him to go to coffee and discuss her teaching Fashion Theory for his department. They sat at Starbucks for hours, discussing her ideas, her teaching style, and her love for nurturing teens. Over an untouched chai latte, she described to him why teaching part-time at that Virginia community college was one of the most rewarding professional experiences of her life. Helping to shape the next generation of editors, stylists, buyers, and designers? She felt like they were doing her a favor, reviving her creativity—and reminding her why she loved fashion in the first place. She was one bite into her croissant when James offered her the job.

Jenna felt lucky. She was a mother to the funniest, sweetest kid in Brooklyn. She had her dream job. Jenna felt like she was in exactly the right place at the right time.

Of course, things weren't perfect. Work was demanding, and even though Elodie and Billie helped, most days she felt like she was barely keeping up. Between running The Baby to and from daycare, trying to devote every second to him when she wasn't teaching, and working insane hours—Jenna was perpetually exhausted. But it was a satisfying exhausted. Like the way you felt after amazing sex or a transcendental workout. Worth-it exhausted.

Yawning, Jenna stretched and took her attention off Gracie and The Baby. She watched the Pratt students in their denim cutoffs and clingy tees, hanging out in cliquey clusters in the park—just talking and laughing and being twenty. And then she squinted. One of the students looked familiar. He was standing near the colorful, complicated playground typing something into his phone, wearing a huge backpack full of camera equipment—a backpack she'd know anywhere.

"Oh my God, Jenna," whispered Billie, slowly lowering her coffee cup to her lap. "Is…that…"

Jenna shot up so fast that her bag somersaulted to the ground. Big boy pull-ups, Transformers and sippy cups went flying.

"ERIC!" she screamed, and everyone at the playground turned to look at her. Of course he didn't hear her, since there was a sidewalk and half a park between them—and he was wearing headphones.

She left her bag on the ground and sprinted in his direction. On her way, she tripped over a double-wide stroller, elbowed her way between two rainbow-haired kids mid-makeout, and lept over a stylish homeless guy trimming his bangs under a tree.

Gasping for breath, she stood behind him, her heart bursting. Was he actually right in front of her? They hadn't spoken since their last day at StyleZine.

She thought about Eric constantly, missed him totally, and always fleetingly wondered if maybe today would be the day she'd run into him. She'd practiced a thousand different things to say to him when this moment happened, and now she'd forgotten all of them.

She ruffled her hair, pinched her cheeks to create a flushed effect, and then cleared her throat. He didn't budge. So, she tapped him on the shoulder. Then, he turned around. And ripped off his headphones.

"Mother-fuck!"

Jenna laughed. "Hi!"

A wide smile spread across Eric's face, the same one she recognized from the first time she met him. The one that, after thirty seconds of knowing him, had turned her life upside down.

"Jenna! You're here! What are you doing here? You're so…I can't….I don't even know how to act right now!"

"Me either!"

"Can I hug you? I gotta hug you."

"You better!"

Then he did, and it was concave, polite—the greeting of two people who were unused to touching each other and not sure how far they should go—but then they slipped into what felt familiar. Eric lifted Jenna off of her feet into a squeezy-tight embrace and, by force of habit, she smothered his cheek with kisses. After a breathless ten seconds, he put her down. They backed away from each other a couple of steps, both self-conscious about how good it had felt.

"What are you doing here?" asked Jenna.

"I'm scouting playgrounds for my new film," he said. "A film? A full-length movie?"

"Yeah, thanks to mad investors and Kickstarter! It's based on the last day of my dad's life. Obviously I don't know what happened, but it's just my way of piecing it all together." Eric was talking crazy fast. It was like he'd saved up years of information to tell Jenna, and couldn't get it out quickly enough. "It's like an ode to throwback BK, lots of color, street personalities. Basically tracing his footsteps around the hood for twenty-four hours. Very *Do the Right Thing.*"

"You've been writing this story in your head your whole life."

"You know me well," he said, smiling. "It's been a little hard to focus, cause I'm always traveling. I just got back from San Francisco, shooting a Travelocity commercial."

Jenna gave him a celebratory shove in the arm. "That's huge! You must've gotten an agent at South by Southwest. Actually, I know you did. Is this the part where I pretend I wasn't Googling your name incessantly during the festival?"

"Stalker." Eric looked thrilled. "Yeah, I got an agent. I started out assistant-directing a director I randomly met in the club with Tim, years ago. I guess I built up a rep, and now I have my own assistant director. I spent most of last year living in Barcelona, shooting international ads. Reebok, Cottonelle. It's been crazy, Jenna. The budgets are insane."

Jenna shook her head, in awe. "I am so proud of you. You're doing well."

"But wait, though," he said. "I even have my own place."

"No!"

"For two years, me and Tim lived in the shittiest studio in Midwood. Our keys never worked, and we only had scalding hot water, which sounds like it would be better than only having cold, but it wasn't. Tim felt like the address was bad for his brand."

"His brand!"

"Right? I was like, what *brand*, son? You have moderate Snapchat engagement and strippers buy your kicks. Explain this brand."

Jenna giggled.

"But now I have an ill spot in Crown Heights. I'm so mature. I have real art and life insurance. And I only smoke weed occasionally." He paused. "Actually I still smoke mad weed."

"Good, I was beginning to think you weren't you anymore."

Jenna smiled. "Wow. Getting fired from StyleZine was the best thing that ever happened to you."

"And you, too. Is this the part where I pretend I haven't memorized your page on Fordham's website and read all of your syllabi and even found a video of one of your lessons on YouTube?"

"I'm the stalker?"

"Six hundred of those twelve hundred views are mine. It feels so good to admit that."

Jenna laughed, and he smiled. And then they stood in front of each other, taking each other in, like long-lost twins reunited on a daytime talk show. Students buzzed all around them. The playground was raucous with boisterous toddlers. The block was alive with action, but they were still.

"I'm so happy to see you," said Jenna.

"Me too," he said. "I need to hug you again."

Jenna snuggled into his arms. This time she stayed there longer. "God, you still hug so good," she said, peeling herself away, with difficulty. She stuck her hands in the pockets of her shorts, and asked the question that she wondered too often. "I have to ask. Are you seeing anyone?"

"Well…yeah, sort of. You know. Here and there."

Jenna's stomach sank. This shouldn't have surprised her, but she couldn't picture him with anyone else.

"Oh Eric," she said, jokily. "You're such a magnet."

"Not even," he said. "I just don't like being alone."

"Why?"

He glanced down at the grass, carefully constructing his answer, and then met her eyes. "Because then I miss you too much. I start wanting to be where I can't be, and I hate that feeling."

Jenna nodded. She knew this about Eric. He couldn't sit for too long with something that was upsetting him.

"I date sometimes, too," she said. "Not often and not very well. It never feels…right."

A few moments passed. A dry gust of wind hit them hard, and Jenna shivered a little.

"Do you think we'll ever get over it?" asked Eric.

"I know that I'll never be over you. But maybe that's okay. Maybe I'll meet someone that I can love in a different way, and be happy."

"You believe that?"

"It's what I tell myself when I want you so badly that I actually get nauseous."

Eric reached out and fingered one of her curls. Then he dropped his hand.

"Well, I should…" started Jenna.

"Me too."

Neither made a move.

"I keep waiting for it not to hurt so bad," said Eric, finally. "Every time I meet a woman, I want her to be you. And these sweet, pretty, smart girls fail so miserably. There's nothing wrong with them; they're just not you. You know that 'other half" people spend their life looking for? I already found her. She's somewhere watching Inside the Actor's Studio and eating yellow Skittles without me. I know who she is. But I can't have her." He paused. "It's like dying of some mysterious illness and knowing there's a cure, but it's just out of reach."

"Don't do this to me," she said shakily.

"I'm sorry," he said, grabbing her hand. "It's the truth."

"For me too," she said, and then kissed him on the cheek.

"Thank you, Eric."

"What did I do?"

"You put me back together when I was in pieces. You gave me confidence, and reminded me that I was lovable. You saved me."

"Nobody saves anybody, Jenna. That was all you. I just helped.

Shone a little spotlight on the parts you forgot were there."

Then they just stood there, fingers intertwined—basking in the charged energy they always generated together. Even though the moment was laced with sadness, it was so good to feel that again.

Finally, Eric pulled Jenna closer and said, "Hey."

"Yeah?" Jenna held her breath. Being that close to him still made her dizzy.

"Do you…think we could ever be friends?" He said this timidly. "Admittedly, I don't know how to be around you and pretend that you're not mine. But I can't let you go, twice."

Jenna smiled. "Let's do it. We can at least try!"

"We can handle this, Jenna. And if I ever accidentally try to ravage you, your job is to remind me that your orifices are off limits."

"I refuse to accept that responsibility. You breathe on me wrong and my panties fly off my body."

"Which is why I gave you that responsibility," he said, his eyes dancing. "Next rule: I can't hear about any other dudes."

"And I can't hear about any of those thirstbuckets you date."

"Stop talking like Terry."

"That girl's catchphrases permeated my brain," she said with a light giggle. And then she let go of his hand and glanced over at the playground. Billie, the eternal romantic, was watching Jenna and Eric with her hand over her heart.

"What are you looking at? Oh shit, it's Billie! Why's she crying?" He waved at her. She waved back, with wild enthusiasm.

"Eric," started Jenna, with trepidation, "there's something I have to tell you. A lot has changed in my life. Before you decide to be my friend, you have to know something."

"What?"

Jenna chewed her lip. After a moment, she looked at Billie and gestured toward her son. Billie called over to The Baby and sent him running over to Jenna, clutching his iPad.

Eric saw the little boy dashing toward them and, just as he was putting the words together to ask Jenna who he was, he went mute. The kid grabbed Jenna's hand and then peered up at him with this curious, intense little face—and Eric stopped breathing.

That curious, intense little face.

"This is my son," said Jenna, with a mixture of hesitancy and pride.

"Oh." Eric nodded with exaggerated slowness. Like he was floating in the ether, gravity-free. Because that kid wasn't just her son. There could never be any question of who his father was. His face was Eric's face. He was even dressed like Eric, in camouflage cargo shorts and a tee that said "Brooklyn Dopeness."

"Go ahead," said Jenna, giving The Baby a little nudge. "Introduce yourself."

He shook his head. "I don't talk to thtrangers!"

"He's not a stranger. It's okay, I promise."

"I'm Otith," said The Baby.

Eric blinked a couple of times. "You're who?"

"Otith."

Eric stood there, gawking at him, feeling like the world was spinning off of its axis.

"I knew someone named Otis." He let out a short, weak little laugh. "H-how old are you?"

Otis held up three fingers.

"Three?" Eric did the math and then looked at Jenna, his expression incredulous. She nodded. Suddenly feeling unsteady, he let his backpack slide to the ground. "Jesus."

"I'm a big boy," Otis said to Eric. "I go potty by myself, well thometimes, and I got a girlfriend named Coco."

"Coco's not your girlfriend, she's your line buddy."

"Applth and orangth."

Eric burst out in crazed laughter. *"Yo, what is happening right now?"*

"Wanna shoot hoopth with me?" He was hopping up and down, so excited to find a guy to play basketball with. "My name is Otith but it should be Lebron, cause I got skillth like him. I'm a problem. Wanna play?"

"Yeah," said Eric, in a faraway voice. "I wanna play."

"Monkey, wanna run back to Auntie Billie and get your ball?"

"Okay. Be right back, bro." And then he held out his little fist in Eric's direction. Eric went rigid with shock and then, swallowing hard, he pressed his fist to Otis' and they both exploded their hands, with a loud POOF.

Otis bounded off in Billie's direction. And then Eric turned toward Jenna. Too overwhelmed to address the real issue, he latched onto the pound bomb thing, babbling in a delirious voice, "Did you teach him that? Did you? Or are pound bombs hereditary? I'm bugging out!"

Jenna grabbed his arm. "Calm down. Breathe. I taught him that. Breathe, honey."

Eric took a couple of deep breaths and then, in a daze, he said, "Jenna, that's me. He's me. He even has my lisp."

"He's more you than you. So braggy and self-assured. He practically came out of the womb screaming, 'I'm awesome!'"

"He's me," Eric repeated, stunned. "And you."

"Us."

"How?"

"Remember that horrible sinus infection I got? Turns out that I, with forty-one-year-old eggs, was one of the small percentage of women whose antibiotics halve the potency of birth control pills," said Jenna. "I was pregnant that last day of work. I thought I was sick from stress, but it was Otis. I found out later, but by then, we were over."

Jenna stopped, flooded with memories from her pregnancy, alone and without Eric. It was so disorienting. She'd been overcome with joy, elated—but thoroughly soul-sick, too.

"It was the hardest decision of my life to have him without you. But I couldn't handicap you. I had my chance to be unapologetically ambitious and chase my dreams in my twenties—and you deserved that, too. I loved you too much to stand in the way of that. I know you. You would've dropped it all for us."

Eric nodded. He would've. He'd spent the last four years working tirelessly, not sleeping, schmoozing, building his brand, chasing (and getting) the splashiest shoots, pooling resources for his film, traveling wherever work took him. No ties.

But for Otis and Jenna, at twenty-three, he would've taken an office job, in any field. He never would've moved to Spain. He wouldn't have done anything. Forget his talent, his training, his lifelong goals. He'd have been finished before he started.

"I couldn't not have him," continued Jenna. "You know I needed this baby, this piece of you, of us, more than I needed to breathe. I…"

"I understand," he said so quietly, she could barely hear him.

"You do?" Every time she imagined breaking this to Eric—and she would've, she just hadn't planned when—it always ended with him hating her.

"I hate that I missed a single second. But I know why you did it. You don't have to explain."

There was more he wanted to say, to ask, but words failed him. After a long moment spent staring at his son on the playground—just existing— he found his voice again.

"He's perfect. And you named him after my dad."

"Yes," said Jenna. "I wanted to honor the man responsible for the two great loves of my life."

Eric looked at her like he was seeing her for the first time.

"I…I never thought…" His voice faltered. He paused, and then started again. "I never thought I could love you more than I already do."

Hot tears sprang to Jenna's eyes.

Just then, Otis ran over to them with his little ball. "I'm back!"

Eric squatted down so he was face to face with Otis. "Yo, you ready? I need to witness these LeBron-adjacent skills."

"YEAH!" said Otis, hopping up and down. Then, he put his hand on Eric's shoulder. "I'm gonna win, but 'member…it's only a game."

"I like your attitude, O." He stood up and then looked down at Otis' Gap knockoff Jordans. "You know, if we're gonna chill, I'm gonna have to step your kicks game up. Your mom's a fashion expert, but her sneaker knowledge is mad iffy."

"I know! Mommy's shoes look like skyscraperth."

"She goes to the bodega in heels, right?"

"How did you know her does that? Do you have thuperpowers?"

"No," said Eric, chuckling. "No, I just know everything about your mom."

"You do? How come?"

Eric looked at Jenna, and they shared a secret smile. "You'll find out soon."

Then, he hoisted his backpack on his shoulder, took his son's hand, and they walked over to the playground together.

Jenna stayed behind, watching them. When they got to the small court, Eric crouched down to Otis' level and spun his little ball on his finger. Otis squealed, clapping his hands. Then Eric coached him on dribbling, before he swooped him up and ran him over to the hoop—and flipped him around in a somersault, ending with Otis slamming in the ball, backwards. It was the most dramatic toddler dunk of all time. Jenna laughed and cheered for Otis—for Eric and Otis—and wiped the happy tears from her cheeks.

Her love and their son.

This moment, the three of them together, it was her default fantasy; always in the back of her mind. But she'd forbidden herself to think it was attainable. After all, was it ever possible to really have it all? Did happy endings truly exist in real life?

Maybe they did. Maybe this was hers.

Jenna walked in the direction of the playground with feet that didn't touch the ground, headed toward her waking dream. Now, all that was left was to live it.

And she did.

CPSIA information can be obtained
at www.ICGtesting.com
Printed in the USA
LVHW112330111218
600144LV00001B/95/P